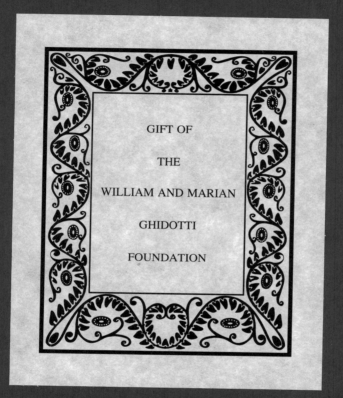

Brothers No More

The Story of Henry Tod
See You Later Alligator
Right Reason
The Temptation of Wilfred Malachey
High Jinx
Mongoose, R. I. P.
Racing Through Paradise
On the Firing Line: The Public Life of Our Public Figures
Gratitude: Reflections on What We Owe to Our Country
Tucker's Last Stand
In Search of Anti-Semitism
WindFall
Happy Days Were Here Again
A Very Private Plot

EDITOR

The Committee and Its Critics
Odyssey of a Friend: Whittaker Chambers' Letters
    to William F. Buckley, Jr.
W. F. B.: An Appreciation
Did You Ever See a Dream Walking?
American Conservative Thought in the Twentieth Century

William F. Buckley, Jr.

Brothers No More

DOUBLEDAY
New York
London
Toronto
Sydney
Auckland

PUBLISHED BY DOUBLEDAY
a division of
Bantam Doubleday Dell Publishing Group, Inc.
1540 Broadway, New York, New York 10036

DOUBLEDAY and the portrayal of an anchor
with a dolphin are trademarks of Doubleday
a division of Bantam Doubleday Dell Publishing Group, Inc.

AUTHOR'S NOTE   This is the eleventh novel in which I refer to historical figures, dead and alive. In this novel there are characters who are related to historical figures. Needless to say, in this novel as in its predecessors, the whole is a work of fiction.

Library of Congress Cataloging-in-Publication Data

Buckley, William F. (William Frank), 1925–
    Brothers no more / William F. Buckley, Jr.—1st ed.
        p. cm.
    1. World War, 1939–1945—Veterans—United States—Fiction. 2. Friendship—
United States—Fiction. 3. Men—United States—Fiction.   I. Title.
PS3552.U344B76   1995
813'.54—dc20   94–24162
CIP

ISBN 0-385-47794-5
Copyright © 1995 by William F. Buckley, Jr.
Printed in the United States of America
September 1995

10   9   8   7   6   5   4   3   2

For (the Reverend) Michael Bozell
el primer sobrino

Book One

One

PFC. DANNY O'HARA had the walkie-talkie in his hand. It was countdown time.

"Thirty minutes," he said in a low voice to Private Henry Chafee, who opened the breech of his rifle for the tenth time. Yes, he nodded to himself, he had confirmed that the cartridge was secure in the chamber. Both men were in sweaty blackface. The sergeant had told them to apply the sooty grease also to their hands and faces—"They'll stand out like flashlights if you don't." Danny looked over at Henry and yes, for a long moment after every explosion, his face was visible even through all the muddy camouflage. If they hadn't blackened their faces they'd have vividly reflected the light of the exploding shells.

These were exploding more rapidly with every passing quarter hour, beginning two hours ago when they occupied their foxhole, cakey-dry, hot, small, smelly, here at the eastern end of the regimental front. The mandate was straightforward: Their regiment was responsible for overrunning the impacted German unit standing in the way of Allied progress. They could not know its size—a company, perhaps; perhaps a battalion—whatever it was that Field Marshal Kesselring had left behind as he retreated from the Arno line north of Rome.

Whatever the unit was, its defensive firepower was seemingly inexhaustible, and Colonel Johnson had postponed zero hour from daytime to dark, resigning himself to the futility of his own offensive, up against the stubborn German unit standing in the way. Nothing had worked against it. The drenching artillery, the close air support, the bombs—they hadn't succeeded in silencing the enemy machine guns and rifles. There wasn't any doubt about it, the American infantry offensive would need the cover of darkness. But it meant also this, that the charge would need to take place before 2200, which was when the moon would begin to shine on the scrubby, bloody hill. "A funny thing," Danny said, "the moon somehow illuminates more vividly than the sun. Did you know that, Henry? A matter of contrast, I suppose."

"I guess so." Henry was fanning himself with the aluminum top ripped off the cartridge case. "God it's hot."

"Yeah, well, we're going to be a lot hotter after we've run the distance." Danny could not be sure exactly how far it was to the firing point he and Henry had been assigned to destroy. He did have the compass bearing on their objective and they agreed that the stars would prove useful in maintaining their course to it. Danny now rechecked the compass and looked up at the stars. "There! That's just a little left of the course we'll be running, see it?" He lifted his hand, fingers extended, moving it up and down, pointing to the star. Henry moved his head behind Danny's to identify the star that would guide them.

"Yes, I see it," he said. "It won't move very much in, what, twenty-five minutes?"

Danny looked at his watch. "I can't make out the time. We'll have to get it from the radio. God, what I would give for a smoke.

Henry! You *don't need to check your rifle breech again.* . . . Sorry, getting edgy. Won't be long now. We've got a full battalion—four companies, sixteen platoons, sixty-four squads. And exactly two soldiers, you and me, Henry, are the little point on the left end of the arc. In a way, that means the whole operation swings on us." He laughed.

Henry didn't laugh.

"If we're lucky, when we charge up on the target we'll discover that our Kraut gunner has already been zapped—" Danny slammed down the palm of his right hand on the surface of his left hand. Another mosquito. His flow of talk was not interrupted. "—hit by one of our artillery shells, maybe. Hell, these guys can't be immortal! What the fuck, Henry, we've been dumping on them since—" He stopped. He would not even try to raise his voice to compete with the two major detonations "—since maybe two o'clock? Oh." Danny stopped talking. He had spotted the spitting light from the gunner ahead and heard the thup-thup-thup of the bullets. They tore into the earth not many yards from the foxhole in which he and Henry were crouched.

"I guess there'll be somebody out there to welcome us after all. *Sheeyit* it's hot. Henry?"

"Yes."

"This isn't much fun, is it. And first battle action for us, too. I forget, Henry. How'd we get into this fucking war? You're so smart, tell me. Come to think of it, I'm smart as hell too. Maybe General Clark will find out who was responsible and maybe—hey, what you think of this, Henry?—maybe the guy responsible will be sentenced to be shot, and maybe you and I, baby, will be the executioners!" He laughed. "That's a good one. When they execute somebody, his hands are tied behind him, he's standing in front of a wall blindfolded—and they use *six* soldiers to fire! But when it's a machine gunner *in the dark* firing at *us,* two of us are supposed to be enough to take him on! Army logic. I wonder, Henry. Do they teach logic at West Point? At the army war colleges?—Give me some of that water, Henry. We may as well use it up. We're not going to be carrying extra provisions on *our* charge of the light brigade." He returned the canteen and put his ear down to the little radio speaker.

"Why do they have to say it a hundred times?—Five minutes-five minutes-five minutes. So?—five minutes! In five minutes we go, Henry."

Danny looked up again at his guiding star, then raised his head just high enough to make it possible to point the compass arrow at his objective. It lay on an azimuth of 290 degrees. Without looking down at the compass Danny said, "Our star's pretty much with us still." He paused. "Great idea, a star lighting your way to the enemy. Well, I guess the Big Star was a light for Herod, right, Henry? Sure. Oh Jesus!" Danny's voice was hoarse now, struggling to make itself heard over the crashing sound of the great detonations.

He brought the radio to his ear, first poking his index finger in the ear to trap a mosquito. "Okay, Henry, *one minute.* They're counting down now in seconds. Fifty . . . forty . . . *get ready!* . . . thirty . . . Henry! *Get up!*"

Henry spoke. "I'm not going, Danny."

Danny looked down at him in disbelief. The explosions had stopped. It was totally dark, silent. He had to guess exactly where Henry's head was.

"Henry! You *crazy?* We got *TEN SECONDS!*" With his hand, he felt for Henry's head. He felt his hair: Henry had removed his helmet.

The fighter plane pilots, moving away from the fire zone, made out below their wingtips what seemed a sparkling tiara: the 3rd Regiment, on the move. And, on the ground, there was thunderous sound and the staccato light bursts of .30-caliber cartridges fired at waist level as the mile-long arc of men roared toward their targets. Danny spat down on Henry—his disbelief was very nearly hysterical—and then launched himself forward toward his star, squeezing the trigger of his rifle every second. He could make out the three GIs on his right, moving parallel. In less than a half minute the floodlight from the bazooka lit up the whole area and Danny spotted the target gun embrasure, ran headlong toward it and lobbed a hand grenade through the narrow opening.

One Mississippi. Two Mississippi. Three Mississippi. Four Mississippi. Five Mississippi. He had counted out the five specified seconds, heard the blast of his grenade. He could now move in, prepared to encounter whatever creature survived the grenade. Cautiously he entered the bunker from the back, with his left hand beaming his flashlight splashily, up, down, right, left, his right on the rifle trigger. The two German soldiers were dead.

Danny paused. The floodlight was now out, the gunfire suddenly ended.

He dropped his rifle and ran the seventy, eighty yards back toward his foxhole. He jumped into it, grabbed Henry by the collar, shook him, and whispered roughly, "Come on! Quick! *Come with me!*" Henry climbed out of the foxhole and, Danny's arm firmly on his sleeve, jogged alongside, back once again in the direction of their star. Danny's star, Henry was thinking, not mine, as he wrested free from Danny's grip, turned his rifle toward his stomach and pushed on the trigger.

Two

D ANNY O'HARA had been instructed by the senior at Yale who tapped him for Zeta Psi to wear informal clothes for the initiation rituals that evening. "You know, khaki pants, whatever. And coat and tie, of course." Coat and tie wasn't any longer quite "of course" at Yale. One master, freshly installed at Silliman College, had specified coats and ties to be worn at meals in his college dining room, and a mere three weeks later the freshly elected twenty-year-old president of the college's student association called on the master to inform him that it was the consensus of the students that to insist on a coat and tie was intrusive and fascistic.

"*Fascistic?*" the master asked. He was a professor of philosophy and frequently took pride in slipping it into casual conversation that he was probably the first academic in the country to start up a faculty chapter of Bundles for Britain. That was back in 1939! "I am about as much a fascist as John Stuart Mill," he comforted himself.

Well. Student ignorance. There wasn't anything—he knew—to be done about that. But he did have the authority to remove any scintilla of evidence that would induce, even if it did not justify, so ugly a label. Accordingly, he repealed his ruling. Undergraduates could henceforth dine at Silliman wearing anything they chose. One student, the next Halloween, took license to do just that, and arrived at the dining room wearing nothing at all.

But the fraternities held on to fascistic standards for a while longer, so that at 4:45 on the Tuesday, Daniel Tracey O'Hara fixed his tie while looking at the mirror above the sink. He was not so distracted by the social ritual that lay ahead of him as to fail to note that notwithstanding his beard, which tended to heaviness, he was incandescently young in appearance and good-looking, his hair light brown with here and there a curl, his eyes brown and penetrating, his lips fixed, it seemed, in a position at once quizzical and patronizing, his white teeth showing between lips that never seemed absolutely to close. He was lithe and strong and tall, and he winked at himself as he left the washroom to return to the student suite he shared with Henry Chafee.

Henry of course knew where Danny would be going. There was not the slightest resentment over his roommate's preferential status. It was two months ago that Danny had asked Henry whether he would be joining a fraternity. He got back the answer —Henry wasn't coy about it—that Henry couldn't afford a fraternity. Danny was regretful about this but didn't distract himself with egalitarian concerns. The administration at Yale forbade fraternity membership to more than 25 percent of the undergraduate body, so that a heavy majority were always on the principal, non-fraternity-belonging side of the tracks, and nobody seemed to have the time to stimulate social resentments. After two years together, Danny had come to terms with differences in economic resources. Danny's mother lived in Palm Beach with Danny's incumbent, affluent stepfather. Henry's widowed mother lived in

Lakeville, Connecticut. Danny's own father had died during freshman year.

"Died of what?" his date Martha had asked him, the night of the freshman prom.

"There is some question about that in our family," Danny said gravely. "There is the school of thought that says Dad died from drinking too many dry martinis. There is the other school that holds that he died because one day he couldn't *get* a dry martini." He then grinned. An infectious grin, so Martha didn't much mind it that Danny was speaking unkindly about his late father.

He would need extra money for fraternity dues. Danny was never absolutely sure who it was—his mother? his stepfather? his father's trust?—that sent him the monthly checks. They came in from different sources, but they always came. When he had special needs (a car, a European vacation) he would write to his mother. She had instructed him, when he got back from the war, to do this. She would forward his request to whichever of his patrons was, in her judgment, either more affluent at the moment, or else more inclined to make comfortable the life of Daniel T. O'Hara; though he would learn, that summer in France, that his suppliers were not wholly elastic in keeping Danny solvent and happy. "I forget, Mother," Danny once asked her after getting back from his vacation. "Did Grandfather die rich?"

"He had money"—his mother referred to her father, the late President—"but not a whole lot of it. Mother needs looking after. Whether there will be much left over after she goes, I'm not sure, and you certainly shouldn't count on it."

"Maybe she will leave me one of Grandfather's postage stamps?" Danny smiled.

"You are a nasty, avaricious boy," Rachel Roosevelt O'Hara Bennett smiled back at him, kissing him lightly on his nose.

Danny had been content to let the matter rest and reminded himself that since he was taking a major in American history at Yale he might at some point pause to examine what if anything the fawning historians had unearthed about the personal wealth of Franklin Delano Roosevelt, his grandfather, who had died when Danny was twenty.

Danny had visited him only once. This was at Hyde Park, the patriarchal estate on the Hudson River where the President spent weeks at a time during the summer. He had been too busy for a leisurely visit, what with the strains of a world war. But a presidential election was coming up, and family photographs were for that reason alone very much in order. The grandchildren were lunched at Hyde Park, were photographed (no interviews), but were not invited to spend the night. His mother had once complained, "Everybody thinks Hyde Park is as big as the Waldorf-Astoria. Actually, it is an *enormous* house, twelve bedrooms." Driving home Danny had said, "Mother, isn't Grandfather going to die soon? I mean, he looks like it, don't you think?" His mother said not to talk that way, that there was a national election ahead. And anyway, presidents get the best doctors in the world.

So in that first summer of sophomore year, Danny had traveled to Europe. Henry stayed with his bursary job at the Yale Library, taking long weekends with his mother and younger sister at the family home in Lakeville. Henry's mother had been widowed when her two children were ten and five. She raised them with eyes sharply focused on the need to economize. Mrs. Chafee worked in the library of Hotchkiss School and budgeted family life as though there were no income except for what her salary provided. Henry suspected his mother had a rainy-day fund hidden somewhere—naturally so, given that both the children had been sent off to boarding schools. This would not have been possible to manage, he explained to his less worldly sister, Caroline, without help from somewhere. But whatever her discreet resources, Mrs. Chafee, when she spoke about money, stressed only the drain of the family overhead, and turned away any question about the expense of boarding schools. When Danny suggested to Henry that he ask his mother for a loan so that he might travel to Europe, Henry was astonished at the mere thought of making such a request. "You don't understand, Danny. You just don't bring up things like that to Mother."

So Danny traveled alone to Europe, and when he got back

from his ten-week trip, he showed 8mm movies, using a bedsheet Scotch-taped to the wall as a screen.

"Certain of the sights I took in," Danny addressed his roommate and four other sophomores from across the hall, tilting his beer bottle up, "the camera simply refused to film. You understand, Josh? It's what Professor Sewall calls 'technological modesty.' " Josh grinned, priming his own bottle. "Can you buy that sort of stuff, I mean, the professional stuff, in Paris?" Danny shrugged his shoulders. "How would I know?" In such moments Danny's patronizing smile was especially beguiling. If only they knew, he thought.

That was last month, before the fraternity elections. It was time now to go—he had been counseled on no account to appear late at the fraternity. But that, and the trip to Europe, and his 1947 Ford Sedan notwithstanding, when Danny opened the door to go to his induction into a fraternity, he sensed that a little curtain, however fine, had been drawn between him and Henry. The luxuries of vacation travel were one thing—Danny and his roommate were physically separated during the summer, so there could be no daily abrasions—it had been only at the moment of departure that the distinction was felt: one roommate whose vacation would be restricted to occasional weekends at home, seventy-five miles from New Haven; the second, off on a vacation that would take him to pleasure spots in Europe, lasting over the entire summer. But this would be different, a little bumpier. Danny's fraternity was only five minutes' walking distance away, and now Danny would be at liberty to go off for dinner or for relaxation other than to the college dining hall or the college's facilities, and of course he would inevitably be making new friends. Invitations to nonmember fellow students were limited, in his fraternity's bylaws, to two invitations per term to the same student.

So, Danny felt a twinge of something—he was not quite sure what it was. Sadness? Well, no, not really. Pride? That figured there, somewhere. Disdain for those who did not do quite so . . . well? Could not afford to be so free? It was all there, somewhere, in greater or lesser measure. Did he feel a whiff of self-isolation? But he had consciously thought the matter out as he walked away from the army hospital in the Arno, after his first visit. What he had said to himself then was foresighted but simple: Either they would remain friends or they would not, but if they attempted to stay on as friends there would be no way to— vaporize?—an experience they had had in common. In fact, only they shared that experience. It was only Danny, and Henry, who knew about the Arno offensive and how Henry had first funked it, then tried to kill himself. If the memory of it was going to haunt them, then better not to see each other at all. But when after their discharge they resolved to apply to room together at college, it had to be on the understanding not that the Arno offensive would be forgotten but that it would be ignored. Either ignored, or maybe even sublimated. But that would be Henry's responsibility. Danny would just never bring it up, not ever. This turned out to be easy. From the beginning, he had been comfortable with Henry, the least demanding of companions; not quite the sparkler, dear Henry, but he could laugh, indeed did so, and he was so very earnest, and so very much devoted to his family, to Caroline in particular.

He was walking confidently now up York Street toward Zeta Psi. He told himself yet again that obviously he could never forget the events of August 12 and the Arno offensive, but that was over three years ago, and they had spent much time together. Would Henry ever be truly independent of him? Danny wondered.

No. But this had nothing to do with the day-to-day pleasure he took in Henry's company. A very nice guy, easy to share quarters with, arousable for a serious conversation, if the urge to have one came up, which it seldom did with Danny.

No, he thought finally, as he approached the graystone exterior of the fraternity, things were fine just the way they were, and Henry was just fine. A real pity, to be sure, that he was a fucking coward. Danny smiled. He savored the formulation.

Three

BACK THEN, in the field hospital, Private Henry Chafee had declined to speak to anybody. After three days of this, the doctor concluded that his muteness was a part of the trauma. On Day Five, the company clerk came around to record the exact circumstances of Henry's battle wound. "I know you can't talk," the corporal said, his notepad in front of him, "so just nod your head yes or no, and if necessary you can write on this pad here, okay, buddy?"

Henry closed his eyes and turned his head away. Only the sound of the big fan was heard, blowing in hot air, it seemed. The clerk faltered; then, after a minute or two, he rose from his chair. "Okay, okay. So you don't want any of this business. We can get the details from O'Hara. Get better."

He walked out of the long, hot tent where the casualties were stretched out, twenty-four of them, on army cots. He wondered to himself whether that was the smell of blood pure and simple. Or was it a combination, blood and all the medications one takes when blood works its way out of where it is supposed to stay. Whatever, it was unpleasant. He resolved, mockingly, not to be wounded. The corporal was glad to breathe air less fetid, though in the hot sun of the Arno Valley it was hotter than in the tent with its two big fans.

Danny thought it prudent simply to leave Henry alone, at least for the first week. What he did was write him a letter, meticulously sealed, on the envelope of which he wrote,

To be opened and read only by Pvt. Henry Chafee.

What he wrote was that, although he, Danny, did not know the correct term for it, he had to assume there was one such word: the word that described the man suddenly frozen in battle, immobilized. "I know enough about people in general, and about you, to know that it isn't a mark of—well, of an organic character defect. So let's let that one lie. Now, what I did on Monday you are free to think of as specially fraternal, or any way you want to put it, but it seemed to me totally logical at the time, and I'm only sorry I wasn't quick enough on the draw to get that fucking carbine away from you. Anyway, I'll leave you alone a few days and then I'll come around."

In fact, Danny mused, Henry's suicide attempt wonderfully capped the subterfuge. The company records showed that Private H. Chafee had been stopped by an enemy bullet while charging forward in pursuit of duty, and was subsequently dragged forward and then carried by his fellow soldier to the medical center. It was too good.

Danny went in on Saturday. He asked the nurse at the desk whether Private Chafee would receive Pfc. O'Hara. "Just ask him. Don't pressure him." An answer came in over the primitive intercom: Pfc. O'Hara to proceed to Ward B.

Danny walked to the designated area and at the entrance to the ward asked an attendant which was the number for Henry Chafee. He would just as soon not need to stare at the faces of a dozen or more mutilated men just to find Henry's bed. But he had maneuvering to do even within the ward he was looking for. A doctor or nurse or aide here, with the need to step around them and the paraphernalia of a hospital, trays at various levels, bottles, tubes, all of them to be skirted.

At number 12A he saw him. Henry's face was unshaven, a blond beard gestating; but his head was intact, the heavy bandages beginning only at chest level. His left arm was strapped to his side to accommodate the two needles, one giving him nourishment, the other blood plasma. Danny said nothing, but took Henry's hand. Henry began to cry. Danny looked around protectively, but in the ambient misery, quiet tears were not noticed. Danny gave him time. Then he said gently, "You got my letter?"

Henry nodded.

"Well, I have a proposal. It is really quite simple. It is that we won't ever discuss what happened at the Arno. And come to think of it, I'm not giving you much of a choice on the question, because that's the way *I* want it, and," Danny pointed to the stripe on his shirtsleeve, "I'm senior over you." Danny had teased Henry when the order was issued at Camp Wheeler promoting the platoon. Three soldiers had inadvertently been left out of the roster. A correction came in a week later, but it left Danny senior in grade.

Henry spoke now. He did not attempt a smile. With his free hand he reached for a limp handkerchief. Danny looked away while Henry wiped his eyes. "Okay," Henry said. "But you can understand I can't take it out of my mind, and won't. Not ever. I don't know if I'm glad to be alive, but I guess I can say I'm glad you are my friend."

The tears were once again visible. "Can you go now, Danny? Maybe come back tomorrow, or the next day? I have to sleep."

He closed his eyes, and Danny got up.

He stared down at his companion-at-arms and felt a great rush of pity, though laced with contempt. He would not conceal the truth from himself, never mind what he had written in the letter. It was simply established that Henry's character was flawed. Danny could never again feel for him quite what he once had.

When they met, soon after arriving at Camp Wheeler in Georgia to take infantry training, the base friendship was conventional: He was dealing with another soldier, on whom he could rely as a comrade in action. No more; Henry was different. But a nice guy, he would certainly not take that away from him.

By the time he reached the door, he had come up with the idea.

So now he went to the company clerk. He wanted to know, he told the sergeant, how to proceed with the matter at hand.

He got back from the sergeant a mimeographed form. He completed it and took it, as directed, to company headquarters, where he got the "Recommended for Citation" form. He relished the words as he inked them down on the form, sitting on a wooden stool in the cramped duty office. The sergeant on duty was preoccupied. He blew his cigar smoke into the air while scanning the freshly arrived directive having to do with a new variety of gonorrhea. He pinned it up on the wall, after spotting a space not already covered by other notices.

I was behind Private Chafee a few yards, Danny wrote, *when the enemy fire struck him down. But before collapsing, he managed to fire several rounds into the bunker, and this made it possible for me to approach the enemy gunners and knock them out with the hand grenade.*

Only Danny knew of the great, hilarious imposture over which he was presiding, and it amused him that its beneficiary, Henry, would be infuriated by it.

But what could Henry do, after all? Danny had taken in hand, at the height of a broad offensive military action, a fellow soldier who might otherwise have been court-martialed for cowardice—*cowardice in the face of the enemy,* as the war codes put it. Instead, a few weeks later, Private Henry Chafee would be discharged from the hospital and given a citation for gallantry in action plus a Purple Heart.

Henry would obviously have to play along. Either that or confess his cowardice—and maybe even get Danny court-martialed.

Henry's mortification, as the colonel pinned the medal on him, was all-consuming—he had been taken completely by surprise, called out of the ranks that morning at reveille. After the ceremony he had refused to speak to Danny. For several days he had needed to concentrate on Danny's impulsive generosity the evening of the offensive before resuming the friendship, which had hardened during the closing, uneventful winter before their discharge, after which they headed for the same university and put in to room together.

Four

THE IDEA was more popular with her children than with Rachel. She didn't mind a sail around the harbor or even a day sail to Block Island, a matter of four or five hours. But once Clement had proposed the longer cruise, there was no reversing the landslide of enthusiasm he triggered. Clement had a way of announcing his celebratory ideas without first checking with her. Sometimes he had already hired the orchestra. This time he did the equivalent, getting the children all excited. Danny's return from freshman year at boarding school was reason enough for maybe a little party for his friends; and yes, Lila had finished the fifth grade at her little school at Newport with the highest grades in the class.

All of this was good, but hardly grounds for major exertion.

When she was a girl, Rachel reflected, nobody made a fuss over what were considered workaday achievements. She remembered the summer in Campobello with her father, stricken by polio. Rachel had been awarded the Canadian equivalent of an Eagle Scout badge for girls. Her reward was a pat on the head from her father in his wheelchair and from her mother a smile, but not very different from the smile she got every day. Most days. On the other hand, true, it was hard to notice such things as children when one's father was campaigning for Vice President, then serving as governor of New York, all of this preparatory to life in the White House. And then too, her brothers never thought to concelebrate their achievements with those of their younger sister. By contrast—Rachel was pleased by the growing intimacy between the boy and his younger sister—on the day Danny came back from his boarding school at Millbrook, Lila greeted her big brother elatedly at the door, presenting him with a beaded belt on which she had worked at odd moments ever since Easter. The border was red, the background yellow, the Indian symbols green, and his name appeared in tiny brown beads discernible a good ten feet away:

◊◊◊ DANIEL O'HARA ◊◊◊

Lila was proud of her artifact and Danny was very pleased by it, and wore it at dinner, drawing Thelma's attention to it when she came in from the kitchen with the soup. When Clement rapped his table knife on the wineglass, demanding silence around the table, the children knew that their father would come up with a celebration. Last year he had made it a visit to Playland at Rye, an amusement park more than three hours' drive away, and three years earlier, just before Clement O'Hara had gone off to England as an official involved with the Lend-Lease program, there had been the trip to Niagara Falls.

"Silence, silence!" The chattering stopped. Mr. O'Hara told them he had accepted an invitation to watch fireworks on the Fourth of July at Nantucket with his old friends the Giffords. He paused.

Danny knew there was something else to come. Anybody can go to Nantucket, a matter of a couple of ferry rides.

"And I thought it would be fun to *sail* to Nantucket on *Listless!*"

The reaction was as Clement O'Hara had expected. That of the children, and that of their mother.

The O'Hara sloop was a quite ancient sailboat, 36 feet long, built during the twenties and neglected during the first years of the Depression. Danny was enchanted by it. The preceding summer, when the *Listless* was pulled out of storage, he had stood by the whole time the hull was recaulked and repainted. He engaged the sailmaker in inquisitive conversation when it was recanvassed, and attentively looked on when the engine was pulled out and overhauled. He signed up at the Ida Lewis Yacht Club for sailing lessons and was soon racing in a 24-foot Star.

He egged his father on every weekend to take *Listless* out. But Clement O'Hara's enthusiasms were short-lived, and *Listless* was used for routine triangular outings in Narragansett Bay. The trip to Block Island was an exception, and it had not been comfortable, the wind coming in that August day as usual, hard and from the southwest. It hadn't helped morale on *Listless* that his sister and mother both felt queasy. Arrived at Great Salt Pond, Rachel had cooked the steak, served supper to her family, then left on the evening ferry for Newport after tucking her children into bed at the motel. Now in prospect was a sail all the way to Nantucket—a forty-mile run, much of it over open water; battling currents pronounced and eccentric was not a venture Rachel looked forward to. Still, she had to admit that it was a novel, and in a way a glamorous outing. Of course, Danny and Lila responded to their father's plan with noisy enthusiasm.

Rachel O'Hara contrived a smile, and rang for dessert.

In the fortnight before the trip, Danny devoted himself to every detail of *Listless*'s needs and appearance. He made innumerable checklists, and when he could corral the attention of his father, insisted he go over them. He told Lila to make up a list of everything that would be needed for the galley, and he, Danny, would go over the list and correct it, and then give it to their mother. Were the necessary tools all there? Danny told his father, who was amused, that it was not safe to set out without a big wire cutter. The purchase was authorized. Danny checked the charts, the batteries, the radio direction finder, the radio; he gave the brightwork an additional coat of varnish and on the afternoon he thought of as devoted to the final details—they would set sail two days later—he stowed in his own locker his three or four most essential personal effects, including his flashlight, his Swiss Army knife, and his .22 Colt revolver.

The weekend before had given them the longest day in the year. Today the wind was sprightly during the afternoon, the sun steady and radiant. Clement left the house late an hour or two before dinner, setting out for one of his meetings in New London with his partners in the oil storage company. He would be spending the night at New London, returning in midmorning.

That night, Danny played cards with Lila and then read from his mother's Agatha Christie collection, finally turning off the light in his bedroom.

But he didn't sleep. He tried counting cricket chirps—he often tried that, during sleepless summers. He explained to Lila that by doing so, counting toward one thousand, you could never actually *get* to one thousand. Because always—"I mean *always,* Lila—you are asleep before you get there."

By the time he got to four hundred, Danny couldn't remember whether he had already done three hundred, or five hundred. He wasn't concentrating on the numbers, or on anything in particular, but he was not dozing off. He was hatching a plan. Danny's plans, beginning when he was a very little boy, had a way of materializing quite suddenly, quite fully.

He jolted up from his bed, flicked his bedside light back on, took off his pajamas, put on his briefs, the white tennis shorts lying on the armchair, and an Ida Lewis sports shirt from the drawer. He squeezed into his tennis shoes, lifted his flashlight from its hook in the closet, and walked silently downstairs to the kitchen. Flashing on his light, he opened the bin where Thelma kept the brown paper grocery bags. He withdrew one, then tiptoed to the refrigerator for an orange and a banana, and to the pantry, where he pulled out a half-dozen graham crackers.

Fully provisioned, he trod quietly to the garage, put his paper bag into the wire container at the back of the bicycle and wheeled it gingerly toward the garage door. This was his only real problem, he figured—opening and closing the wide two-car door without making any noise. He put the bicycle up against the wall, shone his light on the door fastener, and gently but firmly pushed on it until the heavy weights on either side asserted their gravitational authority and the door began to slide open. Danny slowed the movement toward the end of the cycle, to avoid the click-shut sound that might flag the attention of his mother.

It was a difficult maneuver. With one hand he kept the garage door from closing, with the other dragged his bicycle into the open air. That done, he could reverse the door's movements, easing it shut. It would not do for his mother to wake and find the garage door open. On the other hand, she would never notice the missing bicycle.

He thought to himself, pedaling down Alford Lane toward the little highway that would take him to the Bay: This was the greatest adventure he had ever undertaken. He was by himself, propelled by his own power, prepared for the first time in his life to spend the night entirely alone, entirely unsupervised. Where?

On *Listless!* He had never spent the night aboard the boat. Two days from now, his father had promised him, he and Lila could sleep on the boat, at anchor in Nantucket. The senior O'Haras would of course stay with the friends they were there to visit.

As the bicycle drew close to the marina, Danny had it all worked out in his mind. He would open the main hatch to the main cabin, focusing his flashlight on the combination lock. Then perhaps he would turn on the cabin light, pour himself a Coca-Cola from the icebox, maybe eat a graham cracker or two, thumb through a copy of *Yachting* magazine. Then when he felt *truly* sleepy, he'd go forward to the fo'c'sle, unfold a sleeping bag and stretch out.

He wondered for a moment: Should he have awakened Lila and brought her along? It would be nice to have her with him, but he dismissed the thought quickly. He felt only contempt for surviving parental rules governing his own movements, but intuitively he understood any precautions designed to protect Lila. She was just *too young* for grown-up stuff. Maybe next summer.

He thought there might be a security guard, but he had his wallet with him, and the guard could check that *Listless* was owned by an O'Hara. If the guard needed further persuasion, Danny could invite him to be present when Danny opened the combination lock, to establish that he was familiar with it. And, of course, he could describe to the guard exactly what lay in the boat, establishing his familiarity with it.

What reason would he give for boarding the boat just before midnight?

He would tell the guard that he needed to rise early to complete the arrangements for their "ocean trip." He wouldn't say, "the trip to Nantucket." That would sound too routine.

But there was no guard, so Danny bicycled along the marina dock until, against the new moon, he could discern the configuration of the little sloop he had come to know so well.

He put down the bicycle suddenly, quietly. He had spotted a faint light on the *Listless*. The forward hatch, he could see, was open. His heart began to pound. If a light was on, that meant someone had to be on board, because a master blade switch shut off electrical circuitry throughout the boat, and always that switch was disconnected when the last person left the boat. Might it be that a workman had forgotten—left on the master switch, and also a cockpit light? If so, the batteries would drain in a matter of hours.

He walked with extreme caution along the slip the *Listless* was tied up to. Ducking very low, he walked past the fo'c's'le light to examine the cockpit.

Its hatch was open.

That had to mean that someone was below. The yard men would never leave a boat with two hatches open.

One hand on the safety-line stanchion and another on the shroud, he pulled himself lightly over the lifeline to the deck, lowered himself, stomach on deck, and slowly, noiselessly, inched toward the forward hatch. He was several feet from the forward hatch opening when he heard the sound, a woman's moaning. He lay still; and, after a moment, continued to crawl forward. He raised his head only enough to look down into the fo'c'sle. He was looking now on his father's naked torso. A blond woman was gyrating rhythmically above him, looking down on his tortured, pleasured face with a half-smile. . . .

Danny was riveted. The fire in his own loins was instantaneous. He was mortified, entranced, frightened, mesmerized. He thought quickly, silently, to leave, but he could not remove his eyes from the scene below. It was several minutes before his father's moans joined with the groaning of his partner, and then a little animal yelp, after which she bent over, covering his father's body.

Surely, Danny—sweating, breathless—kept thinking, his heartbeat could be heard below? He inched himself back a few feet; then, one leg over the lifeline to the scupper, he swung the other around to the dockside and walked silently back to the bicycle, drawing it along by hand until he had passed a dozen boats, only then mounting it and heading back for home.

In bed again his thoughts were tumultuous, his excitement finally uncontrollable. So much about which he had vaguely wondered was—so much clearer now. It was that way with Danny. What was not clear was what he would say when he saw his father the next day. It was clear to him only what would be on his mind.

"Come on, Danny, let's you and me take this load to the boat, stow it, and I'll come back for the ladies." Clement O'Hara had on his skipper's hat and carried his seabag over his left shoulder, displaying a muscular forearm bronzed right up to the short sleeves of his polo shirt.

Wordlessly, Danny got into the front seat of the boxy Buick station wagon with his father. He wedged his bare knees up against the last-minute grocery bag so that he could close the car door.

"I called the Coast Guard," his father said. "They told me the wind is building. An easterly. Not ideal. But what the heck, it'll probably change, and it won't hurt if we have to tack for a while."

Danny said nothing. After a moment his father spoke again. "If we do tack, I'll make Mom go below, camp down on the leeward side. She'll be comfortable there. Lila can stay in the cockpit—fresh air—and hand us things. You and I, we can alternate on the wheel, and tend to the sails." Clement looked over at his dark-haired son with the trim profile and expressive lips. "You looking forward to it, son?"

Danny said yes, he was looking forward to it.

It was late morning and the day was gray. Newport gray: sullen clouds, leaden seas, wisps of agitated white. Getting the boat as far as the Brenton Reef lightship at the mouth of the Bay was no problem—heading south in an easterly. But father and son had to struggle against the wind pressure to tuck in a reef. While they worked on it, posting themselves on opposite sides of the boom, Lila was at the wheel. Her pigtail swung over her shoulder when the puff was heavy. She focused with fierce attention on the compass, determined to keep the course prescribed by her father.

It was when they got to open water that tacking became necessary. "The course to Vineyard Sound is 110 degrees magnetic," Clement O'Hara pronounced, seated below at the chart table. "We'll do a long port tack, maybe a couple of hours"—he looked down again at the chart—"three hours, maybe, then decide whether to head for the fair current up Vineyard Sound, or go southeast and then on up to Martha's Vineyard. Hit it at the eastern end, go up by Chappaquiddick." He glanced down again at the chart. "Then . . . more beating to Nantucket. Damn"— he looked up and spoke as to himself—"the wind couldn't be worse for our purposes."

And then, to his wife, "Rachel, I'll have a Bloody Mary with lunch."

Two hours later, Rachel pleaded with her husband to return to Newport. "It would be an easy run going back, wouldn't it, Clem? With this wind?" Clement O'Hara was working on his fifth bottle of beer. He tightened the grip of his cap over his head and said nothing to his wife, who was leaning back on the bunk, one foot up on the vertical rail to keep her balance in the rolls. He stood up, leaning his head into the cockpit where he felt the force of the wind and the sultriness of the air. "What course you holding, Danny?"

"One three five." Danny needed to shout out the words to be heard through the din of the wind. The rain had begun to come down an hour earlier. Danny had on foul-weather gear, jacket and pants, a baseball cap, and a towel around his neck. The boat heeled sharply. The wind against the shrouds whistled, the pitch varying with the speed.

"Can you see Gay Head?" Clement shouted out to the helmsman.

"I don't know whether it's Gay Head," Danny called back. "But it's something. At about ten o'clock, maybe eleven; four, five miles off."

Clement went into the icebox for another beer.

"Clement, goddamnit," Rachel struggled against the movements of the boat, her hand clutching the grab rail above the bunk, "you have had *enough* beer. Now throw that overboard or give it to me!"

Clement did not lift his face from the chart. Rachel looked over to one side at her daughter. But Lila worried only about Danny, more than an hour now alone in the cockpit. Clement removed his foul-weather jacket. His sweat shone through the polo shirt. He began to fiddle with the dials on the radio direction finder. He leaned up into the cockpit again and shouted out to Danny, "I'll see if I can bring in Gay Head and New Bedford. That will give us a fix." In the rolling boat, heeled twenty, twenty-five degrees over in the puffs, Clement fumbled with the parallel rules and the dividers and the pencil and the pad over the chart. Rachel, back on the bunk, one foot again up on the rail, could see that her husband was not succeeding in whatever it was that he was attempting. Danny's voice called out, and Clement arched his head into the cockpit to make out the words.

"What you say, Dan?"

Danny shouted out into the wind. "We're getting close to that land, Gay Head, maybe. Should we go on a starboard tack?"

"Yes," Clement said, ambiguously. "I'll come up and do the lines."

It was an unclean business. Danny brought the boat's bow into the wind. His father began to release the jib sheet, became confused and reached for a winch handle, which fell from his hand into the agitated sea, bouncing over the leeward rail which was several inches under water. The jib sheet was now tangled on the winch. Clement had not freed it when the wind batted the sail to starboard, and now, the jib caught aback, the hull pitched and the starboard rail went deeper under water, the end of the boom poking into the sea.

"Loose the main! Loosen the main, goddamnit, Danny!" But the main winch was in the cockpit, not at the helmsman's side—a responsibility of the sail trimmer. Danny was wrestling to get way —with no forward motion, the rudder was ineffective. He had to bring the boat back on a starboard tack until the jib sheet could be untangled.

The maneuver never executed, and the jib back in place, *Listless* continued on a port tack, fifty degrees south of course. A half hour later, Danny could no longer see land. It was after six. The rain ended but fog came in and the wind's velocity heightened. The main's double reef still left the boat overcanvassed.

"We need less sail." Danny's reasoning was in part book learning, in part seat-of-the-pants. *Something* had to be done. He closed his eyes and forced his mind to sort out the alternatives. One was to haul down the mainsail entirely. A second was to replace the jib with a smaller sail—there was a storm jib on board. But, he realized achingly, that operation was complicated. 1) Bring up the storm jib from the locker below. 2) Lower the number 2. 3) Take off, one by one, the number 2 hanks. 4) Hank on, one by one, the storm jibs. 5) Attach the halyard. 6) Switch the jib sheets from the old to the new sail. 7) Raise the new jib.

Even with an able seaman at the helm, the operation required two men forward—though one man alone could do the forward deck, moving deliberately, the helmsman cooperating attentively.

Though Danny had never before put up the storm jib he considered doing it now, for the first time. But could his father, at this point, handle the helm?

No. There was no prospect of success.

The only thing left to do—

Danny peered down into the cabin area. "Dad," he shouted out. His father's bleary face leaned out into the cockpit. "What do you say we take down the main?"

Clement O'Hara pursed his lips, as if giving solemn, profound thought to the suggestion. "Not a bad idea," he nodded.

Danny: "Do you want to go forward and loosen the halyard, or do you want me to? If so, you'll have to take the helm."

It was clear to Danny that his father hadn't understood him. Clement O'Hara stayed where he was, his two hands tight on the handrails, his eyes unfocused, a half smile on his face.

Danny felt a twang of fear in his stomach, a dryness in his throat. The situation was bad. The mainsail had to be let down. How to do it single-handed in a heavy breeze? He took the end of the port sheet, tied a loop, placed it over an appropriate peg on the wheel and, four feet or so from the loop, fastened the line to a cleat. The pressure on the rudder was leftward, the oversize jib pushing the bow of the boat to leeward. The wheel immobilized, Danny sprang forward and payed out the main sheet until the wind spilled and the tension on the halyard was relieved. The boat substantially righted itself; the furious flapping of the mainsail was deafening. Danny maneuvered his way forward to the mast and loosed the halyard, clutching down on the main luff to bring the sail down.

It was heavy work, but finally the sail was down. Danny tossed the end of the halyard over the sail, down, and back, to bind down the sail on the boom, however untidily. Then quickly back to the helm. He whisked off the improvised becket and brought the boat right around, jibing, back onto a port tack. When he had got forward motion and the rudder was active again, he loosed the port sheet and drew it in to starboard. He needed to jump back and forth between the sheet and a wheel that needed constant adjustment.

Finally *Listless* was back on the wind, headed southeast, the heel greatly reduced, but also the boat's speed. She was moving, in all that wind, at only four knots.

Danny looked below. His father's head was on the chart table. He was asleep.

His mother got up and made her way to the companionway—it was easier now to move about. She put her head up over the companionway, protruding to the cockpit. She had to raise her voice to be heard but she spoke gravely.

"Do you know what to *do*, Danny? Can you bring her in? Bring her in *anywhere?*"

Danny was now scared. Once again he forced himself to think the situation through, one step at a time. Over the past excited ten days he had spent hours studying the charts. He drew now from a basic navigator's intelligence and began by asking himself the primary question:

Where were they? Approximately, even. Where—next question —would they find land?

"I think, Mom, that with this fog we don't want to . . ." He stopped and thought. "Dad was doing a course over to the east end of Martha's Vineyard. If we keep this up for two or three hours, then come about again, we should be heading up toward Katama Bay. South of Edgartown. When we get closer to land maybe the fog will clear and we'll see some lights."

He looked at his mother's distraught face. "Don't worry, Mom," he managed.

At nine o'clock Danny calculated he might as well bring the boat about and head north, toward land. The rain had returned, the wind's velocity had stayed steady at twenty-five knots. He let one sheet go and drew in on the other as, in spurts, he turned the wheel. Little by little he was able to winch the sail in tight. They were now on a course to Martha's Vineyard . . . somewhere in Martha's Vineyard, which stretches from end to end over twenty miles.

Rachel passed around a box of cookies. Danny ate two, Lila and Rachel none. Rachel turned to the stove and, after one or two foiled attempts, brought some water to a boil and poured instant coffee and sugar into it. She handed a cup to her son, another to her husband, now showing signs of life. Clement took the cup, stared down at it, shook his head and peered up at the cockpit.

"Everything all right? I had one hell of a headache, Danny, took a five-minute snooze. This coffee and a shot of vodka will fix me up."

Danny lost patience. "Yeah," he called back. "All you need is more booze, Dad." Danny froze, struck by what he had said. He had never before used such language addressing his father. He expected instant furious retaliation.

But Clement retreated to the chart table seat. Danny realized that he was wholly in charge. It was as if he had been anointed.

Two hours went by. Danny's eyes strained in search of lights. The wind had eased. If there had been another hand on board, Danny would have hoisted the mainsail back up. What he needed to know was: Where were they? How far from shore? How far from the Katama channel? East of it, or west? He shouted down to his father, "Dad, can't you get *something* on the direction finder?" Clement's face materialized at the usual spot. His father looked vague, but said something to the effect that he would try.

Danny could hear the static coming in from the RDF and his sea-saturated frame tensed in anxiety. Might his father come up with *some* idea of where they were? At that moment he saw the light dead ahead, and at the same moment *Listless* struck the reef.

The boat pitched over, angled now into the wind. Danny started the motor and shoved the gear into reverse, pressing the accelerator lever all the way down. There was a huge whirr as the propeller blades sucked water in toward the hull. But there was no motion. Rachel shouted out, "There's water coming in!"

Danny left the wheel, turned off the engine, and leaned his head into the cabin. "Dad! Try the Coast Guard. We've got a brand-new radio. *Get the Coast Guard!*"

Clement reached aft for the radio receiver, peered into the fuse box and clicked the toggle that turned the radio on. He pressed down on the transmission key and called out, "Mayday! Mayday! Mayday! Calling the Coast Guard, any station! Come in come in come in."

But only static came in.

"Have you got the right channel, Dad?" Danny was below, tracing the flow of water. He felt the boat tilt and rushed up to the cockpit. Lila squeezed past her father, who was once again calling out the emergency into the microphone. Lila climbed up into the cockpit and grabbed Danny's arm. "Danny, are we going to sink?"

"I don't know," Danny said, struggling to make his voice calm. "But we can't sink very far, Lila. We're on the rocks now, and over there is a shore light. It can't be more than fifty yards away, maybe less. What *is* the matter with the Coast Guard?"

"Maybe he doesn't have the right channel—"

Rachel O'Hara's voice interrupted them. "The leak seems to be slowing. I saw where it was coming in, in the head. I stuffed a towel into it."

"Good work, Mom."

The wind suddenly abated. A few moments later it was totally calm. The only sound was that of Clement O'Hara shouting Mayday! Mayday! Mayday! to the Coast Guard. As suddenly as the wind had stopped, the skies now cleared, and the half-moon shone through. Danny could make out the houses on shore. The light he had first seen was a streetlight. He looked at his watch and called his mother to come to him.

"Mom," he said, struggling to speak evenly. "I'm gonna . . . swim . . . the beach there, right there . . . a coupla minutes is all, no danger . . . I'll take a life preserver . . . I'll head for the house there, and use their phone and call the Coast Guard. Leak's okay, right? . . . Well, we got tide, you know, Mom, the tide . . . If it's coming in, that means a bigger hole as the water lifts the hull. Got to do something . . . Be back in no time."

Danny turned his face away, ripped off his foul-weather jacket, drew down his soggy trousers, yanked off his sports shirt and grabbed a life preserver from the port lazaret. He thrust his arms through it and shouted to Lila to tie the knot while he held the light on the laces. In seconds he was in the water.

They watched him anxiously and almost immediately spotted his problem. The tide. "Oh my God." Rachel grabbed Lila's arm as they tracked Danny's flashlight slipping downstream parallel along the beach. But gradually the light got closer to the shore, and soon they could see the light bounding toward one of the beach houses. Then it disappeared.

"He must be inside," Rachel said tensely. Mother and daughter were hugging each other but their eyes didn't move from the beach house. After a few minutes they saw the bobbing light again. Danny was running in the opposite direction from where he had drifted. They followed the light to about a hundred yards east of *Listless*. Danny had stopped. Apparently he entered the water, because now the light was moving toward them. When the light was twenty yards or so off they heard him shouting. At first they couldn't make out the words.

"The boarding ladder! Put out the boarding ladder! Quick! . . . in the cockpit . . . under the seat!"

Rachel tore back and yanked open the cover. Lila flashed a light into the locker and Rachel pulled out the aluminum ladder with its rail hooks. She fought to free it from entangling lines and in a half minute had it hanging over the boat's rail.

Danny began to climb the ladder but after the first step he paused, gasping for air.

"Come on, Danny!" his sister called.

He hung on to the rail, his knees wedged on to the bottom rung of the ladder. He didn't move. "Danny, Danny, come up!" Lila cried.

Suddenly she understood. "Mom, Mom! He's tired! Quick, help, help!" She climbed over the cockpit coaming and grabbed one of Danny's arms. His mother was there tugging on the other arm. Together they pulled, and his foot caught the ledge of the ladder. He bent over the lifeline, got into the cockpit, and lay face down. His mother dove below and came back with a towel and a blanket. She buried her son in them. Finally Danny whispered, "The Coast Guard's coming."

. . . .

Two days later, Danny strolled from the tennis court in the brilliant sun into the shaded clubhouse. He went into the office, past the corridor with all the photographs of all the famous yachts, going back a half century. He approached the club's secretary. He asked, Could he please use her typewriter during the lunch break? "I just want to type out something, you know, a form." Miss Tarbell offered to do it for him, extending her hand for the document. Danny moved his own hand quickly behind him.

"No, thanks a lot, Miss Tarbell, but the rules are you're supposed to type it yourself, and it's good practice—I use a typewriter at school."

She smiled at him. "Sure, Danny. In ten minutes I'll be going out to lunch. Go ahead and use it. They're all the same, typewriters."

In ten minutes Danny was alone in the office. First he slid an envelope into the carriage of the old Royal. Turning the platen knob, he put it in place. He typed out his mother's name and address.

He pulled out the envelope and slipped in the sheet of paper he unfolded from the envelope. Then he pressed down on the Cap Lock key and with his right index finger punched out:

MRS. O/HARE. YOUR HUSBAND IS FUCKING A BLOND LADY IN HIS BOAT.

He frowned at his work. Should he do another draft? Correcting the typographical errors? He had brought only the single sheet of paper. He opened Miss Tarbell's drawer. But the paper there was all stationery of the yacht club. The other stack of paper was flimsy, suitable for carbons.

He could, using Miss Tarbell's scissors, cut the sheet in half, throw away the top half and type it over on the bottom half.

What the heck. Let it go as it is.

He reflected on how to sign his message. Perhaps "ONE WHO KNOWS." But that, he thought on reconsideration, would be too much. Too . . . melodramatic, like the last act of *Othello*.

Five

DANNY'S BRAND-NEW CAR was a sporty Plymouth convertible and he was anxious to show it off, and this was the perfect opportunity. Henry had never invited Danny to meet his mother and sister but suddenly, after two years, the invitation came. Danny would drive Henry in his new car to his mother's house in Lakeville, Connecticut, and they would both spend the weekend. Early Saturday afternoon after morning classes and a quick lunch at the college dining hall, they walked one block to the garage at Church Street.

Soon after pulling out of New Haven, Danny began his light-hearted interrogation.

"Is your mother—an austere type?"

"I guess the answer is, Yes. Uh-huh. She can laugh, all right, though laughing is not her specialty. She dresses very plainly, reads a lot, doesn't talk much, but listens. She doesn't do the usual things, smoke, drink—"

"Well, she had to do one of the usual things or there would be no Henry, Henry."

Henry laughed. "Yes, Danny, though I suppose when some people do it, it's *unusual.*" When at age thirteen or whatever he tripped over news of the antecedent biological requirements for fresh life, Henry had found it difficult to believe that such a requirement applied also to his own mother. He had closed his eyes to consider it, then quickly reopened them. He would rather not, on second thought, visualize it. On the other hand . . .

"Take a look at the wedding picture. It isn't exhibited, but I'll try to remember to pull it out of the desk. Mother was quite beautiful."

"How could it be otherwise, you handsome blond devil. I don't know about your father, but there must have been a pretty good gene pool there: you, six feet, blond, well built, nice features, blue eyes—"

"Danny. Cut it out."

"Did you know your father?"

"I have a vague memory of him . . ."

But suddenly Danny had braked the car to a halt. It was mid-October in New England, there was a nip in the air, and the maples were fierily exuberant. Danny had spotted a stand selling fresh cider. He was gone only a minute or two and came back not with one gallon of cider but with six. He never underbought, underate, or underdrank, though there was no toll on his figure, or his wallet, though it never seemed to overflow.

"Why six gallons?"

"Make nice house presents. . . . By the way, I hope your ma will serve wine or beer. Will she?"

"As a matter of fact, she won't. That's a good point. We'll have to stop at a liquor store."

"Will she mind?"

"She'd mind if Caroline had anything."

"Caroline's seventeen?"

"Eighteen."

"Smart?"

"She's very smart. She's . . . Well, you'll see. She's"—Henry looked over at Danny at the wheel—"how should I put it? She's —as you would put it, Danny, like me: perfect."

Danny smiled. "Does she know about me?"

"Know what? She knows you are a junior at Yale, that we've been roommates for two years, that you play soccer and tennis, that you . . . served in Italy with me." Henry's voice was suddenly grave. He continued, "Knows that you are studying economics and history, and that your grandfather was President of the United States."

"Is she a New Dealer?"

Henry thought, and replied gravely. "Danny! I *told* you Caroline is smart. Of course not."

Danny enjoyed it all. Grandson of the architect of the New Deal, he more or less accepted it as, at his age, one would accept the Old Testament. Occasionally he acknowledged the existence of fringe dissenters. Henry was one. He went on. "Actually, she doesn't talk about politics, though when we went to Italy she sent a letter to President Roosevelt, told him if I didn't get back okay, she would kill him."

"Kill him?"

"Yes. She was thirteen, something like that. The Secret Service stopped by, talked with Mum, showed her the letter. She gave Caroline a severe spanking."

"How do you know it was severe? You weren't there."

"Caroline wrote me to the APO number. I thought I showed you the letter."

"Well, you didn't. I don't think I'd have spanked her if she had threatened Grandfather. Hmm. Maybe yes. That depends. I can think of some of my cousins, and maybe even some of my uncles, who Grandfather wouldn't have minded a bit if they had, you know, given their lives for their country." Danny made himself sound like a minister delivering a eulogy.

"Cut it out, Danny."

"It's an American sentimentality, the devoted-to-the-death parents bit. My own father was a shit, you must know that. I must have told you?"

"What about his successors?"

"Oh, Henry. Nice, that. 'His successors.' Well yes, there have been three successors. Along the way, I had three stepfathers. Number Two, married to Mom right after Dad, she met on the train. I can remember exactly when it was. The sixth of July, 1941. Mom suddenly announced that she was taking me and Lila to Palm Beach 'to spend a week or so'—that's how she put it, 'a week or so'—with her cousins. They have a huge place at Palm Beach, the Weatherills. Well, to compress that story, she never did go back to Newport—*we* never went back to Newport. *And,* she married a man she met on the club car, a thirty-five-year-old widower whose wife—get this—was killed in the war. She was a passenger on a liner corralled to do duty in the Dunkirk situation. The ship was ordered to pick up stranded British soldiers, which it did, only a German U-boat sank it before it got to safety. Anyway, they struck up a conversation, he was on his way to Palm Beach to visit his mother, and about six months later he was— Number Two."

"Nice guy?"

"I thought so, but two years later, a couple of years after Pearl Harbor, Mom filed for divorce. She wrote me at school. All she'd say was that it didn't, quotes, work."

"He was?"

"He was," Danny ticked off the fingers of his right hand: "Lloyd Rosenthal. Jewish. Loaded. I don't know how much loot old Mom took away, but put it this way: she's never been exactly broke."

"And Number Three?"

"Well now, *that* was a real romance. Hang on." Danny coasted to a stop in front of the liquor store. *"Torrington Spirits. Founded During the Civil War."*

"Couple of reds, couple of whites, couple of six-packs? Have I forgotten anything?"

"Sounds right," Henry nodded. "I'm sure Mother can supply some absinthe for after dinner."

In five minutes Danny was back in the car, the cardboard case of beer and wines reposing on the backseat.

"Okay, got what we needed. Do you suppose" (Danny did not avoid any opportunity to advertise his knowledge of wines) "they'll ever make a wine in California you can drink? Last week I had a California Chablis. Tasted like Coca-Cola poured over old battery acid."

"So you got French at the Civil War liquor shop?"

"Italian. And where was I? Oh yes, the *real* romance. Well, Number Three was an Eye-talian opera singer. He sang in Miami at a big benefit for the USO, and Mom was one of the sponsors, so he sat next to her at the dinner, and she invited him to stay at her place—oh, I didn't tell you: She got Number Two's big place on the water as part of the divorce settlement—because the Eye-talian tenor had two days to kill before his next performance."

"What was *his* name?"

"Brace yourself, Henry. His name was Francantore Incantadore."

"You are kidding me."

"I am not kidding you. Franki's father and mother must have thought they were kidding *somebody*. No wonder Franki looked so sad."

"Did you find him sad?"

"Actually, believe it or not, I laid eyes on him exactly one time. It was just after basic, at Camp Wheeler—when I met you. I had —we had—a fortnight's leave, I went home, late train, Atlanta–Miami, didn't want to disturb Mom, so I got a taxi, drove to the house, got out, paid the taxi, lugged my stuff into the house. But I stopped. I heard this—*voice* bellowing outside, singing an opera aria. I dropped my bags, went around to the back of the house, and there was Francantore Incantadore standing naked on the beach, facing the house and singing like he was in the Metropolitan Opera."

"Where was your mother?"

"She was on the second floor, in the bedroom, standing, the French door open, the moon shining in. I mean it was a great sight, grand opera in the buff."

"You mean she was naked too?"

"No. Of course, I don't know whether she would have become naked if after the aria I hadn't cleared my throat."

"What happened then?"

"Well, when Franki spotted me he dived into the sea. I didn't much know what to do, so I walked into the house. Mom hugged me, told me about Franki, said he was divine and a real nature lover, loved to swim in the sea at night, and maybe I knew or had read somewhere that in Europe, along the Mediterranean, nature lovers don't always use bathing suits? Anyway, by the time I left for Fort Dix they were engaged. That was true love. But," Danny sighed, "true love doesn't always last very long, and when Mom found out—she told me about it—that Franki had taken up with a lady harpist in Mexico, she called up the lawyer."

"Your mom's lawyer must have gotten used to it."

"Yeah. Maybe that's why she ended up marrying *him,* cheaper that way." Danny laughed. "Actually, he's a nice guy. Hard-working, Yale Law graduate, divorced himself, no kids. It's lasted what, five years? and maybe it'll go on— Hey, see that?"

Danny brought the car to a quick stop, reached into the glove compartment and pulled out his .22 Colt pistol. "Keep quiet," he said quietly. He slid out from the driver's seat, closing the door gently, and slunk into a ditch alongside. His body prostrate, he eased his head up to view the field, the pistol barrel protruding through the barbed-wire fence. Seated on the front seat of the car, Henry could see the woodchuck in the farm pasture. He had never himself shot one but that was simply because he hadn't developed the appetite; woodchucks were plentiful in Litchfield County. Usually the opportunist hunters tracked them with rifles, .22s, but if the aim was sharp a pistol would do. Henry had seen Danny shoot and kill squirrels, five minutes' drive past the Yale Bowl.

Danny fired. The woodchuck thirty yards away plunged into his hole. Danny lifted himself off the ground, brushed away stray leaves and thistle, returned the pistol to its holster and re-entered the car. He grinned happily. "I get maybe one out of five at that distance. I cleaned out the whole county at Newport the summer before Camp Wheeler.'' He tossed the pistol back into the glove compartment, put the car back in motion, and exulted in the top-down view of the Berkshire foothills toward which they headed.

As ever, Danny talked, about this and about that, about his pleasures, which were abundant, and his pains, centered mostly on this faculty member or that dean or that cousin, cumulatively not an enormous assembly, given that Danny O'Hara, charmer, led a pretty charmed life, and why not? Weren't the alternatives ugly, he asked Henry?

A half hour later Henry said, "Turn left at the stop sign. You're in Salisbury. We're only two miles away."

Danny drove and admired the elm trees that lined the road. They got to the town of Lakeville and Henry guided him to the northern fork from the town center. "See that house up there?"

"Yeah."

"Wanda Landowska lives there."

"Who?"

"The harpsichordist, Wanda Landowska. She does all her recording there."

"So? Where else would she record?"

"Danny. Most recordings are done in studios. S-t-u-d-i-o-s. It is very unusual to record professionally in a country house a hundred yards from a lake."

"So what happened to Miss Landowska?"

"What happened is she made a great hit, recording the *Well-Tempered Clavier* for RCA Victor. The locals—that includes me and Caroline and Mother; Caroline is a great buddy of the great lady, ever since she was nine years old—got a kick out of it because—all this was written up in *Time* magazine—when she began to record suddenly she stopped. Said she could hear noise from cars driving down along this road. The audio people said there's no noise, but she said she didn't care what the audio people said, she herself was not deaf—*Hi em noht defff!*—unlike the audio people, and—*she heard noise.* So she went to the phone and called the state police."

"Called the police?"

"I mean, called the state troopers in Canaan, said she was the greatest living artist, was recording, and would they please seal off the road—this road, the one we're on—for a couple of hours. And they did!" Henry moved his hand up across the steering wheel. "—Yes, turn into the driveway right there. . . . Speaking of the police, I wonder what—"

The state trooper stationed by the driveway motioned to Danny not to turn in. Henry intervened.

"Tell him it's my house. My mother's house."

The policeman bent down and looked at Henry, then back at Danny. "You'll have to wait. Just a minute. There's an ambulance there. It'll be coming right up. Matter of a minute or two."

Henry opened the car door and jumped out. "What's happened?"

"You the lady's son?"

"I am Henry Chafee. Mrs. Chafee is my mother."

The state trooper, a man in his middle age wearing heavy dark glasses, paused. "Your mother has had a heart attack. She's being taken to the hospital in Sharon. I suppose everything will be all right. But you have to wait—the ambulance," he peered down the road, "they're taking her into it now." He motioned a clearance to the ambulance driver and a moment later it crested the height and turned right, toward Sharon.

They sat silent in the living room, and Danny focused his eyes on Caroline Chafee, struck by her peculiar beauty. She was as plain as a subject of Andrew Wyeth, dressed in the simplest cotton, her hair untended, a lustrous yellow-brown, her brown eyes demure yet searching, intensively engaged, her face oval, her fine nose and ears exquisitely framed, Danny noted, spotting the tension in her hands gripped on the ends of the armchair. Twenty minutes later the telephone rang. Mrs. Chafee was dead.

The telephone rang twice and Henry spoke with a hospital administrator, with a doctor, and then with the family lawyer. Danny took the earliest opportunity to motion Henry to one side. "Henry, at this point I don't think I can be of any help. Would it make sense if I just took off, went back to New Haven,

leave you and Caroline here without me to worry about?'' Henry
didn't appear quite to understand him. But Caroline, grown in a
few moments of tragedy into womanhood, Danny thought—this
morning she must have been a beautiful girl, now she was a
beautiful young woman—Caroline understood, and reacted decisively.

"Please stay, Danny.'' Her voice was soft, yet oddly authorita-
tive in tone. "It will help Henry.'' Danny nodded. He would do
as bidden.

Campbell Beckett, the family attorney, drove in. Caroline
threw her arms around him and, in the arms of her godfather,
let herself cry. The silver-haired lawyer stroked her hair and told
her to try hard to compose herself, to accept the will of God. He
went to the telephone in the little study. Henry was seated on a
stiff upright chair, pale and silent. Danny, standing by the bookcase, could hear the lawyer talking to the doctor over the telephone. When he was through, Mr. Beckett addressed Henry.

"Dr. Coley is coming. He'll be here in a few minutes.'' He
motioned to Henry to step outside with him.

"Did you know about your mother's illness?''

Henry shook his head, no, he didn't know about it.

"Dr. Coley will give you the details. I knew she was having
trouble. After her physical in May she came to see me. She told
me when she came in to make some changes in her will.''

"Was there any sign something was going to . . . happen?''

"No. She said the doctor had told her it could come any time,
probably sooner rather than later. They could not bring her
pulse rate down.''

Henry walked into the study and signaled to Danny to join him
and Mr. Beckett. "Please tell him,'' he asked the attorney, who
filled Danny in. It didn't completely surprise Henry when Danny
then asked, "Are the kids, the, er, survivors, broke?''

Henry motioned to Mr. Beckett. "Please answer the question,
Mr. Beckett.'' He managed a half smile. "Don't worry about
breaking any confidences, Uncle Cam. Danny likes to be in on
everything.''

The lawyer looked over at Henry. "Your mother has—had—

some money. And," he pointed down to the floor and then up at the ceiling, "the house here is unmortgaged." He turned to Caroline. "Whatever you want to do, dear, the estate can pay the bills, if you are careful. You will have to give that some thought. You will talk it over with Henry, of course."

"What has Caroline been doing?" Danny whispered his question to Henry when the lawyer and his goddaughter walked out of the room.

"Going to night school in Torrington, working during the day at the hospital." They could hear the doorbell. "Here's Dr. Coley."

William Coley, all six feet four of him, maneuvered himself into the little study, was introduced to Danny, conferred with Cam Beckett, walked into the house and into the bedroom and closed the door. Fifteen minutes later he came out and sat down by Henry. He looked up at Danny, and pointed his finger suggestively at the door. A New England doctor of the old school was not prepared to discuss intimate matters in the company of an undergraduate from Yale who was not a member of the family.

Danny walked out of the room, onto the lawn. He gazed for the first time at the spring-fed mile-square lake Henry had several times made reference to. At the opposite end he could make out what he assumed must be the Hotchkiss School for Boys, which Henry had attended while Danny was at school in Millbrook, fifteen miles west. The site was quite beautiful, Danny thought, prettier than any of the lakes around New Haven. The afternoon had turned colder but the sky was cloudless, and the sun's rays brightened the foliage, yellows and reds and golds. Danny thought to himself: What a hell of a place and time for this *dumb*—he couldn't find the right word for it—thing to happen. This was his first death outside the battlefield, he reflected. How many more deaths would he come upon before—dying himself? He laughed inwardly. He had forgotten all about dying since the war ended. He doubted he would ever die, he teased himself. Dying was for people less . . . competent than he! Silly thought, sure; he'd die, as everyone would, one of these days.

But for the next hundred years or so dying was for other people. Which reminded him—

What in the hell should *he* now do? After what Caroline said, he'd have to stick around. He couldn't pretend he looked forward to sticking around, though Caroline was an entrancing girl. Woman. It would be good if he could think of something—anything—to *do*.

Henry came out on the lawn. His color had returned. He cleared his throat.

Danny raised his hand. "You don't have to give me the details, Henry. Just tell me this, you want me here—you agree with Caroline?—or should I go back to New Haven? I can find some way of getting back and leave you my car to use."

"Thanks. Caroline has Mother's car. I'd like you here, but only if you . . . if you don't mind staying. Caroline's better. The doc gave her some sort of something." He smiled shyly. "I know something about shock."

Danny's instinct was to be direct. "Well now, Henry, I think I can remember that all right. How many days did you go without talking to anybody? Eh? But you know something, Henry, if somebody is so sick they can't *endure* life, maybe it's good it goes the other way? Maybe she was suffering a lot and you and Caroline didn't know it. Did Dr. Coley tell you?"

Henry looked at Danny inquiringly, as if he had never quite thought about it that way. In fact he hadn't. He didn't really want to talk about it. "We should start thinking about having something to eat."

Danny said he would go out and get some food and bring it in. "You don't know where to go."

"I'll figure it out. You stay with Caroline. Where's a beer-can opener?"

Henry led him to the kitchen and opened a drawer. Danny took the opener and walked out to his car. He was about to press the starter button, but then stopped, took out a can of beer from the box in the backseat, opened it, perched it on the floor of the car and, descending from the car, reached again into the backseat. Under one arm he carried the carton from the liquor store, in his right index finger he dangled one of the gallon jugs of cider. He went back into the house and returned to the car with empty hands. The policeman was still at the driveway entrance. Danny asked him where to go to buy some food.

At ten that night, Caroline was asleep in her room. Danny got up from the chair in the living room and told Henry it would make sense to go for a swim, "especially since we're both loaded." Henry said the water would be pretty cold by now, but sure. He ducked into his bedroom and came back with two towels. He turned the lights in the house out, and passed through the door into the moonlight.

The two undergraduates, trim veterans of a bloody military campaign in Italy, walked the twenty steps to the lakefront, dropped their clothes, and plunged into the cold, pure water. *Everything about this place is perfect,* Danny thought, except that Mrs. Chafee—*Prudence Chafee! What a name she was saddled with*— got sick and popped off! Shit. Life is pretty sticky. Some people's lives. His life was pretty good, thanks; no complaints. He swam on his back looking up at the sky. Then he bit his lip. Was all this booze-thought? Was he on a sentimental high? Four beers and a bottle of wine were threatening to make a philosopher out of him. Oh well, so why not? He smiled back at the moon.

But the water did feel fine, and he thought he caught a little regenerative smile on Henry's face. Can't hide from a full moon, no sir, shouldn't even try.

Six

COMPLETING his junior year, Henry Chafee was busy. Like other students he was taking five courses, and like many of his classmates he was doing a divisional major—in his case, history, economics and political science. And then Henry was active in extracurricular activities. He spent one afternoon every week as duty editor at the *Yale Daily News,* where he was now a senior editor. Three afternoons every week in the spring he spent at the gymnasium, boxing. As when playing football or hockey, his fall and winter sports, Henry had a reputation among his teammates for exposing himself mercilessly to punishment. He would block and tackle with a zest almost singular, and on the ice was all but ferocious in going after the puck. When boxing, his aggressiveness was as marked as his defense was nonchalant. Earlier in the month he had been knocked out—"I'm not sure I was actually unconscious," he said to the coach apologetically, lifting himself off the mat.

"You deserve to have been unconscious," the coach snarled at him. "I don't get it, your right glove was halfway down to your gut and—here, wipe the blood off your lip."

At hockey he was skilled, in football he was fast but weighed only 155 pounds. As a boxer his progress was considerable, and late in junior year he qualified for the varsity team in the middleweight division. Early on a Saturday morning in mid-May he was on the old, rattly chartered bus, headed for the match at West Point. They were approaching Poughkeepsie when team captain Dizzy Koch, a formidable twenty-year-old 200-pounder from Minneapolis, asked the coach, Harry Gulph, if there was a magic way to get tickets for the Joe Louis fight at Madison Square Garden that night. The coach didn't look up from his crossword puzzle but muttered, sure, all you had to do was pay thirty bucks to a scalper.

"If you want to call it 'magic,' " the coach concluded, "say Hesto Presto when you hand over the money."

Thirty dollars was a pretty magical sum of money, Captain Dizzy acknowledged; that would buy you three hundred hamburgers. And then, as if blinded by a revelation, he stood in the swaying bus, hanging on to the baggage rack, prepared to address the team.

Dizzy was an enthusiast, and now he blared out his suggestion, his scheme. Each team member would deposit three dollars into a pool, there would be a drawing. And? And the winner to take the boodle and attend the fight! There was general enthusiasm for the idea, except for Harry Albright, who said he didn't have three dollars, and if he did, he wouldn't risk it on so dumb a game. There were groans all around. The coach was caught up by the idea and confessed that he had twelve dollars left over from expense money, and that he would use that as "scholarship" contributions to the pool, available only for students on scholarship—"Raise your hands, everyone on scholarship." Three, including Henry, raised their right hands. There was animated discussion on whether Harry Albright should be subsidized, it went to a vote of the whole team, and he won narrowly. Everyone was now a participant.

Harry Gulph collected the bills and the boxers wrote out their names on a pad passed around. Dizzy used the scissors on his Swiss Army knife, and the slips of paper were put into the coach's fedora. Coach Harry was by now wholly caught up in the drama and with exaggerated gestures he first blinked his eyes, then raised his left hand to cover them, and then, absolutely to insure that he was not cheating, looked up at the roof of the bus while with his right hand he twiddled the slips of paper, finally drawing one out. Without looking at it, he ceremoniously handed it over to Dizzy.

"Here you are, Captain. You read out the winner's name."

Henry the Winner acknowledged first the congratulatory cheers, then the groans of frustrated disappointment; and later, just before noon, he knocked out his opponent, drawing cheers from ten travelers from New Haven and boos from several hundred cadets.

Henry found the experience exhilarating. At the post-tournament lunch he apologized to his victim, who remarked that he too had been surprised. "Damnedest thing, been boxing three years; never happened before." He felt better when Henry said that he had himself been knocked out only a week or two earlier. The cadet seated on his right asked Henry if he had served in the Army before going to Yale, and Henry said yes, he had been in Italy. This was the formulation he used—he would not say, as most veterans did routinely, that he had "fought" in Italy.

With whom?

He identified the unit. Henry hoped the interrogation would end there, but it didn't.

Had he been in action?

Yes, Henry said, and now he took over the helm, carefully navigating the course of the conversation. To have swerved over to an entirely different course would have struck his lunch mate as rude, or defensive; when intending to divert an inquiry into what kind of a life you had had in the military you don't return suddenly to the subject of boxing. Something nearer at hand . . .

"My roommate was in the Navy in the Italian theater and was in on the landing at Nettuno. But it was successful, initially at any rate; surprise landing—you probably read about it. It was the Navy that delivered an Army corps in what was really total secrecy. It wasn't the Navy's fault that the ground commanders were too timid to exploit the opportunity before them. Kesselring had nothing in the area, largely due to the fact that the Navy conducted a highly successful diversionary landing at Civitavecchia, sixty miles to the north. Here at West Point do you get any training in naval warfare, or does that come only after you get to be a colonel or something?"

The maneuver worked. It helped that the cadet, it transpired, was the son of a naval captain. For the rest of the lunch they fought happily the naval war, 1944–45, and Henry minded not at all when the action moved to the Pacific.

The Yale bus drove to the Greyhound station and when it stopped there to let Henry out, his teammates cheered him. He grinned broadly and, putting his gym kit down on the ground, gave his teammates the boxer's triumphal hands-clenched-over-head salute, and went then to the ticket window to buy a ticket to New York.

The old gray bus was on time, and he worked his way to the rear. It was not crowded, but he did not want to risk sitting down within earshot of the gray-haired scrawny driver who listened to the baseball game on his portable radio as he punched the tickets. Henry was not in a mood for offhand conversation with the driver, or indeed with any one of the dozen riders sitting about the bus, men and women of all ages bound for New York for whatever reason. As the bus moved along on the western shore of the Hudson River, Henry observed offhandedly the light water traffic on the river. But there were a few sailboats, happily confirming the arrival of spring.

It was a good thing that he was unaccompanied, he reflected, since he had no intention of going to the prizefight. He was working in his own way, systematically, to overcome his fear of physical violence and he was making progress in his own deliberate, deliberated way. It is one thing, he told himself, to hit another student with a well-padded glove in a college gymnasium, something else to do the kind of thing that would be done at Madison Square Garden in pursuit of a half-million-dollar purse. He had seen enough newsreels of the great fights in which Joe Louis had been boxing's king almost as long as Henry could remember. Louis was a good clean fighter and often he knocked out his opponent, but almost always there was blood and pain and flesh mutilation. When this happened on the screen Henry would close his eyes, and no one would notice. He would hardly go to see the real thing and run the risk of closing his eyes.

What he would do was listen carefully to the fight over the radio and read accounts of the fight by the sportswriters and—he thought this would be an amusing exercise—perhaps go on and write a column for the *Yale Daily News* on what it had been like, live on Saturday at Madison Square Garden. He smiled confidently. His piece would be full of local color. "At the opening of the third round the fat lady in the front row stood up on her seat and screamed, 'Kill him, Joe! Kill him!' She ran a far greater risk of getting killed than Joe Walcott." That kind of thing. Who would contradict him? He could pick up some of what he needed in the way of atmosphere by listening intently to the radio.

He walked with some excitement across town from the bus station outside the Dixie Hotel and soaked in the excitement of what surely was the most vibrant city on earth. Everyone seemed to strain to welcome the summer. He walked on Forty-second Street and headed west. The streets were being cleaned and a spray truck passed by, dampening the afternoon dust. On Broadway the whole world lit up in front of him, and he remembered his very first sight of it as a little boy, and his settled conviction that he was in Oz, because he had just read a book about the magic kingdom, and surely it was about Times Square?

He walked about, looking for a restaurant that would tune in on the big fight. Perhaps they all would. But he spotted the likeliest of them all on the corner of Broadway near Fiftieth Street.

Where better than the restaurant founded by and, he once read, still presided over by the great king of the sport, Jack Dempsey? He remembered the picture in *Life* magazine when he was a freshman, Gene Tunney dining with Jack Dempsey at Dempsey's bar.

He got the last free table, in the corner of the room. Most of Dempsey's patrons were standing along the bar, their ties loose, half of them wearing seersucker jackets, some of them white jackets and khaki pants left over from army days. They consumed a lot of beer and soon were concentrating intensely on what was being said on the radio by Don Dunphy. Henry ordered the deluxe steak dinner at $3.25. The man at the bar nearest him, wearing a Dodgers baseball cap and a loose-fitting blue jacket, complained that the radio wasn't on loud enough, though Henry had no problem in hearing what the excited commentator was saying as it became clearer and clearer, after the second-round knockdown, what would soon now happen. The kibitzers were demonstrative, and when the champ knocked out the challenger, in the fourth round, the old, imperious lady in dressy satin at the corner gave the signal to the bartender, who acknowledged it by announcing that there would be a beer on the house. Could that be Mrs. Jack Dempsey? The detail would be good in the story he would write, so he motioned to the waiter and asked, and the answer was no, that was Jenny, and "What Jenny says around here goes." Henry drank happily with the crowd, then picked up his little overnight bag and walked out into the sultry heat of Broadway, headed for the Yale Club five blocks east.

"Where you going with that bag, handsome?"

She was slim; her hair covered one of her eyes in the style of Veronica Lake. She swung about her glittery handbag as she approached him, her hips swaying. "How about a little drink before you go to bed? Before we go to bed?"

Henry could not quite believe what he heard himself saying: "Where?" The heat in his loins had been instantaneous, as though his single word were a switch lighting up a huge dynamo.

"I know a place just a couple of blocks away, nice private place.

We can have anything handsome wants—beer, wine, Scotch, gin, sixty-nine." She smiled broadly, her eyes large, brown, alert.

Henry walked with her, nervous but resolute. She had her arm around his. He was surprised that, with his left arm, he was lightly rocking the overnight bag. Like Gene Kelly getting ready to tap-dance. Night-out-on-the-town stuff! He cleared his throat. "Okay, you guide me. What's your name?"

"Lena. What's yours, handsome?"

"I'm Henry."

"I like that. Do they call you Hank?"

"No, just Henry." They came by an old man stirring chestnuts over coals. He had attached a piece of cardboard to a leg of his roasting oven. It said all that needed to be said: "10¢."

"Buy me some," Lena said.

Henry handed the old man fifty cents and opened his hand, displaying two fingers. Under the street light Henry looked down at Lena. She was young—about his own age, Henry guessed—dark, her breasts tumescent. She did not need that much makeup, he surmised. He handed her one bag of hot chestnuts, stuffing the second one in his pocket. She took one, pulled off the shell, tugged Henry to get moving and began daintily to nibble.

"It's hot. But so am I. Are you hot, handsome?"

She moved Henry toward the door of a dark gray building and with her index finger counted down five call buttons from the top. She depressed it, signaling, dash-dot-dash. He could hear the door lock snap open. At the elevator she pushed the button for the fourth floor. Inside the elevator she kneaded him between his legs, smiling sleepily, moistening her lips with her tongue. On the fourth floor she led him to a door which she opened with her own key. Inside was a narrow corridor, a middle-aged woman seated at one corner of it reading a paperback under the light. At her left was a refrigerator and next to it, in what had been a bookcase, assorted liquors.

"What you having tonight, lover boy? You can leave your kit over there." Lena pointed to a closet behind the woman.

Henry said he would settle for a beer, though he felt frustrated by the delay. This he assumed was a part of what he knew to designate as foreplay. But not of the kind he had ever envisioned; his idea of foreplay wasn't something you did in a corridor getting drinks from an old lady.

The woman put down her book, opened the refrigerator and took out two bottles of beer. She poured a rum and Coca-Cola for Lena. "Two dollars," she said, opening the cash box. Henry heard a woman's laughter and a man's voice saying something, but he did not make out the words. Lena motioned Henry to follow her. She led him to a small room with a large bed. She took the beer from his hand, put her own glass down on the night table, slid open Henry's fly, kissed him ardently on the lips, and whispered, "That will be twenty dollars, lover boy, cash up front. Put it there," she pointed to the night table, "and I'll be right with you, handsome." She disappeared into a bathroom.

As suddenly as the switch had turned on, another now took hold of him, and his reaction was instantaneous.

He yanked a twenty-dollar bill from his pocket and dropped it on the bed. He zipped his pants shut, opened the door quietly, walked down the hall, picked up his bag and walked quickly down the stairway to the street. He felt a pang in his groin, but his head was composed, and the hot air tasted summer-sweet.

Seven

T HE PASSENGER LINER wasn't much but the send-off was out of sight terrific, as Caroline's officious friend and classmate Harriet put it. It was just the right time of day for that kind of thing, Danny thought, and Caroline agreed: late afternoon, so that when the sun actually fell, you were snaking out of New York Harbor, traveling to Europe! The *S.S. Continental* was a hastily rebuilt merchant ship designed to help cope with the overflow of Americans who wanted to travel to Europe in the summer of 1949. She was slow, the recreational facilities were limited and the food brought back memories of wartime belt tightening. But she was inexpensive, clean, entirely adequate for Henry and Caroline. The prospect of seeing Europe was the one silver lining in the death of their mother, a death that caused funds to materialize that they did not know existed. Cam Beckett, the trustee, told them at Christmas that their trust could handle a modest trip to Europe, and a few weeks later sent them each a check for one thousand dollars.

The stateroom Danny and Henry shared was a few square inches larger than the room Caroline shared with a stranger, a quite striking, entirely poised redhead who was instantly invited to join the Yale party, did so, and eventually told somebody who asked that her name was Lucy. When the sixth consecutive Yale classmate arrived, Danny said to Henry, Hey, let's call this thing off! It was beginning to look like the famous Marx Brothers stateroom sequence.

Caroline agreed and everyone followed her up to the lounge, which had only the disadvantage that the guests had to pay for their own drinks instead of using up Danny's and Henry's private supply in the stateroom. There were two hundred passengers and at least four hundred well-wishers, a piano player plunking away absolutely outside anyone's range of hearing except the waiter, who kept cleaning the piano player's cigarette tray. The stentorian loudspeakers eventually convinced those who were going ashore that there probably wasn't in fact any alternative to going ashore, unless they wanted to stow away; the companionway was removed.

It was all quite dreamy, Danny thought, looking at Caroline's soft golden hair and oval face and brown eyes with an air of propriety, because although she had spent a total of only six weekends at Yale, beginning when she went to Smith to study after her mother's death, something of a durable nature had begun. Danny had taken Caroline here and there, to campus parties, to fraternities, to sports events, and he liked later to accost his friends and put to them the question, Had they ever seen a dreamier girl? Most of them deferred to Danny. Now, looking at her as she stood alongside her brother peering over the ship's rail at the receding Manhattan skyline, he knew suddenly what it was about her that was distinctive. Because of course a dozen—five dozen—girls crossed the campus every weekend who were knockouts to look at. What gave Caroline that special lift was a detachment from whatever the surrounding focus, never suggesting she wasn't enjoying the hockey game or the post-game cocktail party or, at the moment, the wonderful view of a diminishing skyline, receding from sight even as the sun did; it was the other light in the eye. Required one day to say it in as many words, Danny told his roommate that it gave Caroline "four dimensions." He confessed he did not know exactly what that meant, but then he did not know exactly what was the meaning of that other look in Caroline's eye.

Caroline quite apart, Danny thought, this trip was much more fun than last year's, when he had traveled alone—more exactly, had set sail alone; because Danny was never alone for very long unless he made a strenuous effort to be alone, and he hadn't on the *S.S. Georgic*. He had picked up a girl named Lala and also, he discovered when he got back to Yale, a case of clap.

Caroline was entirely different, in that sense. He would never flirt sexually with Caroline. Besides, he felt in no hurry with Caroline, maybe because her own poise was somehow uninterruptible. There was an intactness there one didn't play with. The first time he had seen her she was desolate, as who would not have been under the circumstances, but she was never quite—vulnerable. He loved to be in her company and when she was with him he was never asking himself, as characteristically he almost always did, what was he going to do next. What he was going to do next, he now reminded himself with pleasure, was sit down at the dinner table next to Caroline. And of course Henry. And, he supposed, the *S.S. Continental*'s management would stick a fourth person down at the table, presumably Lucy. He hoped Henry and Lucy would get on well together, hoped they would absorb each other.

The European holiday would last eight weeks. On September 6 the *Continental* would end its eight round-trip journeys to New York, beginning in Nice. The route was Nice–Cherbourg–Southampton. Caroline would travel, during most of the vacation, with her brother, but the eighth and final week she would spend in Scotland at the summer house of the family of her Smith friend,

Gladys Gibney. After leaving her, Henry would drive south from Paris along the Loire Valley and meet Danny at Nice. Together they would board the boat for the return passage, picking Caroline up at Southampton three days later.

Accordingly they had separated when the *Continental* reached Southampton. The Chafees had their own itinerary, Danny his, which included some sailboat racing in Copenhagen and a leisurely drive in a rented car from Rome through Florence and Monaco to Nice.

On the Monday before meeting up with Henry and boarding the ship for the return passage, Danny was at the Casino Royale. It was one in the morning and the great old gaming palace was still filling up. When he first saw it he wondered if anything at all had changed since the turn of the century. If he closed his eyes he could imagine it filled with men in Edwardian longcoats with muttonchop whiskers and maybe a monocle or two. There were no windows in the Casino Royale, no more than in the Brayeux brothel he had visited in Paris. Everywhere there was velvet. The walls were a shimmering red, broken up only by the gilt that adorned the mirrors and sconces. It must have been a shattering concession by management—surely some duke or count or deposed dowager empress—to have taken down the candleholders and replaced them with yellowed lights? Or were they gas ports? Danny would look into it. He fixed his eyes on the dazzling green of the gaming tables, and on the company at hand.

Only half of the players were Americans, the balance pretty much the same mix as the year before, heavily adorned Frenchwomen of all ages, Dutch burghers, slim-boned Italian polyglots, English aristocrats speaking in single syllables. But during the preceding hour Danny had paid no attention to the backgrounds of the other guests, or indeed to his surroundings; he was aware only of resources suddenly, drastically, depleted.

Danny O'Hara was not used to bad luck. Only the weather, he once told Henry jauntily, had ever really let him down. Last year he had returned to Yale after his summer in Europe with gifts for everybody in sight, with special gift cards written out for his mother, for his stepfather, Harry Bennett, and for Bill Fenniman, the bank official who presided over his inscrutable trust. Even with the gifts all paid for, he had had almost four hundred dollars left over. To each of his gifts he had appended a card, "With love from the Casino Royale, Nice." His mother told him over the telephone that yes, darling, she loved her gift—a Fabergé cigarette case—but that it was really very childish for him to advertise that he had gambled at a casino inasmuch as there was no stupider activity on earth than to gamble when the odds are fixed against you. Danny had handled that telephone conversation with a Yes-Mom sequence while watching television. Television sets were forbidden at Silliman College in students' rooms, for electrical reasons, which made matters slightly inconvenient for Danny, but he quickly devised means to keep his set nicely camouflaged. Now, one year later, he was disporting at the same casino at which exactly one year earlier he had triumphed —and was very hard-pressed.

When the little Neapolitan croupier looked over at him to see whether, in the upcoming round, he was going to put a chip down at the roulette wheel, Danny motioned with his hand, no— he would pass. What he badly needed to do was to check his wallet, but he didn't want to be seen doing so. Certainly not by the blasé chain-smoking thirtyish beautiful blonde with the tiara seated on his right; or by the fat imperious Egyptian on his left— could that be King Farouk? King Farouk was betting ten-thousand-franc notes, the blond lady on his right, a thousand francs. It would not do—no, not do at all!—for the dashing young American *beau idéal,* dressed in black tie as the casino demanded, to be seen reaching into his wallet and peering into it, a beggar foraging for scraps. He would pretend he was going to the men's room.

But what he knew he had to do would take up more time than even a protracted pee, and therefore he mustn't—not in that crowded room—preempt a player's slot at the roulette game. *"Je reviendrais,"* he nodded to the croupier, *"mais ça sera question de quelques minutes."*

There. The croupier was free to interpret "a few minutes" as he chose. He might decide that a few minutes was a modest enough holding time for the comely, urbane young American who hadn't won a hand in an hour; on the other hand, "a few minutes" might be interpreted as just indefinite enough to justify the croupier's giving over the player's slot to someone standing in line to play the game.

What Danny needed to do was something he very much didn't want to do, which was to telephone his mother.

He went back to the Negresco Hotel next door to the casino. Transatlantic telephone calls were something of an operation, so he stopped at the hotel switchboard, slipped five hundred francs into the hands of the operator, kissed her on the forehead and said, *"S'il vous plaît, chère madame, aidez-moi, c'est horriblement"*—he threw up his hands and closed his eyes in feigned agony— *"important. Je vais à mon chambre, trois cent vingt-deux. Voilà le numéro."* He gave her the slip of paper with his mother's number, took the elevator, opened the door to his room, flung off his coat and sat down by the phone waiting for it to ring. His eyes wandered over the morning's paper, without focus. A few minutes later the phone rang. She was on the line.

"Hello, Mom!"

"Danny, how are you, dear?"

"Well, I could not be better. We were runners-up at Copenhagen, got a silver cup. Saw two operas at Milan, including one with that really hot soprano, Licia Albanese."

"Which operas were they?"

"Ah. They were—*Traviata* and *Aïda.*"

"I hope you did not vamp the soprano."

"Oh, Mother, come on. She must be"—what age would Rachel O'Hara think it right that her son should think remote?— "fifty."

He could hear her laugh. Rachel enjoyed her son's verbal raffishness. "I don't suppose you heard *him?*"

"Franki?"

"Who do you think?"

"No. I did ask, but apparently he is in Australia. Do they sing in the nude on Australian beaches, Mom?"

That was dumb of him. Granted, it made him sound normal.

That was good, in one way—he didn't want her to know how panicked he really was. But then she probably did not like being reminded of Franki nude on her beach, doing something she once accepted as romantic.

"You have a lewd memory. Danny dear, why are you calling me? Are you broke?" Rachel could get right to the point.

"Well as a matter of fact, Mom, I wonder if you could lend me a few bucks?"

"Like how many bucks?"

"Five hundred?"

"Five hundred dollars! Danny! Danny? Have you been gambling?"

"Well, as a matter of fact, yes, just tonight, and you know, it sometimes happens, when everything goes wrong? A little like"
—this too was risky, but maybe he could fasten her mind on how proud she had been of her little boy's resourcefulness—"like the weather on that awful sail to Nantucket. . . ."

"Danny." The way she said it, it sounded horribly decisive. It was.

"Don't . . . try . . . to . . . get . . . my . . . sympathy. I told you a year ago you were not to gamble. Now *you* find a way to get yourself out of the mess you're in. I have to go out now. Good night, darling."

His mother hung up the telephone.

He looked in his address book and got out the home telephone number of Bill Fenniman in Hartford, rushed down to the operator and pleaded with her to pry through one more call.

Fenniman was on the line. Danny asked could he borrow five hundred dollars from his allowance?

"Danny, you know I am strictly forbidden by the trust to make any advances to you."

"Well, Bill, could I *borrow* five hundred dollars from the trust?"

"The indenture doesn't permit borrowing against the capital."

Danny's temper was frayed. "Listen, Bill, what the fuck do you expect me to do? I can't get out of Nice without three hundred and fifty dollars. The casino has my note and my passport. Can't you figure *something* out?"

Fenniman reminded Danny that it was after hours. He would need to wait until the following morning, call one of the trustees, maybe talk to the general manager. "I'll see what I can do. I'll wire you by noon. But don't bank on it."

"Noon your time means one whole day away, my time."

Bill Fenniman told him that's how it was, wished him good luck, and said good night.

Danny had less than fifty dollars left, seventeen thousand francs. The roulette table was less crowded, he placed ten thousand francs on the black, lost; put up most of his remaining francs, lost. He told the croupier he would be back, he was going to the bar to have a drink. The croupier nodded. A little less deferentially than before, Danny noticed.

The bar, with its gilt trappings, smoky mirror and tiny lit oil paintings of turn-of-the-century French Riviera, was not crowded, but the half-dozen men and one woman who sat on the fancy stools or stood alongside, drinking champagne, were animated; all of them, it seemed, talking at one time. Danny went to the corner and ordered a whiskey, pulling out one of his two remaining bills to pay for it. *What in the hell do I do now?* Henry would be here the day after tomorrow. But there was no way Henry would arrive carrying three hundred and fifty dollars. Fenniman was the only hope. Would he succeed in scratching up the money?

He noticed the man with the goatee and the cigarette. He was of course dressed formally, wearing black tie like everyone else, but there was a red sliver on the vest pocket that suggested a decoration of some sort. And he acted the grandee in his gesture to the man at the bar. Danny thought his face unappetizing, even rancid. Still, he was happy for any distraction and clearly the man was summoning Danny's attention.

The count, or whatever he was, approached him and said fraternally, in an English heavily handicapped by the French accent, that he had been observing Danny's table and had remarked an extraordinary coincidence—but would Monsieur not join him in a whiskey? My treat? Danny nodded and the count signaled to the bartender.

What was the coincidence? Danny asked.

"That you haff been loossing consistently, even while Madame Déboulard hass been winning consistently."

"She the lady over there, on my right?"

He nodded, extending his long fingers in the direction of the gaming room. "I am Paul. Paul Hébert, at your service. I try to do what I can to make Madame Déboulard comfortable."

Danny put his glass down on the bar and extended his hand. "You undertake to make the lady comfortable. Does that include making the right numbers turn up on the wheel?" He smiled and downed his drink.

Paul Hébert shrugged his shoulders and lit another cigarette. Danny tried to blow the count's smoke away. The tobacco smoke around the bar seemed static. There was no current of air, though the temperature was comfortable.

"I am begging your pardon about that." Paul Hébert waved his right hand about fussily, to help fan away the smoke. "But on ze, er, mattair of making Madame Déboulard happy, it iss just possible you have something that can be of service."

Danny looked at him concentratedly. He paused for a moment. Then, "Like?"

His eyebrows told Paul Hébert, who perhaps wasn't a count after all, that Danny had a good idea what he had that might be of service to a slightly older woman.

"Exactement." Paul Hébert confirmed Danny's suspicion, sipping from his glass of champagne, his eyes on Danny.

Well, Danny thought. He had read about such situations. For a moment it crossed his mind that maybe the roulette wheel *was,* somehow, fixed.

Impossible.

But it was one hell of a coincidence. He had lost practically every time, while the beautiful blonde had won practically every time, he could not help notice. He felt beads of sweat on his brow. He leaned over the bar and finished his drink.

What exactly were the alternatives? Jail? Workhouse? The guillotine?

"I don't give my, er, talents cheaply." His voice was a little hoarse. He paused, and cleared it. "As a matter of fact, I have never done it . . . commercially before."

"Maybe that is why you haff attrack Madame so much. On zee other mattair, Madame Déboulard iss very generous."

"Like how generous?"

"For the evening, seventy-five thousand francs."

"I require exactly twice that," Danny said, breathing deeply; $425—he did the quick arithmetic—would take care of him. But surely any such demand was out of the question? How much did Nana charge? Fanny Hill? Lady Chatterley? He couldn't think offhand of the name of a famous male—gigolo.

Hébert drew deep on his cigarette and exhaled slowly. But this time he made no effort to blow the smoke away from Danny, who pirouetted slowly, to get out of the way.

Hébert was taking his time. "That's very much money," he said contemplatively.

Danny amused himself at the thought of a ribald response, but decided against it. He could not afford to estrange this—procurer. His return on schedule to America the day after tomorrow could well depend on his success. So he just said, "But that is what I need, and I hope Madame will not be disappointed."

Hébert took a final puff on his cigarette, ground it out, and said, "All right." He was all business now. "If she wants you to spend ze night and . . . perrform again in ze morning, you will do that."

Danny nodded.

"And ze price includes—gratuity."

He nodded again. And managed a smile.

He was told to be at the Hotel Ruhl in Cannes at two. He spent his last two thousand francs on roses from the street peddler outside the hotel. He walked by the night concierge unquestioned, gave the operator a floor number one flight above his destination, walked back down to the seventh floor, bit his lip and tapped gently on the door of Suite 7G.

She opened it wearing a yellow silk kimono, only one button attached, at her waist. Her blond hair fell about her now. She was older by perhaps ten years, but Danny could not imagine her any more appetizing when she was eighteen. With her cigarette holder she waved him toward the downy azure couch, pointed to the champagne bottle, smiled at the flowers which she took and deposited in the bar sink. The lights were dim, except over the couch. He sat down and, on instructions conveyed by the movement of her hands, took off his jacket.

Pauline Déboulard—"Pauline"—did not speak English. At least, she said, she preferred not to speak English. Did . . . Daniel mind?

He wondered that she knew his name. But then he was not a stranger to the casino, certainly not to the cashier, and there had been the social item in the paper about the "beau" young grandson of FDR frequenting the Casino Royale.

He said he didn't mind, but warned that his French was not so hot. She said she was not there to give or to take language lessons. She started to disrobe him, he volunteered to do it himself, she said no, she would prefer to do it, but he would need to stand up, which he did. She said rather routine things about rather routine subjects—it was pleasant to have the good luck she had at the roulette wheel early on in the evening—on the whole she thought the casino was well kept up but they would need to consider modernizing after what was going on in Monaco—it was nice to see fewer Frenchmen in the casino than during August— as unhurriedly she unbuttoned her way down his shirt, removed it, unfastened his cummerbund, peeled off his undershirt, unbuttoned and let down his pants and, finally, his shorts. And forsooth! (Danny couldn't help laughing. Just the right word, forsooth, commonly used only by Professor McGiffert in his course on Rabelais.) Forsooth Danny was naked in her hands.

But by now he was seriously distracted. Her perfume nicely overcame the smell of tobacco. He brought up his hands on her kimono and spread it open, exposing breasts wonderfully poised.

She moved his hand down toward a nipple, then the other; then she unbuttoned the kimono and eased herself down on the couch, bending her knees, separating them. She pointed down between her legs, hungrily licking her lips.

Daniel did what was expected, and after a second bout wondered apprehensively whether Pauline would expect yet more. Perhaps if he drew attention to the champagne? He did this, and now she became very talkative and Danny feigned intense interest in everything she said, asking for elaborations and hoping she would tire. Though as he sipped the champagne he found himself face to face with the candor that was becoming his trademark. Actually, he acknowledged to himself as he nodded his head at her story of the fatal accident the week before to her racehorse in Paris, he had in fact thoroughly enjoyed her; indeed, except that he was without the physical reserves for it, he would not mind doing it all over again.

As she talked, he waited for her signal on the matter of spending the night. But very suddenly she had dozed off.

What to do? If he left to go back to his hotel, she might hold him in default, in which event the second payment contracted by Paul would not be made the following morning. On the other hand, if he stayed the night, perhaps moving into the bedroom— she occupied the whole of the couch—might she wake up, offended at the uninvited prolongation of his presence?

He walked quietly about the apartment. He came into an anteroom of sorts. If he lay there, she would be free to wake and remove herself to the bedroom without walking into him. And then if she wished him in the morning, he would be there. No default.

He looked about for his shorts and undershirt and quietly put them on. He wondered where the switch was for the bright overhead light. He tried several, but the light stayed on.

The hell with it. The anteroom was dark.

He lay down and closed his eyes. A hell of a day. He would not gamble again at a casino. Never! Dear Mom, you are something of a bitch, but you're a wise old bitch. Old? Why, she wasn't all that much older than Pauline, and who would think of *her* as old?

Danny smiled as he thought back on the initial rite of the evening with Pauline. He had never done that before. Quickly he was asleep.

Eight

HENRY KNOCKED on Danny's door at the Negresco Hotel intending merely to draw attention to his arrival in Nice. He hardly needed to be invited by his college roommate to come on in. Danny rose to greet him but didn't affect lightheartedness. Something was wrong and Henry spotted it instantly.

He put down his bag, pulled up a chair and sat down. "You want to tell me about it, Danny?"

Danny did. He told it all. His rendering was clipped, his anger convulsive—an anger Henry had never seen before in Danny. But it was an emotion in total control.

Henry spoke. "What are you going to do? I mean," he paused, "what are *we* going to do."

Danny acknowledged, with a nod and a half smile, the fraternal pronoun. "I'm going to where that high-rise is in Cannes where the cocksucker is, going to get the prints, get the negatives, and if he doesn't turn them over I'll toss him out of the window. Maybe I'll do that even after we get the prints."

Henry looked at his watch. "We better go now, skip the lunch business. We got time, but not loads of time. We have to board the boat by seven."

"Yeah, let's go. I have a car outside. I also have this"—he opened the drawer and brought out a pair of handcuffs. "Got them in a toy store this morning, but they'll do if we have to tie him up while we look around. And," he returned to the drawer and brought out a large roll of heavy plastic tape, "we may need to keep him quiet."

Henry said he would go to his own room and come back more suitably dressed.

While Henry was gone, Danny reached into his suitcase and brought out his .22 Colt pistol. He put it into the side pocket of the foul-weather jacket he pulled out of the closet. It was not noticeable in the stiff yellow oilskin. He put on a French cap and sunglasses, walked down the hall to Henry's room and bumped into him on his way out. Henry was dressed in khaki pants, a light sweater and a seersucker jacket.

"You know how to get there?"

Danny nodded. "Just inside the city limit of Cannes."

The night before, Danny, affecting great nonchalance, paid off the casino debt and, for the hell of it, decided he would play Platonic Roulette. A beer in hand, he leaned his back against the red felt wall under the little crystal chandelier and said to himself: Okay, I'll play 10,000 francs—exactly what I pay for my hotel suite for one night. Twenty-eight bucks. *Ten straight rolls on the Black*—and see how I make out. See how I'd have made out using the real stuff.

It was infuriating. Eight blacks in ten rolls! So his 10,000 francs had brought in 160,000 francs. If only he had used real chips instead of fancied chips.

Well, he thought, let's piss it away! So he resolved to bet 10,000

WILLIAM F. BUCKLEY, JR.

francs on the lower third, 1–11. If the ball dropped in any of the eleven lower-numbered slots, he would earn triple.

Incredible! Six of the ten rolls landed on Number 11 or less. He'd have added 140,000 francs to his stake!

He could not leave the casino on so synthetic a high, so he resolved to put up the whole wad! Two hundred and forty thousand francs on—one number.

Which number? Caroline's birthday was yesterday, she was twenty. He closed his eyes and willed the money on Number 20. If it came in he would have eight million-odd francs. About twenty-four thousand bucks. He closed his eyes again and listened for the clickety-clack of the metal ball. He heard a gasp of delight. His eyes opened to see King Farouk dissolved with pleasure as he waited to be paid on the Number 21 on which he had plopped a hundred-thousand-franc chip.

What a bore. Danny was disgusted by it all. He would go to his room and, for a change, read a book. He was well into *Scott-King's Modern Europe.* He went by the dining room and asked for a bottle of Chablis, "And please open it." It was brought to him on a tray by the waiter with his stiff shirtfront and little black bow tie. Danny removed the bottle from the tray, wedged the cork back in, smiled at the sommelier, tipped him, and slid the bottle into his ample pocket.

He was confused by the door lock, fidgeted again with the key and suddenly realized why it wouldn't turn. It was already open. Instinctive caution governed his movements now. He removed the bottle from his tuxedo and then with considerable force burst the door open.

Pauline was there. Danny hadn't seen her like this before, not last night, not this morning. She wore no makeup, no tiara, no furs, no lacy nightgown. She had evidently tossed her raincoat on the armchair. She had a yellow bandana around her head of blond hair and when Danny heaved into the room she began to cry. Danny approached her and embraced her as he might have a mother, not his mistress. And she was there on a motherly mission, to tell Danny he was being blackmailed.

· · · ·

Much later, Pauline had stopped crying. The wine bottle was empty. She stood up and moved her hands in front of her face. She did not want to think of "Daniel," she said, as she would think of a . . . lawyer or a doctor approached for advice. He was something entirely different to her, Pauline. And she wanted a final embrace from her beautiful Daniel. In just ten minutes— that was all the time she needed—she would be back from the bathroom. And Daniel would see the same Pauline he had known the night before, indeed, this very morning *("ce matin si précieux")* at her hotel. Danny nodded.

Yes, this morning had been . . . precious. He had attained an acuteness of pleasure beyond anything he had ever experienced, and he knew that he had given as much as he got; because when the time came finally to leave—Paul Hébert would be coming by with the envelope at noon at the Negresco—Pauline was suddenly inconsolable at the thought of his departure. Her passion had inflamed her resentment over his leaving her. She hadn't even wanted to look him in the face. Danny had dressed, said nothing, only then approached her to kiss her lightly. She had wheeled on him and returned his kiss, but with great ardor; then turned away as Danny went out. She did not expect to see Danny again.

Now, late in the evening of the same day, Danny was putting on his pajamas. Tonight was very different from the night before. This time it was Pauline who was careful about the lights. Only the light from the little sitting room seeped in. Like a little yellow mist issuing through the windows of the French doors. Pauline embraced him, began her caress with such ardor Danny had to reach down and calm her movements. Deep within her he felt her elation and then her exhaustion, and he thrilled in a voluptuous embrace. But this time it was truly over.

He told her he would escort her back to her hotel. She replied that he must be crazy even to consider any such thing. Under no circumstances must Paul Hébert or anybody he knows see them together, not after her treachery. Because now he knew the true narrative of the night before. And, most important, knew where he could find Paul Hébert. Once again, they kissed good night, and goodbye.

The stoplights, though they were few, seemed interminable. The highway was under construction but most of it was still as it had been before the war and during it. The beaches were full but not crowded, as tout Paris edged back toward the capital after a pastoral August, relinquishing the Riviera to its inhabitants and to the tourists—always, the tourists. It was still warm and the salt air came in, tangy and palpable whenever they were stopped at a traffic light; faintly, nicely discernible when under way at 100 kph.

"What does Pauline expect you to do with Mr. Paul Hébert?"

"Oh, that was pretty obvious. She just figures I'll buy him off. Pay more for the fucking pictures"—Danny paused. *"Mot juste,* Henry?—than the tabs would.''

"But she knew you were broke the other night?"

"Yeah, but schoolboy-broke. She obviously figures that for this operation there wouldn't be any shortage of cash. . . . I'd call home—

" 'Mom? Hi, Mom. Fine, how are *you,* Mom? Ah ha. Well you know, Mom, there is this slight problem. There is a dirty old man— A dirty . . . old . . . man. You know, French type? And you know, Mom, when I called the other day, said I needed some cash? Well, the dirty old man saw that I was having trouble so he came and said to me that there was a very beautiful woman around who was so nice and generous he was absolutely sure *she'd* give me some money, or anyway, lend it to me.

" 'Well' ''—Danny's amusement won out for the moment over his anger—" 'well, I went to the lady, Mom, told her about my problem, and she gave me the four hundred bucks. And I just didn't know how to thank her, so I dropped my pants and fucked her.' ''

He roared with laughter, and decided to go on. " 'No, Mom. I didn't pick up any disease, not that I know of. The problem was the dirty old man. You see, he had a camera there and took a bunch of pictures of me saying thanks to the lady.

" 'Yes, Mom, I quite agree. He had absolutely *no business* doing that. Absolutely correct, total invasion of privacy. I must remember to tell him that.

" 'What is he going to do with the pictures? Sell them on the street? Well, uh, no, Mom, he has other ideas. He sells to the tabs. The t-a-b-s. Tabloids. They're pretty raunchy over here, and the idea is, Hey, you want to peek at the way the grandson of President Franklin Delano Roosevelt says thanks to nice French ladies who do him favors?' "

Danny's laugh was truncated.

And Henry's voice was earnest. "Listen, buddy. I think we probably *should* make an effort to buy him off. Did Pauline give you any idea what kind of price the pictures would fetch?"

"No. But if they would fetch more than one hundred bucks, that's more than I've got."

"I've got some."

"I knew you'd say that. But we're probably talking maybe a couple of thousand bucks. After all, they paid me four hundred and twenty-five dollars. So? There's just one alternative: grab them. They're probably still wet, hanging in some improvised darkroom."

The Citroën bounced confidently over all the potholes. Now there was a stretch of beach—"That belongs to Farouk," Danny said. "Where we're headed is the development, over there," he pointed, "at the end of his property."

It was a brand-new high-rise, not yet complete; there were men at work on the top story. The entrance hall was light and large, the salt air providing fine ventilation through the lobby floor. They walked confidently past the desk into one of the automatic elevators. The target was 18B.

Henry was more than willing to act as the man up front, as had been agreed. He would knock on the door, with Danny out of sight. He would tell M. Hébert that he was there to buy some pictures for a British newspaper. If Hébert refused to let him in, Danny would materialize and together they would force their way in and overpower Hébert. If Henry was admitted, he would there and then deliver a knockout blow—in the elevator they had put on gloves to cover their tracks—then open the door for Danny. Together they would tie up Hébert and search for the pictures.

"If we don't find them, we'll need to get serious with him," Danny had said. Henry never remembered seeing Danny more resolute, more vindictive, actually.

M. Paul Hébert, dressed in a sports shirt and slacks, seemed not in the least surprised by Henry's explanation for calling on him, an explanation begun in halting French, but completed, at M. Hébert's invitation, in English. Evidently he was accustomed to doing business thus extemporaneously.

Hébert opened the door. Henry stepped in and instantly delivered an uppercut that crumpled his host, who fell to the floor on his back, his arms outstretched, his mouth open, eyes entirely blank.

The door had not even shut, so that Danny came in by himself. Wordlessly they brought Hébert's wrists together behind him and put on the handcuffs. Then Danny began with the tape. He did not need to pry open Hébert's mouth—it was wide open. He bound him tight.

"Pull up on the desk, Henry." Henry did so while Danny dragged the manacled hands and let the desk leg come down between Hébert's arms.

Danny stood up, breathing deeply. "Not bad. He can't move his arms, can't talk, can't move any farther than the desk can move. Yes, not bad, not bad. Say, Henry, that's a hell of a swing they taught you. I hope you don't ever get angry with me."

Henry smiled. Mad at Danny? Not easy. Not impossible—but very nearly that, when Danny was in a jam, as he now was. Henry had once been in a jam.

Their search was instantly successful. The negatives were there, dangling on clothespins.

"If you don't mind, Henry, I'll do the identifying on those pictures." Danny examined them. He was visibly inflamed by what he saw. He looked down to adjust the lamplight and spotted a small glass tray. On it were a pair of glasses and a key ring. "Looks like he hadn't gotten around to making prints yet. But for the hell of it let's look in the drawers." While looking at a negative he reached for the key ring, slipping it into his pocket.

They did so, and Danny took pleasure in leaving the drawers overturned. "May as well make it look like a robbery. Actually," he smiled, "in a way, it *is*. I mean, the pictures *are* his, technically speaking, aren't they?" Henry said he thought that rather a fine point, but obviously Danny enjoyed making it.

They found nothing, and now Danny turned to the figure on the floor.

"Well, M. Paul. Having fun?"

Muffled groans.

Danny launched now into his deception, an attempt to shield Pauline as his informant. "There is a nice woman in Nice—I know you look after her comfort because you enlisted me in that effort a couple of nights ago. Well, I went to say goodbye to her last night and found she had left town. To Algeria, the concierge told me. Why that upsets me, Paul, is this: I thought if I could find her, I'd tell her *you* were uncomfortable and for a change *she* could look after *you*—see what I mean?"

"Danny, let's get out of here."

"Yeah."

Henry lowered his voice. "We can call the police after we're away and give them the room number, tell 'em we think there's a problem there—"

"Yeah, yeah." Danny's voice was hoarse. He shook his head, as though attempting to wake up.

They went down the elevator together, removing their gloves.

Danny stepped into the car and closed the door. But suddenly he opened it again. "Damn! I got to go back up. I left my dark glasses."

"Well, make it fast—"

Danny was out of the car.

As he rode up in the elevator he studied the key ring and isolated the key likeliest to open the apartment door.

Now he was staring down at Paul Hébert, the dandy manqué with the hint of a decoration on his tuxedo coat, lying now on his side, his goatee protruding under the gag that kept him silent, or rather, just capable of grunting. Danny trained his thought on the Germans he had fired on, thrown hand grenades at. It wasn't at all clear why such as they should die and leave alive such as Paul Hébert. He gave himself a full minute to recapture, step by step, exactly what the vile Hébert had done to him. Tried to do to him. And he imagined what now, if free, and if he settled his suspicion on her, he might try to do to Pauline.

He brought his revolver out of his pocket, approached Hébert slowly, stepping around his thrashing legs, brought the barrel to an inch from the top of Paul Hébert's nose and pulled the trigger.

He tossed the key ring back on the tray, walked back through the room and, in the elevator, tried to concentrate on the question, Was his heart beating faster right now than on that night at the Arno, in the last seconds of the countdown?

Probably less. One gets used to things.

"All set," he told Henry, getting into the driver's seat and adjusting his sunglasses.

Nine

IT WAS ELSIE who had first suggested that Caroline go with her to West Point on the double date, but after Caroline said thanks a lot, no, it was Harriet who more or less put herself in charge of the social agenda.

Harriet Carberry, who roomed with Elsie, was the daughter of a colonel in the army. Her father, notwithstanding his exalted rank, was always something of a drill sergeant. He dealt with Harriet and her two younger brothers as he might have done with recruits. He told them what to do, explained how things worked, supervised their activity, and disappeared from their lives only during their schedule breaks, ten minutes every hour, and the hours after school and other duties. As a boy, Philip Carberry had been sent to Culver Academy, a proud military secondary school whose teachers exercised a comprehensive concern for every detail of the young cadets' lives. Punctuality was central to the working of Colonel Carberry's universe. "If you are not prompt," Colonel—then Captain—Carberry lectured his ten-year-old daughter when she arrived not at twelve o'clock at the corner outside the schoolhouse, as instructed to do, but five minutes later, "you may be the instrumental factor in a breakdown in arrangements whose consequences you cannot estimate." Mrs. Carberry whispered to her husband that he was not addressing a seminar of officer candidates but a ten-year-old girl, but the colonel paid her no heed and persisted in a scolding that lasted so long they missed the train. Mrs. Carberry was amused that the colonel had been the victim of the vice he was so eloquently adjuring his daughter to abstain from, but in fact did not laugh; laughter in the house of Carberry was always suspect, contumacious as often as not, the colonel thought, and also rather effete, like so many of those male leads in Hollywood.

Harriet was a total success, faithful to her father's preachments. And having been born with so exuberant a good nature, she had a difficult time expending it all. She worried about herself hardly at all (what was there, after all, to worry about?), but worried most persistently about Caroline, and about Elsie; and, as a matter of fact, about many of her teachers. Oh yes, and she worried also about the president of Smith. He was overworked, she informed her friends, his office understaffed.

But the object of her concerns at the moment was Caroline Chafee. "Why?—Caroline, don't just say you don't *want* to go to West Point with Lucy, tell her *why* you don't want to go to West Point with Lucy."

Caroline smiled. Caroline smiled a great deal. It was sometimes the sign of understanding, sometimes of gratitude and deference, sometimes a way of closing off a subject she thought it appropriate to close or, in any case, a subject she wanted to close.

She liked Harriet, really did. It had taken her almost the whole of the first two years to get used to Harriet's hectoring. But somewhere along the line it became evident that Harriet simply *cared* —cared very much, the way some people care if other people remembered to brush their teeth that morning. Cared, in this case, very much (Caroline knew this) about her restricted social life. Caroline sighed, seeing no way out of it.

"Darling Harriet, I don't like to repeat myself, but I have told you that I am very attracted to someone, and I don't terribly enjoy myself when I am out with somebody else. Now, is that so unusual?"

Harriet took a deep puff from her cigarette, and then set it down as if to prepare to begin a lecture.

"It is very unusual, very mistaken, and *utterly* wrong, Caroline. We know of course that you are talking about Danny O'Hara. I have nothing against Danny, nothing at all. He is polite, he is handsome, his family is rich and distinguished, he graduated from Yale last spring and has gone to work in New York. Fine. When he was a senior at New Haven he came here what, once a month? And you went to New Haven on odd months. That means that even then, three quarters of the time you spent the weekend—well, alone. But now that he's working in New York he comes only every five or six weeks. . . ."

Caroline had told Danny, at one of her last visits to Yale in the spring, just before his graduation, about Harriet's preoccupation with her lonely weekends.

"What does Miss Harriet do on weekends?"

They were together that evening at the lounge of the Taft Hotel, had walked the short distance from Zeta Psi, Danny's fraternity. It had been a crowded day. That morning, Caroline had taken the train to Springfield from Northampton and there caught the express, Hartford–New Haven. There was a milk punch party at the *Yale Daily News*, then lunch at Silliman, then in Danny's car to the sybaritic crew race with Harvard on the Thames River. Caroline found herself quite carried away—more, actually, than Danny, whose cheers for the home crew she thought perfunctory. Then the cocktail party at Zeta Psi, followed by dinner and two rounds of bridge with Fred Zahn and Charlie Melhado who, some survivors of their game were convinced, were majoring in bridge. Their game was speedy, quiet and ruthless. Danny was accustomed to losing to them but he enjoyed the sport, and the proximity to Caroline.

It did not matter that they were not engaged in conversation during the two hours. His closeness to her was what mattered; and then, during the bidding, he would look at her, the oval face framed by the light yellow hair, her hazy brown eyes looking down at her hand, then up—sometimes, even though she was looking directly across the table, she gave no sense of seeing him. She never lost the train of the conversation, never delayed needlessly in putting down a card or making her bid, but Danny felt that her quiet self-containment was a means of telling those about her that she was quite happy in the private garden in which she strolled, without any need of accompaniment. Danny found this enchanting, but never spoke of the phenomenon, not even to Henry. Surely, he thought, this fascinating faculty of Caroline's must be obvious to everyone around her?

It was after eleven when they sat down at the lounge of the Taft. She ordered Coca-Cola, he a beer. She was at the end of one large leather couch, Danny sat in the armchair perpendicular, his right hand outstretched, his elbow resting on the arm of the couch. She stroked the palm of his hand.

"What does Harriet do on weekends? You know, Danny, I simply don't know. I am sure she has every minute planned of every weekend from now until we graduate . . . she is that way. And I suppose one day she will say to herself, 'Harriet, it is time you got married.' She will then survey the field and notify the lucky winner. And believe me, Danny, he will be lucky to have Harriet."

Danny's shudder was intentionally exaggerated. Caroline noticed it and simply changed the subject. Danny acknowledged the maneuver and commented on it: "You are the least contentious person I have ever known."

Caroline smiled, and replied, "You are *not* the least contentious person *I* have ever known."

He gripped her hand.

And now his voice was slightly hoarse. She sensed what was coming and she was right. "Caroline, I can't stand it any longer. I have to have you. To love you, in my arms. You go up and let me follow in a few minutes, will you, darling?"

"No, Danny dear, I will not. You are my beautiful Danny boy and I do love you, I have told you that, but I am not—"

"—not going to *spoil* your beautiful Danny boy?" He sighed. The spell was quickly broken, his desire sublimated. He removed his hand. The ache of longing was still there, but instantly he recaptured control. He grinned broadly. "Oh dear, I guess I will have to go sleep with somebody else tonight, what a pity."

She didn't say anything, but put down her glass and got up. She looked about the large old-fashioned lobby with its two-dozen leather armchairs, the coffee tables with the day's newspapers here and there, the unused, sleepy, slightly untidy old Negro porter sitting within conversational reach of the night clerk. "It's time, Danny. Time to go to bed."

"That exactly has been my point."

Another of her smiles, but no comment. He walked with her to the elevator. They kissed and he said, "The usual?"

"The usual. I'll walk over to Silliman after the eight o'clock mass."

Danny waved his hand as the elevator doors closed. She blew him a chaste kiss.

Walking back to his college he realized suddenly that if there had been a cat house between the Taft Hotel and Silliman College, with hot and cold running raunchy girls, he would not now —not this very minute—stop to patronize it. After being with Caroline, there was no substitute for Caroline. But, lying in bed a half hour later, he reflected that his self-denial was not, really, all that natural. He was bewitched—that was the best he could make of it. It was a very nice feeling, but the odds were against its lasting forever. He called Sally Smithers in New York and made a date for Sunday night.

Ten

THEY WERE TAKING final exams and there was only one left to go—as it happened, the single course both Danny and Henry were enrolled in, third-year French. They were bone-weary from the studying done to prepare for the exams taken during the preceding ten days, and now Danny was especially, exuberantly restless. He would rather complain about tomorrow's exam than prepare for it, he'd have conceded if asked. So he cranked up:

"You know Clavet'll give us a long, tough passage to translate. Probably from his beloved Racine. But if it is Racine, for sure it won't be anything we've ever laid eyes on before." Danny rose from his desk and lightly tweaked his nose, in the manner of M. Clavet. His voice rose a half octave: *"Rien que vous avez déjà connu*

. . . Henry, I hope what I just said in exquisite French wasn't too complicated for you to understand?''

Henry decided he'd retaliate massively, since his French was much more advanced than Danny's, and so he replied in high-speed French words to the effect, "Obviously M. Clavet isn't going to have us translate a passage we're already familiar with, you—" He had a hard time coming up with French for "jerk." He settled on "—*vous bête.*" And then added in English, "What would be the point of asking us to translate a passage we've already familiarized ourselves with?''

Danny leaned back in his swivel chair, closed his eyes and smiled. "You know what, Henry? You're absolutely right. No point at all. I just felt like dumping on M. Clavet, and then you went and spoiled all my fun.''

Henry enjoyed Danny's spontaneity. Danny was that way. He didn't hide it when he was obviously guilty. It was easier to transform what was previously thought wrong to something freshly recognized as right.

"Screw,'' Danny said. "Let's go to George and Harry's and have a beer. We can talk to each other in French, if you think that's the only way to justify getting away from the goddamn memory work.'' The memory work was a review of five thousand French words the students of M. Clavet were expected to have learned.

"Why not?'' Henry said. "Did you know hamburger is established as perfect brain food?'' Henry's voice was very serious.

"No. As a matter of fact, I didn't know that. When did the brain surgeons come through with that?''

"They haven't yet. I am just anticipating them.''

Danny laughed. Anyway, Henry was all for forgetting the French for a while and having a beer. Or two. If Henry said okay, Danny reasoned, it had to be *okay*. If Henry had frowned on taking off a half hour, Danny would have left anyway. But he wouldn't have enjoyed himself as much.

Henry poked his head out of the open window and looked down on the quadrangle, its dimensions clearly indited by the modest yellow lights under the succession of arcades. A lovely sight. And Silliman was only a block or so from the hamburger and beer joint heavily patronized by students who lived in that area of the campus. "Still warm. Well, why not, June tenth it should be warm."

"I wish your Lakeville lake were around the corner."

"Yeah," they were walking toward the eatery, "that would be nice."

"Hey!" Danny stopped in his tracks. "I got an idea. Let's get a couple of beers, pile into the car, and go to the beach at Savin Rock."

Henry brightened. "What the hell. I mean, *pourquoi pas, Monsieur Daniel? Il faut nous amuser!*"

Twenty minutes later the car was parked. The headlights had detected no other cars along the half mile of sandy stretch by the beach that led to the amusement park at the end of the promontory.

"Monastic community," Danny said, looking about at the empty parking lot. "No lovers." He opened the second beer, handed it to Henry and walked toward the water's edge. A few steps from the water he took off his shoes and khaki pants, stretching the pants out on the sand to sit down on them, beer in hand. Henry joined him. The moon was new, the movements of the seawater visible, but not incandescent. Danny swigged on his beer contemplatively. He was asking himself the question, Now? He answered it. "Why not?"

"Henry? You know something?"

Henry sensed what was coming. The accents, the formulation. An invitation to learning. . . . It had to mean that Danny was ready—finally—to talk about the one subject of common interest never touched on. "You want to talk about Caroline."

Danny was surprised. "Well, yes. I want to marry her."

"I'd have guessed so. And—" he very nearly betrayed an intimacy he had got from his sister, but he caught himself in time— "I suppose you have asked her?"

"Damnedest thing about your sister, Henry. You don't have to formulate things. I mean, not most things. She understands everything. Often she knows what I'm thinking before I'm thinking it. Like tonight, walking to George and Harry's, she'd probably have said when we walked out of Silliman, 'Danny, you'd like to go to the beach, wouldn't you?' . . . No. I haven't asked her. But asking Caroline if she would marry me would feel a little like asking her if she, if she . . . intends to graduate from college."

"You mean—"

"I mean she'd wonder what on earth alternative ever occurred to me. Or to her. She'd say something like, 'What an odd question. Of course we'll be married. The only question is when.' "

Henry was serious. "I know what you mean. She's been that way always. I don't need to tell you that Caroline is—"

"No. You don't need to tell me. I know it. I guess what I'm saying, Henry, is that I hope you approve."

Henry laughed now. "What does it matter? If, as you say, she expects to marry you, that leaves out any leverage I might have on the matter."

"I want you to be happy about it."

"I am, Danny. You know how I feel about you. I won't even mention the most obvious debt I have to you. Well, sure, I will: If it weren't for you I would probably be behind bars right now."

"We agreed never—"

"Yeah, and up until now I've lived up to it. But it's there, the dominant event in our relationship—in our friendship. In my life, come to think of it. And then we've done a lot together since then. Including a little—book-burning in Cannes."

Henry did not see the expression on Danny's face. Since boarding the *Continental* that same afternoon, Danny had never again mentioned Paul Hébert. Or whatever his name was; Henry wasn't sure. "All I can say is that if Caroline loves you the way she obviously does, that fact would eliminate any reservation I had about you. Assuming I had any reservation about you. Though you know, Danny, you are a little . . . headstrong. Probably just your—our—high testosterone level, as twenty-five-year-olds. You probably know that. You should know that it's visible to other people. Like me."

Danny thought this was enough on the subject. He got up,

clapped Henry on the back, pulled off his polo shirt, dropped his shorts, and said, "I got you, Henry; now, *allons nager!*"

He ran toward the water and dived in, followed by Henry. They swam vigorously for fifteen minutes. At midnight they were back with their five thousand French words.

Danny had always had trouble with penmanship. His teachers had always complained about the difficulty in making out what he wrote. One teacher, when Danny was twelve, made him print in block letters, hoping that a departure from the script of the Palmer method would clarify the letters. It helped a bit, but the result, after a year or two, was a strange amalgam of block and script, and the strain on exam readers was such that when Danny one morning got his terrific idea, at the end of the first semester of sophomore year, he found all the examining professors elatedly cooperative.

Accordingly he would arrive at his exams with his portable typewriter in hand and ask routinely for permission to type out his answers to the exam. This he had to do in an adjacent classroom, where he would not disturb other students who were writing by hand on their blue books. Today, at the exam at Strathcona Hall for French 310, the presiding monitor readily acquiesced.

Danny was happy not to have to join the twenty-five students in shirtsleeves bending over, in their standard little desk chairs, the six-page exam paper being handed out. Danny took his copy of the examination paper and walked out of the exam hall with it to a small empty classroom, adjacent. He could tell from the thickness of the stapled sheets that, indeed, there would be a long passage there to translate into French. He closed the door.

Three hours later, he walked with Henry from Strathcona the half block to Silliman. It was sunny and hot. Danny carried a seersucker jacket in one hand, his Royal portable typewriter in the other. The summer was now shimmering about them. It was suddenly sweltering in New Haven: It was now, and would be for three months, a hot, humid little city.

"Funny sensation," Danny said as they walked, slowly, as if

without purpose. "That's it! The end of college life. All that happens now is we fart around for a week, then receive a diploma."

"In Latin."

"Don't worry, Henry. I'll translate it for you."

They reached their rooms. Danny tossed his jacket down on the couch and went out into the community bathroom across the hall.

Henry looked about at the litter in the little study-sitting room, left over from the night before—papers, books, empty bottles of beer and Coca-Cola. Students at Yale hadn't had the luxury of a daily cleaning woman since freshman year.

What the hell. Henry set out to tidy up the room. He began by removing Danny's coat—why on earth did Danny need a coat on June 11 in New Haven, Connecticut? He lifted the light seersucker from the couch and felt the weight of it. Surprised, he looked down into the bared pocket, slipped his hand in and brought out Cassell's French dictionary.

Quickly he slipped it back into the pocket of the coat and laid it back on the couch. He was dismayed.

And then he walked quickly out the door and down the stairs.

He'd wait outside the dining hall until it opened. He didn't want to lay eyes on Danny. He would not have known what to say to him. In fact he did not speak to any of the other students who milled about, waiting for the dining hall to open. Henry was silent, diplomatically diverting all efforts to engage him in conversation during lunch. He tried to sort it out.

Danny.

Cheating.

Eleven

THE DAYS that led to the wedding hadn't been without incident. Soon after Caroline's visit to Palm Beach, where she spent a weekend with her future mother-in-law at her seaside villa, the formal announcement was drafted.

Rachel closely supervised its composition. From time to time the society columns in Palm Beach and Newport reported on Rachel Roosevelt Bennett's activity, and she was entirely agreeable to being referred to as a style setter, and why not? Her father had been President of the United States longer than any man in history and her mother was very nearly as famous as her father. When the King and Queen of England had visited in Hyde Park in 1939 the President had served them hot dogs and all of America had risen to cheer. Rachel was especially attuned to social possibilities to weigh in with The People, her father's constituents, and she was the first, according to the society columnist in the *Palm Beach Daily News,* ever to wear pants—fancy, floral silk pants, especially made for her—at an afternoon garden party at which she was the hostess.

Yes, but Rachel knew that some occasions were born to be formal, and she was not about to deinstitutionalize such a thing as a wedding. Or what came before; and, accordingly, the announcement of the engagement party was entirely conventional, her personal handiwork, even though the stamp was, so to speak, from out there, the provenance of the bride. Henry Beckett Chafee of Lakeville, Connecticut, was proud to announce the engagement of his sister, Caroline Stimson Chafee, to Daniel Tracey O'Hara of Palm Beach, Florida. The announcement recorded the name of Danny's late father and the current name of his mother. And—though Rachel wrestled with this for a bit, but then thought what the hell, why not?—the names of his maternal grandparents. About Caroline, the names of her late parents were given, and it was noted that she would graduate from Smith College in June, and that after graduating from Yale in 1950, her fiancé had joined the Trafalgar hotel chain in New York as a junior executive.

Rachel O'Hara had given a stellar buffet-dance party at her Palm Beach spread for a hundred guests. In the receiving line Rachel introduced Caroline, dressed in yellow chiffon, the light blond hair slightly curled; her son Danny, the poster-boy college grad, in his blazer and white duck pants; her daughter Lila, at six feet one an imposing undergraduate with brown hair, large teeth, and an iron handshake; and Henry, golden blond, with horn-rimmed glasses and a studious air about him, the brother of the bride. The young people stayed on and danced late to Lester Lanin's music and, much later, put on swim clothes and disported in the sea. Rachel spent as much time as she could command closely observing her prospective daughter-in-law. Late in the evening she confessed to her husband almost ruefully that she could find nothing in her to criticize.

"That probably makes her too good for Danny," Harry Bennett grunted, taking off his black tie.

Rachel was half amused (she knew that her self-indulgent son had, well, shortcomings), half resentful (she was proud of him, her firstborn, and utterly delighted by his good looks). She satisfied herself by saying, "If she's good enough for Danny, she's good enough for me."

Henry and Caroline had been assigned the guest cottage, with its two bedrooms and living room. Breakfast was brought in the next morning and Henry, his eyes roaming over the headlines of the *Miami Herald* that came in with the breakfast, complimented his sister on her patience and charm during the long evening. Caroline accepted her brother's bouquet as a routine fraternal courtesy and moved purposively to another subject. "How much do they pay you at *Time* magazine?"

Henry told her he earned one hundred dollars per week. "Eighty-eight fifty after withholding tax."

"How much do you know about our trust?"

"Not as much as I should. We've both been getting the same allowance, seventy-five bucks per month, but every now and then Cam Beckett springs something like a trip to Europe. Are you wondering about the wedding?"

"Yes. It's our . . . treat, right?"

"That's what the book says. I'll call Cam when I get back to New York. Have you set a date?"

Caroline mused, "No, actually, we haven't. Danny, as you would expect, wants it the day after tomorrow. I thought maybe in the fall."

"What do you plan to do during the summer?—and please pass the marmalade. No, that one."

"I haven't told this yet to Danny, but I've told Father Keller I'll volunteer this summer at the Maryknoll Mission in Mexico. I feel I want to do something like that. The Mormons do it—they spend a couple of years doing what they think of as missionary work. I'm not thinking about preaching Christianity, but maybe practicing a little Christianity. I've been given a lot, maybe I should try to give back a little. My Spanish is pretty good but could get a lot better, and the mission—it's just outside of Cuer-navaca—teaches orphans aged six to twelve and looks after them.''

"Maryknollers. Why not Benedictines? You forgetting La-trobe?''

"Hardly."

"You were only five."

"Yes. Funny, I don't remember anything else about when I was five, except for vague memories of Father; and Mother, obvi-ously. But Latrobe I remember—I remember every detail. I re-member Brother Ambrose giving us the first glass of Ovaltine I ever tasted. And I'd hardly forget what you did, Henry."

The memory of it still made Henry shiver.

It was getting late that October afternoon in 1935 and the sun was beginning to go down. Henry and Caroline had spent almost two hours at the forest reserve looking for their parents. They had separated from them in midafternoon, determined to ex-plore the forest all by themselves, unaccompanied by adults. One hour later they set out to retrace their steps. But they were lost, it seemed irretrievably.

Henry, age ten, hadn't known what to do next. They sat down on the scrubby forest floor of decaying leaves, wondering in which direction to set out to emerge from the forest. It was then that he spotted the snake and heard its rattle as it slithered its hypnotizing way toward Caroline's right thigh. Henry felt the hairs stand up on his head and his breath choked but he wasn't paralyzed. He threw himself at the rattler and grabbed it under its oily head, smashing it feverishly a half-dozen times against the big rock.

The snake was dead. Henry struggled to control his breathing. He had been bitten and he knew that rattlesnake bites could be deadly. Caroline seemed to know too because she began to cry. Henry remembered what his Boy Scout leader had told the boys about the blood flow. Accordingly he instructed Caroline. *She must quiet down,* then remove one of her long socks and wind it tightly around Henry's upper arm. Caroline followed his instruc-tions step by step, remaining silent. She was fumbling with the improvised bandage when they heard the evensong of the monks not far away. Henry began to run in the direction of the chant, then remembered what his leader had said: Exercise stimulates the blood flow, spreads the poison. He slowed down to a fast walk, and in a few moments fell into the arms of Brother Ambrose, at the head of the column of twelve Benedictines doing late-afternoon devotions while taking one of their daily walks in the forest surrounding the monastery.

Henry blurted it all out. Brother Ambrose acted quickly. He dispatched one monk to look after Caroline, a second to go at a run to the monastery to call the doctor at Latrobe; and then with a third monk he joined hands-to-wrists to form the classic seat. Brother Ambrose wanted no physical exertion made by Henry, nothing that would accelerate the circulation of the poison.

Accordingly the two monks squatted down and told Henry to sit on the improvised chair formed by their interlocked forearms and to put his arms around their necks. They then dogtrotted the quarter mile back to the monastery. At the infirmary, the matron called the doctor's office to ask if he had brought rattlesnake vaccine with him. He had not. She called the hospital and ordered it sent by ambulance. She made incisions across, and vertical to, the fang mark, renewed the tourniquet, and put a thermometer in Henry's mouth.

Caroline was at his side and would not let go of Henry's free hand. He felt dizzy, then fell asleep, waking to the jab of the needle in his arm. The night was a painful blur through which he remembered nausea, the sound of his mother and father saying unintelligible things to Brother Ambrose, the proddings of a doctor, heavy perspiration.

And, the next morning, a sedated sense of having arrived out of the dark forest onto a grassy plain. He opened his eyes. His mother was sitting in the armchair. One hour later, Brother Ambrose invited the family into the chapel to offer a prayer of thanksgiving. Henry was stretched out on a sofa cushion in the chapel. Caroline knelt behind him during the exercise, and he heard her child's voice attempting to pronounce the prayers of the college of monks, but the Latin was beyond her, as it was beyond Henry.

But from then on, no Christmas went by without an exchange of cards with Brother Ambrose; and when, fifteen years later, word reached them that he had died, Caroline left Smith on a long bus journey, prayed at the grave of Brother Ambrose and, returning to Smith, acted on an impulse she had felt for a year but never yielded to. She went down the hall to talk to her classmate, Maureen Buckley, who had spoken of the work she did during the summer for Father Keller in New York. Would Maureen take her to meet Father Keller and to learn about the Maryknollers? Maureen said sure—she went to New York every month or so and it was always nice to visit with ''FK,'' as his non-clerical associates and volunteers referred to him.

What then happened, one year later—a year ago—was that Caroline had become a Catholic. But for reasons she never explained even to herself, she wished her conversion to be entirely private. Henry had guessed the reason, which was that his little sister would go to great lengths to avoid attracting attention to herself. At one point he had mentioned this to Danny. ''She is so striking naturally, she shies instinctively from, well, from making that light any brighter.'' The last thing she would do at Smith, for instance, was join the drama group, or consent to sing solo in the choir. Anyway, FK baptized her, Maureen served as godmother and another priest in the Maryknoll mission as godfather. She went quietly to church at Smith, and in New Haven when visiting with Danny. But she did not let on, except to Henry, that she had become a communicant.

Caroline returned to her theme. ''On the wedding—you know, Henry, I don't see any need for a big wedding. Even if the trust has money for it, I wouldn't want to spend it. Just—well, we don't have to go into detail.''

''No. No, Caroline. But from what I know of Mrs. O'Hara—of Mrs. Bennett—of Rachel—she's going to think big about the wedding. You'll need Danny's support.''

Caroline paused. Then she turned inquiringly to her brother.

"Henry, I know I'm doing the right thing. I'm sure you think so too. But maybe, I don't know, maybe I want to hear you say it, in your words. 'Is there anyone in this company who has reason to object to the bonds of matrimony? If so, speak, or forever hold your peace!' " Caroline laughed when she spoke the words, but she didn't do so in such a way as to repeal their having been spoken. More gravely, she went on, "Is there anything about Danny you, well, you wonder about?"

Henry thought it best to adopt his technique of evasion, which was slightly to divert. "Danny is my best friend. What more can anybody say?"

The telephone rang. "Yes, Mrs. Bennett. Okay, thanks— Yes, *Rachel*. Of course, I am happy to call you Rachel. Yes. It was terrific. Terribly nice people. Yes, I thought the music wonderful. No. Not quite, but I can be over there in fifteen minutes. We don't have very long before flight time, do we? See you in a bit, Rachel."

And on Wednesday, Caroline had the letter. General Bennett was taking over. *The wedding would be in Palm Beach. . . .* There were plenty of precedents for orphaned young people turning the responsibility for a wedding over to parents of the groom. *The Episcopal minister at Palm Beach was an old family friend, indeed as a younger man had served as assistant rector at the church in Rhinebeck, New York, to which Danny's grandfather repaired on Sundays while governor, and, later, President. . . .*

Well, Caroline sighed, it had to come. She thought of telephoning Danny to discuss it with him. Then she thought better of it: If she talked it over with Danny, he'd then have to tell his mother he had had a discussion with his future bride and— lost out. Because he would from sheer inertia side with his mother, and then lose out to Caroline. So would Rachel Roosevelt O'Hara Rosenthal Incantadore Bennett.

"Dear Rachel: You are wonderfully kind to offer to relieve Henry and me of all those responsibilities, but we've talked about it and we think Mother and Father would have preferred that we act as hosts. The house at Lakeville isn't much, but it has a very nice lawn. And, Rachel, I haven't spoken about it, though I wouldn't be surprised if Danny has suspected it, but I became a Catholic a year ago and, as you probably know, the laws of my church specify marriage by a priest. The priest at Lakeville is a very nice man, and I hope you will like him. On the matter of the date, I will talk with Danny. I have in mind something along about the middle of September. As I said in the letter I sent you on Monday, I was enchanted by the whole affair on Saturday and was happy to meet some of your friends. Love from—Caroline."

"Mom, it's *not* an insulting letter." Danny grasped the telephone in his left hand. His legs were stretched out in exasperated anticipation of a long exchange with his mother. He closed his eyes as Rachel Bennett fired on. Volley after volley. *"How* do I know it's not insulting? *Because,* Mom, *you just finished reading it to me.* Do you want to read it to me *again?* Go ahead, I'm listening."

Rachel read out loud again the letter from Caroline.

Danny responded: "Now, what's *insulting* about *that?* You can say her letter is *disappointing.* You can say it's *shortsighted.* Dumb. Stupid. Ungrateful. But look, Mom, if that is the way she *feels* about the wedding, it's not 'insulting' to say so. And anyway, it's not the end of the world, is it? A couple of weeks down the line you can give us a party in Florida with Frank Sinatra and Judy Garland singing—the wedding can be a simple affair in Lakeville— No. No, I *didn't* know she was a Catholic. I *did* know that on Sundays in New Haven she went to the Catholic church at Yale to mass, but I assumed it was just one of those, you know, ecumenical things. But apparently she's quite serious about it. What? Al Smith? Al Smith was a Catholic and hated Grandfather? *Mother!* Al Smith was *nominated* by Grandfather. It's just not *correct* to say that Catholics were against Grandfather; hell, they voted *for* him, most of them. . . . Well, I mean, that's too bad, and I see what you mean. I mean, I'm supposed to be an Anglican. Okay, so she is more of a Catholic, I guess, than I am an Anglican. But what are you saying I should do about it? Call the Ku Klux Klan? . . . No, I know, Mother. That was a joke. —A what joke? Yes. A bad joke. How about if I agree to call it an *insulting* joke? Does that make you feel better? I'm sorry, Mom, I really am. But I really don't think, six months after the wedding, anybody will remember where the wedding was, or what the religion was of the guy who married us."

Danny motioned to Sally Smithers to bring him a drink. *Such a good old shoe, Sally, provides me with everything I want, including her comfy apartment, and in three years she never once suggested we get married, I mean, how perfect can a girlfriend—a lady friend—be?* He sipped his drink while letting his mother smolder out her indignation at being tamed by a twenty-one-year-old indigent Catholic convert. He more or less agreed with her as, little by little, she reduced the charges against Danny's future wife: Yes, he said finally, that was a suitable compromise, a really terrific idea, Mom. Rachel would give a big wedding party—at Lakeville.

He would call Caroline. But not right now. Later that night, maybe; or maybe the next day. Caroline could always be reached by phone at lunchtime at Haven House at Smith.

He put down the telephone, got up, gave Sally a kiss and said, "Sorry about that; yes, it was awfully long. Do you have a mother, Sally? I mean, *obviously* you have a mother, and you must know then that mothers sometimes get out of hand. But your mother wasn't out of hand when she had *you,* you bet."

He loved being with Sally, more actually, than he loved Sally, and it was that way too with her, who loved her time with Danny but would not want to be with him full-time. She always made herself available to him, or mostly always, since once in a blue moon her ex-husband hove in, exercising squatter's rights. It was wonderful that he could talk to her about all the plans he had to make in connection with marrying Caroline, but then these plans didn't necessarily mean discontinuing visits with Sally Smithers, who always smelled like sweet hay. Funny he thought that, because he didn't know what sweet hay was, or what it would smell like, except that it would smell like Sally.

Twelve

T HE WEDDING wasn't going to turn out to be all that modest, Caroline realized as the date neared. Cam Beckett had told Henry that the family trust could come up with three thousand dollars for "such an important event." And then word got around, in Lakeville and in neighboring Salisbury and Sharon, that the daughter of the late President was the mother of the groom. It was even rumored that the widow herself would turn up for the wedding of her dashing grandson—after all, Lakeville was only an hour away from Hyde Park.

Friends popped up, resourceful friends, anxious to help; many of them volunteering to put up for Friday and Saturday night members of the wedding party, or even just plain guests from out of town. "In Lakeville, guests-from-out-of-town means practically everybody," Caroline chatted to Henry about their home town with its twenty-five hundred inhabitants.

She sat allocating expected guests to hostesses, all details carefully logged in her thick white-leather register designated to keep a record of everything that pertained to the wedding. Already a half-dozen pages listed presents and the addresses of the friends and acquaintances who sent them. Preponderantly, they came from friends of the groom. That was to be expected. Henry looked over his sister's shoulder. "Caroline, you will be glad to know that you will begin married life owning three toasters."

"Yes. I'm beginning to hope that somebody will send us some bread. Have you counted the pitchers?"

"What did Mrs. Bennett—Rachel—contribute?"

"The honeymoon. Sweet. I persuaded Danny to take our two weeks in Scotland. He's never been. We'll fly Pan Am on the twentieth. Wish you were coming too, Henry. No! That isn't a proper thought for a honeymoon. I'm *glad* you won't be there, Henry!" She laughed and went to answer the telephone in the study.

Henry could hear her talking to Cam Beckett. The conversation ended and she returned to the living room. "He is a sweetheart. If I hadn't decided on Danny, I'd have proposed to him."

Henry said that conceivably Mrs. Beckett would have been uncooperative.

"She certainly hasn't been uncooperative about the wedding." The Becketts were moving into the guest house on their property, vacating the five-bedroom house for Mrs. Bennett and her retinue. "I wish we could think of something really nice to do for them."

"Maybe I can persuade Henry Luce to put Mr. Beckett on the cover of *Time*?"

"Yes, Henry, that would be very nice. 'Portrait of a Connecticut Yankee.' 'New England Lawyer Lightens the Load of Orphaned Smith Grad Marrying into Royal Family.' How'm I doing, Henry?" She scratched an entry into the wedding-present list.

"Fair. How many people is Rachel inviting to her party on Friday?"

"Danny said she didn't place any limit on it. I shouldn't think all that many people would want to come in on Friday for a noon Saturday wedding. It means finding someplace around here to spend the night. My invitation list is only about forty, counting Smithies. Danny, needless to say, is inviting half the Yale class of 1950. —Henry, I haven't told you about Madame Landowska."

"Don't tell me *she's* coming? Will she bring her biographers? The studio technicians?"

"Henry, quiet. No. Actually, I rather hoped she would come. Every now and then . . . did you read the *Time* magazine article about her? Dumb, of course you read it. Did you do any legwork on it?"

"Actually I did. I went and spent three hours with Denise Restout, her librarian, researcher, counselor and cook. She's not yet thirty, you know. I gave Max five thousand words of Landowskiana I got from Denise."

"Well then you know she has been *known* to attend a party, though maybe only one every couple of years, and usually it's a party for the fiftieth anniversary, or whatever, of a Caruso or Schnabel type, you know. But she's been nice to me since I was ten and she made me play on her Pleyel harpsichord. She would just sit there and mumble in French to Denise, and Denise would then tell me what I was doing wrong, and the old lady would just nod. It is such a glorious sound and when she plays her fingers are like little pistons, straight up and down. So anyway, I thought: Why not ask?"

"How'd she take it?"

"It was wonderful. She got up from the chair and sat down at her harpsichord. You know, the famous one, yes, the Pleyel, and she played something very simple, not anything I knew or recognized. Just a couple of minutes, then she told me it was an epithalamium—she taught me that word, taught it to me in French, Henry—a lyrical wedding ode. It was written for her by Poulenc, who was just a young man, as a tribute to her husband when he died in 1919."

"What did she say about the wedding?"

"She said," Caroline's voice was excited, "she said no, she would not come. But that she would give me a wedding present. On Thursday or Friday before the wedding I can bring up to eight people to her house, and she will play for us, for one hour. Henry! A private concert by Wanda Landowska! How do you like that!" She was radiant. The telephone rang; she darted out of the room and was back in a minute or two and returned distractedly to the acceptance list she had been discussing. "Yes, I told you Danny was inviting half your class."

"What's the matter with the other half of the class of 1950?" Henry got up from the floor. "There," he said, putting down the scissors. "That's the lot for today. God knows how many more packages will arrive tomorrow. But you'll be on your own, Carol. I leave for New York after supper." Impulsively, Caroline got up and embraced her brother. She hung on to him for a full minute.

Mrs. Bennett had been in residence at the Becketts' for two days before her party began. For it, she brought in caterers from New York. A large tent, in red and white vaulted stripes, materialized on the lakeside lawn of the Becketts'. Inside the tent were chairs and tables for two hundred guests, a wooden platform for ten musicians, a substantial dance floor, clusters of roses and chrysanthemums and azaleas punctuating the seemingly endless circular buffet.

Cocktails were served in the Beckett house from two bars. The guests began to flow in at seven. By eight, the older generation was overwhelmed. Jeff Lowry suggested to Danny that Zeta Psi could proceed to do its business—"we've got a quorum!" Harriet bounced about, a pinball touching every base. They filled the house's rooms, upstairs and downstairs. The buzz of animated conversation became seamless, as incessantly exuberant in the little study downstairs as in the little drawing room on the second floor.

—*"She is ever so pretty, Rachel. And the expression on her face is heavenly."*

"What else would you expect? She spent the entire summer sprinkling holy water on Mexican orphans. You would look heavenly too, Alice, if you did that."

—"*I don't mind telling you, Jim, that girl is something else. And she adores me. But that doesn't surprise you, does it, Jim? I mean—Jim, do you adore me?*"

—"Gus, cut it out. You're making me sick. Come to think of it, you've made me feel sick every one of the five hundred times I've been with you in the past four years."

—"*So what I'm gonna do, Johnny, is— Listen. Well, get closer then, I'm not going to go to a loudspeaker t'tell you. What I'm gonna do is spend the night at Millbrook with the Abbotts, then I'll pick you up at the Coleys' at—exactly, exactly 10:25. That way we'll get to the church by 10:40 which is when we have to begin ushering the—ushering the— Aw, screw you, Johnny. Can you remember just one thing: 10:25? At the Coleys'?* . . .

—He pressed her hand. "You having fun, doll?"

Caroline nodded. "As long as you're here, Danny, I'm having fun."

The party was down to the twenty or thirty bitter-enders. The bandleader sent in his question: Did Mrs. Bennett want the musicians to go beyond one o'clock? The same messenger who brought back the word ("No") then went to Danny and whispered to him that his mother wished to see him right away in the main house. "In her sitting room."

Danny got up, clutched his glass, thought better of it and left it on the table. "Be right back," he said to Gus and Amy.

He walked up the two flights of stairs to the sitting room. "Hi, Mom, terrific party—"

Silent, she motioned him to the chair. He stopped talking. His eyes looked furtively around the small room with its dressing table, armchair, and couch.

"Somebody has stolen my necklace."

Danny shook his head. "Which necklace?"

"What do you mean, *which* necklace. The one I was wearing tonight. The one Harry gave me. My *diamond* necklace."

"When did you take it off? Why did you take it off?"

"Because it was irritating me," she barked. "I have a little rash back there," she pointed.

"Are you absolutely sure, Mom, that you had it on tonight?"

"Sure I had it on?" Rachel Bennett was incredulous. "Are you drunk, Danny? I could hardly *imagine* having it on, or *imagine* having taken it off before dinner—"

"Have you looked everywhere?"

"Well," her eyes were spitting out contempt for her only son, her *stupid* son. "No, I haven't looked *everywhere.* For instance, I haven't looked in the coffeepot downstairs. I haven't looked inside the bassoon or whatever that thing is they're blowing into down there.

"The questions you ask! When I took it off before dinner I stuck it the only place I ever stick it"—she pointed to a small velvet jewel case sitting on the dresser. "I put it *in that case* and stuck the case *in that drawer."* She opened the drawer in question, shut it, opened it, shut it, opened it, finally slamming it shut. "Obviously somebody stole it."

"Mom, I feel terrible about this, but what—"

"We are talking about a piece of jewelry worth fifty thousand dollars."

"Is it insured?"

For a moment, Rachel Bennett calmed down. "Yes. Of course. But not for its present value. . . . But that's not the point. We have to do something about it."

"What? I mean, Mom, exactly *what?"*

She gritted her teeth. "I'm going to go and talk to Cam Beckett."

"Mom, he's undoubtedly asleep. And if he isn't, what could he *do?* And besides, Mom, he might feel a little guilty just because it's, well, his house. . . . Is it his servants around, or people you brought from New York?"

"Hal. Al, Cal, whatever his name, he's with the Becketts. The rest were with the caterers, except, of course, for Helen. . . .

Obviously Helen didn't do it. Why should she wait eight years, if she was going to steal my necklace—she's been with us eight years.'' Impulsively Rachel got up, opened the door to the little study and called out to straggling members of the staff on the floor below. ''Is Helen down there? Please ask her to come up.''

She came quickly and Rachel reported the missing necklace. Helen looked perplexed.

''What is it, Helen? Do you have any ideas about it?''

''Mrs. Bennett, I don't think you brought that necklace up from Palm Beach.''

Rachel was dismayed. Was she losing her mind? Helen didn't make mistakes of that kind. But Rachel was not about to rebuke Helen using the same kind of language she was prepared to use with Danny. ''You are wrong about that, Helen,'' she said impatiently. ''But never mind. Thank you. Good night.''

Danny didn't think it wise to revisit the question whether the necklace had actually been worn, and so said, ''Mom, I'm truly sad about this, but since there isn't anything I can do, shouldn't I get back to the party? You, er, you don't want me to say anything about the necklace to, I mean, let the word out, do you?''

She shook her head and motioned to him brusquely to go.

''Anything wrong, Danny?''

''Not a thing, Caroline. . . . Only thing that's wrong is that tonight is still twenty-four hours away.'' They kissed. There was a round of applause. The following day, after a telephone call to the caretaker at the Palm Beach estate, who verified that he could not find the necklace in the room upstairs where he had been instructed to look, two state troopers quietly questioned members of the staff, those who worked for Cam Beckett and the half dozen there from New York who had catered the night before and would do so again after the wedding at noon. Helen continued to insist the necklace hadn't been brought up, that it would turn up in Florida. Inevitably, the word got out that Mrs. Bennett's necklace was missing. But there was nothing like an uproar over it. ''She might have left it in Newport and just forgotten," Danny said to Henry dismissively. Henry demurred, saying he thought he remembered its being worn during the cocktail party the night before. But other matters pressed, and the state troopers soon left, while others prepared to go to the church.

Book Two

Thirteen

LILA O'HARA, someone remarked to Lawrence Callard, the Director of the Franklin D. Roosevelt Library at Hyde Park, went from adolescence to matronliness, eschewing all stages in between as—well, as a waste of time, really. Lila was a feverishly diligent woman. She had breezed through her Ph.D. in history at Harvard, the envy of those of her colleagues who labored on at normal metabolic speeds. Lila read quickly, remembered everything she read, wrote quickly and made decisions quickly. Her style, whether speaking or writing, was not distinctive, but it was orderly. She was conscious of her work habits and liked to remind all who would listen, which meant everyone Lila could corner, of the effectiveness of the work habits of Anthony Trollope.

He was, Lila would inform you, the "greatest nineteenth-century novelist, when you really come down to it; yes, greater than Dickens.'' Trollope, Lila had discovered, began to write at six every morning. He pre-marked his writing tablet at calculated intervals into which Trollope could fit 250 words, written in his customary hand. ''So,'' as she detailed it to her older brother Danny when first she read about it, ''at six-fifteen he would look for the mark he had etched on the pad. If it was farther down on the page than where he was, why—he would write faster until the thirty-minute check. If the mark came *before* he finished, he would slow down.'' This for Lila was a metaphor of her working habits. She would decide what she wished to accomplish in a day. If it was necessary to work harder in order to accomplish it, why she would do so. If she found herself advancing toward the end of the day, her work mostly done, she would simply slow down. She was greatly satisfied by the handle she had on her scholarly, clerical life.

She did her major in modern American history, writing her dissertation on her grandfather's fourth presidential race. She was disappointed that one publisher after another declined to publish her thesis. She received her fifth rejection at Palm Beach where she was vacationing during the spring break with her mother. Lila had permitted herself a total relaxation—this too was a part of her programmed life: When you go to Mom's house in Palm Beach, take advantage of the beach, of the sea, of the swimming pool, of the large staff, and *do nothing*.

She was told at the pool that the telephone call was for her.

It was her roommate at Cambridge, staying in for the holidays to make up for the three weeks of work missed earlier in the season, when she was doing volunteer work for Senator John Kennedy's campaign against Hubert Humphrey in West Virginia. Clara had been instructed to open any letter from Cornell University Press addressed to Lila. Clara read her the rejection letter, including the sentence to the effect that the editors would be willing to reconsider if Miss O'Hara, in a future version, succeeded in introducing more ''fresh material.''

Returning to the pool, she sat down on the beach chair, waiting for the Bloody Marys before lunch. She did not usually share professional developments with anyone, but this time she blurted it out to Rachel: Her thesis had been turned down yet again.

"I hope you can see what they're up to, Lila dear," Rachel commented.

"What you talking about, Mum?"

"Well, it's pretty obvious to me. You are my father's grand-daughter, and they'd like it very much if you would stir up Daddy's files at Hyde Park and scoop in some sexy stuff."

Lila looked at her mother, took off her heavy black-lacquer glasses and said, "Ah. Yes. I understand."

She might have been a little late, this time around, in tying all the loose ends together, but now it was incandescently clear: She needed her mother to lean on Hyde Park, pure and simple.

The only teaching offer she had received had been from a respectable but unexciting college in the Midwest. Accordingly she had been exploring an alternative, an opening not to teach, but to engage in library work at a college that did not have a library comprehensive enough to permit her to continue the research to which she was attracted. She could not *understand* why she hadn't thought before about the obvious direction to go.

She should be working at Hyde Park, exploring the volumi-nous collection of material assembled around the career of her grandfather. This, after all, was the first formal presidential li-brary in American history funded by the government and de-signed one part as an academic and scholarly trove, one part as a memorial.

"Mum," Lila said, peering through her glasses and adjusting the straps over and under her bathing suit, "are you on . . . very good terms with Grandmother?"

"Sure. She is always very busy, of course, and isn't well. I plan to go up to see her sometime this summer."

"Would I have any problem making an appointment with her?"

"No, I don't think so. I hope you sent her a Christmas card? I think I see what you have in mind. You want to go through the archives?"

"I want more than that. I want to be hired full-time to work in the FDR Library. Then I will put in a lot of time researching the 1944 campaign. Then I will rewrite my dissertation. Then it will be published. Then I will be famous as Dr. Lila O'Hara, not just a social footnote as granddaughter of Franklin Delano Roosevelt."

Rachel patted her daughter on the back. "Careful, dear. Thou shalt not be overbearing." Rachel reached for her drink. "But don't worry, darling Lila. I'll write Mother this afternoon and ask her to see you. And . . . I'll tell her what you have in mind. Mother prefers it that way.

"Now, come along to lunch."

Fourteen

DANNY PICKED UP the phone on his desk. It was Cutter Malone, chief accountant, full-time employee of Martino Enterprises.

"I'm ready with the second-quarter reports. Shall I come up? Or you want to do it at the hotel?"

"No. Here's okay. Nobody's going to interrupt. But tell you what, Cutter. Let's wait . . . meet at five-thirty."

"Okay, I'll come by then."

Danny buzzed Margie. "I'll be staying on for an hour or so, but don't worry about me, just a meeting with Cutter to go over the financials. Please call Caroline. Tell her, oh, sometime before eight, I figure I'll get home."

"All right, Danny. Some coffee?"

He turned down the coffee and, Montblanc pen in hand, checked the list of things he needed to do, the people he needed to call. On that list of things to do, every morning and every afternoon of his life, was a call to the old man, to the boss. To Mr. Martino. To Giuseppe Martino. Giuseppe. Might as well get it over with.

Giuseppe Martino answered the phone and spoke with a tremolo that had got much wobblier since the death of Marita. In part this was owing to age—next week Giuseppe would be eighty-four —but a mini-warble had been there even when Mr. Martino was young. Generations of employees of the Trafalgar hotel chain had amused themselves by imitating it.

"The curse, Danny"—Giuseppe had tremoloed yesterday, during one of the daily telephone talks with Danny—"is mine, not Marita's. The curse to live on and on, childless. You are very lucky, with five beautiful children." Danny knew that, in Giuseppe's idiom, there was only a "beautiful" child. If Danny's five children had been chimpanzees, Giuseppe would not have referred to them otherwise.

The exchange, the reference to children, did not on this occasion immediately speed on to Giuseppe's recounting the details surrounding the death of their only son, by drowning, thirty-three years ago. He had done that once to Danny, and Danny thought that once quite enough. Not that Danny wasn't sorry about the death of thirteen-year-old "Gippy Jr." by drowning, just that Danny simply found it difficult to activate any retroactive grief: What happened, happened, he figured. So Gippy Jr. died, too bad, but what is the point in bringing it up all over again? He had been required to weep, that first time around, when Giuseppe gave in to his own convulsive grief. Danny's histrionic skills were well developed, but he had not that often had occasion to make himself weep, so he had thought it best to turn his head, spread open his left hand, raise it fatalistically to his forehead, and then let his shoulders palpitate in little forward thrusts. It was a tribute to Danny's performance that Giuseppe had ended by consoling Danny—the surest sign of success, Danny, gratified, thought.

Giuseppe always initiated a conversation, whether with Danny or anyone else, with a personalized remark or a question. The one exception to this rule had to do with his sister Angelina, whose calls, however infrequent, he attempted to cut off as quickly as he could; Giuseppe would rather abandon congenital protocols than speak to his sister more than the required time to exchange vital information.

So that when Danny said, "Hello, Giuseppe, it's Danny," Giuseppe replied by saying, "You do not need to tell me it is you, Danny. I know your voice as I knew the voice of my own son." Danny reckoned he had better get on with the business of his call, but he felt a filial need to acknowledge the gesture, and so said, "I am flattered, Giuseppe, that in any way I should remind you of your son." And then, quickly, "The Chicago hotel is not going very well. The usual business. The labor unions. The slowdown of last spring lost us the patronage of some of our regular clients. I am sure we will get them back, but probably we'll need to coax them with a schedule of special rates, that kind of thing."

Giuseppe was not much interested. "Whatever. Of course. Remember the Martino formula: Every hotel has to do its own borrowing. No holding-company debt, no credit exposure. I know that you will make the right decisions. Chicago, you know, was my first hotel."

"Of course I know. That's why the picture of the Trafalgar-Chicago is the frontispiece of the book. Your book."

"My book?"

"Giuseppe, I'm talking about *The Great Martino.*"

"Of course. 'My book.' It is not *my* book, it is *your* book. *You* wrote it."

"Well, I think of it as *your* book, and so does everybody else. In any case, you hardly need to tell the author of *The Great Martino* anything about the history of the Trafalgar chain."

"Danny, do you *really* think Mrs. . . . your grandmother . . . actually *read* that book, my book?"

"Giuseppe, I told you she did. When I last visited her, a year ago, she had that book on her *lap*. And we talked about you."

Danny could hear the old man's sigh. It had been worth it.

Danny resented the high price he had paid the wretched ghost-writer, but clearly it was worth it, and Angelo Price had kept his word—no one knew (except Caroline) that the book extolling the life and accomplishments of Giuseppe Martino had been written by an old retired hand living in Greenwich Village, for hire but, as Angelo had said to Danny, "Remember, O'Hara, you're paying for quality bullshit; I have my standards." He did, and the book, though unnoticed by the critics, was praised by the whole Trafalgar circle.

"It is the highest honor I have ever been paid, to have *her* read a book about *me*. I have read one hundred books about your grandfather."

"Yes, Giuseppe, I know that, and you know how much I appreciate it. And how much *she* appreciated it."

"So what else, Danny, except the Chicago business. Are you and Caroline going to have another baby? It is about time, no?"

Danny was glad that his grimace was over long distance. "Ho ho, Giuseppe. Don't you think five kids is about enough?"

"My mother had twelve. But maybe you are right, because Momma had one too many."

Danny laughed. It was not necessary to feign ignorance of Giuseppe's feeling about Angelina, his one remaining sibling. Clearly he wished she had never been born.

It was fortunate that Giuseppe tired so easily. Five years ago the telephoned conversations would go on a full hour. But always Danny knew to leave it to Giuseppe to take the lead in calling the conversation to a close. It was that way with presidents. His mother had told him when he was a boy that visitors to the Oval Office were always warned never to say, "It is time to go."

"Wait until the President makes the move. As long as the President is disposed to have the company of his visitor, the visitor is at the President's disposal."

Danny was—always—at Giuseppe's disposal. Danny was president of Martino Enterprises, Inc., yes, but Giuseppe was chairman of the board and sole owner of the corporation's stock. It greatly amused Giuseppe that the board of directors was made up of Giuseppe, his valet, his chauffeur, his cook, and his housemaid. "Board meetings go very smoothly, Danny. No one has any problems. Of course, after every meeting I give each one of them a nice tip. . . . But one of these days you will find out all about boards of directors." The tremolo here was so pitched as to be pregnant with meaning. Giuseppe did not know that Danny was familiar with the old man's will. Both wills.

Cutter Malone walked in, shut the door, sat down in the black leather chair with the fluted brass legs, then abruptly got up, went back to the door, opened it slightly, squinted into the neighboring office and returned to his seat.

"Do you want to sweep the room for phone taps, Cutter?"

"In my profession we are trained to be careful," Cutter said, drawing a silver cigarette case from his pocket. The hand that brought the lighter to his cigarette trembled slightly, though Cutter was not yet fifty years old. He could use some exercise, some diet, and easy on the booze, Danny thought. Maybe someday he'd tell him. Meanwhile, to more immediate business.

"In your profession you are trained to harass otherwise enterprising people. What have you cooked up by way of reports for the quarter?"

"Well, Danny, I will certainly concede that you are one of the most enterprising people I have ever known. No, a correction: *the* most enterprising. Anyway, have a look at this."

He handed him a bound manila folder. "That's the consolidated balance sheet. These"—he handed him six more folders—"are the quarterly returns on our major league. I have the minors, if you want them."

Danny spent a full half hour, first on the consolidated returns then, one after another, on the individual hotels. At the direction of the chairman of the board and sole stockholder, Giuseppe Martino, quarterly contributions were to be taken from company profits and paid over to the Hyde Park Fund. Danny had shepherded a "Hyde Park Fund" through Internal Revenue, getting for it a tax-exempt charter, and giving as its purposes to assist in scholarships focused on the twelve years of Franklin Delano Roosevelt's presidency. Simultaneously, Danny had organized a corporation licensed to engage in any activity. It was called the Hyde Park Capital Fund, Inc.

For three years, a diminishing sum of money was remitted to Giuseppe Martino's personal account by Martino Enterprises, Inc. Substantial sums were paid over to the Hyde Park Capital Fund. Mr. Martino had never complained about the reduced returns from his twenty-two-hotel chain. Danny had explained how heavy the pressures were on the hotel business; and anyway, it wasn't as if the enterprise were collapsing. Substantial profits were still turned in to the shareholder. That they were less than they had been was a development one needed to accept philosophically. And to the extent they were diminished by the contributions to Hyde Park, why Giuseppe was glad to reaffirm concretely his devotion to the memory of President Franklin Delano Roosevelt, and no, he would not diminish his annual contributions to Hyde Park—Danny must see to that: "Don't reduce that contribution by five cents, Danny!" If Giuseppe had been surprised to be told that 75 percent of the profits of his corporation were now going to Hyde Park, he'd have been even more surprised to learn that a log of his verbal instructions given to Danny O'Hara over the past three years sat in the safe, initialed "G. M.," and that these instructions had been to convey to the Hyde Park Capital Fund twenty million dollars from the profits of Martino Enterprises, in five annual payments.

It was grand larceny. Cutter opened the little refrigerator, brought out a bottle of champagne, poured two glasses, and raised his to Danny.

"Rather neat, isn't it?"

Danny handled the compliment nonchalantly. "One has to take opportunities that come up. We aren't really depriving the old man of anything. He has everything he wants."

Cutter entered a cavil. "But you know, Danny, everything depends on your continued relationship with the old man."

"Well, yes and no. If ever he got, well, mutinous, what do we do? A little paperwork, fuse the two Hyde Parks, get out of the way, point to the telephone log, shake our heads and wonder if the dear old man has truly lost his senses."

"I wouldn't do this if the old man were ten years younger."

"Maybe I wouldn't do it if I were ten years older. Cheer up, buddy."

Caroline O'Hara reminded herself that she loved Harriet Carberry, really did. And reminded herself that Harriet's prying was motivated only by a desire to help her friends. But this was only the first day of a three-day visit, and she confessed she was glad that tomorrow and Wednesday Harriet would be in New York during the day, returning to Greenwich only in time for dinner and to spend the night. That would complete Harriet's annual New England tour. She would return to Pasadena, and the prying would be only over the telephone, attenuated; once or twice every month, until her next visit East.

Harriet had put on weight, perhaps because she was almost always nibbling at something—at the moment, she was nibbling at the big bowl of M&M's. But she was still a handsome woman, determined to oversee the happiness of her friends.

"Well, does Danny have to call in on every one of the hotels in the Trafalgar chain?"

Caroline knitted as she talked. The long table behind the couch was crowded with framed pictures of her handsome brood, two girls and three boys, all of them now visiting with their aunt. She had not changed, but now her lips were slightly parted, framing a smile lit by quiet pleasure and giving pleasure to those in her company. Father Kevin, at the Riverside Church she attended, had remarked that Caroline had acquired a maternal beauty, which was different from the maidenly beauty he had merrily praised at the party after he married her and Danny, twelve years ago.

Caroline answered Harriet's question. "Danny likes to be able to tell people—I've heard him do it—that he has in fact visited every one of Mr. Martino's hotels. But of course he doesn't do it every year. Though every year he looks in on the major hotels."

"Is the one in Los Angeles one of the major hotels?"

"Of course. Los Angeles, Chicago, Miami, Boston, New York, Detroit. How'm I doing?"

"You're doing good, Caroline. I wouldn't be surprised if you could name the sixteen other cities where there's a Trafalgar."

"Even if I could, I wouldn't. Why do you ask?"

"I was just wondering. You know, I spotted Danny in Los Angeles just a month ago?"

"Oh," Caroline said, not looking up from her knitting. "Is the music too loud?" She got up and turned down the volume. Just a hair. "It's the memorial album, Landowska. That's the twenty-fifth Goldberg. She makes it so sublimely sad. You spotted Danny in Los Angeles? At the Trafalgar?"

"No. At the Bel Air."

"Looking in on the competition, I guess," Caroline said.

That's one way to put it, Harriet thought. Assuming Caroline was willing to acknowledge that there was such a thing as competition for Danny, as distinguished from Danny's hotels. She grabbed another handful of M&M's from the bowl and decided to drop the line of inquiry.

The telephone rang, Caroline put down her knitting and reached for the receiver.

"Yes. Well, thank you for calling, Margie." And, to Caroline, "Danny will be late. But not too late. By eight he'll be here."

Danny was in a convivial mood, which was good because Caroline had invited his sister, Lila, to join them for dinner. Lila had finally stopped going away for more and more schooling. And, Danny remembered, it seemed back then as though she would never stop growing. She was as tall as her brother and very talkative about her work at the Hyde Park Library, to which she drove every day from her house in Millbrook.

It was she, Lila O'Hara, she explained to Harriet, who passed on the credentials of visiting scholars. She puffed avidly on her cigarette and drank her gin and tonic in businesslike gulps. "We had someone last week, said he was preparing a life of Sidney Hillman. He was the labor leader—remember? CIO? In case you forgot, FDR—'Grandfather,' as I guess I'm entitled to refer to him in this household—said, 'Clear it with Sidney,' when he decided at the convention in Chicago to drop Henry Wallace and give the vice presidency to Harry Truman—1944, remember?"

"For heaven's sake, get on with it," Danny said to his sister. "We all remember 1944, we all remember reading about dropping Wallace, taking Truman, et cetera. So?"

"*So*—don't be so impatient, Danny. I'm not one of your hotels. So, this 'scholar' said he'd like to examine White House correspondence with Hillman during 1943, '44, and up until FDR died, April '45. I asked him who was his publisher, and he said Henry Regnery, Chicago. And then he said, 'Chicago made special sense to me, of course, since Hillman operated out of Chicago.'

"Now, in my business you get to know a fair amount about publishing. And it makes no difference—absolutely zero difference—to someone writing a book about somebody who lived in Chicago, whether the publisher who's going to distribute the book also operates out of Chicago. The principal publishers are in New York City. It was clear to me that this 'scholar' was giving me an excuse for using Regnery. Why? *Because*"—Lila thrust her drink up above eye level, as if to declare independence, or proclaim emancipation— "*because Henry Regnery is a conservative, reactionary publisher* who has published several books critical of FDR, including the book by Tansil. His thesis—get this—is that Grandfather wanted the Japanese to attack Pearl Harbor, so he'd have an excuse for going to war!"

"So what did you do?" Caroline asked. "You can't, can you, refuse material to scholars just because they publish with a conservative house?"

"Not so easy when it's scholars you're dealing with, but I had Mr. Henningson—that's his name, Cyril Henningson—fill out the form we have, and told him he'd hear from us within a week. So I looked up the references, made about fifteen phone calls, and it turns out that young Mr. Henningson is a stringer for . . ."

Obligingly, they all waited for the revelation.

"Westbrook Pegler! Pegler is the angriest man in America and he fuels his anger by attacking FDR and Grandmother. So what he was up to was having one of his researchers, posing as a scholar, come to Hyde Park looking for dirt."

"Is there dirt there?" Harriet asked matter-of-factly.

Lila looked at her. She knew from one or two past experiences that Harriet was unusually direct in her manner of speech. But was she also dumb? She trained her eyes, after adjusting her horn-rimmed glasses, on Harriet and said in tones she might have used at a history seminar, "Harriet, FDR was a politician. Politicians do things, make commitments—the kind of thing, well, the kind of thing you don't want to shovel out to somebody who isn't going to put it in the proper perspective. If he were, oh, Arthur Schlesinger, we'd know that there'd be a historian's . . . sense of—"

"History?" Danny volunteered.

"Exactly, Danny. Exactly."

Danny gave his sister a sly wink. Lila permitted herself a trace of a smile. Both took care to effect their exchange so that Harriet would not be privy to it.

Lila left, an hour and a half's drive ahead of her. She kissed Caroline, her brother Danny, and—she thought, Why not?—also Harriet. After they were gone, Danny asked Harriet if she would like to swim out in the Sound. "The water temperature's real nice." She declined, but urged Caroline to join her husband. "I have a long day tomorrow. I'll turn in."

Wearing terry-cloth dressing gowns, Caroline and Danny walked hand in hand to the water's edge. It was just after Labor Day, still summer, but the heat shimmer had gone and the air was fresh and bracing. The property was pretty well sheltered from neighbors at either side by leafy trees and tall bushes. Danny dropped his robe and dived in. Caroline followed him. In the water Danny ducked and a few seconds later, sputtering water from her mouth, Caroline giggled her remonstrance.

"Stop that! Danny. You are a silly boy." He surfaced and made out Caroline's eyes, and her little smile, in the new moon light. He sank underwater again, his two hands on her breasts. She threw herself to one side, swam vigorously toward the beach, her foot reached land and she ran toward her dressing gown, followed closely by Danny, who threw himself over her on the grass. His hand reached between her legs.

"Danny?"

He only just managed to reply, through his ardor. "Mmmm?"

"I'm not safe yet. Not for two more days."

Activity froze. Then Danny pushed her away brusquely. "God-*damnit*, Caroline. Why don't you wear some protection? Or is it that you want *another* baby? How many more, ten? Twenty?" He flung his bathrobe across his lap. "Nine fucking days—no, nine *non*-fucking days—because Mother Church won't allow you to take *civilized* measures to guard against having thirty-five children. I happen to be a *normal* man, Caroline, and it's not *normal* to go nine days every month without—"

"Danny, Danny." She stroked his hair. "Just try to understand how I—we—feel. Please, darling. Let's go up to the house, have a nightcap, maybe. The children will be here first thing in the morning."

Danny had put on his dressing gown. He was not yet smiling, Caroline could see. But the immediate crisis was over.

They walked toward the house and Danny reminded himself to pay greater attention to the timing of his out-of-town trips. They should more closely correspond with Caroline's periods. Dumb of him not to have thought of that before. He wondered whether he would also have to worry about Florry's periods.

Fifteen

FLORIDA CARMELA HUERTA left home when she was six-teen. Her mother, Jeanne, a native of France married to a Mexican-American soldier, had been widowed when only thirty (Enrique, wending his way more or less home from El Cielito Lindo one night, was run over) at which time ten-year-old Florida had two younger siblings, a boy (Raul), and a girl (Conchita). Their mother grieved the loss of their father and was so lonely, she shared her bed with attractive substitutes and in six years had three more children by three more companions.

Her most recent lover had attempted to seduce Florida. Jeanne, ever obliging, tried to persuade Florry in seductive French to be accommodating, whereupon Florry bashed her mother over the head with a table lamp. At this, the lover brought out his belt, grabbed her left wrist and beat Florry over head, shoulders, legs—whatever part of her was exposed—for ten full minutes. Raul, age twelve, tried to restrain the assailant, who grabbed him, pulled down his shorts, and beat him raw on the naked buttocks.

Florida was left weeping on the floor of the room she shared with her five brothers and sisters. She writhed in pain through the night, tiptoed early in the morning to her mother's room, drew the wallet of the lover from his pants, and left the house with a canvas suitcase in which everything she owned fitted comfortably. She had the address of a friend whose parents had moved to Los Angeles.

Dorothy's mother had met Florida back in San Diego a year or so before. She liked her, knew about the parlous situation at her mother's little apartment, consulted with her husband in their two-bedroom cottage in Santa Monica, suffering from old age on its fifteenth birthday.

They agreed to cooperate in the fiction that Florida was an only child whose mother and father had both drowned in the terrible ferry accident a month ago in San Diego Harbor. Finding herself alone, Florry had made her way to the address of a girlhood friend in Los Angeles, and now, they hoped, "Sister Alicia, that the convent will take little Florry in, make room for her with the other orphan girls you and the other sisters so generously look after."

It worked, and in a few months the nuns learned that Florida Huerta was badly underinstructed but extraordinarily gifted. It was only a matter of weeks before she caught up with other girls her own age. Her behavior was exemplary. She studied and read six hours every day and did chores for four hours, everything from cleaning toilets to teaching the little girls how to read.

After eighteen months, Sister Alicia told her that she was going to give her special training to study for the college boards. But how could she afford to pay tuition? Florry asked. Sister Alicia said she should set her sights on earning a full scholarship. Florry bowed her head in bewilderment. Sister Alicia looked at her, her hair braided and pinned behind her oval face, the large eyes, the full figure. Sister Alicia sighed. If she prevailed and won the scholarship, Florida would be an alluring target. But that was, very simply, the way things were. Sister Alicia closed her eyes and recited a Hail Mary, beseeching strength for little Florida to resist temptation.

Florida did yield completely, though the importunate male was not after sexual favors. What Nicola Agrippo wished to cultivate was the knowledge of Spanish and of Spanish literature. It was toward the end of her sophomore year and Professor Agrippo had become her tutor. He had officiated over the impact on her of the Spanish language. To be sure, her father had known Spanish, but conversations at home were in English, or in her mother's hectic French. Florry knew nothing of the structure of the Spanish language, which she had never used or heard used at home.

She raced through the first year's formal course and was ready for the final examination halfway through the first semester. Mr. Agrippo took her out of the intermediate class and entered her in advanced Spanish. Before the end of her freshman year she was reading Spanish classics. Now he encouraged her to compete for the student exchange seat endowed by the University of Salamanca, designed for two California undergraduates who were well on their way to proficiency in Spanish and were inclined to the study of Spanish history, literature, and culture.

The qualifying round was conducted by teachers of Spanish within a competing jurisdiction. Those students who passed the qualifying round went into a final round. The six finalists would be examined by Professor Juan Gustavo Amador, who traveled from Salamanca to examine finalists in six American cities.

The nervous students, two boys, four girls, met for lunch at the home of the Spanish consul. All of them were seniors in college except for Florida. Their genial host suggested that it might be both amusing and appropriate to speak to one another, and to their hosts, only in Spanish during lunch. The contenders did so, at first tentatively, then rather garrulously. They were seated around a table presided over by the consul and his wife. From the living room they could look down on the city of Los Angeles, and inevitably there was talk of smog. "Sir," one student asked her host, "how do you say 'smog' in Spanish?" The consul was startled by the question, and said he would defer to Professor Amador for the answer. Professor Amador spent fifteen minutes discussing textual descriptions used by Cervantes to describe the air, from pure to extra-polluted, in his epic, then wandered over to note how Dante had handled the phenomenon in the *Comedy*. He did not answer the question, and nobody took the initiative in pointing this out to him.

After about ten minutes, Florida was pleasantly surprised to conclude that her Spanish was distinctly better than that of one of the girls, and infinitely better than that of everyone else. She had not quite got used to her remarkable fluency, never having tested it in a competitive situation. But it was also the case, she reflected, that she was improving every day. Her peculiar capacity to ingest Spanish was churning so intensively, she had learned a great deal even since the competition was initiated, just two months before.

To be sure, it wasn't merely conversational fluency the visiting professor would want to satisfy himself about. What exactly he'd ask, Florry didn't know. She did know that there really wasn't very much she could say in English that she couldn't find a way of saying in Spanish, possibly excepting the best word for smog. That was a comforting thought.

Florida caught the eye of one of the two male contestants, a trim blond young man from Berkeley who had traveled down to Los Angeles for the examination. His eyes were pale blue. From his slightly parted lips white teeth showed, and his smiles were easily ignited, though mostly he kept within himself whatever it was that amused him; Florry watched him a full five minutes, and never quite knew what it was that brought on the quick, amused, inscrutable reactions. She noticed that although it was only May, he was nicely tanned—either he had spent a week or so in southern California, or he had spent long hours lying in such sun as they got in the San Francisco area in April and May. His glance at Florida was candidly covetous. After lunch, as they walked out to the little *capilla* where the examination would take place, he approached her and reintroduced himself: "Nobody can remember names when more than two people are introduced—I'm Tracy Gulliver, and you're—?"

"Florida Huerta."

"Look," he said, his smile now full, beguiling, "the shooting match will be over by five o'clock, and, win or lose, I don't have to go back to Berkeley till *mañana por la mañana.* So what do you say we have *una cenita, entre los dos?*"

Florida was attracted to him and inclined to accept the invitation to a little dinner between the two of them. There was the one problem, that Professor Agrippo had said that if she won the scholarship, he would host a little celebration at his apartment. Florry was reluctant to tell the young man—to tell Tracy—that she doubted she would be able to dine with him because she expected to win the competition. She had to devise a more modest way to plant the problematic . . .

"That would be nice. There is a complication, and I won't know whether I can work it out until after—"

"After they award me the scholarship?" Tracy asked, affecting guilelessness.

She wondered—did he actually *expect* to win? Or was it merely braggadocio, the kind of thing to expect of preying young males? She merely smiled at him and waved her hand, a "let's-see-what-happens" gesture.

It was the practice of Professor Amador to conduct his examination in front of all the candidates. He liked to explain that, by doing so, the applicants were themselves able to evaluate contending talents. As often as not, however grudgingly, his election of the winner was unchallenged by those left behind. The burden was heaviest on him, since he would of course not put the same question to more than one student.

"Well, Tracy, I wish you good luck."

"Thank you, dear Florida. *Aunque no estoy seguro que necesito buena suerte.*" That riled Florry: Tracy, saying he didn't think he needed good luck to win.

Yet somehow—the way he said it?—she didn't mind his self-confidence, though it had to mean that he hadn't taken the measure of her skills during the random conversation at lunch. Well, he would soon hear her perform.

The competitors drew straws.

Tracy would be fifth, Florida last.

Her confidence was fortified as she heard the first girl, a deadly serious student from the Santa Barbara campus, exchange conversational patter with Professor Agrippo.

Yes, she was very anxious to get to know Spain. . . . Yes, the University of Salamanca must be a very exciting place to study, and she knew of course that it was the second-oldest university in Europe. . . . Indeed she intended to pursue her Spanish studies, having given four years to the study of the language, spending two summers in Mexico.

It was a good performance, but hardly memorable. Obviously Fran (Frances Weymuller was her name) needed to run her thought through her mind in English before translating it into Spanish. The mark of the amateur. But after all, they were all amateurs, including herself, Florry forced herself to admit.

But she was gaining in confidence. The performances of the ensuing three competitors didn't disturb her. It was now Tracy's turn.

She listened dumbstruck. She was both flabbergasted and furious. He spoke with near-native fluency, at high speed, about subjects not entirely prosaic. Clearly he had, for histrionic effect, disguised his achievement during the badinage at lunch—it would be more fun to spring his fluency on the competitors than to let them have a preview of it at lunch. The examining professor was also struck by the proficiency, and after ten minutes asked where and how had Mr. Gulliver prepared his Spanish? Tracy said that he had studied it beginning junior year in high school, that he had been attracted to the language as the result of an early love for Cervantes communicated to him by his mother; and that he had been coached during summer months by his father's . . . gardener, who talked to him by the hour, and together they would go to Spanish and Latin-American movies every week. He was now, he said, attempting to write poetry in

Spanish. Give us a sample, Professor Amador asked him. Tracy recited a sonnet.

After fifteen minutes Professor Amador thanked and dismissed him. He looked over at the other contestants, satisfied that when the decision was handed down no one would question the verdict.

He signaled to Florida. She rose and sat in the examination chair opposite Professor Amador. She was flustered, demoralized, having in a matter of minutes traveled from confidence that she would win to sure knowledge that she would not. But the examiner gave her the full fifteen minutes and even told her that he was impressed by her quite unusual handling of the language, that he had never examined any student who had done so well after only a single year's application.

That was sweet music for Florida, but didn't vitiate fully her resentment at Tracy Gulliver's deceit; though she could not help but be awed by how he spoke, and what he had spoken about.

Professor Amador went through the ritual of retiring from the chapel to the sacristy adjoining, in effect, the jurors' room. He came out a few minutes later, accompanied by the consul. He smiled at the contestants and, speaking in clear, melodious Spanish, complimented them all on their performances, expressed his wish that they would all visit Bologna sometime, and that they would continue their Spanish studies.

He then walked over to where Tracy was seated, extended his hand, and said, "I hope you will have a fruitful year at our university." Everyone in the chapel applauded.

The consul's wife invited them to take iced tea on the terrace.

Walking on the well-tended lawn toward the gazebo with the tea and cookies, Florida asked Mrs. Trevino, her hostess, if she might use the telephone for a local call?

Of course.

Professor Agrippo received his star student's news and proceeded to say all the right things. "You can't protect yourself against a senior who has been working on the language for six years. But remember, no one else who was there can compete again next year because the scholarship is open only to undergraduates. You can—and if I know my Florry, you will overwhelm the judge next time, the way your Berkeley boy did this year. So I plan to just stow away the food and drink I had prepared for you —we'll use them for the celebration next May.''

Florida, flush with pleasure, her self-confidence renewed, joined the party, and when Tracy asked, Had her telephone call succeeded in removing the obstacle? she had answered, *Sí,* and forty-five minutes later they thanked their hosts, Professor Amador, and their fellow competitors, and strode out to the street. Tracy hailed a taxi, after reminding Florry that out-of-town finalists had a generous travel allowance. "I am loaded with counterpart Spanish dollars, imported from France, and don't ask me to explain how that's possible."

Florida had never eaten at a restaurant in Los Angeles, and Tracy took her to Romanoff's. She was staggered by the luxury of the experience, the opulence of the surroundings, the glamour of the clientele. Tracy's poise impressed her, and she grew giddy with excitement, giddy, too, from the wine, and infatuated by the lively conversation—at first they had spoken in Spanish, now he was talking animatedly in English, and she learned that his father was a vintner, and that not only had the one man he had spoken of coached him in Spanish, but so had several other grape tenders from Madeira, immigrants from the island's devastated wine region. He was an only child. "My mother is dead. At the funeral they played a large part of Scarlatti's Mass. She was very, very beautiful. She had a heart attack when I was sixteen."

When he was sixteen! Florida was tempted to tell him about how *she* had left *her* mother when Florry was sixteen, but thought better of it. As the first hour, then the second, went by, she sensed what would now happen. She had wondered, often, when and under what circumstances she would submit to the initiation her mother's lover had first attempted on her, then beaten her for resisting. When Tracy said that it would be a glorious end to a glorious day if they could spend another hour or two together in his hotel room she merely nodded, and when an hour later he gently guided her movements, and asserted his own, she felt she now knew ecstasy, *éxstasis.*

. . . .

In the last week of the school year Professor Agrippo motioned to Florida Huerta to come to his office after class.

He was very pleased with the news he had for her. Florida had been trying to find summer work more demanding than the camp counselorship Sister Alicia had found for her, and Professor Agrippo had assigned himself the responsibility of looking around.

"Listen!" he said, speaking in Spanish. "The big hotels are in great competition for traveling businessmen from abroad. In Europe all the concierges are fluent in three, four, or five languages. Here our people know only their own language. I have gotten you a job as Spanish translator when there is a need. The balance of the time you will serve as an assistant receptionist. It is a very good hotel, one of the very best. The Trafalgar."

Florida was very pleased, and very grateful.

Sixteen

D ID IT EVER occur to you," David Abshire asked Henry at the Metropole Bar where, in 1963, the foreign correspondents gathered, "that your nice Thank You—"

"Than Koo."

"—that your omniscient, resourceful Than pause Koo might be a Vietcong?"

"Sure it 'occurred' to me, in the sense that one is supposed to play with such hypotheses about everybody here. Is it possible that Henry Cabot Lodge is on their side?"

"No reason to make a joke of my point." David Abshire from the *Boston Globe* was very young, and perhaps for that reason sensitive to sarcastic thrusts from such veterans as Henry Chafee. "Your twenty-one-year-old boy-translator-informant happens to be from Hué. On the other hand, Henry Cabot Lodge is from Boston."

"These days, there are probably more pro-Vietcongers in Boston than in Hué." Henry did not like criticisms of Than Koo. He did not hear many, but he treated none casually that he did hear.

"Okay, Henry, I give up. But I get more fucking rumors passed along from you, which you in turn get from Thank You—"

"Than Koo."

"—and this one has got to be the best, that President Diem and Brother Nhu are thinking of assassinating the U.S. Ambassador to South Vietnam. As Anthony might have said to Brutus, *Cui bono?*"

"Koowee what?"

"Oh, sorry. I forgot you didn't go to Harvard. That's c-u-i. *Cui bono?* Who benefits? If Lodge is murdered by the government we are spending billions to protect, that would mean one thing for sure: a U.S. pullout from the scene. And that would mean Communist invasion from the north. End story, end silly rumor. Are you *quite* sure Thank You isn't one of . . . them?"

At this point Henry had no alternative than to accept the thrust as humorous. Though the message was anything but humorous. There was already demoralization in South Vietnam, never mind any plots against our ambassador there. "We've pretty well got that breakdown in morale already," Henry said, lighting a cheroot and acknowledging the bartender's offer of another glass of white wine. "I personally don't think an assassination would be attempted. But there isn't any doubt that Lodge has gotten to hate Diem, and we have to suppose that Diem reciprocates the sentiment. And there isn't any doubt that Lodge thinks it's more than merely a street rumor."

"Lodge *knows* about it?" David Abshire was genuinely surprised. "Why? Because you told him?"

"No. It's true Than Koo passed the rumor on to me, but then I checked with—with a friend in the embassy. They had picked it up three days ago."

David Abshire was now all professional. "Did your friend analyze the rumor? If so, what did he say?"

"It's this simple, David. Everybody in town knows that Lodge has gone over to the Harriman wing in the White House. And what they want is Diem out. Out! They've been hoping for an army coup for two months. They're not disposed to wait any longer. Diem could plausibly be calculating that if Lodge is bumped off, his own life and government might be saved."

David looked thoughtfully at Henry. He would try one on him. "Have you run into the rumor of Brother Nhu dealing with Hanoi?"

"Yeah. That's another one I don't believe. Nhu wouldn't deal with Ho Chi Minh except to get something from him. And all that Hanoi wants is the surrender of South Vietnam. This side of that, the North Vietnamese aren't playing. At least that's how I read it."

"And how the readers of *Time* mag will read it, Henry. Well, let's have something to eat."

"I can't join you, David. I've got an appointment."

The two correspondents walked out of the bar, one into the hotel dining room, Henry to the hotel entrance. Than Koo would pick him up in the car at exactly 8:05.

Henry had met Than Koo in Hué. Minh Tong, the interpreter on whom Henry had relied in the spring and early summer, was a retired schoolteacher, a gaunt, ascetic member of the Vietnamese mandarinate. In July, while tending his little garden on Nguyen Trai Street in Cholon, on the outskirts of Saigon where he lived with his sister, Minh Tong fell gracefully to the ground, a three-step ballet of death: one more Vietnamese—the record keepers put the figure at 22,000—executed by the Vietcong for the capital sin of "consorting with the imperialists." Henry had attended his funeral. The eulogy by the priest was in French; most of Tong's friends spoke in French. Leaving the church, Henry tendered his condolences to Minh Tong's sister. He paused outside to observe the mourners filing out of the little church and wondered how many of them had been condemned to death by the Vietcong. The American presence in Vietnam had reached 13,000, and a dozen correspondents were now doing full-time duty. Americans soak up native help wherever they go, he reflected. About how many South Vietnamese might one say that, by midsummer 1963, they had in some way "consorted" with an American? Were we talking about one hundred thousand people, or maybe a million? He would reflect on that point in a future dispatch to *Time.*

Whatever the exact figure, that meant a lot of potential executions, any way you looked at it.

The taxi took them from Cholon to the airport. He was bound for Hué, the old South China capital of Annam, in the north. The road, now being expanded into a highway, was heavy with military traffic; indeed, the flight to Hué would be on a military plane. Someone in the pool would act as his translator. Aboard the plane he pecked away on his little Hermes typewriter.

". . . *few Americans are fluent in Vietnamese, and the graduate schools are only now offering the language to specialists. Accordingly, Americans in Vietnam rely on natives. But it is hazardous duty, especially resented by the Vietcong, who deem it intimate servility to the imperialists. . . .*" Henry would work that, or something like it, into his next dispatch to New York. And, as he had done now over the dozen years since he went to work for *Time,* he would slip into an envelope a copy of his dispatch and mail it to his sister Caroline. He would scrawl a word or two in the margins. That way he thought himself as always in touch, and of course there were the letters, back and forth. It didn't much matter where he was, Henry reflected. Caroline was there, just around the corner.

Than Koo rang the bell at Henry's suite at the Grand Hotel, the gilt from the French colonial period fraying, the ceiling high, the fan functioning. Henry opened the door. Than Koo bowed his head and introduced himself: He was prepared to serve as guide and translator.

Henry motioned to him to sit down. He had got used to adult Vietnamese who appeared to be much younger than they actually were. But Than Koo looked a mere seventeen or eighteen. Rather feminine, with high cheekbones, eyebrows that tilted up, white teeth and pink lips, the hair running just behind his ears.

"Do you speak English?"

Than replied in French that no, he did not. Was French satisfactory?

Henry nodded. After three years in Paris as a foreign correspondent he was as much at home speaking in French as in English. He rang for tea and started to dig in. He began by asking Than Koo about his schooling.

Than had graduated in June from the university, where he studied history and French literature. His mother worked as a nurse at St. Joseph's Hospital. His father had served the French as an infantry captain. He had been killed in the Indochina war.

Henry asked him a question he had already asked the major whose office had recommended Koo: What screening had he got from the Vietnam officials who had assigned him for duty?

Than asked if he might smoke a cigarette. Henry nodded, and lit one of his own little cigars. Than seemed reluctant to answer the question, but then closed his eyes and said, "Well, we are in a civil war, monsieur. And I felt I had to do it."

"Do what?"

"Excuse me. Turn in my teacher."

"Why did you turn him in?"

"Because I discovered that he was linked to the Vietcong."

"He was your teacher of what?"

"He was a Balzac specialist—"

"Was?"

"He has been executed."

"Was there a trial?"

"A military trial."

"Were you a witness?"

Than looked down at the floor. "Yes. I told them what I had seen."

"Which was?"

"A copy of his dean's memorandum to Colonel Thuc. It gives the special qualifications of forty or fifty seniors who might be most useful in the war effort. It is a very confidential list, because in the hands of the enemy, it becomes a 'hit list.' "

"Is your name on that list?"

"Of course."

"Did you find it in time to keep it from the VC?"

"What happened was that Pen—another student—was looking in the briefcase of our professor to find out what grades he was giving out for the semester. He is a scholarship student and could not afford to get low grades. While going through the briefcase he found a list—he was puzzled by it, and showed it to me. I recognized it right away."

"Why?"

"Because I typed it. I had been cleared to work with classified documents. That happened during my junior year. That's how I knew how important the roster was."

Henry puffed on his cheroot and scratched at his blond beard. "Well, as you say, it *is* a civil war. But as you know, Than—"

"Please call me Koo."

"As you know, I am a journalist. My magazine, *Time,* is preparing a cover story on the Vietnamese situation and I want to spend four or five days inspecting the progress of the strategic hamlet program. I got a couple of memos—hell, you don't read English?"

Than Koo shrugged his shoulders.

"Well, I'll go over the suggestions that have come in on a few sites we ought to pay special attention to. But the army is cooperative, I know. On the other hand, I want to go to at least as many hamlets not recommended by ARVN as to those that are—you get my point?"

Than Koo nodded.

And that was it. The next hour was devoted to preparations for the trip. They set out the next morning for Thon Hai Cac, on the west bank of the Perfume River.

Hai Cac was twelve kilometers from Hué. There were seventy or eighty villagers there, a dozen families plus the retired elderly. Heavy coils of barbed wire surrounded the hamlet, almost a half mile of barricade, Henry calculated. Entrance to the hamlet was effected through an opening guarded by two men armed with rifles. Twenty yards behind the gate, a third guard sat behind a second barricade that shielded his machine gun. In the morning, the gate would open and in the early, yellow light, the farmers, as old as seventy, as young as thirteen, would file out and attend to their fields and paddies. Rifles were stacked nearby, readily accessible to a half-dozen farmers trained to use them. In the late afternoon they would file back to the security of their hamlet.

That was the idea: to give the little farming communities security from the Vietcong killer squads. Henry questioned the arthritic senior councilor and weighed carefully what Bao Tin said. It was to the effect that 15 percent of the hamlet's working force was now for all intents and purposes fully occupied in providing security, which meant a proportionate decrease in the produce that sustained the village. "If, monsieur, one year ago I had been told that we would produce fifteen percent less than the year before, I would say: Hai Cac cannot afford to do that. Take from us our production—take from us the little revenues we get from the one, two hundred sacks of extra rice—and you have truly doomed our little village." He acknowledged that the army had promised to supply soldiers from its own reserves. "But that was eight months ago, monsieur, and where are they?"

Had there been enemy action during that eight-month period?

Bao shook his head. "But maybe we have just been lucky. We do not let down our guard."

Successive hamlets, most of them larger than Hai Cac, told pretty much the same story. Henry sensed the fatigue brought on by the stalemate. The peasants seemed to have no confidence that the danger was diminishing, that the Vietcong, day after day, were growing weaker and tomorrow would be extinct. Almost every night the radio blared out news of military operations that had resulted in heavy losses to the enemy, but there was no corresponding relief, no letting down in the precautions required by those who secured the hamlets.

Thon An Van Thuong sits twelve kilometers east of the eastern mountain range that flanks the Ho Chi Minh Trail and the same distance south of the DMZ, the line that separates North and South Vietnam. It was the last of the hamlets Henry had scheduled himself to visit. At the gate, Than Koo got out of the jeep to show the guard his identification. From where he sat in the jeep, Henry could see him exchanging what, with all those gesticulations, could only be heated words with the guard. He hopped down from the passenger seat and approached the gate. "What's going on?"

"He says after what happened last night, his instructions are to take extra precautions. He wants me to give him my identification and then radio in to the military to confirm our identity."

"What happened last night?"

"Somebody—somebody *in* the hamlet—got into the quarters of the chief councilor, put a steel wire around his neck and garroted him. He left a note: 'One less imperialist lackey.' "

"Oh God." Henry drew in a breath. "Koo, *quick*—find out if the body is still there."

Than Koo asked the question, and turned back to Henry: "He says they've left him the way they found him because a police constable is coming from headquarters."

Henry paused. He spoke in very low tones, against the possibility that the guard understood French. "Look. A picture of this situation would be very useful to *Time*. Tell him that if he can arrange to get us where the . . . body is, so that I can take a picture, it would be very valuable to the war effort, and to Vietnam's . . . allies. Offer him two thousand piastres."

The guard summoned his relief and motioned Henry and Than Koo to follow him. In a few minutes they were at a straw-thatched cabin elevated on stilts ten inches from the ground. They heard voices inside. Henry motioned to Koo to go up the little companionway and explain to whoever was there what was planned while he gathered his camera equipment. In moments a short, grizzled elder dressed in a cream-colored smock emerged. He addressed Henry in French, told him to proceed; they shook hands.

The dead man was lying on his stomach, dressed in pale blue pajamas. The telephone cord around his neck had left a mauve, puffy collar. He had died from the classic commando strangle. At each end of the executioner's cord a wooden dowel was attached. The cord had been crossed, giving the assassin the leverage he sought. No doubt his knee had ground against the small of Bui Minh's back while he tightened the stranglehold.

Henry raised the pajama top. He bared a large mauve area. Minh's bare arms dangled over the edges of the cot. The sheet of paper bearing the VC's epitaph had been stapled into the nape of the neck. Henry looked up: On the little desk alongside he saw the chief councilor's stapler.

The note had been written as if by a child, the letters incompletely formed. Henry took six pictures.

They retreated to an empty hut maintained for visiting military, assigned for this night to Henry and Than Koo. The deputy chief, succeeding now to the position of chief councilor, had verified by radio their bona fides and was glad to learn that the American newsman and his translator had brought their own provisions; he would not want the American people to be informed that An Van Thuong was inhospitable, but in fact supplies were very scarce, in particular of specialty foods.

The provisions from the jeep were hardtack and canned fruit. Henry removed his sweat-soaked T-shirt, lay down on one of the cots and let his head rest on the bedroll that passed for a pillow. Than Koo sat on the wooden floor, his own shirt dry, intact.

"You yellow-skinned prodigies never get hot, Koo. What is your secret?"

"We grow up in the wet heat, Mr. Henry. It takes a little training. In ten, fifteen years, you will become accustomed to it."

"I'm beginning to think it's going to take about that long . . . *merrrrr-de*—in English, Koo, that's *sheeyit*—what a bloody situation. Let's just think about it. You got a hundred and eighteen people here according to the new boss-man, and one of them sneaked into that hut last night. Made himself right at home. Used the stapling machine to leave his message. The killing area is *congested* with clues. A couple of pros from L.A. or New York could track down the killer in what, a couple of hours? Especially —if you will permit me, Koo—availing themselves of some techniques of interrogation in your country that are frowned upon by Mr. Earl Warren. Earl Warren, Koo, is the head of our Supreme

Court. He is very protective of the rights of— Oh, never mind. Just— Shit. The fact is, *they're* not going to find him. And it's creepy that they don't know who he is. Is he the guy next door? Or maybe he is one of the guards?"

Henry shook his head. "This is not a good situation. Koo, be a good boy and go to the jeep and bring me my typewriter. And yeah, bring a couple of beers. Nothing like steamy hot beer. Hell, may as well bring the overnight gear, yours and mine. We can't leave here now until morning."

A few minutes later, Henry Chafee had propped up the Hermes on a wooden drawer turned upside down and resting on his lap. He typed slowly, decisively, page after page, pausing to wipe his face and to sip his beer. Finally he finished. He had fifteen pages.

He got up off the cot and went to his seabag, where he foraged and came up with his plastic bottle of brandy. He looked about him at the bare quarters. "What in the hell are we going to use for cups?" Than Koo motioned to him to wait just a minute. He slipped out of the hut and was back with two thick drinking glasses.

"They—we—use these for tea also."

Henry poured himself two generous jiggers and then looked over at Than Koo. "You want?"

No, he said, the beer was enough.

Then why did he bring two glasses? Henry wondered. But he had long since decided that there was no purpose in choking up on alien inscrutabilities. He would simply designate them as such when he wrote his articles.

Henry leaned back with his brandy glass, clutching the sheaf of papers with one hand. "Wish to hell you could read English, Koo." He brightened. "Hey, I have an idea. Would you like me to read it to you in French—translate my article for you?"

Than Koo said he would like that very much. But Than sensed Henry's general restiveness. The heat, the general oppressiveness of the climate, the isolation. Than felt an obligation to come up with some kind of relief. . . . Would Mr. Henry like it if Than Koo sponged him with some cocoa oil? It was abundant in this part of the world and he had brought in a small bottle of it when he went in search of the glasses. It would cool him off and make him feel a great deal better, something the French military had taught the Vietnamese.

"Sure," said Henry. "You want me on my stomach?"

"Yes," said Than Koo. "And you should remove your shorts. The oil is for the whole body." Henry paused, then decided that any prolonged hesitation would send the wrong signal, as if he had detected an impropriety. He pulled down his shorts and removed his socks.

Than Koo worked on his back, traveling from neck to toes slowly, consuming four or five minutes.

"Now turn around."

Henry did so, and Than began at the neck, worked on each arm, back to the chest and, slowly, down to the waist, and headed south.

Henry clasped a hand smartly over the sponge and the hand that held it.

"You can skip over that. Go down to my legs." He paused. Perhaps he was upsetting some convention for a body massage done with cocoa oil. He felt a need to mollify Than Koo, and so he said, "I'm a little sensitive there—in between."

Than Koo said nothing, but began again the massage, on Henry's thighs.

"That feels real good, Koo. Real good, thanks."

Two minutes later it was done, and Henry admitted that he did indeed feel better. He put on his shorts and a fresh T-shirt, took a swig of brandy, lay back on his makeshift pillow, holding the little gas light in his left hand, and began to read, pausing here and there to reach for the appropriate French word. . . .

"In the . . . steamy hamlet of An Van Thuong, a half hour's walk from the heavy-laden trail down which arms travel from the Communist expansionists in the north to the insurgents in the south, a . . . mere half hour's walk from the border of North Vietnam, the natives did not sleep soundly on the night of July 12. Early that morning they had been given a . . . grisly reminder that the enemy wasn't . . . safely outside the barbed wire surrounding them. The enemy was also inside their . . . enclosure. That morning, Bui Minh, the august chief councilor of An Van Thuong, was found face-down on his cot, strangled by someone who had professional training in the . . . discipline. Behind the body there was a convenient stapling machine. The killer used it—to pin to the back of the neck of the chief councilor the Vietcong's calling card. It proclaimed in a childish scrawl that, now, with the death of Bui Minh, South Vietnam was relieved of one more . . . 'imperialist lackey.'

"The killing of Bui Minh is the story of a whole country, six hundred miles, from the DMZ to the Gulf of Thailand, a country tormented by tens of thousands of killer germs that, undetected, undetectable, swim about the organism with their little poison darts, wearing the body down. . . .

"—You sleepy, Koo?"

"Forgive me, Monsieur Henry. I think I did close my eyes. Please, go ahead."

Henry drained the last drop from his glass. "No, I'll do the rest tomorrow if you want. I think we should leave the gaslight on, low. Good night, Koo."

"Good night, Monsieur Henry."

Seventeen

ON OCTOBER 3, Oliver Simpson checked in at the Trafalgar Hotel in Los Angeles. The reception desk was standard Trafalgar. The men and women attending it, as also the Cashier and Reservations section, all wore the Trafalgar blue—blazers with gray pants for the men, V-necked light suits for the women. Every month the legend changed on the little pin they wore on their lapel. This month it read, "Go Trafalgar!"

Oliver Simpson, an unsmiling middle-aged man with close-cropped hair, spectacles, and a heavy briefcase in hand, had a reservation for two nights. He handed over his American Express charge card before filling out the register.

After a minute or two he said, "Well? Where is my room key?"

"Oh, sorry, sir. We seem to be having some difficulty with your Express card."

"What do you mean you're having a problem with my Express card? I use it every day." He grabbed it from the hand of the clerk. "What's the matter with it?" He held it to the light and scrutinized it. "Must be something wrong with your verifying machine."

"Well, sir, would you by any chance have any other credit card on you?"

Impatiently, Simpson brought out his wallet, pulled out a wad of cards, spread them out on the counter, stopped, picked up an Express card, looked at it. "Hmm. It appears I gave you my son Ollie's Express card by mistake. An old one, it must be." He tossed the correct card to the clerk, who picked it up.

"No problem, Mr. Simpson. It does get confusing, all these cards." The verification was done, and a young porter took the two bags and led Simpson to his small suite.

"Can I bring you some ice, sir?"

"You can bring me more than that. I haven't had lunch."

"Sir, the room service is open until midnight. Just dial 234."

"Why can't I give you the order?"

"Well, sir, the hotel isn't organized that way. They need me to carry bags."

"I should think they'd need you to accommodate the guests."

The young man blushed slightly. "Will that be all, sir?"

"Under the circumstances, yes," Mr. Simpson said, peering down at the menu card. The porter hesitated for a moment. Mr. Simpson made no movement toward his pocket. The young man turned and left.

Mr. Simpson examined the printed menu, dialed 234. "This is Room Service, can we help you?"

"Yes. I want onion soup, a hamburger steak, tomato salad, orange sherbet, coffee, and a half bottle of dry red wine."

"Which wine would you like, sir?"

"Which wine do you recommend?"

"We have a very full selection, sir. If the wine list isn't in your room, shall I send one up?"

"No. Just give me a half bottle of the house wine." He put down the receiver, looked at his watch, and made a notation. He then dialed Laundry/Dry Cleaning.

"I have a suit to be cleaned and three shirts to be washed. How long do I have to wait? . . . All right, send up for them, Room 782."

He then dialed the assistant general manager.

"This is Mr. Patton. Can I help you, Mr. Simpson?"

"Yes. I need to send a telegram. Can I give it to one of your girls over the telephone?

"I'm sorry, sir, we're not set up to take Western Union over the telephone. Can I send up a bellman to take your message?"

"Does that mean I have to pay extra to the hotel for sending the telegram?"

"There is a fee, sir, but I think you would find it reasonable."

Simpson put down the receiver and made another note. He dialed the Trafalgar Athletic Club.

"I want to arrange for a massage in my room. When, and how much? . . . Twenty-five dollars is too much." Again he put down the receiver.

He dialed the desk. He wanted a car and driver to take him out to the Santa Anita racetrack.

"You wouldn't get there until four-thirty, Mr. Simpson. Is that all right? We can have a driver within fifteen minutes."

"No, four-thirty is too late. Forget it."

He called Reservations. "I want to know the difference in fare on flights to Tokyo via Pan Am and JAL, and how frequent is the service and is it non-stop."

"Can we call you back on that, sir?"

"Yes." He made another note. When the lunch was brought in he tasted the wine. "No good, take it back." He lifted the aluminum cover and sliced the hamburger in half. "Too rare. Cook it some more."

The waiter's response was something less than automatic. But eventually he said, "Yes, sir. It will be a few minutes. You wish a different wine?"

"I wish a drinkable wine."

"Yes, sir."

In the dining room that night, Simpson ordered the chicken and then ten minutes later told the waiter he would have the fish instead. He lit a cigarette. The maître d'hôtel approached him. "Sir, if you wish to smoke, I'm afraid we'll have to change your table to the other end of the dining room." Simpson looked at him, glared, and put out his cigarette. "Sorry about that, sir. It's a hotel experiment."

Back in his room, he turned on the television set. He called the desk. "The reception on my television is no good."

"Oh? Well, I'm sorry. I'll try to get hold of a technician. Your room number?"

"Seven eighty-two."

"All right, sir, we'll see what we can do." Another notation on the pad.

The television man came, tested the image, brought in a half-dozen stations.

"Seems okay to me."

"It's working now. Wasn't before."

"Well, good night."

"Good night," Simpson managed.

He told the operator to put him on Do Not Disturb and to wake him at seven. He called for the porter at 7:30, stopped at the cashier, turned in his key and said, "I've got other plans. You can cancel the balance of my reservation."

The clerk nodded his head, made his calculations on the cash register, and handed the bill to Mr. Simpson. He looked down it, item by item. "You've charged me for a restricted TV channel that I didn't put on. It was put on by your technician. He was testing."

The clerk looked at the bill, examined the notation, hesitated for a minute, then deducted the item from the bill.

"I hope you enjoyed your stay, Mr. Simpson."

Oliver Simpson did not reply. He turned to the porter, and followed him out the door to the taxi.

.　.　.　.

General Manager Bradley Jiménez knew something about the methods used by President Daniel O'Hara for checking on the operation of his hotels, but even knowing about them, there was no absolutely safe way to guard against accidental bad service or incivility. Usually the phony guest, in fact an undercover employee of Martino Enterprises, materialized sometime during the month before the inspection visit by the president. But sometimes Danny tripped up his general managers, sending in the informant two months before his own visit; sometimes—he especially enjoyed this, and had pulled it on Bradley Jiménez—his informer would check in only a day or two before Danny. Several years ago, Bradley had told the desk to report to him anyone whose requests or complaints were egregious. When that happened—and such alarms were rung at least once a month—he sent out a Golden Alert on that person's room. A "Golden Alert" was done routinely for VIPs. If Room 808 was occupied by Elizabeth Taylor, any request to any division of the hotel that registered as coming from number 808 got instant service—other postulants went to the rear of the bus. Bradley Jiménez had decided to do a Golden Alert on one Oliver Simpson, but by that time Simpson had checked out.

They drove from the airport in the hotel's stretch limo. Danny put his legs up on the car's facing seats. "How're things going, Jiménez?"

"Pretty good, Mr. O'Hara. We had a fair quarter—"

"I know exactly what kind of a quarter you had. Do you think we don't look at the records in New York?"

"Well, I thought you might be pleased with it."

"It shows practically no growth. And an average occupancy rate of seventy-two percent. What is the occupancy rate at the Ambassador?"

"It isn't any easier to get those figures than it was last year."

"But you got them last year. At least, from the Ambassador."

"Yes. But the lady got fired."

"Fired? Hmm. Who's she working for now?"

"Us."

Danny nodded. Fair enough. "She must still have a friend inside the hotel?"

"Mr. O'Hara. Look, we are trying. But we don't have the figures right now."

At eleven o'clock, the section chiefs were assembled in one of the hotel's meeting rooms. Danny O'Hara addressed about fifty men and women responsible for making available 126,200 man-beds per year, serving up to three times that many meals and maintaining appropriate hotel space. Danny was introduced "—for the benefit of those of you who haven't already met with Mr. O'Hara, our president."

He greeted them cheerfully, and without the aid of any notes, recited to them the hotel's performance during the last quarter, compared it with the same quarter a year earlier, spoke of the need to put money aside for capital improvements, possibly including an auditorium for the use of convention guests, and then he said that the board of directors had specified that there would be no general increase in salary, beyond such increase as was necessary to compensate for inflation, until the operating figures showed an improvement. The "directors" (Danny never mentioned Mr. Martino) were willing to share the profit—"for every extra dollar made by the hotel, we'll put half of it in salary increases. Yes, you have a question?" He pointed at a very young redhead man seated in the first row.

Bradley Jiménez broke in. "That's John Purdy. He is a recent graduate of UCLA, he's with our accounting department." The young man's voice rang out loud and clear.

"Mr. O'Hara, would that be profits before tax, or after tax?"

"Before tax."

"Well, sir, I read in *The Wall Street Journal* a while ago about your speech to the Teamsters Union, and you said that hotel expenses, including food, labor, maintenance, tax and debt service, account for ninety-two percent of all income—"

"Leaving only eight percent for the stockholders—stockholder. That is correct."

"Well, doesn't that mean that we have to increase productivity by nine units, in order to increase your profits by one unit? And if that's right, does that mean we have to double our productivity in order to earn a two-and-a-half-percent increase in salary?''

Danny was momentarily at a loss. He turned to the general manager. "Explain it to him, Jiménez."

Bradley Jiménez sounded very much like a political candidate, Danny thought after sitting down on the chair onstage and looking faintly bored. Jiménez was going on and on about depreciation, taxes, competition, the need for productivity, the recession about which President Kennedy had made frequent references during the past year. Danny reconciled after a while that he had better bail out his general manager. He rose.

"Thanks, Jiménez. It is, as you can all see, a complicated question, hotel economics. But I think we have to applaud the decision of the directors to share their profit, dollar for dollar, with us. Are there any more questions?"

No.

Jiménez had instructed three subordinates to begin the applause. They did so, and their colleagues joined in. Danny thanked them, told them that on the whole they were doing a good job, and followed Jiménez to the dining room in the executive suite.

The lunch was immediately brought in. Danny went to what had once been a French window that opened out into the tiny porch. The handle no longer operated. "I hate these damned sealed-in windows."

"I do too," Jiménez commented, "but I can understand why you ordered them installed a couple of years ago. They are economical."

Danny had to admire Jiménez's preemptive strike. "Yes." Danny turned his head slowly to look into the face of his general manager. "Yes. They are economical. But it's all right to hate things that are economical, isn't it? I hate vending machines, don't you?"

"Actually," Jiménez permitted himself to say, "I don't. I get a kid's sense of omnipotence from them."

"Are they heavily used here?"

"We have them only in the basement rooms, with the Ping-

Pong, bowling alley—that floor. Yeah, they're popular. How about in New York?"

Danny poured himself a glass of wine, carefully inspecting the bottle. He grunted his approval and tasted it. He was ready to change the subject.

"I'll spend a couple of hours with you and the accounting people. Then I want to talk with what's-his-name—Nash?—hear what he has cooking in the way of promotion."

"George Nash. He's put his major effort into how to get the President to stay here on his next trip."

"That's easy. Put Marilyn Monroe in the adjacent room."

"We've already done that."

Danny smiled. "You kidding?"

"Not completely kidding. We got word to the White House, through who I think is the right person, that every effort would be made to make the President comfortable, and that if he consented we would invite some of his oldest Hollywood friends to meet him for a drink or a cup of coffee."

Danny smiled appreciatively. Then, after a pause, "On the matter of making people comfortable, everything set for me tonight?"

Bradley Jiménez reached into his pocket, took out a key and handed it to Danny. "Bel Air 807A. She'll be there at eight. I've taken the liberty of specifying the food and the wines."

"Good ho! Jiménez." Absentmindedly, he tucked into the caviar.

There was plenty of time ahead of him before Florry would arrive at his suite at the Bel Air. He decided to walk down Rodeo Drive, which was achieving something of a reputation as a fashionable shopping center. He liked to have a bauble at hand to give to Florry. He directed Jiménez to have his driver take his overnight bag and briefcase to his Bel Air suite, and sauntered out into the California sunshine, and the sweet air.

He ambled past a gallery exhibiting oils of Maurice de Vlaminck, dead only a few years. A fancy haberdashery featuring custom-made shirts, ties for an extortionary twenty dollars. He looked at the vintages in the wine store. A 1959 Château Lafitte —why not? He entered the store and billed it to the Trafalgar.

The next store was run by Dominique LaBrave. It traded in old jewelry. He admired the Fabergé egg in the corner, and then looked up at a diamond necklace.

Danny stared. Was this a hallucination? No. He looked intently at it once more. It was unmistakably his mother's necklace, missing since his and Caroline's wedding. The ruby-sapphire design at the center of the pendant that hung down from the rich baguette loop had been designed for his mother by the jeweler at Palm Beach to simulate a tiny R for Rachel.

He reached for the handle, but the door was locked. He rang; a buzzer opened the door. He greeted a middle-aged woman, distinguished in her dress, bearing and manner.

"I was looking at that necklace in the window, with the ruby-sapphire design."

"Yes, it is very beautiful, isn't it?" the woman said, walking over to the window and bringing a key from the pocket of her trim suit. She laid the necklace on a velvet pad.

"What are you selling it for?"

The woman looked down at the coded scribble on the attached label. "That is sixty-five thousand dollars," she said. "A lovely piece."

"How old is it?" Danny asked.

"Not so old. World War Two. Perhaps middle forties."

Danny's mind was racing. The Dominique LaBrave establishment was manifestly not engaged in fencing stolen goods. He would proceed cautiously. "Do you have a provenance for it?"

"Yes, of course. And of course, we guarantee the authenticity of all our jewelry. This necklace," she studied the label, "has forty-two carats of diamonds, and two each of rubies and sapphires." She left the showcase and went to a recessed bookcase, brought out a thick ledger, opened it and turned to the page she was looking for.

"It was purchased at auction in Geneva from the estate of the late Viscountess Asquith."

"Does it indicate how long she had it? Where she got it?"

"No, sir. It doesn't. But as I say, it has been appraised, both by the auctioneer in Nice and by our own establishment."

"That necklace was stolen from my mother," he said.

The woman treated the declaration with equanimity.

"Perhaps you are right . . . perhaps not. But there is no legal question about our title to it. Or, for that matter, yours, should you decide to purchase it. I'm sure Lady Asquith bought it on the assumption that it was the seller's to sell."

"Tell me, from your experience. Am I bound to inform the insurance company that I have happened on a diamond necklace stolen from my mother?"

"I think that would be courteous. The insurance company is of course at liberty to attempt to trace its purchase back to when Lady Asquith, or her late husband, acquired the necklace. These things are not always easy to do, as you can imagine. And then, of course, we don't know now how many generations of owners figure in between your mother and Dominique LaBrave. May I ask, when was the robbery?"

"It was in September 1951."

"About ten, twelve years ago. Yes. Well."

"You would sell it at a discount, I suppose?"

"We like to oblige, especially younger men who might make a habit of patronizing our store." Mrs. LaBrave smiled lightly and studied the necklace, though her appraisal was of the man who made the offer. He was a cosmopolitan man in his mid-thirties, perhaps not the killer-handsome he must have been a decade earlier, but nevertheless strikingly pleasing to look at. His nose and upper cheeks showed a trace of pink. Either he had been drinking at lunch or else the strain was now ineffaceable, years of heavy drinking. His brown hair was plentiful and carefully brushed. The light blue shirt was button-down, his custom-fitting suit made of the lightest gray flannel.

"I could let you have it for forty-seven thousand five hundred dollars."

"How about thirty-five?"

She smiled. "No," she said sweetly. Then: "Forty-five, period."

Danny smiled back at her. "Well," he said, "no harm in asking, is there? Dear old Mum will have to do without her necklace. But for the hell of it, I'll take your home number." She gave him a card. He was talking with Mrs. Dominique LaBrave herself.

At the hotel he checked his watch. It was 9:30 P.M. in Palm Beach. His stepfather would be relaxed, enjoying the general amplitude of life. Danny rang the house; his mother answered.

"Hi, Mom. It's me."

Rachel Bennett sounded genuinely pleased. "Hello, darling. How are you? Where are you? Why are you calling, since you have all the money you need these days?"

"Los Angeles. You know, the usual. Hotel duty. I'm fine, but want to have a private talk with Harry about your—I won't tell. Promised not to."

She laughed. "Dear Harry. He thinks the party is secret. Every other person I walk into at Palm Beach whispers to me not to betray the confidence, that they're coming to my surprise party. Are you and Caroline going to surprise us?"

"I hope so, but of course it depends on whether one of the children is about to be baptized or confirmed or ordained. You know, we have divine priorities in our household."

"Now, darling, don't be so negative about Caroline's faith. I pause to say that it is in refreshing contrast to your own. When last did you attend divine service—at your wedding?"

Danny decided he would take the fork on that road. "No, really, Mom, we'd like to be there. Some things are coming up in the business so I can't say absolutely for sure, but we'll—"

"Surprise me?"

He laughed. "Yes, surprise you. Now let me speak to Harry. But you are not to be in the room when I talk to him. Promise?"

"That's easy, darling. He's upstairs in the study, watching television. I'll buzz him on the intercom. Hang on."

"Harry? Hi, Harry!"

"How are you, Danny? You and Caroline coming to the"—he lowered his voice—"surprise party?"

"We're going to try. But let me tell you something exciting. You know the stolen necklace? The one you gave Mom on your first wedding anniversary?"

"They catch the thief?"

"No. But guess what, I *spotted* it! It's in a very reputable store here, Beverly Hills. It really is a stunner. That design of yours, fantastic!"

"But—what kind of a price? Where did they get it?"

"We went all through that. Legitimate auction, all certified, estate of Lady Asquith, Geneva."

"What a hell of a present that would be! To give it to Rachel on her birthday! What do they want for it?"

"They want eighty-five. But I prodded the lady real hard, told her it had been Mum's, that you designed it. I think—I think—I could get it for seventy-five."

Harry Bennett prided himself on being a tough man of business.

"Offer her seventy, and just walk away if she says no. Well, no, don't walk away. Call me from the hotel. When can you get back to me?"

"Well, the store's closed now. But I'll get to the woman first thing tomorrow. I'll let you hear from me as soon as possible after noon, Florida time. If she says yes, how do you want me to handle it?"

"Call me, I'll call the bank, they'll have a certified check by the end of the week. Hell, that's terrific news, Danny. You're a hell of a thoughtful guy. The perfect surprise! Her missing necklace!"

Danny dialed, Mrs. LaBrave's voice came on, soothing, poised.

"Mrs. LaBrave? This is my mother's son."

"That's nice," she said. "Yes, of course. You wish the necklace?"

"Yes, but there is one string attached. Not one, I'm sure, that will bother you. You will receive a certified check for seventy thousand dollars, and you will give me cash, twenty-five thousand dollars. Broker's fee."

"I understand," she said. "I see no problem."

"Good. You will be receiving a check from Mr. Harry Bennett, to whom you will send the necklace. When you get his check, go to the First National Bank at El Camino and ask for Mr. Umin.

Tell him to credit Windels and Marx, attorneys, Fifty-one West Fifty-first Street, New York, the account of J. Taggart. Got that?''

There was the briefest pause.

Yes, Mrs. LaBrave said, she got it and was certain his mother would be very happy to have back so beautiful a piece of jewelry.

Danny thought the whole thing amusing. Cashing in on dear old Mom's necklace when she lost it, then cashing in on it when she retrieved it. He could only top that one, he thought wryly, by stealing it again from dear old Mom.

Fun thought. But that would be gilding the lily.

He would have liked to share his escapade with Florry. Florry loved to hear about Danny's maneuvers, though she would never have had reason to suppose that there was anything unconventional in Danny's relationship with Mr. Martino. Florry was intensely interested in Danny, in his business, his thoughts, his insights and, sure, his potency. She would even argue with him on this point or that: Was it likely that a piano player in the large lobby, playing in the afternoon, would amuse the guests, tend to bring them back? She thought not, but she let Danny persuade her that he was right, and he felt after all such exchanges with her both a sense of accomplishment and a closeness with the person who had challenged him, and then succumbed to his reasoning.

He blurted out the story of the necklace. But he did not get from her, after telling it, the collaborative enthusiasm he was looking for. In a strange way, Florry was all . . . middle-class. It amused Danny, the fruit of Hyde Park vineyards, to think that of someone brought up as Florry had been, reacting as she now did. Well, at least he scored on the matter of his cunning. Artistic cunning, he thought it appropriate to describe it. At least it would make him smile every time he thought of it.

Eighteen

AT THE ARVN OFFICERS CLUB at Tan Son Nhut airfield outside Saigon in the late afternoon of November 1, 1963, a dozen Vietnamese off-duty officers, including two generals, were relaxing. Four of them played cards; the bar dispensed wine and beer. The day's newspapers, in Vietnamese and in French, lay on the wide table at one end of the large room, along with bulletins from Agence France Press. At one corner of the common room the television set was on, its sound muted so as not to interfere with those who sought other distractions. Even in November, the heat was felt, the distinctive jungle heat, in an area only twelve teasing degrees north of the Equator. The air conditioner pumped in shafts of cooler air, but fitfully. The card players arrested their game when the chief steward came in from the office next door obviously with an urgent message.

"General Nguyen, a call from the presidential palace."

The steward led the general to the ornate carved telephone booth in the foyer, opened the door to let the general in, closed it, and walked away toward the door leading to the common room. But as soon as he was safely out of sight of the booth he circled back and, moist ear to the wooden panel of the telephone booth, listened intently to the conversation. He had no difficulty in making out the words spoken by General Nguyen Khanh.

"Yes, Mr. President. I shall most instantaneously convey your message. But, sir, exactly to which gentleman do you expect me to convey it? . . . Well, Mr. President, if you do not know, sir, who is in charge of the . . . insurrection you speak of, I can certainly report your message to the Chief of Staff, and surely he will get it to the right gentleman? To the right party? . . . The Chief of Staff is with the insurgents? Well, Mr. President, in that event, he surely *would* know to whom to convey your message? . . . Yes, sir. I repeat it: You agree to resign the presidency in exchange for safe conduct for yourself and your brother. Mr. President, I will telephone you within the space of one-half hour. I shall drive instantly to the headquarters with your message."

And then, in French, his voice muted, *"Adieu,* Monsieur President."

General Nguyen walked briskly from the anteroom, opened the door and slammed it shut. His voice, commanding his aide's presence, resounded through the flimsy wall of the common room.

The steward, his face held tight against the side of the phone booth, had escaped detection. Now he ducked into the booth and, his foot tapping out his impatience, dialed the number he had dialed so often these past months. He was grateful to hear the voice of his younger brother at the other end of the line.

"The coup is on! I have overheard this end of the conversation.

General Nguyen Khanh, talking with the President. Diem offers to resign in exchange for safe passage for him and the family."

"To whom is General Nguyen reporting the President's offer?"

"I don't know. The best I could make out was that the President doesn't know who is heading up the coup."

"Surely it is General Minh?"

"I think so, and that fits with other information I have given you. But I could hear General Nguyen distinctly, and he said, *'If you don't know who is in charge of the coup, Mr. President, I'll have to report your offer to the Chief of Staff.'* "

"Then the President is still in the palace?"

"Yes. Because I took the call myself, and it came from the palace, and General Nguyen said within one-half hour he would call the President back, obviously in the palace."

Than thanked his brother. And then, "We will use our customary signals. Do not leave the club, Tri. Stay as close to the telephone as you can."

Than Koo put down the telephone and walked quickly across the hall. He opened the door into the sultry office, Henry's typewriter clicking away, without knocking.

Mrs. Fuerbinger, wife of *Time*'s managing editor Otto, told Henry that her husband was in South Africa and was "just plain inaccessible." Henry then dialed the home number of Chief of Correspondents Richard Clurman, his own direct boss. When no one answered the telephone—it was just after six in the morning in New York—Henry Chafee very nearly rang the home telephone number of Henry Luce (he had secreted it when, one evening in New York, he had heard it read out by Clurman to a telephone operator at the Council on Foreign Relations). But he stopped himself. Wake up Henry Robinson Luce, the most formidable publisher in America, at 4 A.M. Arizona time!

Besides, there was only one thing for an enterprising journalist to do, and he would do it, with or without the explicit sanction of New York. He must follow President Diem, wherever he went.

The only way to peer into the presidential compound was from

Han Thuyen Street. The large house on the corner, directly opposite the palace, was the property of Ngo Viet Thu. He knew of Henry Chafee as the author of a *Time* profile on American architects, and early in the summer had asked Henry to introduce him to architect Philip Johnson at a convention he would be attending in New York City. Ngo Thu could now return the favor.

But on November 1, he was out of town.

Than Koo moved dramatically and convincingly, and persuaded the housekeeper to let them in and give them access to the study on the third floor.

Henry Chafee took his station there, binoculars in hand. Than Koo returned to the car, put on a chauffeur's cap, and waited at the wheel, his walkie-talkie in hand. The sun had just now set and the relief in temperature was immediate.

"There's a car coming out of the palace"—Than heard Henry's voice crackle—"no flags or anything. But that doesn't surprise. Let's see what the guards do. . . . They're checking an I.D. Obviously not the car we're looking for."

At eight, Henry thought it time to check in with Koo's brother at the Officers Club. "Any way you can patch in from your phone to your brother?"

No, Than Koo said. But he would take the radio with him and duck into the café at the opposite corner and use the phone there. Meanwhile, if Mr. Henry spotted the presidential car he should alert him through the radio and Than would immediately make chase. Okay?

"Okay. Go ahead."

Moments later, back at the wheel of the car, Than Koo signaled. "My brother says the Officers Club is practically empty. Wherever General Nguyen went to call back the President, it was not there—"

"Hang on, Koo." Henry trained his glasses on the car making its way to the entrance gate. It was very far from a presidential limousine, a simple sedan. The two guards leaned down to peer through the windows. But then they snapped to attention and saluted.

"Go! Go! Go! Koo. Quick! Quick!" Henry looked down from the window and saw his own car speeding off in chase of the suspect car that had just passed through the gates of the presidential palace.

He stood by the radio. In a few moments Koo was on.

"I've got them. They turned off Hoc Lac Street, onto Tran Hung Dao. They are heading toward Cholon. Driving quite slowly. They are stopped at a light right now. I'm leaving two cars between them and me . . ."

Than did not release the channel. He described the route he was following. "We are still on Tran Hung Dao. Driving about forty kilometers per hour. Traffic is easing up. Suspect car stops to let a pedestrian go by. Taking left onto Phung Hung."

A few minutes later, "They're pulling up. Don't know what it is, the house on the side. A house on Tran Hung. *They're getting out!* First two men have raincoats over their heads. The third man has rushed past them. He is opening the door to—I cannot read the number of the house. The two men have disappeared inside. . . . Mr. Henry, I think that was President Diem and his brother Nhu. No. I do not *doubt* it is them. I *feel* it."

"What happened to the car?"

"Someone has just come out of the house. He is getting into the car. . . . It is driving down the road. Turning right. It looks like a small driveway. It is covered by trees. I can no longer see the car. I do not want to risk turning in to that road."

"No, no. Now listen, Koo. Seems to me obvious they're going to stay where they are for a while—if not, why did they go there in the first place. Now I've got to get back to my office, cable New York. Figure a half hour. I'll approach to within a half block of where you are after I spot your car. I'll bring food and something to drink. I'll charge up my radio in the office, but will keep it on. Turn on the car radio low and keep listening in case there's an announcement. You won't hear from me for thirty minutes unless it's an emergency. I have eight twenty-three. I will signal you at eight fifty-five." Henry opened the door at the moment the tropical shower hit. He took off his seersucker jacket and improvised a hat, charging off toward the street where he could hope to flag a taxi, or even persuade a Vietnamese with a motorbike.

Than Koo would do as instructed.

The telephone rang insistently at the winter house of Henry Luce at Scottsdale, a suburb of Phoenix. It was 6:30 in the morning. The housekeeper shook herself awake and finally agreed to knock on the bedroom door of Mr. Luce.

"What time is it?" he bellowed through the door.

"Six-thirty, Mr. Luce."

He grabbed the telephone from the bedside table. "Yes," he grunted. "Luce here."

"Harry!" His Chief of Correspondents explained to a sleepy tycoon what was going on. In a matter of seconds, Luce was transformed into an excited journalist. He took in the story and then issued instructions.

"We've got one important decision to make. Whether to tell the White House. Can you get through to Chafee without any trouble?"

"Yeah, for"—Clurman looked at his watch—"exactly ten minutes. After that he plans to stake out the house where they're hiding out. Only his interpreter is there now."

"That's no good. Tell Chafee to put off going back to his station until he has somebody standing by the phone in the office. Somebody with a radio who can relay my instructions. I'm not sure I can decide on this—decide what to do—in less than an hour or two. I assume President Diem will stay wherever he is overnight, with Nhu. I assume that, but of course we can't be sure. But the interpreter is there, you say?"

"Yes, Harry."

"Probably they'll stay put. Now what I need is a telephone operator. Damnit, it's only what, eight o'clock your time? Can you get through to the home number of one of the office operators? Tell somebody to get the hell over to the switchboard to handle my calls?"

"Harry, we've got six operators, and they're probably all having a cup of coffee and getting ready to get into the bus or subway to go to the office. There's no way I can make them get in any faster than they'd get there anyway."

Henry Luce was not patient in such situations.

"All right. All right, Dick. Get the switchboard to stand by for me at exactly nine your time. Now I want you to read all the cables from Chafee and from everybody else you can get your hands on who's up on the Vietnam situation. Do our people know about the coup? If so, when did they find out? And if so, who is conducting the coup? Has there in fact been a coup, or is Diem just going into hiding?

"And what are our people in Saigon going to do about it? Are they prepared to look after the physical safety of the President?— *of course,* you won't let on we know he isn't in the palace any longer. Can we assume that some of the military will stay loyal to him? If so, do they anticipate an armed struggle? Are there any indications that the enemy might move if there is disorder?"

When Henry Luce's curiosity was stirred he wanted to know everything there was to know. "What time will you be at the office, Dick, eight forty-five? Where in the hell were you at six when Chafee tried to get you. Duck hunting? Hmm. Don't suppose you know how to work a switchboard. . . . Here's an assignment for you. Round me up the home telephone numbers of McGeorge Bundy, Bob McNamara, Averell Harriman, Ted Sorensen— What? Slow down?" Henry Luce puffed at his cigarette. "Yes, okay. McNamara . . . Harriman . . . Sorensen—Bobby? No. If it comes to that I will talk to the President myself. And yes, the home telephone number in Saigon of Cabot Lodge. I'll talk to you at eight forty-five. The White House number, that's 456-1212, right? Yes. Goodbye."

The housekeeper brought in coffee. Henry Luce called the White House. "This is Henry Luce. I'm calling from my number in Phoenix. You have it. I want to talk to Secretary Rusk. I know how these things are, I know, I know. Just you call him, tell him I need to speak to him on an emergency matter, give him my number. Thank you."

He put down the telephone. Five minutes later it rang. "Mr. Luce?"

"Yup."

"This is Virginia Rusk. Dean spent the night in Atlanta and should be on the way to his plane now, because he's due here before lunch. The White House can probably put you through to SAM-118 as soon as he gets to the airport."

"Oh. Well, I'll take it from here. Thank you very much, Mrs. Rusk. I'm sorry to disturb you."

He swigged down his coffee. Might as well take a shower. Can't call Clurman back for—twenty-three minutes.

At noon Eastern Standard time, the conference call was in place. Henry Luce in Phoenix, Richard Clurman in New York, Henry Chafee in Saigon.

Luce took the floor.

"All right. Chafee?"

"Yes, Mr. Luce."

"For security, we will refer to 'Subject.' You're telling us—I've read your cable—that Subject is asking for a guarantee for his physical security and his brother's. Does Lodge know that?"

"I don't know. I haven't told him. I don't know whether General Nguyen passed out the information, or maybe one of the people who heard about it from him."

"Does anybody at our embassy know that Subject has left the palace?"

"Again, I don't know. I don't think General Nguyen knew Subject was skipping out, because our man heard the general promising to call him back *at* the palace. Now maybe he did, and maybe Diem—Subject—is following the general's instructions. Maybe the guy who drove him to the safe house is acting on military orders, maybe acting for the general who pulled off the coup—if it has been pulled off."

"Your cables tell us it's been all over Saigon for weeks that the White House is encouraging a coup. They don't tell us whether Kennedy-Rusk-Lodge have done anything about the physical security of—of Subject. Know anything about that?"

"No. No, sir, I do not."

"Dick?"

"Yes, Harry."

"This is a hell of a situation. If we let Lodge know where he is, does that a) increase Subject's chances of getting away? or b) diminish those chances? If Lodge fingers him, somebody has to go rescue Subject. I can't believe Lodge wants to shelter him and . . . brother . . . in the U.S. Embassy. So if Lodge gets into the act, he'd have to protect him without offering diplomatic sanctuary. But that may be a lot harder to do if he knows where Subject is than if he *does not* know. What you think?"

"I think, Harry, we've got to tell the White House—"

"Tell the White House what? That Subject is out of power? Or tell the White House that he's out of power and hiding in a house known only to *Time* magazine's Saigon correspondent?"

"Begin by telling the White House that in case they haven't heard, President Diem has been overthrown."

"How does that advance U.S. interests?"

"Harry, the White House will want to have it both ways. They'll want to say they had nothing to do with it. And then they'll want to wave to the new Administration—Big Minh, you agree?— and to the Buddhists and to the hate-Diem crowd, which is much of the world, and say, Look how smoothly we Americans can handle the situation when it gets out of hand! Look what we did to Lumumba! Look what we did to Trujillo! Henry—Henry Chafee—is it your impression that the Lodge crowd want Diem killed?"

"That is my impression. It would be simply more convenient. With Diem still alive, his whole establishment in South Vietnam is still alive, and potential avengers of the government in power. Yes, he'd prefer Diem dead, but Lodge isn't going to line up a firing squad."

"Where exactly are you now?"

"It's near one-thirty. I'm at a bar a couple of blocks from House X. We've taken over the bar, made a deal. The bar owner is a lot richer. I'm wearing out, but my man and I are taking watches, one of us snoozing in the back of the car, the other at the wheel."

"What happens when your bar closes?"

"Mr. Luce, the bar won't close to your Saigon correspondent. I've made all-night arrangements with him."

"Good. Call this number, my number—602-555-8738—at, er, call it two hours from now. Got that?"

"Yes, Mr. Luce."

"But, obviously, if Subject goes somewhere else, call in as soon as *that* happens." Henry closed his eyes, committing the telephone number to memory. He had lost all desire for sleep. He could not imagine that he'd sleep again.

But Than Koo had dozed for an hour. Now he got out of the car and opened the door to the driver's seat. "Your turn, Mr. Henry."

"Get in the other side, Koo. I've been thinking."

The nearest street lamp was on the left. The house they were watching was opposite it, thirty or forty meters down the street, its dull yellow paint all but covered by the leaves and ivy that shrouded it. The traffic was very light, one car every fifteen or twenty minutes. There was no sign of police or military.

"Koo," Henry said, "you should go to the telephone in the bar—I'll bring you in, give an okay to the bartender to let you stay, use the phone, etc. Call your brother. If he's not on duty, call him at home. It's been six hours since we've been in touch with him. I can't believe there hasn't been military traffic in the club during the last few hours. After that, call Tran Tuyen. He's been pretty valuable to us in the past. See if he has anything. Okay?" Henry knew that Koo did not relish talking to Tran, whom he considered as something of a rival informant. But he would of course do so.

Koo was gone twenty minutes. He sat down on the front seat by Henry. "You're right. Tri said a lot of officers started coming in just after our call. There was a lot of drinking, a lot of yakking. He heard every kind of rumor, heard there was a countercoup, General Minh arrested, heard Lodge had flown out of the country, heard Diem had flown north. Heard everything.

"But then I got hold of Tran Tuyen. He has one very specific piece of information. At seven forty-five last night—that would be less than a half hour before he left the palace—Diem called your friend Colonel Conein." Than Koo's reference was to the CIA colonel who occupied the office opposite Henry's. "Said he wanted safe passage out of the country and who if not the CIA would provide it? Tran says apparently Conein stalled, said that to fly Diem out, CIA would need to bring in a jet transport from Guam, and that that operation would take twenty-four hours. Diem said to Conein over the phone, 'Twenty-four hours is too long.' "

Koo paused. "Sounds to me like the CIA doesn't want to get involved in an escape operation. Diem figured out they were closing in on him and decided to go to—well, to come here." He pointed offhandedly to the yellow house they were covering.

Henry Chafee was silent. "I'll try"—he knew he had to try— "to sleep for an hour, before it's time to call New York. Call Phoenix, I mean." He opened the door and moved into the back of the car. He closed his eyes, but did not sleep.

"All right. Dick?"

"Here, Harry."

"Chafee?"

"Here, Mr. Luce."

"What time is it there?"

"Just after seven. It was dawn a few minutes ago."

"No movement?"

"No movement."

"Well, I've talked to everybody involved. Just about everybody. Haven't talked to the President, don't need to. Your cables are on the mark, Chafee. Getting rid of Subject is a U.S. operation, at least getting him out of office is. But zero plans were made to provide for his safety. Oh, they think he's still in the palace. I pitched real hard with Rusk—Subject should be taken to the embassy, I said. It's the only way; he'd be safe there. Never mind the diplomatic fuss—hell, U.S. embassies have been used before.

And anyway, the White House objective, getting Subject out of the way, would be accomplished.

"Rusk wouldn't buy in, but he did say we'd provide sanctuary if he actually showed up. So?"

"The time has come to tell the State Department that Subject has left the palace with—with his brother; that we know where he is, and they can send a car to pick them up and take them to the embassy—"

"But, Mr. Luce, if Lodge or any of his people delay or if they pass around the address, then it seems to me there's a hell of a risk—"

Henry Luce was terse. "I have considered all of the angles. I have come to this conclusion. What is his address?"

Henry paused. Then he said, heavily, "It is 322 Phung Hung Street."

"How you spell that?"

"P-h-u-n-g H-u-n-g."

"Good. Stay where you are. I'd guess the embassy people will get there within the hour. Call me back in two hours."

Henry Chafee hung up the telephone behind the bar. The bartender bowed—oriental punctilio. Henry was halfway to the door when he stopped, turned, and said, "Dong, give me a double whiskey."

He gulped it down and walked back to the car. He told Than Koo about the conversation.

"So they have the address?"

"Not quite. I gave them number 322."

"But it's 342!"

"Yes. But where we are parked we can see 322. If it is Americans who show up there, we can lead them to the correct address. If it isn't Americans, why, tough shit—ARVN got a bad lead from New York."

"Mr. Chafee!"

Henry looked up. The car was pulling out of the drive. It did a U-turn and pulled up by number 342. Immediately the third man came out of the door, followed by his two august guests, once again with raincoats draped over their heads. They entered the rear of the car, the first man was at the wheel and the car slipped forward.

"*Careful, Koo!* They might be looking back. Wait another few seconds. . . ."

The traffic was picking up. It was early, but already it was hot. The rain of twelve hours ago was used up, and the dust rose from the wheels of the car on which their eyes trained. Than Koo followed.

The lead car went only a few blocks, coming to a halt at Hoc Lac Street, outside a church. The passengers walked out of the car into the church. It was clearly labeled, the Cha Tam Church.

"I'll be damned. Either they've gone in to mass, just to worship, or maybe they have an appointment with the priest or somebody else, to hide them. Well, we'll find out. I wonder if there's a door into the church that we can't see from here?"

"Do you want me to walk up and look?"

Henry reflected. "Why not? If there's any question, you're just another parishioner, coming in for early service. But come back —Koo! *Hold it!*"

An armored personnel carrier shot past their car and, alongside the church, screeched to a halt. Six soldiers jumped to the ground, pistols in hand. They barged into the church.

Three minutes later the President of the Republic of Vietnam and his brother and chief political adviser, their hands tied behind their backs, were dragged from the church and thrust up into the back of the van. Its hatch door quickly slammed shut. The carrier roared away.

Henry nodded his head as he tapped Than's shoulder. Than Koo slipped the car into gear. In ten minutes they had left Cholon. The carrier swung left onto a rutted side road, macadamized perhaps twenty years ago by the Japanese.

"Don't get too close," Henry said. "Hold it here."

The carrier had come to a stop a quarter of a mile ahead.

They could hear six shots. A man in uniform jumped out of the back section. There was blood on his bayonet, reflected in the early sun. He walked up to the front of the carrier and spoke with the driver. Then back, and into the carrier. The driver executed a U-turn and sped past the station wagon with the bearded American and the pale young Vietnamese who sat silent, apparently asleep in the front seat.

Nineteen

AT THE BEL AIR HOTEL in Los Angeles, Florida Carmela Huerta knocked on the hotel door a few minutes after eight. She was wearing the gold-white bandana. A waterfall of Aztec silver rippled down from her neck to the cocky breasts. Her floral-patterned dress was drawn tight, and around her waist a wrought-silver belt with a large turquoise buckle hung loosely. Turquoise stones dangled from the ears, her sleek brown hair swept back over her head into a bun in back. She wore very little makeup on her bronzed skin. Her smile was at once poised and vivacious.

"It's good to see you, Danny." Her voice was alto in pitch, her accent urbane.

He got up, kissed her lightly on the forehead. She looked up at

him and returned the kiss, on his lips. She lingered there ada-
mantly. His response was immediate and acute.

"Now?"

"Will we be interrupted?" she whispered.

"I ordered dinner for nine-fifteen."

"Then now."

He bolted the front door and led her into the bedroom. She
kissed him again before sliding into the bathroom. Danny unbuttoned his shirt, tossed it onto the chair, followed by his undershirt. He took off his pants and climbed into the bed. She came
from the bathroom, opulently nude, lay down on the bed, and
stretched out on her stomach.

"Danny, remove my necklace. I couldn't get it."

He turned on the lamp, found the clasp, unhooked it, slid off
the massive silver, letting it drop to the floor. Then with his left
hand he pinioned her neck as she lay, and with his right lifted
her hips. She gave no resistance, raising her hands behind her
instead, to complete an ardent linkage.

Fifteen minutes later she moved her mouth next to his ear.
"Better get dressed." She giggled. "Dinner is on its way."

"Good idea. Better one: Maybe I'll tell 'em to go away, come
back at breakfast time."

She pushed him on the shoulder and he got up. A few minutes
later the doorbell rang. Danny opened the door, smiled at the
waiter, and pointed his finger to a recess in the room. "Set up
the table there, that's fine."

He sat, and then tasted the first of the three wines. "Go right
ahead with the soup," he told the waiter. "My wife is dressing,
and will be here in a minute."

He and Florry amused themselves with the banter about their
"children," done for the benefit of attending waiters. They became so enthusiastic about their imagined family they sometimes
found themselves going on with their act even after the waiter
had stepped out, as the waiter had just done to bring in an extra
fork.

"I agree, Danny. Judy should be prepared to go away to school
in the fall."

"Have you selected the victim school?"

"Now, don't talk that way about our eldest child."

"What other way is there to talk about that monster?"

"She'll grow out of it. Pour me some more wine."

"If she doesn't, she'll end up in Sing Sing."

"You never really understood Judy."

"Dr. Spock wouldn't understand Judy."

The dessert was served; the waiter left and was told not to bother to return for the dishes. They sat on the couch, their cordials on the coffee table in front of them.

"How's it going at school?" he asked.

"If I thought you cared, I'd tell you. —That's not fair. After all, you care enough to pay my bills. Anyhow, it's good. Even though I'm an undergraduate, I sit for my orals in the advanced class next month, Professor Bergin examining. A tough hombre. If you forget when Dante had his first communion, he'll flunk you."

"When did Dante have his first communion? If you forget, call my wife. She'd know."

"I like it when you take an objective view of . . . your marriage. Speaking of our 'Judy,' how is your brood? Your real brood?"

"My brood is, among other things, expensive. Actually, the youngest, Suzy, can talk now. Come to think of it, that's the bad news. Tommy, the oldest, will be eleven, I think, the day I get back."

"Does Caroline pay a lot of attention to the kids?"

"Caroline is either taking the kids to school, coaching them in their homework, doing their homework, or driving them to the skating rink or to church. Sometimes she gets a free minute. That is when she knits."

"Doesn't sound like the most fun in the world."

Danny didn't answer. Instead he asked, "You going to be able to pull away for the weekend in Acapulco?"

Florry lit a cigarette and let the smoke out of her mouth wispily. "I'd like to. I can work on my thesis pretty much anywhere."

"I didn't have in mind a weekend in Acapulco to explore *The Divine Comedy*—"

"I'm not doing my term paper on the *Comedy.*"

"I know. I know."

Danny stood up and began to pace the room. Absentmindedly he flicked on the television set. He heard the voice of Henry Cabot Lodge. He was expressing official regret at the violent end of President Ngo Dinh Diem. "He was my friend, and a great patriot and leader."

He turned to Florida. "Did I tell you Caroline's brother is there? He's a correspondent for *Time* magazine." Must drop him a note, he reminded himself.

"Is he—"

"His name is Henry."

"Is Henry like—Caroline?"

"Henry's a nice guy. Sort of a plodder. We . . . fought together in the last days of the war. Landed in Italy straight after basic training in the fucking infantry."

"Were you in action?"

"Yes. Henry wasn't quite ready for it."

"What do you mean?"

"He froze. I had to go on my own, then come back to pull him out of his funk."

"Henry a fag?"

"I don't think so. He isn't married, but I don't know that he's ever had a boyfriend."

"Close to Caroline?"

"He idolizes Caroline, and vice versa. They glow when they're in each other's presence. I used to think it was nice. Now I find it disgusting."

"But it sounds very romantic."

"In a way, it is. No, I guess not. Brother-sister love is in its own category."

The telephone rang. Danny was surprised. Only Jiménez knew where he was. He picked it up.

"Real sorry to do this"—it was Jiménez—"but Cutter Malone said to track you down wherever you were. I told him you had gone to the football game. He didn't tell me what it was, but he's waiting at this number."

Danny put down the telephone. "Florry, excuse this. Watch the TV for a few minutes; I'll go into the bedroom and use the phone there."

He recognized Cutter's home telephone number, and rang it.

"This is Danny."

"Danny, Giuseppe Martino has had a stroke. He's in the hospital. He can't talk well, but the doctors can make out that he's asking to see you."

"Is it—the end?"

"They're not saying that, obviously. But I called Dr. Jerry Cash, gave him all the details I could get from the doctor at the hospital, and Jerry says from strokes like that, people eighty-four years old don't usually recover. How soon can you get here?"

"Dumb question, Cutter. You know as much as I do about coast-to-coast airline schedules. There's an eight A.M. Unless you hear from me, send the car to meet that flight. . . . Have we forgotten anything?"

"No. The . . . document with the correct Hyde Park . . . address is the one that will turn up."

"Good. See you, Cutter."

Danny emerged from the bedroom with a wide smile. He poured himself another glass of wine.

"Good news?" Florry said.

"Yes." He walked over to the light switch and the room was suddenly in shadows.

"The news . . . is so good . . . I need to . . . communicate it to you . . . joyfully." All his clothes came off and, on the couch, in the dark, he began to undress her. "Florry. Do I mean more to you than Dante?"

"How much do I mean to you, Danny?" She was helping him pull up her skirt.

"More than anybody, Florry. More than anything. As you can tell. . . . There, see what I mean? And—*control* yourself, Florry, sweet Florry, though with you, I'm not much good at—control. . . ."

Twenty

T HE FLIGHT was very long. The U.S. military was obliging
to U.S. newsmen, who regularly hitched rides to Guam,
connecting with the commercial carrier there for Honolulu. But
the transports designed for the military were not to be confused
with luxury carriers. Henry slept—slept in the sense that he lost
consciousness, or thought he did. He had long since learned that
the kind of sleep one falls into from undeniable biological need
somehow does not provide rest. So that when he woke up, as the
plane landed in Guam, which still showed signs of the face-lift
required after the war with Japan, he felt wretchedly tired.

The Pan Am plane for Honolulu would leave two hours later.
He put down his typewriter and heavy briefcase and stretched his
arms. It was midmorning and the military airport was thrum-

ming with activity. What seemed like an endless row of trucks loaded with supplies squatted edgily, each waiting its turn to load up the C-124 Globemaster cargo planes. Henry's instinct was to search out someplace to shower, then he remembered he had showered an hour before boarding the airplane, nine hours ago. He walked into the large hangar, signed the registry, confirmed the departure time of the flight, then wandered into the PX. He picked up a copy of *Stars & Stripes*. At the cafeteria he took coffee and leafed through the paper. It featured the release by the Soviets of Professor Barghoorn of Yale.

Henry had followed the story eagerly, in part because the behavior of Communists had become a professional concern, in part because he remembered well the self-effacing, scholarly professor of Russian studies with whom he had studied only ten years before. Barghoorn had been picked up by Soviet policemen in Moscow, charged with conducting espionage activity against the Soviet Union. Offhand, Henry could think of no unlikelier person to conduct espionage. Fred Barghoorn could not have hidden a piece of cheese from a mouse. The result had been a great furor in the academic-literary world, and it had had the desired effect: President Kennedy denounced the detention of Mr. Barghoorn. "He was not on an intelligence mission of any kind," the President insisted. Two weeks after the U.S.-sponsored assassination of Diem, Henry was not in the right frame of mind automatically to accept the word of President Kennedy, but in this case, what the President said Henry knew to be plausible.

He smiled as he read on. There was something so . . . reassuringly, doggedly predictable about Soviet polemical warfare. After putting the professor on a London-bound flight, a Soviet spokesman "confirmed" that Barghoorn had "committed espionage" and "could have been made to stand trial," but that since President Kennedy felt so strongly on the subject, the professor was released. Nice, Henry said to himself, that the Soviet authorities go to such lengths to avoid hurting Mr. Kennedy's feelings.

He went on to read the feature profile on Mr. Barghoorn, written by his sometime colleague in Saigon, David Abshire.

Barghoorn, the report read, had made six trips to the Soviet Union since the war. He had "always been very careful, while in the U.S.S.R., to avoid any actions that could be construed as espionage, even refraining from carrying a camera or engaging in overlong conversation with Soviet citizens." The purpose of his recent visit was "to gather evidence for a book . . . on the Soviet political system . . . and on political instruction and indoctrination." Henry's smile broadened as he read that Barghoorn "had informed Soviet authorities of this before his trip." He wondered whether old Fred had stipulated the maximum length of any conversation he would have while in Moscow.

He put down his cup to turn the page, and learned that the Institute of Strategic Studies estimated that the NATO countries had outpaced the Soviet bloc by five to one in numbers of intercontinental ballistic missiles. Skipping about, he noted that Supreme Court Justice William O. Douglas had married again, as had Gary Powers, the U-2 pilot shot down by the Soviet military —Henry had covered his release, in Berlin, with Powers set free in exchange for the U.S. release of Soviet superspy Rudolf Abel.

He wandered around the PX, and suddenly it occurred to him that he hadn't bought a gift for Caroline or for the children. He looked about at the heavy-laden shelves. Booze was manifestly a big favorite of military clientele and occupied row after row of shelf space. Conventional fifths of liquor sold either for a few cents less than one dollar (Old Crow), or a few cents more (Jack Daniels). His eye caught the bottle of cognac selling for forty dollars. *Forty dollars in a PX?* Was it taken from Napoleon's private collection? He brought it down from the shelf and turned it around in his hand. What-the-hell—he plucked it down in the trolley he was dragging along. For the children he purchased games—Parcheesi, dominoes, Monopoly for Emily (she probably had two sets). He thought to telephone Caroline, but after looking at his watch decided against a call that would ring in Greenwich at close to midnight. He could call from Honolulu.

Or he could wait until getting to New York.

He sat down in the lounge. He knew that he needed to question himself. What was going on? How was it that he was finding reasons to postpone calling Caroline? *Caroline*. He opened his large briefcase, reached into the farthest compartment, took out the manila folder with her letters and pulled out the one that had arrived only a few days ago. It was her P.S. that roiled in the memory. He read it again. "You ask how is it with Danny. Dear Danny, he has very heavy responsibilities and is away a great deal. I'm afraid he doesn't see the children, at least not as much as I'd like. And then, too, Danny just doesn't understand why religion can be so important for some people. Some people—me, for instance—feel the complexity of things and we know that there are beacons that guide us, help us make our way. In that sense, he doesn't understand me. But he is dear, and beautiful, and doing very well in his hotel business, so don't worry."

But Henry did worry, and felt he had to prepare himself, when he did see Caroline and talked with her, for a metamorphosis— or was it a mutation? The evolution had been from Danny-Caroline, absolutely perfect marriage, to Danny-Caroline, less than absolutely perfect marriage, to Danny-Caroline. . . . Could it be that she was actually unhappy?

He put back the letters and wished that the next hour, sixty everlasting minutes, would fragment into one second, allowing him to board his flight. He was itching with fatigue. Should he take another cup of coffee? Maybe a drink?

He would take a bottle of beer.

The middle-aged bartender managed to display what had been a sergeant's chevrons on the khaki shirt he wore as a retired civilian employee of the military center. The bartender was glad for a customer, glad for the opportunity to chat. "You press?"

"Yes. *Time* mag."

"I don't read *Time*."

"Oh? I'm sorry." Henry knew, from much experience, that in such situations as this the antagonist wished to be asked *why* he did not read *Time*. Henry would not give him the satisfaction. The bartender waited, then picked up the conversation again.

"Did you cover the Diem funeral?"

"There was no Diem funeral," Henry said, lighting one of his cheroots.

"Well, I'm not so sure he deserved one."

Henry bit. "Why?"

"He was persecuting the Buddhists."

Henry shuddered at the inevitability of a hundred such conversational encounters in the thirty days ahead of him before his return to duty in Saigon. He would need to develop little escape hatches. "My mother was a Buddhist."

"Oh? She oriental?"

"No, actually. Her mother and father were Irish Catholics, but when she was in college she spent junior year in New Delhi and was converted. I'm on my way to her funeral."

"Oh, I'm sorry. What happened?"

"She burned herself to death."

"Why?"

"To protest Diem." Henry put down the empty beer glass, thanked the bartender, and walked mournfully in the direction of the boarding area. In fact, he felt slightly better, awakened by the exchange. A little infield practice, he thought.

He did a lot of sleeping between Guam and Honolulu, San Francisco, New York. But when he landed at Idlewild Airport he began to suspect that his fatigue might have another cause than merely the very long hours he had spent awake in the last week in Saigon. And he didn't want to see Caroline until he was well.

It was too late to see a doctor, but he called Miss Allison at *Time,* who did everything for the magazine's foreign correspondents, and told her he might be sick. She told him to call in the next morning. She would tell him who to see, where, and at what time. "Symptoms?" she asked.

"Just total fatigue, can't seem to shake it."

"Maybe you've picked up mononucleosis."

And yes, that was what he had picked up.

For one week he would be an outpatient of Lenox Hill Hospital, taking antibiotics and Vitamin B shots, drinking lots of water, getting lots of sleep. He should be fine in about a week. A week! Twenty-five percent of his leave.

He would not go to Greenwich until he was fit. And he would not tell Caroline that he had been one week in New York without calling. Let alone Danny.

Twenty-one

I T WAS ON THE FIFTH DAY of Henry's stay in New York that he saw the *Herald-Tribune*'s obituary on Giuseppe Martino. Henry learned details about Danny's employer he hadn't known before. Giuseppe Martino had immigrated as a very young man to New York, went to work at age fourteen as a busboy at the Fifth Avenue Hotel, left New York to fight in the First World War, returned to Chicago, formed a syndicate, built a hotel . . .

And so on. He was the sole known stockholder of Martino Enterprises. The only surviving member of his large family was Angelina Martino of Phoenix. The funeral would be at St. Agnes Church on Forty-third Street and Lexington Avenue, at 11 A.M. on Wednesday.

Tomorrow. Henry went to the telephone and called his sister.

She was overjoyed to hear from him. "You said you had a leave coming up soon but you never gave the exact dates!"

He didn't tell Caroline when he had arrived. He gave the impression he had just got to town: "I saw the clipping this morning on Mr. Martino. Was it sudden?"

"He lived four, five days after the stroke."

"Was he seeing people?"

"Danny went to the hospital—he called for Danny. But there wasn't any conversation. It was good that Danny could hold his hand."

"Yes. Danny okay?"

"Yes, he's fine. When will you come to us?"

"You'll be at the funeral. Shall I go to Greenwich after that?"

"You will go to Greenwich this afternoon. At the latest."

Henry felt better.

Giuseppe Martino was hardly a member of the family, so the death of the eighty-four-year-old did not dampen the spirits of the house. Uncle Henry was a great favorite of the children, and Henry was there to play with them when they came back from school. He went with the two oldest to catechism class at St. Catherine's, Riverside, nearby. Sitting behind the children in the large new church with its modernist stained-glass windows, Henry was reminded by the nun that the twenty docile but animated children sitting in front of him with their catechism books were actually thought to be capable of sin. "Jesus died for all our sins. That means your sins too, Tommy. And don't just stare at me, trying to look like an angel. You have probably sinned at least twice since breakfast. Right, Tommy?"

"Right, sister."

"And you, Emily. Have you been patient and helpful to your sisters and brothers?"

Emily giggled.

"I thought so," said Sister Aloysius, her whole face a doleful frown. "You see—we all commit sins. Now we will say one Our Father and one Hail Mary, and I will see you next week. Don't forget to say your prayers at night and in the morning."

The children scurried out, Emily and Tommy into the backseat of their mother's station wagon. Henry sat in front with his sister. The children chattered and giggled, and when the car drove up to the entrance of the house after a short drive, they threw themselves out of the car and ran at full gallop into the large, gabled house to which a wing had been attached since Henry last saw it, nine months and one baby O'Hara earlier.

It was cold and windy, the trees were bare, the Sound gray. Caroline fastened the brake. "You look tired, Henry, and thin. We'll have to coddle you." She kissed him on the cheek.

Not the time to talk to her, Henry decided, returning her kiss with a playful hug.

Danny was, by contrast, very talkative. He had three times filled up his own glass with gin and tonic before dinner, and forced Henry to have a second. After dinner he ignored Caroline, who nursed a single glass of wine as she knitted. Danny spoke at unconfined length about the political situation. "I don't see how they can beat JFK next year. It actually looks as though the GOP will put up Barry Goldwater. Suicide time, right, Henry?"

"I don't know. Kennedy's got a lot of—"

"I mean, Goldwater will scare people to death. He's thought of, by an increasing number of people, as a wild man. Look at Vietnam. I mean, what would 'President Goldwater' do there? Well, Henry, Vietnam—you're on. Tell us about Vietnam. . . . Though come to think of it, since both of us"—he nodded at Caroline—"read *Time* magazine every week, I guess we both know what you think about— Is everything we read in *Time* about Vietnam something you wrote?"

"Well, there's the editorial—"

"Well, sure." Danny poured himself another glass of wine. "There's that, of course, editing at headquarters. There always is."

Henry decided to stray from the subject. "Speaking of editorial processing, how active was Mr. Martino in the affairs of the company?"

"Not at all. Last couple of years, I doubt he knew where he had hotels."

"Well, Danny, now that he's gone, who'll get the stock? His sister, the old lady in Phoenix?"

"Angelina?" He laughed. It was a little raucous, Henry thought, that laugh. "Giuseppe couldn't *stand* Angelina. I'm sure he made some arrangement to make sure she'd be comfortable. But give her the stock?"

"Well, who *does* get the stock?" Caroline asked the question.

Danny's face turned grave. For a moment he was silent. "Nobody knows. Probably some foundation, with the voting stock kept separate. Maybe a self-perpetuating board of directors, that kind of thing."

"When will it be known?" Henry asked.

Danny sighed. "I just have no idea how these things work. Giuseppe did all his legal work with Lombardo Cellini, and after he died, with Lombard Junior. He'll be at the funeral." He paused. "I think it's perfectly okay for me to ask him. You know, ask him about the voting stock, who gets it. After all, I am accountable to the board of directors of Martino Enterprises, which means right now I answer to Giuseppe's chauffeur, cook, maid and valet. Yes, I'll ask tomorrow. When do you go back to Saigon, Henry?"

Henry told him he'd be back inside of a month, and that during his stay he intended to spend time in Washington talking with people at the State Department and with Indochina experts at Georgetown. "You've never been to the Far East, Danny. Why don't you and Caroline come on over? Exciting things are happening in Tokyo. I could meet you there for a few days."

"Take Caroline away from the kids? She'd faint with longing. Might as well propose she go around the world in a sailboat. Well," he laughed heavily, "at least in a rocking sailboat it wouldn't be all that easy to create more little O'Haras." Henry stole a glance at his sister. She didn't look up.

"Tell you what I'm thinking." Danny now seemed truly interested. "What I'm thinking—I haven't told this to you, Caroline—what I'm thinking is maybe to run for the Senate. Now listen." Danny stood up and walked over to the fireplace, placing his right arm on the mantelpiece.

It was rather a heroic pose, Danny thought. He looked over at Caroline. She had resumed knitting.

"I don't care what they say. Ken Keating is vulnerable. This is a *Democratic* state. Keating beat Irving Ives in fifty-eight, so who *couldn't* beat Irving Ives—Wallace Beery? Ken has had his day in the sun, predicting that stuff about Castro and the Soviet missiles. So, he had a pretty good informant, I grant that, and he milked the hell out of the missile crisis a year ago. But really, he's going too far. You know his last thing, don't you?"

"About how the Soviets left a missile or two in Cuba?"

"Yeah. Well, he's getting close to kook time. And there's been a solid reversal of public sentiment. The John Birch Society has done a lot to discredit anticommunism. So I figure this: If Rockefeller pulls out of Albany and beats Goldwater for the GOP nomination, there'll be a serious fight for the White House, and Keating might have a chance to slide back in. But if it's Goldwater versus JFK, Keating's got a problem. And that problem could be—"

"You?" Henry volunteered.

"That's one way to put it. A better way is, 'Me, FDR's grandson.'"

"What about the problem of financing a senatorial campaign, Danny? You're not a political figure."

"I don't think financing is going to be one of my worries."

This time Caroline met Henry's glance.

Twenty-two

HENRY WAS BACK at the same PX in Guam where he had bought the forty-dollar cognac. He recalled the genuine pleasure he had given a couple of his *Time/Life* colleagues and a few old friends with his forty-dollar bottle. He amused himself recalling Danny's theatrical whiff from the glass. What was it about the presidency of Martino Enterprises, Henry wondered, that had caused Danny to put on such airs? He had always behaved naturally. In the army, at Yale, even at Nice—naughty-natural. But affected? More and more, Henry thought, Danny was becoming Mr. FDR's grandson. A seigneurial afflatus. Born to rule. And now, at age thirty-eight, he had the U.S. Senate in mind. Henry thought a great deal about Danny, even as he attempted, for some reason, to think as infrequently as he could about Danny. But however he might manage that, there was no way to think infrequently about Caroline—which ended up with thinking a lot about Danny.

Caroline was becoming cloistered. The right word? Yes, but the unfortunate word, given the now near-strident hostility Danny showed for the Catholic Church. It was plain to Henry that the intensity of her involvement with the Church was a measure of her alienation from Danny, or, rather, his from her. The Church asked nothing of Caroline that imposed at all on Danny, save whatever restrictions on sexual congress affected the size of the family desired by both parents. Henry was made overpoweringly sad as he thought about it, what seemed the impending destruction of what had seemed a perfect union. He found himself flirting with the wish that Caroline had never come near a Catholic priest. But then he was forced to ask himself whether he was sorry his own life had been saved—by Brother Ambrose, a Catholic monk. And, finally, he forced himself to ask the question: Could it all be Danny's fault? Was Caroline responsible in some way he hadn't detected?

Meanwhile, Henry was pleased fully to have recovered his energy. He pondered whether to buy another bottle of the forty-dollar cognac. Henry would never engage in such an extravagance merely for himself. If he bought it, it would be to give to somebody. But who? Henry Cabot Lodge? General Big Minh?

. . . Than Koo? He paused. Koo liked the wine they sometimes shared at dinner in the field. And once Henry had offered him Scotch, which he had taken, perhaps for the first time—he had refused it during their inspection trip of the hamlets.

But no. Not a forty-dollar bottle of cognac for a twenty-two-year-old Vietnamese boy. Well, no, Henry should stop thinking of him in that way, never mind that he continued to look like a sixteen-year-old. Than Koo was a grown man, a college graduate, a skilled interpreter, a shrewd and resourceful sleuth wonderfully skillful in ferreting out newsworthy tips and information useful to a correspondent. And, Henry allowed himself to think it in as many words, Koo was a very graceful, arrestingly attractive biological specimen. No doubt the Vietnamese ladies lusted after him, though come to think of it, he never saw Than in feminine company, but then he was wholly devoted to his work. He felt an impulse quite alien, distinctive, stir within him. He did not analyze it, but it moved him. He suspected it was such a feeling as fathers have for their sons.

He placed the bottle in the trolley. He would give it to Koo on his birthday. Or before that, if Ho Chi Minh surrendered to Big Minh. Fuck, Henry thought. By the time North Vietnam gave up, the cognac would be worth eighty dollars.

He boarded the plane. It was an improvement over the troop carrier that had taken him from Vietnam to Guam. The government was now chartering conventional 707s. It was after midnight, Guam time. The plane was not full. It carried perhaps fifty men, a half-dozen women, one of them Marguerite Higgins of the *Herald-Tribune*. Henry occupied the aisle seat in the first row and could stretch his legs outside the bulkhead. He dozed.

What was it, one hour, two hours later, the shove on his shoulders?

He looked up. It was a steward. Evidently he hadn't wanted to turn on the overhead lights—too many people sleeping; everybody was sleeping, Henry guessed woozily. But the steward's flashlight shone *right into Henry's eyes,* causing him to blink and pitch his head forward. He reached up with his hand, an effort to deflect the light.

"What's going on?" His voice sounded testy.

He heard the shocked voice wrestling with the words.

"Kennedy. President Kennedy. Shot. Dead."

Henry yanked at his seat belt, stood up, one steadying hand on the bulkhead, the other on the shoulder of the steward.

"What did you say?"

He just nodded, as in a daze, moved to ease Henry's hand away from his shoulder, and stepped forward to the next row of seats. There he shook a sleeping soldier. Henry stared at this man, transformed into a death courier. He was mouthing the words when suddenly all the lights in the large cabin flared up and the voice of the captain came through the loudspeaker.

"Ladies and—" No, that wasn't right. There was a little static, the sound of the voice clearing itself. "I have news. The radio reports that President John F. Kennedy is dead. Shot by a sniper in Dallas. I'll fill you in when more details come in. Ladies and gentlemen"—the captain had recovered his bearing—"the President of the United States is dead."

The passengers were instantly awake, mostly mute, were staring at one another, repeating, "Dead? . . . dead . . . dead?" And going on to, "How? Who did it?"

After what seemed an eternity the captain's voice came on again. "The President's body has been taken to Air Force One. A judge has administered the oath of office. Lyndon B. Johnson has been sworn in as the thirty-sixth President of the United States."

The steward and the stewardess were summoned to the pilot's cabin. They emerged with instructions to open the bar, in the captain's words, "to give everybody anything they want." Henry turned to Marguerite Higgins. He could think only to say, "It's a hell of a story, isn't it."

"Yes," she said. She made it plain she didn't want to talk about it.

Henry had to talk with someone. He made his way to the seats opposite where an army captain, a glass of Scotch in his hand, was staring down at his drink. Henry couldn't think what to say, and could not believe it when he found that he had actually spoken the words, "Did you know him?"

The captain looked at him, startled.

"Sorry. I meant, Did you ever lay eyes on him?"

The captain shook his head. "No. But my father did. Dad was on the PT boat with the President."

So it went during the long four hours. Before the plane landed, a man named Lee Harvey Oswald had been arrested.

Henry walked down the gangway, shielding his eyes from the bright sun. Than Koo was there. His face was stern.

"Now Americans will know how we felt." Henry had never before heard Koo sound bitter.

They shook hands. Than Koo took the typewriter from Henry. They walked silently into the terminal. The whole airport was silent, except that over the loudspeaker an organ played sacred music. It was a more resonant stillness than that of twenty days earlier when Diem was killed. Even the dispatcher out front hailed the cabs without blowing on his whistle. What mattered was decorum, even as decorum sometimes matters on the battlefield.

Book Three

Twenty-three

BEFORE LEAVING on his trip into the northern sector, Henry slipped a sheet of paper into his typewriter and addressed a cable to Richard Clurman, his boss. He knew Dick well and trusted him. But he didn't want to reveal the nature of his anxiety—not to Dick, not to anyone. The tangled domestic situation had something of a scandal value: Danny O'Hara was bordering on being a public figure now, having quietly advertised his availability for the Democratic nomination for Senator.

When Bobby Kennedy, nine months after the assassination of his brother, announced that he would seek the Democratic nomination in New York, Danny was grown up enough to get the message, which was, roughly, Get lost. But, having ventured into the race, Danny was widely accepted as a political contender, the young, glamorous hotel tycoon, grandson of the most towering figure in United States politics—well, there were those who felt that John F. Kennedy, for all that he had only one thousand days in office, had moved FDR over on the historical stage.

Still, Danny had got a fair amount of publicity, and in some of it a reference could be found to his brother-in-law, Henry Chafee, whose own reputation as a dogged and lucid foreign correspondent was rising as the U.S. commitment in Vietnam occupied more and more of the public's attention. Dick Clurman would notice it if Henry spoke of family problems, because, among other things, Clurman noticed everything.

So Henry wrote to him: "I'm a little ashamed, and also a little sorry, to be asking to go home after only fifteen months. But if it works out, I'd like a tour in Washington or New York, or for that matter, anywhere in the States, New York being best. The reason for this request is personal, but it has to do, also, with the feeling that I need to whiff firsthand U.S. air on the whole Vietnam business. So much has happened, between the death of Diem and the Tonkin Bay business in August and then LBJ's bombing of North Vietnam installations. I could use time at home to sharpen my perspectives.

"I'm about to take off for Hoile Lang Miet. ARVN maintains a small unit there, and the gooks keep up sniper fire, even though the area has been swept three or four times. It's a good illustration of what we need to get a handle on: If ARVN doesn't succeed in absolute pacification, then we have a situation in which a single Vietcong sniper can keep a platoon of ARVN immobilized. I'll try to get you some good copy on this."

What accelerated Henry's thinking on the request to go back had been yesterday's letter. Caroline had closed by saying, "There is something going on, something of a corporate nature I don't understand, and Danny is not about to explain it to me, but he is on the phone what seems endlessly, mostly to Cutter Malone and to Mr. Martino's lawyer. He is terribly distracted, and leaves home sometimes for periods of four or five days without letting me know that he's going or when he's coming back. If I need him (I try not to bother him) I have to call his office and try to track him down. Say a special prayer for Danny, as I think he needs help.''

Henry was not a churchgoer but he believed in prayer, and did as his sister requested, except that his prayer sought help not for his brother-in-law but for his sister.

He got up and walked over to the air conditioner to turn it off. It would stay off for as long as he was away. Now the usual plunge into the hot, wet air of Saigon. Always he would put on his sunglasses—that helped to prepare him psychologically for the shock of moving from fairly dry 80-degree air to very wet 100-degree air.

He walked, briefcase and typewriter as ever in hand, to the driveway outside the office building, now guarded by two ARVN soldiers with automatic rifles.

Than Koo was ready, the baggage was in the station wagon. They made their way through the mopeds and motorbikes and jeeps and trucks, through security at the airport, and boarded the plane. Once again Henry found himself in Hué.

Nobody was a better guide in Hué than Than Koo. On the other hand, at this point Henry was willing to say that nobody was a better guide anywhere than Than Koo. In the past year he had become fluent in English. He and Henry still spoke together in French, but only out of habit. Beginning in the spring, Henry had given his dispatches to Koo to read and pass judgment on. Henry admired the shrewd appraisals. From time to time Koo would recommend including this or that datum, or putting greater (or lesser) stress on this or that development. He remembered the deferential smile on Koo's face when months earlier he had returned the dispatch in which Henry wrote of the ascendancy of Tran Kim Tuyen as the new security head. "Tran will get nowhere," Koo said simply. "Nhu does not trust him." A few weeks later, Tran was deposed.

Two hours after landing in Hué, they checked in at Lang Miet. It was a "strategic hamlet," in the formal designation. But in the past year its resident military population had evolved from a single soldier per hamlet to a full platoon. This was the dismaying change in equilibrium on which Henry wanted to report.

He was given a hut to share with an ARVN lieutenant, a wiry young grizzled veteran of three years in the field. His name was Tu Da, and Henry was gratified that he spoke French. This, Tu recounted, was his third tour of duty at Hoile. "The first time I was here with two soldiers, we were told to hunt down a sniper who, at night, was firing into the village rather lackadaisically. I got the picture after talking to a dozen villagers. They contradict themselves, you know. But it came down to this. Over a couple of weeks, this sniper had fired forty, fifty rounds of rifle fire."

Lieutenant Tu's face was grim now as he described the demoralizing effect of this random firing into Hoile. "It meant that after dark no one could walk from any place in the village to any other place because there was always the possibility of a stray bullet. Have you ever been in London?"

"Yes," Henry said.

"It must have been like that in London at the time of the V-2 rockets, you agree?"

Lieutenant Tu, it transpired, had learned recent European history from a Frenchwoman who had fought in the resistance in Bordeaux during the war. Tu spoke with animation about the great events in England, France and Belgium in the closing months of the war.

"So your mission when you first came was what?" Henry asked, taking notes on his pad.

"To find the bugger."

"Did you?"

"Oh yes. My men and I hid out late in the afternoon, nicely concealed. The hills surrounding Lang Miet are of course ideal for the single, hidden sniper. But I calculated that he was firing from between one hundred and one hundred and fifty meters away, so we took stations two hundred meters back, and waited. It was a good wait; we saw nothing on the first night. But on the second night I heard a shot. It came in at about ten o'clock, but a little closer to me than to my corporal over on the left. So I began to crawl toward him, hoping he would keep firing. I knew that my corporal would be advancing from his other side. Well, we were successful."

"You caught up with him?"

"Oh yes," Lieutenant Tu said, drawing deeply on his cigarette. "Yes, I crawled up to within firing range, made out his profile and fired a bullet into the back of his head. We searched him, no papers; usual thing. He was maybe nineteen years old."

"Mission completed?"

"Well, Mr. . . . Chafee?"

Henry nodded, Yes, that was his name.

"Yes, *that* mission was completed, and I went back and joined my unit, and exactly five days later we had radio word from the chief here: another sniper. Exactly the same fucking thing. So the captain sent me back, not with three men, but six men. Our mission now was not to kill him on the spot, but to track him back to the village or the military unit he came from.

"So we did. Just after daybreak the sniper headed back; walked from the edge of the field, coming out of the forest, across the field, into Khe Sanh, several kilometers to the east. He was wearing black pajamas. We were on his tail.

"How would you like the assignment, Mr. Chafee, of isolating one twenty-year-old Vietnamese from a band of thirty or forty of about the same age? Most of them wearing pajamas? Exactly. So, what we did was plant one of our men in the village, to try to ferret out the Vietcong insider."

"Any luck?" Henry was writing swiftly.

"If you want to call it that. Our man reported after a month that he figured the Vietcong cadre had maybe four people in it."

"So you arrested them all?"

"Hell, we shot them all. The trouble was that two months later the sniper fire resumed. So this time the captain sends a full platoon with orders to go through the four villages that surround Lang Miet, offer rewards, make threats, that whole business. We've been doing that for over four weeks."

"Successful?"

"Well, we've lined up a lot of suspects, shot a bunch of them, sent some of the kids to a prisoner camp. But as of a week ago— the sniper firing again. So we have no alternative. We've got to keep men here and go after the snipers, one by one."

"Will you permit me to go with one of your sentries?"

"Risky business, Mr. Chafee."

Henry did not comment. Instead he asked, "Will any of to-night's sentries speak French?"

Tu paused for a moment, his mind going down the duty roster. "No."

Than Koo spoke. "I will accompany you, Mr. Chafee."

"No, Koo. As they say in the States, this is beyond the call of duty."

Koo smiled. "If you do not take me along, I will follow you fifty meters behind. That would be more dangerous for me, and I would not be very useful to you as a translator."

Henry turned to Tu. "Okay?"

He cocked his head up, snuffed out his cigarette. "That's up to you."

Shortly before dark Henry and Than Koo applied the blackface, beginning at the hairline down to below the neck, and then on their hands. They were each handed a carbine. Henry had his own binoculars. The duty soldier was a corporal, Vo Dung. Lieutenant Tu briefed the three stalkers, indicating the positions they should take while awaiting sniper fire.

They filed out at dusk, gratefully feeling the relief of a fallen sun. They made their way through the field, then into the wood, climbing up the gentle hill, headed for the hollow dug up over a year earlier behind the far end of the forest. They carried three days' supply of food. One sentinel stood watch, the other two lay in the hollow. The silence was total.

Henry, on watch at midnight, stared at the stars. He wondered, might he—*conceivably*—succeed in identifying the Arno star? The star that, twenty years ago, had guided him and Danny in the assault against the Nazis? At Hué, he calculated, their position was approximately twenty degrees north latitude. Twenty years earlier when he and Danny had fixed their eye on a star to guide them, the north latitude was more like fifty. Henry had never paused to study the star cycles, but he had a good eye for configurations, and, yes, he thought he spotted it! Just there, under

Cassiopeia and to the right. What were those twenty years in the lifetime of a star? So brief as not to be susceptible to measure. For Henry those twenty years, he hoped, had worked a decisive change in him. It was inconceivable to him that his courage, if tested, would now fail him.

Those years had certainly changed Danny. Though he wondered, Was Danny, after all, the same person now that he had always been? Henry remembered his agony on learning that Danny had put him up for a decoration. At the time, he succeeded in putting the episode behind him, as nothing more than an act of misdirected playfulness—pulling the tail of history. He was no longer so certain. There was a trace of cruelty in what Danny had done—after saving him first from a court-martial, then from dying of a self-inflicted wound.

Henry put it out of his mind and forced himself to listen attentively for any sound of rifle fire. For any sound at all, for that matter.

It came toward the end of the watch, a single rifle shot. It appeared to have been fired by someone directly ahead of them, somewhere between their own position and the hamlet. If the sniper was in the forest, he might have needed to climb up a tree to get the desired angle. Either that, or he might have been prepared merely to fire up into the air, satisfied that the bullet would fall down into the compound, even as a rocket would come down. It would be almost as lethal brought down by gravity as at the end of a bullet's life, fired horizontally.

He looked to the corporal, instantly awake, instantly in charge.

Vo Dung said nothing, not a word; there was only the incessant sound of the crickets. Vo simply moved up out of the hollow and began to make his way forward, traveling at a snail's pace, body bent over, his torso horizontal to the ground. Above all, sound was the enemy. Henry waited until the distance between him and the corporal was about twenty meters. Before moving forward, following Vo, he turned his head and whispered to Than Koo, *"Keep same distance."*

At this rate, Henry thought, it would be an hour or more before Vo Dung reached the middle of the forest, two hours before he got to the end of it, where the field outside the village began. The night was dark but not black; visibility extended the distance between him and Vo. Looking up at the trees, most of them dense with foliage, he could see only up to where the branches began. He was sweating now and it seemed almost as though the surrounding trees were weeping into him. If the sniper was perched on a tree branch it would be impossible to spot him until he was directly overhead.

Henry began to conclude that this was a mad, suicidal mission, but then remembered that Lieutenant Tu had twice apprehended a sniper. They had to hope that the sniper would be incautious. At least they knew this, that he would eventually have to crawl away in order to return to his own village. Maybe that was the witching hour.

When would it be? Nearer to dawn? But that of course would depend on how frequently the sniper would fire his rifle. The conventional pattern had been a half-dozen shots in the course of the night, though the psychological impact of the earlier shots greatly exceeded the later ones when the villagers, except for the guards at the gate, were asleep. Henry felt the full, raw taste of terror. It was so much easier to do that—to *feel* the danger—in the dark. Especially when crawling, a few inches at a time, in total silence, the ear blocking out the crickets' monotonic chirp.

A shot rang out again. The man in front of him rose and began to run. Vo must have spotted the sniper and elected to charge him. Henry stood up and turned his head back to alert Than Koo. But he did not see him. He turned and walked back a few paces. Still no Than Koo. He began to jog back, even as the exchange of fire ahead began. He was carrying his carbine. Sheltered by such noisy cover, Henry could afford to call out. It was an audible husky whisper. "Koo! Koo!" He stumbled over a body. He threw himself down.

"Koo. *Koo!*" He shook Koo's head, slapped him on the cheeks. He knew suddenly the presence of the killer. He yelled a strident savage yell, swung the butt of his carbine with a boxer's swiftness at the human frame in front of him, felt the heavy thud, righted the automatic and fired three rounds. He reached now into his pocket and yanked out the flashlight. The pajama-clad young man lay gasping for air, his right hand clutching a large knife. Henry fired into his mouth. Then he shined the light on Than Koo and saw the blood on a throat slashed ear to ear. Koo's lips were parted, framing a disoriented smile, one eye peering to one side, the other eye in the other direction. When Corporal Vo arrived on the scene Henry was on his knees, his hand on Than Koo's chest, sobbing quietly, his flashlight still lit.

Twenty-four

D R. LILA O'HARA hadn't ever met Giuseppe Martino. Never mind, said Dr. Lawrence Callard, the director of the Franklin Delano Roosevelt Library at Hyde Park. "I still think it would be a good idea for you to attend his funeral."

"Why? There's no relative, according to the *New York Times,* except an old lady who lives in Phoenix. Whatever Martino has left us in his will, he's left us."

"Yes, I know, I know. But he gave us fifty thousand each year for the past four years; that's a lot of money, and of course we hope to hit it big in the will. There'll be some press there, and your brother is a central figure in Martino Enterprises—yes, Lila, you must go."

Lawry Callard knew that from time to time it was necessary

quite simply to tell Lila what to do. And it was of course a little easier to handle her now that the grande dame was gone. It wasn't that Lila had ever taken to going across the lawn to cry on the shoulders of Grandmama. At first Dr. Callard had been a little skeptical about taking on the staff a granddaughter of the President, but Lila's credentials were excellent, and the request from her grandmother was pretty pointed. He really had no alternative. In such matters, one didn't say no to Eleanor Roosevelt.

It had been difficult at first to acclimate to Lila's officiousness. She was a hard and intelligent worker and no assignment was too tedious for her. On the other hand, any assignment given her became a Lila project, and the orientation was not always exactly as Lawry Callard had intended, though he would admit, if pressed, that Lila's ideas were sometimes inventive and useful.

A few months ago Dr. Callard had had a query from a historian at Oxford. He wanted to know whether Colonel McCormick's *Chicago Tribune* had ever hinted at a liaison between President Roosevelt and Marshal Pétain—he had addressed the query to the *Chicago Tribune* and got back a letter from the successor to Robert R. McCormick, who manifestly sought to keep the colonel's spirit alive: "The files of the *Chicago Tribune* are not copious enough to record all the iniquities of Franklin Delano Roosevelt. Perhaps you can apply to the Marshall Plan for aid in retaining a researcher." Dr. Callard was amused, Lila not at all. But she went diligently to work, reading through every reference to President Roosevelt published in the *Chicago Tribune,* in the Hyde Park files, over a period of thirteen years. She found nothing that linked FDR to Pétain. She undertook, on her own, to write to the Oxford historian to ask what had been his lead in suggesting that there had been a back channels contact. She heard in turn that in one of his numerous appeals, Pétain had hinted that he had had an understanding with the American President. . . .

So: Lila would go to the funeral.

There weren't many people at St. Agnes's Church. Indeed everyone there was an employee of Martino Enterprises or a member of the family of an employee. Danny was afraid that someone, he couldn't quite figure out who, since he himself had made the funeral plans, would suggest that he should intone a eulogy. He was relieved to hear from Caroline that in a Catholic funeral service, eulogies are not generally given.

So the little assembly of fifty or sixty people sat through a sung mass, there was some conversation outside the church, and everyone went home. Henry joined the O'Haras—Danny, Caroline, and Lila—for lunch at Voisin restaurant, to which Giuseppe Martino had introduced Danny shortly after he came to work—an elegant, quiet, old-world restaurant in the Sixties, serving French cuisine. Danny ordered a Scotch on the rocks, Henry joined him, the others ordered coffee and juice.

After they had looked at the menu, Lila addressed her brother. "When are they going to make the will public?"

Danny looked up at his sister and noticed that Henry and Caroline were looking at him. "Oh well, I asked Lombardo Cellini. There are apparently some formalities to go through, but he said that probate would probably release the general contents of the will within a couple of weeks."

Lila made plain her interest. "How much for Hyde Park, Danny? Any idea?"

"Well no, not exactly. I hope the entire estate will continue to give you people the fifty grand you've been getting."

"Is that *all*?" Lila was clearly put out. "In one of the letters he sent to Grandmother a couple of years ago, enclosing the annual gift, Mr. Martino said something about how he would make a 'significant' bequest when he—I think he said—went 'on to another world.' Sound like him?"

"Eh, yes, Giuseppe was given to very sentimental formulations. But, Lila, you ask if that is a significant bequest? Fifty thousand dollars a year? At, say five percent, it takes a million dollars of capital to spin off that much money. A million dollars is still a significant amount of money, even if Grandfather did everything he could to diminish the value of the dollar." He laughed. Much more robustly than Lila laughed, but her brother's analysis satisfied her. Yes, a million dollars was a lot of money.

.   .   .   .

Lawrence Callard had taken to assigning Lila to answer letters
addressed to the Library asking questions to which the response
could be indicated by Dr. Callard in a word or two, leaving it to a
subordinate to explicate. It struck Lila, now familiar with her
grandfather's modus operandi, that Dr. Callard was imitating her
grandfather's ways. On the other hand, she reasoned correctly,
that probably was the way of all busy men—to indicate pithily
what was to be replied, leaving it to someone else to fill in the
language.

This was a letter addressed to the Hyde Park Fund by a lawyer
in Poughkeepsie, New York. The lawyer wrote to say that he had a
client who wished to establish a fund that would concern itself
with the environment in the area around the Hudson River, in
the general vicinity of Hyde Park. The thinking was to give the
charitable enterprise the name "Hyde Park Nature Fund," and
the lawyer wished to inquire whether the trustees of the Hyde
Park Fund would raise any objections to the similarity between
the two names.

In handwriting, Dr. Callard had written, "Tell them why nix."

Lila knew Lawry's mode of thinking. She had reached the
point of understanding fully even instructions given thus laconi-
cally, instructions others might have found inscrutable. Her assignment was to write a tactful letter to the lawyer explaining why
the confusion of a "Hyde Park Nature Fund" was not something
the Hyde Park Fund would put up with. "Tell them why nix" was
a way of saying, Forbid them to do it but be diplomatic about it.

So, later in the day—Lila would not rearrange the order of
things she had set out to do, unless it was an emergency—she
went over to the huge current reference section of the library
and searched out the New York State Corporation Index. She
went down the list—

Hyde Park Auto Service
Hyde Park Capital Fund, Inc.
Hyde Park Fund, Inc.
Hyde Park Funeral Home, Inc.
Hyde Park Pharmacy, Inc.

She paused. Hyde Park Capital Fund?

What was that? If it was okay to set up something called the Hyde Park Capital Fund, why was it not okay to set up something called the Hyde Park Nature Fund?

Maybe the Hyde Park Capital Fund was so unrelated to FDR and the Hyde Park with which she was associated that confusions weren't possible. She needed to find out exactly what the Hyde Park Capital Fund *was*. She went to the Register of Corporations and looked under "Hyde Park Capital Fund." The reference book in hand was for the year 1963. She read, "Incorporated June 1959. Address, P.O. Box 1776, Grand Central Station, New York 10017. Incorporator, C. Malone. Capital, $1,000. Shares, par value 10 cents."

Cutter Malone? She had met him, a great friend of Danny's; an officer in Martino Enterprises.

She looked in the library to inspect the volume for 1962, but it wasn't there. She spoke to the librarian and learned that super-annuated corporation registers were thrown out at the end of the year. Lila went back to her office, looked through the Pough-keepsie telephone directory and dialed the number for the public library.

"This is Dr. O'Hara at FDR Library, Hyde Park. I wish to know if you have back copies of the Register of Corporations, New York State."

She was put through to a librarian.

No, they didn't keep the old Registers. A lot of lawyers kept them, but probably the best thing would be to go to Albany, to the Secretary of State's office. "They would have everything you'd want."

The following morning, Lila drove the sixty miles to Albany. The uniformed officer at the entrance to the capitol told her where to go. She knew the city well. She had explored the governor's mansion where her grandfather had held court, dauphin to the whole English-speaking world. Lila felt the pulsations of the modest city that had sent the governor on to the White House to save the day for democracy.

She entered the reference library and quickly confronted a file on a dusty shelf of Registers of Corporations going back through the years.

For 1962, the entry for the Hyde Park Capital Fund was indistinguishable from the entry for 1963. The same was so of the registers for 1961, 1960 and 1959, the year in which the Capital Fund was established.

She went now to the librarian. Her heart was beginning to pound. Where could she find a record of substantial transactions in New York corporations? She was directed to the Corporate Reference Service for the current year. "That service picks up transactions, filings, references, that kind of thing, to a corporation. For instance, transfers of shares usually require a stamp tax, and the Reference Service records stamp taxes paid, and the sums of money represented."

She was handed the reference manual and took it to a work desk. Her eyes scanned down the first-quarter report. There was no change. She turned to the second quarter.

"Hyde Park Capital Fund. Address, P.O. Box 1776, Grand Central Station, New York 10017. New York State Stamp Transfer Tax paid on 2,875,000 shares of Martino Enterprises, Inc."

She stared at the entry. She removed her glasses. She heard the librarian giving out instructions to someone, answering questions. She did not make out the words being spoken. She got up, finally.

"Is there a way to make a copy of a page in the Corporate Reference book?"

She was told to take the volume to the basement floor. "The fee is twenty-five cents per page."

Lila nodded, opening her purse.

"No. Downstairs. You pay downstairs."

She nodded, and walked off toward the staircase.

Twenty-five

PESQUITO has got to be the most optimistic human being in the western hemisphere."

"Umm."

"You know, I don't think you particularly care. You've got that thesis on your mind. What century was it written in?"

"Seventeenth. Cervantes died the same year as Shakespeare."

"And the way you tackle it, it might as well be this week's issue of—*Life* magazine. What were they doing in the seventeenth century that's so engrossing."

"Fucking."

Danny smiled, and leaned down and touched a kiss on her head. Then, his beer bottle in his left hand, he turned to Pesquito for the fourth time. "Damnit, Pesquito, you said you were *certain* we'd run into some good fish—you said sailfish, in fact—today. It's almost twelve o'clock. How far out are we?''

"Mabee ten, twelf kilometers."

"Is this the best spot? I can't imagine why else you'd choose it. It has got to be what, 110 degrees?" He tilted back the beer bottle. Maybe he'd look in on Augustino on the top deck. Why not?

He climbed the companionway of the 54-foot fishing launch. The trolling speed was a leisurely eight knots, 9.2 miles per hour, 14 kmh—approximately. He felt the wind in his face and the hot sun overhead. "Hey, Augustino, feesh? Soon? Beeg feesh?"

He got the *Sí, señor,* but Augustino did not smile, perhaps because he had no teeth. What he did was smoke. An old aluminum ashtray did heavy duty at the bottom of the control panel. The gauges had long since lost out to the weather, and Pesquito did not trouble to polish them, or the wood in which they were emplaced.

Danny thought to make conversation. "What is the range of this boat?"

Augustino looked up. "Raich?"

"Range. How many mi— how many kilometers can it go before we stop to take more . . . *gasolina?*"

Augustino nodded his head. He understood. He left the wheel and his cigarette, raised his two hands, all the fingers outstretched in his left hand, two in his right. "Seffen hours."

Danny acknowledged the information, decided it was too arduous, too hot, to pursue the conversation. At that point Pesquito's voice cried out from below, "*Strike! Strike!* Come, Mr. O'Hara, come!"

He turned and made his way down the companionway steps two at a time and saw the rod bent over, Pesquito's right foot on the transom, straining. *"Sit! sit!"*

Danny sat in the fighting chair and buckled himself in. Pesquito, though pitched forward by the diving fish, edged over and thrust the base of the rod into the receptacle rising from under Danny's crotch. Danny grabbed the rod with his left hand, and with his right made contact with the reel. "I got it, I got it!"

Florry had put down her book. She brought out a camera from her purse.

"Good, Danny, good!"

She looked up again when his rod line went slack and she saw the great swordfish thrash, all silver and blue, soar up toward the sky and then plunge down. "I got him too," she said, "got him, terrific!"

When they got back to the succulently air-conditioned suite they were wet with the heat but exhilarated. "You go ahead," Danny said to her, pointing to the shower. In a few minutes she came out, dressed in a light terry-cloth dressing robe, her hair tucked up into a white-towel bandana. She left the shower running. Danny, in undershorts, moved into the bathroom and stayed under the cool water a full two minutes. He came out, a towel wrapped around his loins. He was very pleased. "That was pretty out there, no? That was a lot of fun. Did you time how long it took?"

"At least twenty-five minutes," Florry said, stretched out on the bed, the top part of the bathrobe separated, her eyes half closed. "You got the hang of it in a hurry, Danny."

"Well," he lay down beside her, letting the towel fall to the side, "it isn't all that hard. Takes a little coordination. A certain amount of strength. Hell, I'm what, thirty-nine years old?" He looked down at his right arm, flexed it, and tweaked his protruding muscle with the fingers of his left hand. "Want to feel, Florry?"

"Not *that* muscle," she replied, her voice gone husky.

Good old Florry, Danny said to himself, easing his pelvis up toward her and, with his right hand, edging her head toward it. *She never waits for me, she's always there, willing, anxious, loving, soft, luscious. . . .* He was moaning now, his eyes closed. What a perfect day, and the whole evening stretched before them.

The Hotel Mirador was where the divers performed. The restaurant's thirty tables sat on a terrace one hundred feet above the waves that tore snarlingly into the base of the cliff at irregular but frequent intervals, momentarily raising the water level from inches above the coral ocean floor, when the wave ebbed, to eight or ten swollen feet. It was during those few precious seconds of elevation that the diver, plunging down off the edge of the cliff, could safely penetrate the water without hitting the jagged rock inches under its low-ebb surface.

It was cool now, and Danny wore a white linen coat and tie without complaint. They had wanted a Mexican meal, but the maître d' had looked blank when they started by ordering tamales and enchiladas and frijoles refritos, as though Mexican food were something people outgrew in their teens, certainly before they began patronizing the restaurant at the Hotel Mirador.

"Okay, okay. No tamales today." They ordered fish. Danny was talking about the growth of Acapulco. "I was here once before, yeah, I told you; I was fifteen, and there were only three hotels. We stayed at the Papagayo, three bucks per day including breakfast. I'm thinking of putting in a Trafalgar Hotel here. Either buy one and transform it or build one new. I wanted to talk to you about that."

Florry sipped on her wine and said she thought it would be a very good idea, why not?

"I had a nifty idea. What would you think of making Acapulco your home and taking a job in the hotel? Pretty much anything you liked in the hotel business."

Florida Carmela Huerta put down her fork. "Danny. You do know, because we have discussed it maybe one hundred times, that I am studying Spanish? That I am working on advanced work that will roll into graduate work and a dissertation not far down the line? That they might want me someday at Salamanca on the faculty, at some point, after I get my Ph.D.?

"Now I have a suggestion for you. Why don't you give up the hotel business and come and keep house for me while I study and teach? . . . Okay, I agree, that's not very funny. But you know that I love you very much. But you should know that I am not going to live the rest of my life as your Acapulco concubine."

She looked down at the table for a minute, and he could see the moisture in her eyes.

"We've edged up on the subject before." Florry did not look at Danny as she spoke. "If you want me to become Mrs. Daniel O'Hara, I will say yes, I will do that, I will put away my books—though I'll do my dissertation—and live with you. But not in Acapulco. In Greenwich. Or wherever your main residence is, if Caroline gets to keep Greenwich."

Danny didn't reply. He was grateful that, suddenly, all the floodlights on the cliffside had dimmed, arresting everyone's attention. A slim young olive-skinned man was poised on top of the cliff ledge, a spotlight on him. A second light trained on the roiling water twelve story-lengths below. The diver was waiting for just the moment when the water would be rising but had not yet quite reached maximum height. The diners held their breath. One wave, apparently all-enveloping, roared in. Danny tensed his muscles—but the diver let it pass. Seconds later he dove—and a half second before he made contact, a huge wave, bigger than its predecessor, roared in. The diners exploded in applause.

There was a pause at the table. Danny spoke. "I understand, Florry. I do. And you know how much I love you. But you know I have five children. And there's something else—"

"You're *his* grandson. And you might want to run for senator in 1968."

Danny did not reply.

"All right, Danny. I get your signal. Only just remember: *You're* not committed, *I'm* not committed."

"But I'm committed to taking care of your school bills. You know I wouldn't welsh on that—"

"I'm sure you wouldn't. And—shall we be grownups about it? —you get something in return. But you have a, what, transcendent commitment? Well, I don't. I don't need to make that any plainer, do I, Danny boy? Danny badboy?"

He smiled, taking her hand under the table.

"No. And, you know, me and Caroline—that may change. Who knows? Getting married more than once was certainly okay by my mother. And she's closer to 'him'—FDR—after all, than I am. So, who knows?''

He motioned to the waiter. And beckoned to Florry, ''Dessert?''

''Liqueur,'' she said. ''Crème de menthe, green, and coffee.''

''You ask for it, Florry. I like to hear you speak Spanish.''

Twenty-six

HARRIET CARBERRY, age thirty-five, had got married. Her husband—Giacomo Orsini—was not exactly what Harriet's friends would have guessed Harriet would choose as a husband. For one thing, he was a pianist, and Harriet had never, while at Smith, shown any particular interest in music, though she kept a photograph of Frank Sinatra on her wall right under the photo of Ronald Colman. And then Giacomo Orsini had no right arm. Harriet had sent a letter to her numerous friends, a letter she hoped would arrive before any newspaper notice of the betrothal.

". . . It's quite possible," the form letter read, "that you have heard him play. He is quite magnificent! If you have, then you know the truly miraculous thing about 'Jackie' (that is what they call him—I call him Giacomo) is that he is one-armed. Yes! A piano player with only a left hand! Like the great Paul Wittgenstein, who died in March. Maybe you never heard of him, the great left-handed pianist, brother of the famous philosopher? Ravel and Strauss wrote music just for him. Oh well, we never said a Smith education touched in at *all* bases, did we? Anyway, with Giacomo it's congenital, but he started as a little boy in Italy (his family didn't come here until just before the war), and I swear, well, you'll know for yourselves when you hear him play— with one hand he can accomplish more than some pianists with three hands. Musicians who have heard him play (he went through Juilliard) are so inspired by Giacomo that several have written, or have promised to write, *one-handed piano pieces!* dedicated to him! Aranjuez (the Spanish composer) wrote one for him just last year. It is very substantial, fifty-two minutes, and very beautiful. Maybe we can have a party one day soon (at Smith? At a reunion?—I'll write Polly and propose it!) and he will play it for all of us. Giacomo has been married before, it was a terrible mistake. If I had known him, I mean, even as a friend, I think I could have steered him away. There's a little girl, but she lives with her mother in Wisconsin. Anyway, our wedding will be 'private'—just his parents, his sister, my brother (did you know Mom died last year? What a saint!). But after that we will drive through New England so that as many of my friends as possible in that part of the world can meet Giacomo. And the month after, we'll drive through California so he can meet my western friends. Our permanent address is 100 West 75th, New York 10023, the phone is KL5-7223. I can't wait to see you again and for you to meet Giacomo. Thank you for sharing this special joy with—Your friend, Harriet."

Caroline bundled off a wedding present and wrote to say she would be delighted to meet "Giacomo/Jackie" whenever they passed by. She was surprised when, only two weeks later, Harriet rang. She was in Boston, she had planned to drive with Giacomo on a leisurely swing south, but he had got a call from his agent and would be performing in Dallas, replacing a pianist who had taken ill—"Giacomo played for the Dallas Music Development

Center two years ago and they loved him, so they're having him back." Under the circumstances, Harriet was going to drive by herself straight to New York, but if convenient, would have dinner and spend the night at Greenwich—"the last day of my honeymoon!" Of course, Caroline said, and the schedule was confirmed for the following day.

Danny groaned on being told Harriet would be there. "She's such a talkative old bag."

"In the first place," Caroline continued her knitting, "she is a very pretty woman, not an old bag. In the second place, yes, she talks, but she talks mostly about other people. About their concerns—"

"I suppose you will now tell me that to talk about other people is the Christian thing to do."

"Well, yes it is. Christian doctrine tells you to love your neighbor. Harriet loves her neighbor. She is bent on finding out how she can help her neighbor—well, her friends. She can't do that without asking about them. Asking about their family, their problems."

Danny continued reading the afternoon paper.

Caroline put down her knitting and went over to Suzy, the four-year-old playing in the corner of the room with her giant jigsaw puzzle. Caroline looked over her shoulder. Suzy was attempting to squeeze the rear end of the horse behind the head of a cow. She had begun to hammer down on the plywood piece.

"Not there, darling. Over there."

"I don't like it there."

"Well, that's where it belongs. Have you ever seen a cow with the tail of a horse?"

"Yuss."

"When?"

"Yussterday."

Caroline laughed, bent over and picked her up. "We have to go to bed now, darling. Go kiss your father good-night."

Danny looked up from the *New York Post*, tousled Suzy's hair, returned to the paper and said, "Good night, sweetie."

The following afternoon Margie called from the office. Danny had asked her to call, she said, to say that a business meeting would keep him so late in New York he would spend the night in town. Caroline thanked her. Danny had decided to give Harriet a wide berth.

Harriet brought presents for all the children, told the three youngest a ghost story during the children's dinner, kissed them all good-night and, accepting a glass of wine, sank back into an armchair, chattering first about the children and how beautiful and gratifying they were, and didn't Toby have a little bit of a temper? She then spoke about Giacomo and how wonderful it was to be married to someone she could not only love, but also admire. Caroline felt it coming, and it did.

"Now," Harriet said, "since Danny isn't here, it's really easier to talk. How is everything going?"

"Danny is distracted. His business—the hotels—takes a lot of time, and keeps him away. . . . On the other hand, you know, Harriet, it's probably not altogether a bad thing that he is away— I figured it out the other night. Last year he was gone a total of a hundred and twenty days—"

"About a third of the time." Harriet would file that datum, Caroline knew. "That means two plus days per week, average of, say, ten days per month."

"Well, I didn't figure it out that way. I counted the nights he spent away—away either from here or from the family when we're in Newport or Palm Beach. My point is that when he *is* here, he is not completely happy. He quarrels with me, and doesn't pay very much attention to the children, though I do think he has a sneaker for Suzy. So? Better he should be away one third of the time than the whole of the time."

"He's—talked about breaking up?"

"No. No, no. But when he is here he does perfunctory games with the children, plops down with the newspapers, magazines, occasionally a book. Drifts into his study and is on the telephone for as much as a half hour. If there is a guest, somebody he likes, or—let's face it—somebody who is influential and might be helpful if he runs for the Senate, his face lights up."

"Does he have a mistress?"

"Yes," Caroline said, turning her glass on its coaster.

"How do you know?"

"I think I'd probably have pieced it together from this and that. The occasional very discreet phone call—door closed, phonograph record on—the difficulty of tracking him down when he is away and I actually need to consult him—Toby's polio scare, for instance. I found a matchbox, cleaning out his jacket one day, from the Bel Air Hotel. Why should he pick up a match-box?—he doesn't smoke—at a hotel he doesn't stay at—the Bel Air is a competitor of the Trafalgar. But then—"

"Smoking gun?"

Caroline nodded. She bent her head down more sharply to her knitting. When she spoke her voice was unsteady.

"Yes. It was an anonymous letter." She laughed briefly. "You always think of anonymous letters, at least I do, as made up of snippets from newspapers of different-size type, different fonts, maybe a little ungrammatical, like 'WATCH FOR YOUR LIFE BECAUSE YOU WILL SOON MEET YOUR MMAKER.' Two M's in 'maker.' But this was really odd."

Caroline paused to think. Then, "Harriet?"

"Yes."

"Do you want to hear it?"

"God, yes."

Caroline put down her knitting, left the room, went into the hall, and in a few minutes was back, a sheet of paper and envelope in hand.

"The postmark is Berkeley, California. The letter is typewritten. It is even dated—March 1, 1965. Ready?"

Harriet poured another glass of wine. "Ready."

" 'Dear Mrs. O'Hara: You will perhaps be less resentful of my anonymity if you force yourself to answer the question, "Why *should* an informant, on such a mission as this, identify himself?" There are reasons why it does not make sense to divulge my identity, none that argue any use in doing so, let alone any obligation to do so.' "

Harriet whistled. "He sounds like Lord Chesterfield."

Caroline continued. " 'Your husband, Daniel O'Hara, has been—I use a Spanish idiom—"making house" with a young woman in Los Angeles. When Mr. O'Hara is in town, he spends the night with her at the Bel Air Hotel. Occasionally they travel together, as for instance to Acapulco not long ago. I cannot absolutely predict the intended arrangements between them, but the liaison has lasted two years.

" 'What is my purpose in writing to you? I am of the young generation who believe in women's rights. If a man betrays his vows, his wife should know it, as this will widen the choices she has: to ignore the infidelity, to confront her husband or to terminate the marriage.

" 'What is my proof? I am not in a position to give you proof— I am not, for instance, a freelance photographer—but even if I were, I'm not sure I'd be disposed to give it to you. It is this simple: If you wish proof, the next time your husband travels to Los Angeles, retain a private investigator to follow his movements. For your convenience, I enclose the relevant listings from the Los Angeles Yellow Pages directory. You will see there are a number of agencies ready to help you, should you wish to get professional help.' "

Caroline paused and Harriet spoke gravely. "Is that it?"

"No, actually. He adds a P.S. 'If your husband gives you a hard time and you want to slow him down, ask him what really happened to his mother's necklace the day before you were married.' "

"What's that all about?"

"I don't know. I dimly remember Rachel losing a necklace. It's hardly important." Caroline then held up the enclosure that came with the letter. "Here are the listings from the Yellow Pages."

Harriet's eyes stretched up, then down. She was silent. Then, "As Jackie—Giacomo—would say, What kind of a cat wrote that letter?"

Caroline picked up her knitting. Thelma came in. Dinner was ready.

The two women, seated in the candlelit dining room at one

end of the Sheraton table, had a problem trying to focus on other subjects while dinner was being served. But they made the effort, and Harriet talked about Giacomo and his practice routine, about the recording he would make next month of Ravel's "Study for a Left Hand," of Harriet's decision to apply for a job with an advertising agency in New York, to which she could bring the experience she had accumulated in Los Angeles. Caroline talked about the children, their schools, and about Henry, and the tragic death of his interpreter, who over the year they were together had become like a son. Both agreed that the situation in Vietnam was bad, but certainly, with the infusion of a quarter-million U.S. fighting men, the war would be soon over.

At last dinner was finished and they went back to the little living room. Harriet wasted no time.

"Have you any idea who wrote that letter? I don't mean what *person* wrote that letter, but what *kind* of person wrote it?"

"No. It's postmarked Berkeley. Sounds to me like an academic type, maybe a graduate student. But begin with the beginning: You've heard it. Do you doubt that what he says is true?"

Harriet shook her head. "No. I don't. What are you going to do? Have you decided?"

"Yes—I have decided. I mean, I have decided what should be done, and what I want done. What I can't be absolutely certain of is that I'll have the strength to do what I have decided to do. Is that too complicated, Harriet dear?"

"I understand what you are saying, but not what your decision is."

Caroline reached for her coffee cup. She spoke, it seemed, to the cup, not to Harriet. "I think there is a point in trying to do the 'right' thing. And for quite a few years now I have thought that the right thing continues to be—right—never mind what its appeal. I have a moderate amount of pride, and I'd satisfy it hugely if I changed the locks to this house before Danny comes in tomorrow. I could easily get the private eye in Los Angeles to lock up the legal case for me—that would be good economic footwork, right, Harriet? Then . . ."

"Then what?"

"Exactly. Then what? I get the house, maybe five thousand dollars a month. The children are without a father, I am without a husband."

Harriet began to speak. Caroline raised her hand. "Wait. You're about to run into the business of how can I sleep with a man who's sleeping with another woman. I don't pretend this is a so-what question. It's been rough, that part of it, since I found out. And it's for that reason, because it's rough, that I quickly had to come up with it. Meaning, to say to myself: I'll have to find the strength. I *know* what is the right thing. For my children, for me. And guess what, Harriet? For my husband. After this run with the lady in Los Angeles he may have got it out of his system. Granted, he may end up wanting a divorce, in which case there's nothing I can do about it. But both of us know, from personal experience but also from our reading, these things happen—and marriages survive. Not always, but sometimes. And . . ." Here Caroline needed her handkerchief, the tears streaming from her eyes. She had to pause before she could pronounce the words she wanted to speak. "I feel that if I do what God would want me to do, I can't be doing the wrong thing."

She had said it and now, her eyes dry, and she looked up at Harriet, and her eyes had back the old spark, and that little buoyant sense of detachment. Harriet extended her hand, Caroline took it.

Twenty-seven

LILA DIDN'T OFTEN press him so insistently, so over the telephone Danny said okay, okay, but why did Cutter Malone have to be there? Technical questions? Too technical for Danny? Okay, four o'clock, Union Club.

He buzzed Cutter. "Lila—my sister—has set up a meeting, absolutely insists you be there, she says it's something very important to her. She is my kid sister, you know. I wouldn't be surprised if it was some appeal centering on the FDR business, or maybe it has to do with her dissertation—yes, it's got to be that. Because I received the galleys last week with a covering note from her. Gibbon couldn't have been more excited when the *Rise and Fall* galleys came in. Maybe she'll put in to have us order a copy for every room in the Trafalgar chain, along with King James.

Anyway, she said it wouldn't take too long. Four o'clock, Union Club, *mañana. Hasta mañana,* Cutter."

His private line rang. Caroline. Did Danny plan to drive with her to Canterbury on Friday? Danny remembered—Tommy would be interviewed for admission to boarding school. Caroline said she thought his mother and father should be there for appearance's sake. "Seems to me the right thing to do," Caroline said, letting just an icicle into her voice. "And Canterbury—Kent, Connecticut—is exactly an hour and a half away."

"Friday. Friday the . . ."

"Friday the eleventh."

"Yes. I think I can change my schedule to make it. Put me down, yes."

"Thank you, Danny. I'll see you tonight."

"Yup. Say, Caroline, what's Lila so anxious to see me about in New York tomorrow?"

"I don't know, Danny. I suppose one of her projects. She's a dear. Help her if you can."

Danny grunted and put down the phone.

Cutter and Danny got out of the limousine together and walked into the ornately decorated club. Danny wasn't a member—"I belong to too damn many clubs, thanks," he had said to Henry, who had proffered him an invitation some years back—but he knew his way around and went right to the steward. He nodded his greetings and said, "We're here to meet with Dr. Lila O'Hara"—Danny liked to throw that around, "Doctor Lila," sort of a *mélange de genres,* as the French would put it—"Lila O'Hara." Camelia O'Toole. Sacheverell Jones. . . . The steward looked down at the day's schedule. "Yes, that's third floor, Room E."

Danny climbed the stairs and opened the door. He stared at the end of the table. At its head sat his godfather.

He had not laid eyes on Francis Biddle since his wedding. How old must he be? Eighty? Francis Biddle, Attorney General of the United States in the third Administration of Franklin Delano Roosevelt, a United States Judge at the Nuremberg trials. One of the four judges who sentenced twelve German generals, admirals, diplomats to hang, seven others to jail. The aristocratic, French-born, scholarly, rectilinear friend of civil liberties. The conscience of the legal fraternity, one biographer had called him. And who was that, next to Lila? With the stony face, double-breasted gray suit. And Lila, who was not smiling.

Danny knew, knew instantly.

His face broke into a broad smile. "Uncle Francis!" He walked over and shook his hand. "Haven't seen you since . . . since Lakeville. This is Cutter Malone, my associate. Cutter, you know Lila."

Lila shook hands. "This is Ernest Rhodes, my attorney." They shook hands again, Lila sat down and motioned to Danny and Cutter to take the chairs opposite. She came instantly to the point.

"Danny, we have all the documentation here. Uncle Francis has been over it in great detail as has Mr. Rhodes. If you feel you want to argue about it, we can stick it in front of your eyes. It's likelier that you're thinking it's time to bring in a lawyer, and of course you can do that any time you want. But I think it would make sense for you to listen to me and to Uncle Francis first. Okay?"

Danny kicked Cutter on his shoe, a signal to tell him to keep quiet.

"Dear Lila"—Danny thought he might try his characteristic approach to tough situations, just *try* it, see what happens—but then he saw the look on the face of Francis Biddle. He felt the look on the face of Francis Biddle. Abruptly he changed his tune. "Lila, let's hear what you have to say."

"It's harder for me, Danny, for the obvious reasons. So I'm going to turn the chair over to Uncle Francis."

Mr. Biddle put on his glasses and moved the yellow pad up closer to him.

"Daniel, if I were the state prosecutor, here is how I would address the court:

"The prosecution, your honor, undertakes to prove that the defendants, Daniel T. O'Hara and Cutter Malone, exploiting a professional and personal relationship with the late Giuseppe

Martino, the founder and chairman of the board of Martino Enterprises, Inc., and the sole stockholder of that corporation, conspired to tamper with Mr. Martino's will, to defraud the Franklin Delano Roosevelt Library, and to embezzle sums of money in excess of two million dollars. We will present irrefutable evidence of these felonies, in violation of criminal conspiracy, theft, fraud, and embezzlement statutes and will ask for the maximum penalties on each count, which add up to forty-five years in jail."

Danny was white. He did not look to one side to Cutter.

Francis Biddle put aside his notes. "Even though I am your godfather, Daniel, I would willingly see you sent to a state prison for the rest of your life. But I am also a trustee of the Franklin Delano Roosevelt Library. And I consider myself also a trustee of President Roosevelt's reputation. Of his legacy. I would not relish a public prosecution of the grandson of Franklin Delano Roosevelt, accused of cheating the Franklin Delano Roosevelt Library."

Mr. Biddle waited. Danny made an effort: "It honestly was kind of complicated, Uncle Francis. You see—"

Judge Biddle slammed his open hand on the table. "The last thing we want from you is sniveling lies. We are here to discuss the scope and the mechanics of restitution. After we have made those arrangements, we will fix a date for your resignation as president of Martino Enterprises. You, Mr. Malone, will also resign on the indicated day, after the transactions have been completed. And if you are detected any time in the next ten years working as an accountant, a sealed complaint, with all the particulars, will be mailed to the office of the District Attorney.

"Mr. Rhodes here has worked out a schedule. Some of the figures are missing. Mr. Malone will furnish those figures. Mr. Rhodes will then specify exactly what is expected of you both.

"My presence is no longer needed. Lila," he turned to Lila, whose expression had not changed during Judge Biddle's summary, "there is nothing further for you to do, and I would be grateful if you escorted an old man back to his apartment."

She rose. Everyone rose. Danny wondered whether his sister would address him.

Not today.

Francis Biddle took her by the arm. "Mr. Rhodes, kindly call me later in the day, as convenient."

"Yes, sir," Rhodes said, sitting down in his chair. He leaned down and brought his briefcase up on the table. He withdrew a large manila folder.

"Ready, gentlemen?"

Twenty-eight

DANNY DID NOT TROUBLE to advance this trip to Trafalgar–Los Angeles. No anonymous agent had been sent out from New York to test the hotel's pressure points. What did *he* care—whether, in the days and years ahead, the Trafalgar hotel chain prospered? One week from today he would resign as president. He envisioned the scene at Trafalgar–New York when word got out. It was gratifying that people would be stunned, having for so many years dealt with him as though he were the owner of the chain. And a little frightening, the obvious speculation: *Why? Why was Mr. O'Hara leaving?*

He had had of course to be very careful, back at the office, not to arouse suspicion that his mind was elsewhere. Granted, even before that terrible session at the Union Club it had been speculated that Daniel Tracey O'Hara would probably not spend the rest of his life serving as president of Trafalgar. "Remember," Jill from the accounting office said, sitting at the table in the Trafalgar–New York cafeteria reserved for employees, "the glint in O'Hara's eye a couple of years ago when he thought he might be running for the Senate? Those glints don't go away, not unless just about everybody who votes seizes up one day and mutters, *'Anybody but O'Hara!'* "

Ginny, from advertising, nibbled on her avocado salad. "Nobody would *ever* say that to Our Danny!"

Ginny was a political activist. She had volunteered to work for Danny's campaign, but the sudden entry of Bobby Kennedy into the political race kept her on the sidelines. "Keep your eyes on 1968," she said now to Jill, almost in a whisper. "Jack Javits is getting old. He's ripe to be beaten." . . . That exchange, overheard by Danny's secretary, Margie, seated at the next table, was quickly repeated to Danny. He feigned indifference. In fact it had delighted him.

The in-flight movie was *Goldfinger*. It caught Danny's attention, but after a half hour or so he ordered another Scotch and let his mind turn back to his own concerns.

The Biddle plan for restitution called for the quiet transfer by the stockholders of Hyde Park Capital Fund—Danny and Cutter Malone—of all their stock in Martino Enterprises, Inc., to the Hyde Park Fund. Ernest Rhodes and his accountant had diligently examined financial records going back for three years. Disgorgement would be primarily by Danny, given that he held 75 percent of the stock of Hyde Park Capital Fund. At nine in the morning on the day following the meeting at the Union Club, the bank balances of O'Hara and Malone were reviewed, as agreed upon, and also their portfolio of stocks and bonds.

Ninety percent of these were ordered liquidated, the proceeds remitted to the Hyde Park Fund.

Two weeks ago, Rhodes served notice on Danny that he was to put his summer house in Newport on the market and remit the proceeds to the Hyde Park Fund.

"How'm I going to explain that to Caroline? To my wife?"

"That is your concern, Mr. O'Hara," the lawyer said. Ernest Rhodes was not a talkative man. His conversational bluntness stopped only at the boundaries of civility. Where on *earth* had Lila found this creep? Danny wondered.

Lila. That was another problem. He waited for several days after the Union Club Massacre to see whether she would make an initiative. She didn't. He didn't think it wise to give her the impression he didn't care about her, though, in fact, he didn't care all that much about her, but his future, such as it was, was very much in her hands, so on Day Five he composed a careful note. Its design was to convey to his little sister that he was truly sorry about all that. But he needed to be careful in exactly what he said, and it was not a bad idea to pluck a violin string in it.

"Dear Lila: It was grand [this would show that Danny's old fortitude was still there] *to see you the other day at the Union Club, and to get acquainted again with The Scourge of Nuremberg* [just a little devil-may-care was okay, just a little]. *There were some painful things to go over* [there, that was pretty contrite, no?] [not contrite enough] *—and it truly grieves me that you have been put to such* [such what? trouble? humiliation? fright? horror?]*"*—he scratched out *"to such"* and substituted *"through such an ordeal."* [That would give her the credit she probably thought she was entitled to, for having gone through all that trouble. On the other hand, she was certainly being well rewarded. She had got her beloved Hyde Park enterprise about a hundred million in common stock! Probably she was given a raise!] *One of these days, maybe on a sail—not to Nantucket* [that might soften her up a little, the memory of that experience]*—I can tell you how it all happened, sort of little by little. Unlike the New Deal!* [She'd like that. Lila was forever speaking of the New Deal as distinctive because it came in as 'a full-blown package, a complete political-philosophical program.'] *Much love as always from your big brother* [that would arouse any fraternal enzymes floating about in his sister's scholarly mass], *Danny."*

He would have to tell Caroline that the summer house so popular with the children would not be theirs come June. Rhodes was tough, yes, and even unfriendly, but at least he did not set out to do impossible things. He did not, for instance, try to reclaim the salary paid to Danny and Cutter over the felonious years, 1959–64. There would have been no practical way to do this. Beginning way back in 1951, Danny had set up, unknown to any living soul in America including Cutter, beginning with the proceeds from the sale of a valuable diamond necklace, a personal bank account in Geneva into which he made systematic deposits, sometimes from his salary, sometimes from his vastly overstated expense accounts. That morning he had established the value of his Swiss account. After decoding a statement sent on plain paper and retrieved from the New York office of Crédit Suisse, he saw that he had husbanded assets of almost a half-million dollars. Dear Uncle Francis would never know about that, the son of a bitch.

Meanwhile—and this really needed to be done before tomorrow night, when he would be with her—he had to make the agonizing decision about Florry. Danny closed his eyes, crossed his legs, and gave himself a few moments to luxuriate at the thought of Florry. At the feel of Florry.

He sighed. It would no longer be possible to sidetrack funds from the hotel to maintain her. And, of course, trysts with her in Acapulco, Vancouver, Hawaii—where he had taken her just two months ago—would no longer be possible, not after leaving his post as president of the Trafalgar chain.

He would have to marry her. Or give her up.

Of course, when he was *reestablished,* he could contrive to resume his trips to the West Coast. But that was for tomorrow. Perhaps even for the day after tomorrow. He was, after all, seriously interested in the race for the New York Senate in 1968 and had to set himself up financially to make that race, only a couple of years off. He would need to maintain himself before he could resume maintaining Florry.

Maintain himself how? He brought out his Montblanc pen and lifted a notepad from his briefcase.

He could list the Astor hotels from memory: Baltimore, Washington, Atlanta, Dallas, Chicago, San Francisco, Denver. A young chain, ambitious, well managed. Let's face it, O'Hara, he said to himself, what you know how to do, what you're good at doing, is to run hotels. So? So that, obviously, is where your financial future lies.

There were two problems. About one, he was fairly confident of finding a workable outcome. When Biddle had said to Cutter Malone that he could no longer engage in accounting work, O'Hara was alarmed. Did an equivalent interdiction apply to him? *Danny would not be permitted to reenter the hotel business?*

After analyzing the question he was able to persuade himself, and later persuaded the awesome Mr. Rhodes, that there was a genuine difference between Cutter's going back to accounting and Danny's going back to the hotel business. He counted on Rhodes's persuading Biddle that any prohibition affecting Danny's line of work would not be comparable. Danny's crime hadn't been, so to speak, a crime intrinsic to the hotel business. It had simply been a crime, period. He struggled to make this point appealingly to the earnest Ernest Rhodes. By contrast, Cutter Malone's crime had required him to traduce his own profession, the practice of accounting.

He felt confident that Rhodes would consult with Mr. Biddle and report back with a clearance for Danny to continue in the hotel profession.

The other problem was young Tony Astor. Using family money, to be sure, Astor had resurrected the dilapidated Mark Henry Hotel in Chicago. So the capital wasn't his, but the creative work was, and at the time he waded into the Chicago situation, Tony Astor was only two years out of the University of Virginia. Tony was not yet thirty, but he was president and had a controlling interest in the Astor chain with its seven hotels, splendidly located. Tony Astor had a reputation—he paid large salaries to quick-minded and industrious young people.

Danny closed his eyes. A light fog was lifting, and he was achieving perspective.

It would be humiliating to go from president of Trafalgar to vice president of Astor. And what would they think at Trafalgar of a move so transparently a demotion? Wouldn't it then be conjectured that some undisclosed pressure was responsible for his resignation?

No. He would have to move in on Astor in a different way. He would set up as hotel consultant—that's always good. And all you need do is—open an office!

"Daniel T. O'Hara, Consultant to Presidents."

He laughed. But in fact everybody recognizes that there are advantages to working for yourself, to making your own schedule; so that to quit as president of Standard Staples in order to become president of Daniel T. O'Hara Consultants—consultants to the Staples industry—was not by any means a step down.

After setting up shop, he would stage his advance on Tony Astor. He complimented himself on his forethought in sending a half-dozen letters over the past few years to Tony, congratulating him on his serial conquests in the hotel business. They had met from time to time, had even played tennis and sailed together. It would all pay off.

Now, Florry. Would he tell her before . . . or after?

But then, *just why* did he have to tell her *anything* on this trip? No one (who mattered) knew he was going to resign next week.

Danny was delighted with the speed of his thinking on the subject: He could write Florry when he got back to New York, or even telephone her.

He needed only to answer for himself a single question: Was he willing to say to her, "Okay, Florry. You win. Divorce ain't easy, especially if it's a Catholic at the other end. But it can be done. So, come and be Mrs. O'Hara."

His eyes registered again on the image of the airplane's movie screen. He winced. *That man in the movie!* Whatever he was called in Hollywood, his *real* name is: Francis Biddle! He stared at the screen, squinting his eyes for focus . . . until reality took over.

Of course, it wasn't Biddle. He ordered another drink.

What had brought Francis Biddle to mind?

Yes, face it. Granted it would not help politically, far from it. But the real obstacle, the conclusive obstacle, was dear old Uncle Francis.

Danny would have to figure out a way to get himself to Los Angeles frequently. If absolutely necessary, he permitted himself a silent smile, he could pay for the round trips and the hotel rooms himself! He could not bear the thought of indefinite absences from Florry. There was of course the obvious sensual joy, but her company was so special, her understanding of everything he said, her curiosity, the resilience of her mind, exactly complementing his. Et cetera.

But it would not do—certainly not for the time being—to bring Florry to Greenwich.

With Bradley Jiménez, everything was as usual. Danny made all the appointed rounds, visited with all the key personnel, showed the usual keen interest in the figures, gave a nice pep talk to key members, and confirmed at lunch with Jiménez that the arrangements for that night were as usual. He was through with his rounds by four.

Florry arrived on time, as ever. And, as had become now a fixed habit, or obsession, they made love before dinner. She looked especially ravishing, Danny thought, looking down at her, her head on the pillow, her long eyelashes closed. Oh God, how he loved her, loved loving her, loved making love to her, her responses so copiously reciprocal. Whatever he did, he must plan to be with her once a month, no matter what. They kissed tenderly, he dressed minimally, went into the living room and, in a few minutes, the dinner was served. She joined him, radiant— had that blond gleam in her hair escaped his attention until now? Or was she simply experimenting with some new gold-exfoliating hair wash or whatever? He would ask her. No, he would not ask her. Private business, hair color.

Florry chatted. She would compete the following week for the Salamanca scholarship. Danny noticed that she seemed much less eager than when she had first told him about the contest, almost three years ago. Florry had after all not even tried out for it in her sophomore and junior years—she would not leave Danny. Well then, why was she competing this year? Danny asked.

"I really have to, to appease Professor Agrippo. He has given me so much of his time, so much guidance. I had to make very elaborate excuses to skip the competition last year and the year before. But this is my last chance, of course—after June I'll no longer be an undergraduate. I hope to win the prize, of course—for the record. Then I'll wait a week or two, and tell the committee I can't leave my—*amante!*" She laughed. "No. I'll tell them Sister Alicia absolutely needs me to take over the orphanage. Something like that. Don't worry."

"You don't doubt you'll win it?" Danny tucked into his asparagus and poured them both more wine.

"At this point only a native-born Spanish poet posing as an American could beat me. You know the rules? Nobody can compete who spoke Spanish as a child or who has traveled to Spain or spent more than two weeks in Mexico. Otherwise they'd just be handing our scholarship money to Spanish expatriates.

"But how goes the hotel business? I know the Trafalgar is doing well, at least during the twenty hours a week I'm there. You were nice to give me the job three years ago, but for a long time now I've really been earning my keep. There is tons of Latin-American business. And, by the way, the Ambassador has a Spanish-speaking person at *both* their desks."

If he were going to tell her *anything,* now was the time. He was tempted. Well, he'd take just a *tiny* step in that direction.

"There's a board meeting coming up. They're bringing in trustees. You know that the stock is held by the Hyde Park people? I assume they'll bring in trustees I can feel happy with. So I guess it's safe to say: not much change."

Florry looked slightly distracted. Suddenly she turned to him. "Danny, I can't stay the night. Because—this is no fabricated excuse—Sister Alicia does need me very early in the morning. Three girls, sisters, are coming in to the orphanage, don't speak any English, Mexican uncle is driving them up from San Diego. The mother disappeared—that kind of thing."

Danny said he was disappointed, but she didn't have to leave right after dinner, did she?

No, but maybe after an hour? He leaned over and kissed her deeply, lingeringly.

"Or so," she managed.

. . . .

She gave their coded knock on the hotel door: *dot-dot-dash-dash-dash*. The tall blond young man with the light blue eyes and the pearl-white teeth opened the door. They spoke only in Spanish. After a year at Salamanca, Tracy Gulliver could speak as well as any native Spaniard.

"Did you tell him?"

"Well, no, Tracy, I didn't."

He offered her a glass of wine, but she said no, she had had enough wine tonight.

"Why not?"

"After I was there for a while, I figured—"

"He . . . did it with you?"

Florry pushed him away. "Of *course* he did it, Tracy. I mean, grow up! If I *wasn't* going to *do* it I wouldn't have gone up to his room. He has paid over six thousand dollars for me during this year, plus the extra stuff I get in the hotel." She smiled suddenly, and looked up at him coquettishly. "I mean, do you want to make a dishonest woman out of me?"

Tracy found it hard to smile, but finally did so. What, really, did it matter, one more time? But *the last time.*

"So when will you tell him?"

"I decided I'd write to him from Salamanca!" She kissed him lightly on the cheek. "On stationery from Assistant Professor and Mrs. Tracy Gulliver."

His smile was now radiant. " 'Tracy Gulliver' said in Spanish isn't easy."

"I'll practice."

Twenty-nine

A CABLE was waiting for Henry at Hué. It was from Richard
Clurman, who advised Henry that his request was granted,
that he could return from Saigon for a six-month leave. "At least
six months. We'll talk about it in New York."

Henry spent two days attending the funeral of Than Koo, consoling his relatives and writing a detailed cable on the events of
those terrible hours. In an entirely separate cable, addressed to
Clurman, he acknowledged gratefully the considerate treatment
of his request to leave Saigon for a while, but now he confessed
that the experience of Hoile had "wiped me out. I know it's only
temporary, Dick, but honestly, I feel now no curiosity, no desire
to write down what happened, to interview anybody about anything. I'm afraid I'm not going to be very much use to you out in

the field for a while, and I don't mean out in the field in Saigon, or Rome or Moscow or Paris. I mean out in the field *anywhere.*"

After writing so solemn a sentence, his spirits lifted, and he went on, "Did you spot what Nelson Algren said a while ago? He captured my mood exactly. Somebody asked him how up he was on world affairs and Algren said, 'Put it this way, if Marjorie Morningstar married the man in the gray flannel suit on my front stoop at noon, I wouldn't bother to go to the wedding.' I'm afraid I feel a little that way, but obviously I can't take that out on Time Inc., so maybe I'd just better have a leave of absence without pay."

When he got back to Saigon, Clurman had already responded: "I HAVE AN IDEA. WHEN DO YOU GET TO NEW YORK? ADVISE."

At Guam there was the usual layover. He found himself walking into the PX. He stared at the bottle of forty-dollar brandy. He was no longer tempted to buy it.

He bought more of the usual things. For Tommy and Emily he got the new Japanese Olympus radios—one each. Children do not like to share toys, he reminded himself. Though Caroline had always offered to share hers with her older brother. That was true except for the little mother-of-pearl binoculars; she had wanted those so badly she simply hid them. He longed to see her again, and to tell her about Than Koo. She would understand.

He arrived in New York at noon on Saturday, called Caroline, and agreed to go to the country that afternoon. He bought the *New York Times* on the train and was astonished to read, on the business page, of the resignation of Daniel T. O'Hara as president of Martino Enterprises. What was going on? He read the entire news story and then turned to *The Wall Street Journal,* where he found a personal analysis combined with an interview. He read it hungrily.

"The resignation came as a surprise to Mr. O'Hara's associates. It is known among his friends that O'Hara is interested in politics. In 1964 he put in an early bid for the Democratic nomination for the Senate, but was blown out of the political water when Robert F. Kennedy announced his own candidacy. One associate speculated that Mr. O'Hara wished to devote much of his time during the next two years to lining up support for a race in 1968 against Senator Jacob Javits. The leading contender for the Democratic nomination is now Paul O'Dwyer, but Mr. O'Hara is young, well connected (his grandfather was President Roosevelt), and has built a reputation as a skillful manager.

"Questioned about the 1968 race, Mr. O'Hara said it was too early to talk about it, but he did not deny an interest in it. What will he do in the meantime? He will, he said, open a consulting business specializing in the development and maintenance of hotels. The firm will be called O'Hara Consultants. Two 'skilled executives' have agreed to join the firm, he said, but he declined, as premature, to give their names."

Caroline was waiting for Henry at the Greenwich railroad station. Their embrace was intense. It struck them both at that moment that their reliance on each other was critical. Henry could sense that the union—Danny and Caroline—would not survive.

"Henry, let me suggest something. We go by the house, you can give Suzy a smooch—she's the only one at home at this hour —and leave your bag. Then we'll get into the car and drive off, have lunch somewhere, maybe the Red Barn at Wilton, get right away from it, what do you say?"

A half hour later, Caroline was at the wheel of Danny's convertible. She left the station wagon for Thelma, who would crisscross the children in midafternoon to their various classes in piano, art, religion, typing, First Aid—whatever the schedule was for that day; it was all neatly typed out and tacked onto the bulletin board in the kitchen.

It was a soft day in spring, the azaleas on the Merritt Parkway sleepy and seductive, the air still and fragrant. Caroline drove slowly. Henry asked, How bad is it? She confessed that she felt in Danny a deep restlessness, a sense that an explosion had to come.

"What's the business about his quitting Martino?"

"Believe it or not, I learned about it yesterday. But in talking with Lila a week ago, I now know that she knew it was coming. Something she said that made no sense when she said it comes to life now. She said something like, 'I don't worry about what Danny will do.' I thought it was some vague reference to the running for Senator business, but Lila doesn't much go in for speculative thought. She obviously knew that Danny had to do something because Danny was no longer going to be president of Martino.

"But that's *all* I can tell you."

"And on the other front, Carol?" Carol. Only Henry called her that.

"On the other front, he is more distant every month. He has a girl, Henry, in Los Angeles. He goes there a lot. I had an anonymous letter. I assume it was written by the girl's other—gentleman. Pretty conclusive stuff. The letter had an odd P.S., said that if ever I wanted to prove a point to Danny, or something of that sort, I should ask him about his mother's necklace. What's that all about?"

"I don't remember whether you knew about it. Somebody stole Rachel's big diamond necklace the night of her party before the wedding. The state troopers were all over the place the next morning."

Caroline reached over and put her hand down on Henry's shoulder. "Henry. You know what that has got to mean?"

Henry paused at some length. But finally he said, "Yes. I can't believe he'd bring up the business about the necklace to anybody . . . I can't believe it. But then I guess I can believe anything about Danny at this point. . . . So, Carol, what now? You want me in the act?"

"No. When the moment comes, and I guess yes, it's coming, I'll tell you."

"Is your priest—still . . . useful?"

"He's been perfect. Has kept me slowed down to just the tolerable speed."

"I don't mean to diminish for a minute the importance of the spiritual question, but could it be that at this point your commitments, or what you think of as your commitments, are hurting you? I mean, more than helping you?"

Caroline was obviously glad to be able to address the question with the only other person she had ever spoken to about it.

"No no, Henry. You truly do not understand—no, that's the wrong word. You aren't—*familiar* with—the Christian complex. I was with Father Kevin yesterday. You may remember that he officiated at our—funny, how subconsciously I avoid the word 'marriage,' now that I propose to—I have to get the terminology right here, Henry, because it's important to me. I'm not about to 'dissolve' a marriage, because in my understanding I don't have the power to do any such thing: the vows were exchanged, the marriage was consummated. I am Danny's wife, he is my husband, as long as he lives. He will be free in conscience, and of course in law, to remarry; I won't be. Not unless it proved that for whatever reason, the marriage didn't take place. Have you ever heard of 'psychic consummation'?"

"No. What is it, Carol?"

She laughed. "What it probably is, is liberation theology. A fancy way to deconstruct a marriage. What it says is that a marriage isn't consummated merely by the physical transaction on the wedding night. It can only be consummated when there is a psychic union, an emotionally evolved decision by husband and wife to stay together forever. I mention this primarily to make the point that Danny has been—in every sense of the word—my husband. When we married, he wanted very much to marry me, and I don't doubt the sincerity of his wedding vows, though I guess at this point I have to say I wouldn't be surprised if all along he had dalliances, perhaps going right back to the period when we were first married.

"But Father Kevin helped a great deal. His technique is really wonderful. It sounds obvious, but it isn't. What his technique is, is never to answer a question, only to ask it. So he asks, 'Do you still love Danny?'

"Answer: 'Yes, I do.'

" 'Does he still love you?'

"I answer, 'That depends what you mean by love. If you mean exclusively enamored by, the answer is no. If you mean merely, "has tender feelings for," I'd say yes.'

"Next question, 'Does his presence in the house affect affirma-
tively, or negatively, the lives of the children?'

"And now for the first time, Henry, I'd have to say, 'negatively.' Because the children are growing, and they begin to notice their father's aloofness, the lack of interest he has in what
they do—in them. His neglect of their mother.

"So I've had to answer, 'On the margin, negatively.'

" 'Will the children suffer materially from a separation of their
parents?'

"I answer to that one, 'Modern divorce laws pay reasonable
attention to the needs of mother and children.'

"He then asks, 'Are you satisfied that if you proceed to separate, you are following the dictates of a conscience guided by
your understanding of Christian priorities?' "

Caroline did not proceed, as she had done until now, to answer the final question she had posed. Henry said nothing, but
clearly he was waiting for the resolution. Only her answer to this
question mattered.

Finally Caroline spoke. "I said to Father Kevin, 'I'm not quite
ready yet to answer that question.' "

"What did he say to that?—No, I shouldn't ask; that is an
improper question."

"Yes it is, Henry. But I'll answer it just the same: He said,
'When you are ready to answer that question—answer it.' "

Henry opened the door. "Come, Carol. Let's go in, have
something to eat."

Together, hand in hand, they walked into the restaurant. Suddenly Caroline stopped. She lifted her finger to her lips. "Don't
say anything, dear dear Henry, that suggests Father Kevin has
been anything less than saintly to me, through it all."

Henry nodded. And squeezed her hand.

On Monday, Clurman absentmindedly lit a cigarette while his
other lit cigarette lay on the ashtray only half consumed.
Clurman was absentminded about such matters (he had once
ordered two complete meals sent to his room at a hotel). He was
not in the least absentminded about the hundred-odd correspon-

dents posted nationally and internationally to serve *Time/Life*. Henry Luce had for many years put heavy emphasis on contracting to the extent possible the time between the event and his readers' survey of it, through the instrument of *Time*'s reporters, researchers, and writers. No expense was inordinate. When Marilyn Monroe was found dead in Los Angeles on a Sunday morning, one million copies of *Time* had already been printed and were on their way to subscribers. Yet purchasers of *Time* could buy the magazine on Monday morning with twenty-nine inches of detail on her death: a technological miracle over the news-gathering part of which Clurman had presided, two or three telephones ringing at one time, two or three cigarettes, as often as not, burning at one time.

The Chief of Correspondents had sensed the closeness between Henry and his interpreter, whom Clurman had met and admired on one of his trips to Saigon. Clurman had authorized an under-the-table special bonus for Than Koo's work in bringing together invaluable information on the last hours of President Diem. He knew that a sharp break from conventional journalism for Henry would be good therapy.

"We got a request a week ago." He leaned back at his desk. "Columbia School of Journalism. Paul Appleby has had a stroke. They are left without an up-front ex-reporter star professor. School starts in a week. They want a replacement, somebody who's served as a working journalist. One semester is all they need—they're working on a permanent replacement. Ten grand, and Time Inc. will pay an extra five. I think it's just right for you, what do you say?"

Clurman could never quite understand that subspecies that needed to deliberate. He was pleased, but not surprised, when Henry said, "Sounds good."

They spent three hours, and then lunch, discussing Vietnam. Clurman had concluded that President Johnson would not pull out and possibly couldn't do so, and what he wished for most was any evidence of internal weakening in North Vietnam. He wanted to know how Hanoi could take the punishment. "How can they get ten, fifteen thousand troops down the Trail every month? How can they stand the damage we're doing to their shipping? How do they succeed in replacing the people we apprehend and imprison or execute?'' Henry said that no one was theoretically better equipped than he to try to answer such questions, but that he couldn't do so. ''My experience at Hoile is—the national experience.'' It was not easy to satisfy Clurman, and Henry did not succeed in doing so.

The class Henry was to teach was made up of eighteen students, one or two freshly graduated from college, the majority in their mid and late twenties, two or three in their early thirties. These last had engaged in newspaper work mostly in outlying parts of the country. They had been picked by their editors as especially promising reporters/analysts who needed that odd combination of book learning, competitive writing experience, exposure to historical texts, deep drafts of newspaper culture that the journalism schools seek to provide.

Henry was the complete professional. In fourteen years he had done everything, specifically including a few paragraphs for the Encyclopaedia Britannica's Yearbook, a historical update on Vietnam. He had interviewed and conversed with many of the men and women who dominated the news, had done reporting for twenty cover stories and had himself written eight for *Time*. He was inexhaustibly patient with those with whom patience was merited, or necessary. If it required twenty hours at the Quai d'Orsay to get something from President Charles de Gaulle, Henry would wait as patiently as, only a couple of years ago, he had waited, in a car, outside the last building President Ngo Dinh Diem had spent a night in. If a student was deeply troubled in a search for the best way to frame a story, Henry would stay with him (or her—ten of his students were women) as long as required.

But if a student was frivolous or exhibitionistic, Henry could be as unsparing as he had been in the boxing ring. The second day of class a tweedy young man with a wispy mustache, who affected a stutter and walked about with a gold-topped cane, raised his hand after the week's assignment had been read out and said, "What's the point in reading *The Taming of the Shrew*?"

Henry answered, "The point in doing so is that you will then have done what I have told you to do."

The young man twiddled his mustache, took in the look in his teacher's eyes, and decided to let the matter drop.

A month later, taking lunch in the cafeteria shared by faculty and graduate students, Barbara Horowitz asked if she might sit with him. By all means. Henry was struggling to his feet when she touched him on the shoulder and restrained him.

"Miss Horowitz," as Henry referred to her in class, was in her thirties, dark, sturdy, her hair provocatively set in a Dutch-boy bob utterly incongruous with her brassy temperament. She had attended Reed College in Oregon and gone to work in Walla Walla for the daily newspaper. After a few years she quit to join the staff of a weekly whose guiding lights were *Rolling Stone* magazine and *The Village Voice*. For *Beetle* she wrote about rock music and the shooting stars of rock land, and about civil rights, racism, imperialism, the military-industrial complex and nutrition.

The magazine folded, but her contributions to it had been noticed by regional editors, and now the editor of the *Seattle Post-Intelligencer* had sponsored her for a Columbia School of Journalism slot. Her ideological zeal was at missionary-high level and in class she was provocative but never ill-mannered. Henry would not argue with Miss Horowitz, but in correcting her papers he would indicate where she was simply attitudinizing. Henry was quick to acknowledge that the line between reporting and editorializing was not clear, that as a writer for *Time* magazine he was hardly equipped to be censorious on the point. But the writer absolutely needed to know, and to communicate to the reader, that he knew what he was up to. "Otherwise you are engaged in guile, and you don't want that, or, at least, shouldn't want that." Miss Horowitz listened to what he had to say and paid attention to what he wrote on her papers.

Within ten minutes, Miss Horowitz had persuaded Mr. Chafee to call her Barbara. He said he was prepared to do so from now on, that he inclined not to use first names unless asked to do so. Whereupon he asked her to call him Henry.

"You are a quiet fascist creep, Henry, you know that?"

"Yes," Henry said, sipping his iced tea. "Would you rather I were a noisy fascist creep?"

She laughed. "While I'm at it, why did you land so hard on Little Lord Fauntleroy that first week?"

"You're referring to Andrew Bradford III."

"Who else?"

"Imagine exposing yourself to such ridicule, asking out loud, Why read *The Taming of the Shrew?*"

"You're evading me. Remember, Henry, I am a skilled journalistic interrogator. I didn't ask you why people should read the *The Taming of the Shrew.* I didn't even suggest it's dumb to ask the question. I asked you why you knocked little Andrew out of the ring just for asking?"

Henry sighed. He was about to reply when Barbara interrupted him—"God, I wish you would shave off that beard, so I could find out what you look like."

"Now who're you picking on?"

"Whom am I picking on."

"I don't use the objective whom except after a preposition."

"In that case you can edit *The Taming of the Shrew.* Shakespeare didn't know about your rule. 'Of all thy suitors, here I charge thee, tell/ Whom thou lovest best: see thou dissemble not.' "

"Nice going," Henry said. "And what's more, I give up. What do I have to do to get just a little quiet from you?"

"Denounce U.S. imperialism in Vietnam, contribute to the fund to build a sanitarium to park Barry Goldwater in, and go march in Mississippi."

Henry laughed. At the end of lunch he felt ten years younger.

And at the end of the semester he asked Barbara Horowitz if she would marry him.

"Are you sure you're not a homosexual, Henry?"

"At this point," he said, "I am quite certain."

They were seated at Maxwell's Plum. Her hand reached under the table and gripped his. She lowered her head to hide the tear, but he had seen it. He felt within him an irrepressible devotion to this independent, raucous, opinionated woman with her bob-cut hair and flashing eyes. She had become everything, and more, as he discovered how urgent was an appetite he had kept in place all these years. She tightened her grip on his hand and Henry Chafee felt an elation he hadn't ever felt before, some-thing so deep and consuming he knew of it only as an abstraction he had encountered in his reading. He knew now that it really existed.

Thirty

THE *NEW YORK TIMES* gave Barbara Horowitz a job. She
had elected to retain her maiden name. At the little civil
wedding ceremony Danny served as best man (Caroline agreed
with Henry that at this moment there was no alternative to tapping Danny). Henry, straight-faced and clean-shaven, asked her
whether she desired him to change his own name to Horowitz.
She had already changed the name of Henry to "Henny." "I
don't want to call you by the same name everybody else does,
and you've made it clear you don't much like 'Hank.' So it's
Henny, same thing Ann Boleyn called Henry the Eighth." Henry
—Henny—let it go, along with his beard. At the newspaper she
quickly earned the respect of her editors and was soon writing
features under the supervision of the style setter, editor Char-

lotte Curtis. It was the year of a heated municipal campaign in New York City, with rising Republican star John Lindsay ready to abandon his seat in the Congress in order to run for Mayor. She was assigned to do several stories on Lindsay's background and temperament—his public life had been well chronicled over the years.

She did a series of six stories on the enormously tall, extraordinarily handsome congressman, about whom it was pretty much taken for granted that he would one day make a bid for a presidential nomination. What stood most stolidly in his way was of course Governor Nelson Rockefeller, who wished to be President, and who dominated New York politics.

Barbara Horowitz explained to her readers that John Lindsay's inner circle reasoned that he would need to appeal to liberal circles in New York to win support. He was, after all, a Republican seeking voters in a city resolutely Democratic. In one story she predicted that if Lindsay won, there would be tension between him and the Governor—whose problem was the opposite of Lindsay's: Nelson Rockefeller needed to woo conservative Republicans. Rockefeller was the principal liberal figure in the Republican Party. He had contended against Barry Goldwater for the Republican nomination a year earlier and, when Goldwater won, pointedly refused to campaign for him. "Governor Rockefeller is mending fences on his right while John Lindsay is using a battering ram to attract New Yorkers on the left," Barbara Horowitz informed her readers. The city editor then assigned her to do a portrait of Abraham Beame, the City Controller and likeliest winner of a Democratic primary. "Horowitz"— she liked to see herself thus identified—found the assignment tough going, inasmuch as the short, elderly candidate was resolutely uncolorful. She complained one afternoon to her editor that Beame "has never ovulated."

"Has never what?"

"Just an expression."

"Well, find a different expression," Curtis said. ". . . I know, I know, Abe Beame isn't John Lindsay, he doesn't make the ladies swoon over him, doesn't go to Broadway shows, didn't shine as a student at Yale, doesn't represent the Silk Stocking district. So he wears black socks on the beach. So he's a pol? So write something interesting about pols.''

Barbara Horowitz did, and Henry, reading her story in the morning paper, told her she was an alchemist. She affected to be indifferent to the compliment. "Have you ever done a cover story on a pol?'' she asked.

Yes, he had done Mayor Daley.

"That doesn't count,'' Barbara objected. "Daley's fascinating.''

Henry explained that pols become fascinating if they exercise power, but in order to do that they generally have to win elections.

To round out the political coverage, the *Times* told her to do a feature on Conservative Party candidate William F. Buckley, Jr. She spent a few days reading his books, his columns, and listening to one of his campaign speeches. She reported to the City Editor that she could not do a feature on him, but would gladly volunteer to serve on it if ever an execution squad were organized. Charlotte Curtis told her to do her duty, goddamnit, and she ground out a story about one third of which was blue-penciled as too tendentious.

She was pulled away from municipal politics to do "a big story'' on the FDR Library—the paper would publish several features on the twentieth anniversary of the death of President Roosevelt. Barbara called Henry at *Time* and told him of the assignment. "Stop everything and quick, call your sister-in-law, Lila, tell her what a sweet and talented thing I am, and would she please give me the next four days of her time.''

Lila O'Hara hadn't been at the small wedding and had never laid eyes on Barbara Horowitz. She insisted on being told which train Barbara would be on—Lila would meet it. "Tell Barbara to look for the tall lady with glasses and an ice-cream cone in her hand. They've got the best ice cream in Dutchess County at the drugstore across the street.''

· · · ·

No fewer than six scholars were at work on some aspect of the Roosevelt story. And one of those six, Max Huxley from the University of Chicago graduate school, was writing not about Roosevelt, but about the Library. He was twenty-five years old, slim, studious, direct, persevering, and attracted to unusual juxtapositions; he tended to look out for relationships, e.g., between the style and dimensions of FDR's tombstone and the period during the war when he specified what these should be. He was a steadfastly curious young man, familiar with the protocols of academic scholarship but unfamiliar with the ways of journalists. Working side by side with Barbara Horowitz, he saw an opportunity to learn exactly how a reporter from a serious daily newspaper met deadlines and crashed through obstacles that would hold up an academic researcher for a week or a month or a year.

And Barbara saw in Max Huxley an opportunity quickly to accelerate her knowledge of the Library, that extraordinary complex founded by Roosevelt himself in 1941, which had become a permanent repository for over two hundred separate collections making up over seventeen million pages of manuscripts, over a hundred thousand photographs, and thousands of feet of motion picture film. Already there were over thirty thousand books covering the life and times of Franklin and Eleanor Roosevelt.

Barbara gravitated toward Max and he was obliging. He let her spend several hours reading his tidy notes, from which she got a quick general, and also profound, idea of the activity of the Center.

Barbara Horowitz, accustomed to writing under every kind of pressure, marveled at young Huxley's notes, which appeared to have been prepared and written without any trace of pressure or haste. After a few dozen pages, Barbara wondered if Max had ever—ever in his life—made a simple typographical error. ("You might as well look for a typo in the text of Lincoln's Second Inaugural Address on the monument," she told Henry over the telephone.) For that reason her attention was arrested on one page where in ink he had placed three question marks (???) at the margin of a paragraph that dealt with recent contributions to the Library, listed for 1964. The documents revealed the receipt of 2,875,000 shares in Martino Enterprises, Inc., at an appraised value of over one hundred million dollars.

She walked over to Huxley, who was taking notes at another desk in the library. "Max, what're the question marks all about?"

There were others in the large room, working within earshot, so Max answered in a whisper. "The gift didn't come from Martino. It came from something called the Hyde Park Capital Fund. I never heard of the Hyde Park Capital Fund. And how did they get the stock? I'm going to Albany tomorrow to look up the records of the Capital Fund."

"Anything screwy going on?"

"I hope so. It would certainly liven up my thesis."

"Let me know if you find out anything interesting?"

Max smiled. "Waal," he drawled out the word, "why give the *New York Times* a scoop that belongs to the University of Chicago?" And then, after a pause of exaggerated concentration, with a little smile, "Sure."

And Max did.

Late the following afternoon he told Barbara that the Hyde Park Capital Fund had for two years owned the Martino stock. And that the two listed officers and directors of the Capital Fund were one C. Malone, and D. O'Hara. "Obviously that's Daniel O'Hara, since he was president of Martino Enterprises until a few days ago. But what was he doing with all that stock for almost two years? And where did the dividends go during that period? But it's easy enough to take the next step."

Of course. Just ask Lila. . . . Did Max mind if she tagged along?

No. Sure, come along.

Lila O'Hara received them together: Max Huxley, with whom she had dealt for the better part of a month, rounding up information he requested—whose scholarly attitude she approved of; and Barbara Horowitz, whom she had met only two days before, at the railroad station, and instantly liked.

What, Max began by asking, was the Hyde Park Capital Fund?

"Oh, I'm not all that sure. Old Martino was a man who liked to do things his own way, and I guess he told Malone and my brother to hang on to the stock for a year or so, for whatever reason—maybe the hotel chain was being reorganized, or something like that—and then to turn it over to us. Sorry, can't be more detailed than that."

"Well, who *can* be more 'detailed' about the arrangement?" Max persevered.

Lila now turned cold. "Max, we are a research center, but this doesn't mean that we encourage the dilettante. Some Chicago University don with nothing very important in mind wants a graduate student to spend a hundred pages in a thesis nobody's going to read on what happened between Monday and Tuesday; I mean, who cares, Max? I certainly don't, nor do my colleagues."

Barbara was startled. Max turned to his notepad.

Lila lit a cigarette and said, "Do you have any more questions?"

Max said yes, but he'd rather put them to her the following day, as he hadn't arranged them in the proper order.

"What about you, Barbara?" Lila's voice was back to normal.

Barbara said she was getting along fine but would certainly call on Lila before she began to write her story.

Max and Lila walked out of the library. Max said to her, "You know where my favorite place is to sit down around here for a few minutes?"

No, Barbara didn't know. Max motioned her to follow him.

They walked to the front entrance of the mansion. Max showed the guard—he was friendly with all of them, at this point —his working pass, Barbara showed hers. She followed him into the oaken hallway, up four stairs to the central corridor. Over to the third door. It was open. He turned in, showed his pass again to the guard standing by the velvet cord. Max lifted it from the hook attached to the stanchion and signaled to Barbara to walk on through. They passed across the thick embroidered carpet, around the bookcase that jutted into the room, to a couch in the little alcove from which they could view the imposing desk at the other end of the large, comfortable study of Franklin Delano Roosevelt.

"He had the couch here for an assistant to use while FDR was examining any of the books around us. You can take notes on the table here"—he pointed to the heavy unadorned table with the black leather stretched across. "FDR dictated a lot, reading from the table, to his secretary, seated where we are. It's kind of fun sitting here. The tourists don't get this deep into the FDR study. But the guards give us scholars the run of the house. Barbara?"

"Yes?"

"What was that all about with Lila? That outburst? Not at all like her. Something's fishy. The records show that Martino Enterprises spins off three and a half to four million dollars a year. So where did that money go between November 1963, when the old man died, and April 1964, when the dividends from Martino Enterprises began to flow into Hyde Park?"

"I don't know. But Lila was pretty tender on the point, I agree. I just don't understand it. What are you going to do?"

"I'll begin by asking Mr. O'Hara for an appointment. Then I'll get a copy of the will from probate. Then I'll ask to see the accountant of Martino Enterprises, whoever he is. Then I'll look for the tax receipts, from the day Giuseppe Martino died."

"Have you any idea what's going on, Max?"

"No I don't. But I can't figure out what the purpose was of the Hyde Park Capital Fund. Whatever its purpose, it belongs in my thesis."

"And in my newspaper. Max. Dear Max. I have to tell you this, that I'm going to have to pursue this story on my own. But if it turns out to be a story and if we publish it, I'll give full credit to you for raising the question in the first place."

"I understand. But don't get ahead of me on trying to get the interviews with O'Hara and Martino's accountant; give me a couple of days."

"Max, what on earth is going on? What do you think?"

"That depends. . . . I wonder what FDR would have said, if this kind of thing had been plopped on his desk there?"

"Maybe he would have said, 'You need a good lawyer,' and quoted his rates."

Thirty-one

M R. MALONE on line two, Mr. O'Hara." Danny picked up the telephone.

"Morning, Cutter. . . . What? Hold it. Cutter, call me back, but on my private line."

"Okay." They both hung up.

The second line came directly to Danny's desk. It rang. "Yes, Cutter, tell me about it. . . . Max Huxley. Yes. Well, he called in here a few days ago, wanted to see me about Martino's will. Margie put him off—till one day next week, I think. Why? . . . You *saw* him? —Cutter. Where are you?" Danny looked down at his watch. "Meet me at the Yale Club. I can be there in fifteen minutes."

He told Margie he was going to the Yale Club to meet a prospective client. On arriving at Vanderbilt Avenue, Danny went to the bar on the third floor. He ordered a gin and tonic and walked with it to a card table in the rear of the room. Cutter showed up, carrying his inevitable briefcase. He declined a drink, and sat down.

"Okay, from scratch."

Cutter writhed about in the big armchair trying to make himself comfortable, but the chair wasn't the problem.

"He got me on the phone. That's easy, you know, Danny. Anybody can get me on the phone these days, since nobody in New York is less busy than I am. So he says he's doing a thesis for the University of Chicago on the FDR Library and he'd like to talk to me about the Hyde Park Capital Fund. What was the purpose in founding it, what did it do with the money that flowed in from Martino before the stock went to the other Hyde Park fund."

"What did you say?" Danny's voice was edged. He signaled to the steward for a refill of his drink before he had finished the first.

"I said that my understanding of the matter was that the enterprise was confidential and therefore I was not free to discuss the matter with him."

"That shut him up?"

"Hell no. He said he had already tried to get an appointment with you to discuss the matter, that he intended to examine the will of Giuseppe in order to unearth who authorized the Capital Fund to hold the stock for two years. The son of a bitch means business, Danny."

Danny stroked his glass. "Hang on, Cutter. I'm going to call Lila."

He got his sister on the phone.

"You alone?"

"Yes. How are you, Danny?"

"Not good. What do you know about a little turd from Chicago called Max Huxley?"

"Has he been to see you?"

"He's tried. He got hold of Cutter. He is asking all the wrong questions. What do you know about his background? Don't you vet those people before letting them camp down at Hyde Park?"

"Hang on."

She was back in a few minutes. She read now from the application letter. ". . . Maxwell Huxley. Born Grosse Point, Michigan, 1940. High school—Grosse Point public schools. B.A., University of Chicago 1961. Admitted, Graduate School, Department of History, September 1961. M.A., 1963. He is doing a dissertation under Professor George Callard, no relation to our Callard. You want to hear what Callard says about him?"

"Yeah."

" 'Max Huxley is an impressive student. He is very meticulous, a resourceful researcher with an eye for the interesting historical detail. He wrote his undergraduate thesis on FDR's third term and is now embarked on a dissertation on the FDR Library, its background, its objectives, its resources, with the view to informing future presidents on the ideal arrangements for their own libraries. I earnestly recommend to the administrators of the FDR Library that they give Huxley access to the archives and help him in any way possible and convenient.' Signed, G. Callard."

"The son of a bitch has all the qualifications we'd most like him not to have."

"What are you going to do?"

"I don't know. But I don't think it's a good idea for me to be in New York while young Huxley is in heat. I got plenty of excuses for going to France. Or Switzerland."

"You can study up on hotels. Danny?"

"Yes."

"How's Caroline doing?"

"Screw Caroline."

Lila shook her head. There was no way of dealing with Danny, not anymore. So she said simply, "Let me know what you plan to do."

Thirty-two

DANNY PACED THE FLOOR of his study in Greenwich. He paused every few minutes to stare vacantly at the memorandum from his secretary. It recorded the request of Mr. Max Huxley for an appointment and gave Huxley's telephone extension at the FDR Library and the telephone number of the hotel at Rhinebeck where he was staying. Danny walked over to the nicely camouflaged little refrigerator in the corner of the study, pulled out fresh ice and mixed another drink.

What in the hell was he going to do?

He found his mind canvassing possibilities almost preposterous, on quick second thought. Might the great prestigious Francis Biddle be able to intervene? But how? By calling the president of the University of Chicago and asking him kindly to tell graduate student Max Huxley to lay off FDR's grandson?

Could he get a forger to concoct a letter of instruction from Giuseppe Martino, directing Daniel O'Hara to hold on to Martino stock after the old man's death for a couple of years, before turning it over to the Hyde Park Fund?

But why? And if such a letter existed, why hadn't Cutter mentioned it to Huxley when asked about it?

Gradually, two alternatives crystallized. One of them was perfectly straightforward: Bribe him. . . . A truly imposing bribe.

How much? Well, if Huxley wavered, Danny could be flexible. He might begin at twenty-five thousand dollars, and be prepared to go to double that.

What if he wanted one hundred thousand dollars?

One million dollars?

He forced himself to sit, calm down. A million dollars was a silly sum of money even to think about. It was just a metaphor, a way of saying he would not accept any bribe. But the lesser figure?

He knew that the salary of assistant professors beginning in college was about twelve thousand. So by offering him twenty-five he was offering him two years' compensation—among other things, compensation he wouldn't even qualify for until *after* he earned his Ph.D. And, tax free. Danny was hardly going to write it off as a business expense, and Huxley wouldn't likely list it as compensation. And if Danny let Huxley move him up to fifty thousand, that was *four* times the salary he'd be getting.

He'd have to try it.

He made his plans carefully. He wrote out the schedule in painstaking detail, leaving out nothing. Like a choreographer's ballet: one step after another. He recited the schedule to himself. Spoke it out, his eyes closed, a half-dozen times.

When he was fully satisfied, he lit a match to the sheet of paper and watched it burn. He poured himself another drink and took it up to his bedroom, at the other end of the hall from Caroline's.

. . . .

His first call in the morning was to Cutter Malone.

He spoke next to Margie, told her he would be out most of the day. He would be driving with Cutter to look at a site in the Berkshires, near Great Barrington, where a resort hotel might be constructed. The project was confidential, at the request of Malone's client.

He went then to Crédit Suisse, exposed his credit number to the cashier, and withdrew twenty-five thousand dollars in one-hundred-dollar bills.

Shortly before eleven, Cutter Malone was easily overheard by his wife speaking over the telephone. She heard her husband say, "Yeah sure, Danny. I'm available. I'll meet you at the railroad station in Greenwich. No point in your having to drive in to New York—we can shoot up toward Great Barrington from there." Cutter told his wife he'd be away most of the day, to look at a possible hotel development with Danny.

At about noon, Danny set out for the Poughkeepsie Inn. When he checked in, he was bearded and dressed in a tuxedo. With his left hand he carried a saxophone case, with his right, an overnight bag. He left a cash deposit of sixty dollars for one of the hotel suites and signed in as Peter Espinoso. He asked that his suite be as far as possible from other guests, as he might wish to practice his instrument. "Just one night," he told the clerk. "Wedding reception."

In his living room he settled down. First he put on the silk gloves, then changed his clothes in the adjoining bedroom. Now he wore a simple gray suit, a soft blue shirt and discreet striped tie. The traveling case with the tuxedo was in the closet, along with the saxophone case. He looked at his watch, and flicked his mind back to the sheet of instructions from last night.

At 3:15 he put in the telephone call. He rang through to the FDR Center and gave the operator at Hyde Park the extension number.

"Mr. Huxley? This is Cutter Malone. I'm in Poughkeepsie, looking in on the Poughkeepsie Inn on behalf of a client. I've thought over your request and decided to give you the information you want. I'm going to France in the next couple of days, but I know you said it was urgent to see me. Could you come right away? This will be the last chance for me for at least a month. . . . You don't have a car?"

Fuck! Danny hadn't thought of that.

"Well, is it worth it to you to hire a cab? What is it—less than a half hour, no? Can I hang on for a minute? Sure. . . . You say you can borrow a car? Oh. Well, that's fine. So you should be here, what, a couple of minutes before four o'clock? Fine. Now since we're going to be touching on some confidential matters, I don't expect you to mention our meeting. That is a condition of my cooperation. Is it acceptable? . . . Good. Come right up to number 811. I'm in one of the manager's side rooms. If he happens to be consulting with me when you come in, I'll ask him to leave and wait till we're through. Okay? Good."

Sounds very calm, Danny thought. Very measured. Huxley had spoken slowly over the telephone, deliberately. He must have been within earshot of the person who so promptly offered him the use of a car.

Danny poured himself a drink of Scotch from the plastic container. He kept his eye on his watch. He moved the dresser in the bedroom, a waist-level table with three drawers on either side, away from the wall opposite the window that looked out onto Cannon Street.

He thought to turn on the television set and just coast about, see what was playing. He began to do so, but the sound of the voices coming in over the various channels provoked him, he didn't know why. He looked again at his watch. Huxley might even come in as early as 3:50, if he got the car right away.

One more shot would help. He poured it into his glass, gulped it down. That was one thing he hadn't thought of, hadn't written down. Breath.

He didn't have any toothpaste. He must do something about his breath. He fiddled inside his pockets—perhaps he had left a cough drop, which he sometimes carried. No. *Nothing.* He went to the bathroom and put the soap into his mouth, lathering its disgusting waxy-oily taste on his tongue. With toilet paper he wiped his tongue and breathed out into the mirror. He huffed into his right hand, held up to an inch from his mouth and tried to smell himself. He was satisfied.

He was back in the room and heard the knock on the door. Danny opened it.

Max Huxley wore gray flannels and a blazer. Danny shook hands with a serious young man, hair close cut, briefcase in hand. Danny motioned to him to sit down and went back to his own chair behind the dresser.

Huxley spoke. "You're Mr. O'Hara. I've seen a lot of pictures of you. Including," Huxley smiled, "when at age fourteen you visited your grandfather. I was supposed to see Mr. Malone."

Danny was prepared for that one.

"I didn't want to advertise my presence in this part of the world. My autocratic sister would not forgive me for being so close and not calling on her. Anything Mr. Malone can tell you, I can tell you. You have a question, Mr. Huxley? We may as well get on with it."

"I have a few, yes, sir." Huxley opened his briefcase and brought out a clipboard. He drew a manila folder from it. "I guess the first question is, Why did the Hyde Park Capital Fund turn over the Martino stock to the Hyde Park Fund?"

"That was what Mr. Martino wished us to do."

"Why did Mr. Martino deed the stock to the Capital Fund in the first place?"

"He told me he wished me and Mr. Malone to benefit for fifteen months from the proceeds of the Trafalgar chain. A reward for the time we had put in."

"Where is there written evidence that that was his design?"

"There is no written evidence. His instructions were oral."

"My research shows that during the period the Capital Fund owned the Martino stock, the company generated dividends of just over four million dollars. Do I understand you to be saying that Mr. Martino wished you and Mr. Malone to receive a bonus in that amount?"

"He did not specify the amount. We were to receive whatever the proceeds of the enterprises yielded during this period."

"How is it that no publicity was given to the arrangement?"

"We didn't feel any need to give publicity to it. Mr. Martino had no wish to give it publicity."

"A copy of the probated will arrived in the mail this morning. There is no mention in it of the stock moving from your hands to the Hyde Park Fund after two years. Where are your instructions to do this?"

"I told you the instructions were oral."

"That means that if you wished to do so, you and Mr. Malone could have kept that stock forever, doesn't it?"

"That would have been dishonorable," Danny said, leaning back in his chair, a trace of a frown appearing on his forehead.

Huxley paused. Then, "Well, there is no point, is there, in maintaining the confidentiality of the arrangement? I mean, it is very unusual, and for that reason newsworthy. I will of course do what I can to verify all this, that is my duty. But I cannot see why anyone would have any objection to this—"

Danny interrupted him. His voice had a new hardness in it. "To tell the truth, Mr. Huxley—Max, may I?—I do not want publicity given to the arrangement. There are good reasons for this. Associates of Mr. Malone and of mine would—I mean, some of them—would resent it that they were not also beneficiaries of the estate, even if in lesser amounts. An incitement to jealousy. And we are not anxious for the trustees of the Library to know that—that there was a distribution in advance of the funds that went to the Library. They might feel compelled for fiduciary reasons to file some sort of an objection—"

"Mr. O'Hara, are you saying I should suppress this arrangement?"

"That is exactly what I am suggesting, except that I wouldn't use the word 'suppress.' I'm suggesting you simply *ignore* it. It's hardly a major story. In fact, I'm here to *request* you do this. Mr. Malone and I would be willing to make a substantial contribution to you and your research, in exchange for your cooperation."

Max Huxley's mouth opened, his eyebrows lifted. And then, "Mr. O'Hara—"

"I am talking about twenty-five thousand dollars in cash, which I have here with me in my suitcase." Danny leaned down as though to rehearse the opening of a suitcase and the removal of a package from it.

"Mr. O'Hara, please. There is no way that any such exchange would be taken other than as a—bribe. I mean, anybody who knew about it would say just that, that I had accepted a bribe. I mean, you can see that, can't you?" Max Huxley's voice was that of an elderly man pleading for understanding by someone less worldly, less sophisticated.

"You will learn, Max, when you are a little older, that people throw terms like that around—'bribe'—for personal convenience. Somebody who wanted to think ill of you would interpret helping a lady across the street as sexual harassment. Forget it. The best rule in life, whatever your profession, is to be practical. To take . . . practical . . . opportunities. . . ."

Huxley knew he would get nowhere. He decided to leave the room. He was flushed when he rose from his chair.

"Come on, Max, sit down. I mean, what's the hurry, let's just go over it one more time."

Max remained on his feet. "I've said everything I have to say, Mr. O'Hara. But if you want some reassurance, I'll give it to you: When I publish the story, I will omit any mention of our encounter here. Any mention of any attempt by you to keep me from— going ahead." He started toward the door when the bullet pierced his back.

Huxley toppled over onto the floor, one hand reaching behind his back. He gave out a soft moan. Danny rose, approached him and fired a second shot above Huxley's ear. Blood flowed now onto the carpet, from Huxley's mouth and stomach.

Danny closed his eyes. His mind turned to the memorandum he had committed to memory the night before.

A B C D then E then F.

He had instructed himself what to do at every point. But he had not anticipated the working of his mind. Now he opened his eyes and stared at the young man with close-cut hair on the floor, bleeding to death. Maybe he was dead already. Quickly Danny closed his eyes. He held them tightly closed. He needed to do this before doing anything else. He would not look again at what he had done. And it would help him to have a deep swallow. Turning his head away, he walked to the bathroom and brought out the bottle. Again he shut his eyes. He must go back now to the schedule, must go past F on to G. Everything depended on self-control. He was good at that, he remembered, he was always good in a crisis, whether sailing in a boat or finding just the moment to toss a grenade into a pillbox; he was good up against heavy weather in a casino, calm and steady when face to face with a grim judge-prosecutor like his godfather. . . .

He would need to test himself again, though he had not imagined how difficult it would be. . . . The next step. Ah. Yes.

He put his gloves back on, went into the bedroom, took off his clothes and put on his tuxedo. He reattached the beard. Now he needed to approach . . . the body, alongside which the briefcase lay. He opened it and surveyed the neatly indexed manila folders. He removed the two files marked ''Hyde Park Capital Fund'' and ''Hyde Park Fund.'' He replaced the other files and closed the briefcase. He felt inside the pockets of Huxley's coat, brought out a little leather appointment book, examined the page with the afternoon's notation, tore it out and put it in his pocket. He paused and thought better of it. He reached down and put the entire notebook into his pocket.

He picked up the saxophone case, went past the elevator to the staircase and walked down eight flights. At the bottom of the staircase he peered over to the main entrance. A guest with a raincoat slung over his shoulder was checking out. Danny turned left, leaving the hotel through the side entrance. He walked a block to the outdoor parking garage, got into the car, paid his parking bill at the checkout counter and set out for Greenwich. Nearing Putnam, he slid off his beard and took off the jacket to his tuxedo and the black tie. In the men's room of a diner, he slipped off his black trousers and put on gray flannels. Back in the car, he put away the evening clothes and put on the jacket to his gray suit and the striped tie. He resumed driving. He'd be in Greenwich in plenty of time. At exactly 6:25 he would stop opposite the Greenwich Library. Cutter Malone would be waiting for him and would step into the car. They would park at the Pickwick

Arms Hotel and go into the bar, where they would order a drink and ask the bartender please to hurry, as they needed to catch the 7:05 express for New York.

When Danny got home he told Caroline he had had a most enticing offer and had agreed to meet with a French hotelier. "I'll be flying to Paris tomorrow, then maybe Geneva, Nice, Zurich, Lyons—depending on how it goes. I'll be checking on one, or more than one, of the chains."

Caroline asked him if a week's supply of clothes would be enough.

Danny nodded. "If I have to stay over, I'll have my stuff washed. Yes, three suits should be plenty. Thanks, Caroline. I'll go say goodbye to the kids."

Thirty-three

WHEN HENRY RETURNED to *Time* from the Columbia School of Journalism, he was grateful to learn from Richard Clurman that he was not being reassigned to Saigon. "I think you had enough of Vietnam. Besides, I gather that if Barbara went there she'd root for Ho Chi Minh."

"That's a little exaggerated." Henry had got used to being teased about his wife's expressive political sympathies and thought maybe he should do something about the exaggerations before they calcified. "Barbara's gradually pulling out of that whole scene. She still thinks we shouldn't be in Vietnam. But she doesn't pipe up anymore to defend what the Vietcong does, though she defends what they want—"

"Yeah, independence. Like the North Vietnamese have independence. Never mind"—Clurman didn't allow such matters to get in the way of business at hand—"we're going to leave you here in New York. Meanwhile, we have an immediate assignment." Clurman lifted a cable from Stockholm.

"The Nobel committee, our book people think, is going to give the prize to Georges Simenon. Otto's pleased as punch because nobody can be more fun to write about than Simenon. He boasts—did you know this about the great novelist?—of having had ten thousand different women."

"Ten thousand? I remember reading about him that in one year, back in the thirties I think it was, he managed to write forty-four novels in one calendar year. It's hard to figure out how he had time to log in his yearly ration of women—he's how old?"

"Sixty-something. Born 1903."

"How can you have that many women and write that many books? Hell, forget the books. How can you have that many women and—read the morning paper? We doing a cover?"

"It'll be a cover if he gets the Nobel. We'll write it as a cover. If Nobel passes him by, we'll run big inside. For your information, Georges Simenon is at this moment the world's single best-selling author."

"I am impressed. Where do I go?"

"Cannes. He rents a big place there. He knows English but doesn't like to give interviews in English, so your French is critical." Clurman was reading from the bio attached to the cable. "He lived in Connecticut for five years—hey, aren't you from Lakeville, Connecticut?"

"Yup."

"Well, Simenon lived there for five years in the fifties, it says here. His son, Marc, went to Hotchkiss. Kicked out."

"Why? Procuring for the old man?"

"Doesn't say. Anyway, he's agreed to cooperate. He doesn't much mind the idea of being on the cover of *Time*. Don't tell him he won't be if he misses out in Stockholm. Just the usual, you know—'It's-not-my-decision. . . .' "

. . . .

Henry was surprised on reaching the Pan American counter to see Danny standing in line.

"Danny! Paris?"

"Yes."

It was clear that Danny was less than overjoyed at the prospect of seven hours on a 707 seated next to his brother-in-law. "You too going to Paris? Traveling first class?"

"No," Henry said. "The stockholders of Time Inc. don't think first class is absolutely necessary for first-class work from their reporters. I suppose you *are* first?"

"What else?" Danny said, ostentatiously adjusting his tie and looking up in the general direction of the balconies. "I'll cross the tracks somewhere along the line and have a drink with you. Now I got to get to the newsstand. Want anything?"

Henry shook his head. "I've got ten novels by Georges Simenon to read. That's a week's work for Simenon, twice that for me."

Several hours later, Danny moved back to the tourist section. His face was flushed, his words a little garbled. He told Henry he'd be moving about a bit, Paris, Geneva, Nice—where would Henry be quartered? And for how long?

Henry gave him the name of the hotel at Cannes.

"Ah, Cannes/Nice. Reminds me of juvenile delinquency, that part of the world. As a matter of fact I'll probably be going to Nice. There's a succulent hotel there. And other succulent things. When I'm there, in Nice, I always stay at the Hotel Negresco, you know, next to the Casino Royale. You remember it?"

"Yes," Henry said as Danny took down the name of the hotel in next-door Cannes where Henry would be staying. Danny promised to call in if he got to that part of the world during the next few days.

Henry stayed overnight at the Sofitel Hotel near the Paris airport and took the flight to Nice the next day. He checked into his hotel and was given the telegram: "CALL IMMEDIATELY. NEVER MIND HOUR. URGENT. LOVE BARBARA."

He walked quickly to his room and went to the telephone. It was four in the morning in New York.

"Listen, Henny. Goddamnedest thing. This morning—yesterday morning—about the time you took off from JFK, the people at the Poughkeepsie Inn in Poughkeepsie found a corpse—a *corpse*—yes. His name was Max Huxley. He was shot. Shot in the stomach and shot in the head. No apparent motive, the police say. His wallet was untouched.

"Now listen, Henny, I spent *hours* with Max Huxley right up until yesterday."

"You did?"

"Yes. A really nice guy, lovely guy, a scholar who digs like a good reporter and who has bright and funny ideas—serious, a little bit of romance there, he liked to sit at FDR's desk—"

"You knew him all that well?"

"Henny darling, I *leaned* on him the moment I got here, four days ago. He went out of his way to help me in every way. Day before yesterday, we had a joint session with Lila. Henny, I got *close* to Max."

"Tell me more about him."

"He was a graduate student, doing a dissertation on Hyde Park. Two days ago he told me he had got hold of an interesting wrinkle . . . involving a hundred million dollars. A hot lead. You ever hear of the Hyde Park Capital Fund?"

"Isn't that where Martino left the money? For the Library?"

"It's where he left the money, yeah. Only the Hyde Park Capital Fund was owned seventy-five percent by—Danny. Daniel Tracey O'Hara. Max couldn't figure out why the stock passed over after Martino's death to the Hyde Park Capital Fund and then, after two years, suddenly was transferred to the Hyde Park Fund. So *for two years* Danny and his partner, Cutter Malone, who was the principal accountant for the Trafalgar chain, sopped up all the profits of the corporation. Did you know anything about that?"

No, Henry said. He knew nothing about the other Hyde Park fund.

"My point is, Henny, there *was* a motive for killing Max. He was onto a hot story."

"Barbara. You're not suggesting Danny—or the Malone guy— went to Poughkeepsie to bump off a graduate student?"

"No. All I'm saying is, there *was* a motive. So my question is: Do I go to the police with what I've just told you?"

"God, that's a hell of a question. Funny . . ."

"What's funny?"

"Danny was with me on the plane yesterday. Prospecting for hotel business. On the other business—your business—I don't think it's right for us to throw out a lead so obviously crazy that implicates my brother-in-law."

"Darling? *Darling Henny.* In this situation I am not 'us.' I'm me. A reporter for the *New York Times.* There is a murder. The victim, a good person, was working side by side with me for the better part of three days. He was onto something he thought might be—might still be—a life-sized scandal. Forget you're my husband, forget Danny's your brother-in-law, the best man at our wedding. You are Professor Chafee and I'm Barbara Horowitz, a student at Columbia School of Journalism, and I give you this situation. *What do I do, Professor?*"

Henry breathed deeply, thought quickly and said, "Yes, you're right. But listen. To the extent you can, Barbara, be 'Miss *New York Times*' in your dealing with the police—not a friend of the victim-friend of the family."

"That will be easy. Remember my name, darling; I'm Barbara Horowitz, not Mrs. Henry Chafee."

"I don't know what time I'll get back from seeing Simenon. Whatever time it is, I'll call you. Will you be at the *Times* or back in Hyde Park?"

"I'll be wherever the police tell me to be, is my guess. Call person-to-person for me at the Library. And don't go through Lila. Goodbye, darling. Say hello to de Gaulle. Congratulate him for getting out of Algeria."

The villa where Simenon lived and wrote was larger even than Somerset Maugham's, only a few miles away, about which Henry had written four years previously. Looking at the imposing villa, a reconstruction of a nineteenth-century château, Henry estimated from the driveway that there might be as many as fifteen or more bedrooms there. Enough for a moderate man's purposes.

But then it was a complex household. One story about Simenon, one of the many Henry had perused in the past few days, published in *The New Yorker*, described the great author's entourage at one point in the fifties. Henry had copied out, possibly to quote in his own story, the passage exactly: *"The ménage consisted of the Master; his first wife; his soon-to-be second wife; Boule, the faithful maid-companion-mistress who has lived with him for twenty years, and two children by the two wives."*

Henry had decided there wouldn't be any point in attempting to probe Simenon on family matters; no reporter had ever succeeded in getting Georges Simenon to talk about any aspect of his home life with the single exception of his mother, for whom he would take any opportunity to reiterate his loathing. His mother had wanted him to be a pastry cook and was terribly disappointed when, at age twenty-one, he went instead into writing. Almost there and then, it seemed, Simenon published not one dozen, but several dozen novels, all of them successful, gradually becoming the toast of the international literary set with his Inspector Maigret series. Simenon liked to talk about his books. Henry had been especially struck by one published interview. Simenon was asked how had he thought up such an extraordinary array of criminal situations around which to center his sixty-five Maigret books, to which Simenon had answered: "I have no imagination of my own. Everything I write is based on something that happened somewhere."

He found Simenon in an agreeably talkative mood. The butler had led Henry into a wing of the palatial villa. The study was, as one would expect, book-lined. On one side of the desk reposed the famous typewriter—for the first decade or two, Simenon had written everything by hand. Now his typewriter was greatly fancied and admired by the legion of journalists and writers who interviewed him. Uniformly they stared at it, wondering what was its talismanic secret.

Henry noted that notwithstanding that he sat in what amounted to a literary factory, there was no disorder. Well, perhaps that was why: In factories there can't be disorder, or the flow of . . . sausages is interrupted. He knew, had read all about, Simenon's famous working habits: up at six in the morning, six hours of uninterrupted writing, an hour or two in the afternoon to survey yesterday's work or even to attack an entirely different book. Or short story. Or movie script. Or play. Simenon writing fiction was an undisturbable phenomenon, like the rising sun. No one who himself wrote—no one like Henry—could begin to understand how it was done. But all were curious about the physical arrangements of Simenon's workshop. He was neat.

Simenon sat deep in a leather armchair, legendary pipe in mouth, wearing his glasses over what had so often been described as his hound-dog eyes. An olive-and-green bandana hung loosely but neatly around his neck.

Simenon took the initiative. His greeting in English was more guttural than, for some reason, Henry had expected, given the five years he had spent in northwestern Connecticut whence he supervised the training of his son at prep school. The boy's instruction had been comprehensive, including, at age thirteen, sending him to New York City where, at the great Simenon's request, a friend of his editor at Doubleday had arranged a night for the teenager with an accomplished and motherly whore, to "fix him up," as Simenon had learned to put it. Henry would need to make some reference to Simenon's extravagant sexual life, always the talk of the literary world, but he knew better than to dwell on it. Perhaps Simenon would say what was foremost on his mind? Simenon did:

"I see *Time* magazine has picked up the Nobel rumor in Stockholm. I will not believe it unless I see it in the newspapers. But perhaps it will happen—who knows? I suppose it is true there is no single writer alive who is better known than I am. Certainly none who is more productive. I correct that, monsieur. There are no *dozen* writers alive whose work, cumulatively, is as extensive as my own. I do not deny that. And there is always this possibility too, that Sweden will rise above those dreary accusations—that I collaborated with the Nazis during the war. It is true that I continued to write in Paris during the war. What was I supposed to do? Take up music? In Sweden they should understand.

"Yes, Sweden. You will remember, Monsieur Chafee—you are so young—Sweden did not engage in the war. In that sense the whole of Sweden was, by fashionable ideological standards, a 'collaborator,' right?

"Did you know," Simenon's lips crackled into a smile as he reached into his pocket for a different pipe, "that when it was proposed, at the founding conference in San Francisco, that Sweden, Switzerland and Ireland be admitted into the United Nations, they were all three vetoed? On what grounds? Monsieur, guess. On what grounds?"

Henry said he could not remember.

"On the grounds that they were not *peace-loving nations!*" He let out a whoop of laughter. "Three nations that did *not* go to war were not *peace-loving!*"

Henry did not want to interrupt the soliloquy, and didn't do so. A half hour went by before Simenon asked, "What do you want to talk to me about? I have told my wife I will no longer discuss with anybody the matter of fornication. What else?"

Henry popped the question. He said, "Beyond fornication there is imagination. Tell me about yours."

Simenon welcomed the query. He spoke of his last three novels as handy reference points. Had Henry read *Le train de Venise? L'homme au petit chien? Le petit saint?*

The first two, Henry said, not *Le petit saint.*

"Well," Simenon said with relish, "all three of them were based on events that happened between the first day of April last year, and the last day in April. And the one before, *Le rond point* —that one was not published in English—did you read my novel about the pornographic photographer, right here in Cannes?"

No, Henry said, he had not read it.

"Well," Simenon explained, "a middle-aged—procurer?—no, he wasn't a procurer, not exactly. He had two or three beautiful women in his stable, one of them apparently a knockout and privately wealthy. His specialty was to find socially conspicuous men—somebody like me, for instance. He would represent himself as someone anxious to please that beautiful lady over there—this would be at the opera, at a nightclub, at a casino. He would tempt the person to bed with one of his ladies in a room especially equipped with a camera. You guessed it?''

Henry found himself leaning forward, listening acutely. "And then?''

"And then he would take the pictures and do one of two things. Either he would blackmail the man, or he would sell the pictures to the underground tabloids." Simenon sighed. "It was an exciting life, but not a very long one.''

"What happened?''

"Somebody put handcuffs on him in his apartment over here'' —he flexed his finger in the general direction of the sea—"and shot him. That was an intriguing one, because the police found one photographic negative—it had been separated from the roll. The lady was readily identifiable, one of the photographer's regulars, but the man, you could see only his backside. All you could tell was that he was young and well shaped.

"They did track down the lady. There was no way for her to deny what she had been up to. I mean, a screw is a screw, is it not, monsieur? But she insisted that she and her lover were entirely unaware what the pornographer was up to, said she didn't know anything about the cameras, said she kept no record of who her lover was.

"Of course they cannot fool my Inspector Maigret. He pieces it all together, with his characteristic skill and delicacy and self-effacement." Henry knew that the fabled creation of Georges Simenon, the Inspector Maigret who figured in sixty-five novels, was a special enthusiasm of his creator. "Yes, Maigret of course penetrates the operation and comes up with the identity of the killer. It happened that it was a young man who was in these parts to frolic. He was the grandson of Franklin Delano Roosevelt—''

"Excuse me." Henry's impulse had been to shoot up from his chair. He clenched his left hand on his steno pad and continued to write, controlling his voice. "But how did you come up with *that?*"

"Simple. I told you, I have no imagination. But I read everything. I looked at the society columns during the period and there were two references to a grandson of President Roosevelt, who apparently frequented the same casino the dead man operated in."

"Do you have, for instance"—Henry struggled to affect only a journalist's interest—"the date of the murder?"

"Not in my memory, and I'd have disguised the date in the book. But in fact it was," he closed his eyes for a moment, "it was in early September 1949, I believe. Maigret of course assembles the evidence."

"What"—Henry's voice was remote, as if he were speaking to himself—"what happens in the book to Roosevelt's grandson?"

Simenon laughed. "Oh, he beats the rap. Of course I change his identity, I make him out to be a young Arab prince, and the French authorities succumb to pressures from Saudi Arabia. But Maigret's record, I am happy to say, is unspoiled. That's what counts, you know, monsieur. The reader has no doubt that Maigret was right when he fingered the grandson as the killer."

Much later, Simenon rose. It was time, he said, to prepare for dinner. Yes, he would agree to see Monsieur Chafee again tomorrow or the day after, if there were more questions to be asked. And yes, the morning would be satisfactory for the *Time* photographer. "But not more than one hour. Tell him eleven to twelve. Photographers rule the world. They tell kings and queens and prime ministers what to do. But they do not tell Georges Simenon what to do. They take more time shooting a portrait than I require to write a book. Good day, Monsieur Chafee."

Thirty-four

A T NINE, Henry was at the Bureau de Police in Cannes. The sergeant at the desk rang a supervisor, relayed the request, received back instructions, and told Henry to proceed to the second floor. In Room C, Inspector Gilbert would be waiting for him.

Henry was surprised and pleased that the older man, tall, slim, balding, well-dressed, was cordial from the start. This was unusual in his experience with old crime cases and brusque and bored police officials asked to look into archives.

"My son is also a reporter," Gilbert said after a few minutes, during which he offered tea or coffee to his guest. "Roland is with *Paris Match,* studying English at night. He hopes to be sent to New York for a tour of duty.

"Of course I will help you in any way I can. *Time* magazine is a very distinguished publication. I do wish they would come out with a French edition, like *The Reader's Digest.* Because—I am ashamed of this, but I have the excuse that I fought in two wars which . . . engrossed my attention . . . consumed a great deal of time—I don't speak any English, or read it. A most difficult language!"

Henry sympathized, and then told him that in connection with a very important story planned by *Time* on Georges Simenon, Henry was doing research on some of the plots used by M. Simenon in his novels, and that yesterday the famous author had told him about the background used in the novel *Le rond point.* Henry's request was to examine the police files. Henry had got the date he was looking for, the day the *Continental* sailed from Nice with Danny and Henry aboard in September of 1949. He got the exact date not from Caroline—the last thing Henry would do at this moment was speak to Caroline, not knowing what if anything had come up between her and police investigators. He supposed it likely that the police from Poughkeepsie had approached her, or would at any moment. He had got Margie, Danny's secretary, to do him the little favor of calling Caroline, who had always kept a diary. Caroline reported to Margie, after digging back in her files, that the *Continental* had picked her up on September 8, 1949, at Southampton.

That meant that it had sailed out of Nice on September 6.

Henry Chafee was looking for police files recording the murder of a man who, if Georges Simenon was talking about the same man, had been murdered on September 6. "M. Simenon reports that the murderer was never apprehended. Would that mean that the file on the victim is still live?"

"Live?"

"Open. I mean, still open."

"Technically, yes," Inspector Gilbert said. "But after five years, if the case is not active, the file goes into a separate division. But with the details you give me, there should be no problem in finding it. You are comfortable where you are sitting? Here," he handed them over, "are the morning papers."

Inspector Gilbert was back in fifteen minutes. "It is not too thick a file. You are most welcome, if you desire to peruse it in detail, to do so over there." He pointed to an empty desk. "M. Raymond is off duty today, so help yourself to his facilities."

Henry sat down at the battered heavy desk of M. Raymond, with the overflowing IN and OUT boxes and the two telephones and two ashtrays. He opened the fifteen-year-old file.

It began with a typed six-page police report. The typist hadn't made an effort to avoid typographical errors. Several of the words were XXX'd out, and there were emendations in a large circular hand. Attached was an autopsy, written in dense medical language. Several clippings from the local newspapers were in the next folder. And, after them, a folder containing a half-dozen photographs of the dead man, taken in his apartment, as he was discovered.

He was Paul Hébert. And, Henry stared at the picture, transfixed, he was exactly as Henry and Danny had left him, hands handcuffed, the heavy desk leg resting within the loop of his arms. The difference was that when Henry left, Hébert was merely shackled; here, Hébert's head lay flat on the carpet, stained with blood.

Henry inspected another photograph, stapled to a sheet of paper, and translated the caption, which read: *"Photo retrieved from deceased's atelier. Found on floor of cabinet with developing solution. Possible suspect. See appended material for interview with woman."*

Henry stared at it. The angle of the camera highlighted the face of a full-featured woman, her blond hair disheveled, her eyes half closed, a gratified smile on her lips. Her lover was presumably fondling her breasts. Was she Danny's woman?

Henry looked even more carefully. The lover's buttocks were tightly drawn, his shoulders slightly lifted.

Henry had often seen Danny's backside, walking into and out of their common shower; swimming, in the old days, at the gymnasium at Yale. He could not identify Danny from the picture, but Danny had said enough to suggest it could have been he, the night before—the photographer had caught a lover in a copulative thrust. When they had retrieved the pictures, that day in

September fifteen years ago, Danny had snatched them up, the print and the negatives, and stuffed them into his jacket pocket; he had no wish to let them be seen, even by his co-conspirator.

Still, if it was Danny that Henry was looking down on, not another young man in bed with a whore, it was a deduction, not a positive identification, though a deduction backed by over-whelming circumstantial detail.

Henry wanted more. He turned to the coroner's report with the autopsy.

The estimated time of death was given as 1400, September 6.

Henry closed his eyes.

How was it possible?

His memory then relived the moment.

Danny turned the car key, started up the motor; the air was very hot. Then suddenly Danny said—yes, the memory was now vivid—*Damn! He had to go back up to the apartment; he had left his dark glasses.* He had left the motor running.

Danny—it was now as clear to Henry as though he had seen it all done on film. Danny had gone up in the elevator and shot Paul Hébert.

How had he got into the apartment?

He must have pocketed the key when he and Henry left the apartment to go down to the car. Either that, or he had contrived to leave the apartment door unlocked when they slipped out. Either way, it could only mean that Danny planned all along to go back, after Henry was safely out of the way, to carry out the capital sentence.

And during the drive back to Nice—it all came back now—Danny had been exultant over the success of what Henry now knew was a mission much more ambitious than the mission in which Henry had collaborated. That mission was simply to re-trieve the photographs. Danny had a larger view of it. It was to kill the blackmailer.

Back in the hotel, Henry called Barbara. It was 8 A.M. in New York.

What was going on?

Three volleys of "official New York" police had come to question her, she told him. "The third was the District Attorney. He told me it made good sense to be completely quiet about me and Huxley and Hyde Park. I told him of course. "I'm not about to circulate stuff that might publicly incriminate Danny. I mean, unless he's guilty. Obviously," Barbara Horowitz's voice trailed off just a little, "—obviously he isn't.

"I said all the right things, but I did remind the D.A. that I am a professional reporter, and have professional duties too. He clucked an understanding cluck. The D.A. rewarded me by telling me that they were grilling Cutter Malone about the Hyde Park Capital Fund. Danny was with Cutter the whole day, Tuesday, on a hotel-inspection tour of some kind up in Massachusetts, so at least we know they weren't personally involved. Beats me. How's it going at your end?"

Henry found it hard not to share with her the stages of hell he had visited. But not yet, not yet. So he answered the finite question. "Very interesting, Simenon. Great talker. Great reader. Not much on imagination, though. I'll be seeing him again this afternoon, and writing out my notes tonight." Henry was eager to end the conversation, eager to get back to his work. To thinking. But he needed to say one thing. "Barbara, it would be great if, somehow, you could make contact with Caroline. Just—I don't need to tell you what to say—at least say this, that I called, wanted to know about her, told you how much I love her, that kind of thing." And then, abruptly, Henry said, "Call me back if you have any news."

Barbara did call again, late in the evening, Henry's time. Henry was alone in his hotel room, typing his notes and translating passages from a book of essays by Simenon and putting off a final moment of self-examination.

"Henny, soon after lunch the D.A. sent somebody to take a long deposition from me about Max. Then the D.A. came back to see me, said the French had been asked to track down Danny in Paris, but he had checked out of the Ritz Hotel. They weren't saying anything more to me, but a minute ago I had a call from Caroline—yes, I had already called her, as you asked. . . . She had just put down the phone with Mrs. Cutter Malone, you remember who *he* is? . . . Yes, well, Cutter Malone has been arrested, his wife said."

"On what charges?"

"Grand larceny. They want a hundred thousand dollars in bail, Caroline said, and Mrs. Malone asked if she had any *idea* where in France they could locate Danny because, she said to Caroline, Danny undoubtedly could clear up the whole business."

Henry didn't want to prolong the discussion. He told Barbara he'd have to call her back because a cable from *Time* had just been handed to him by a bellboy.

He needed to think—Henry was perspiring when he put down the telephone receiver. And the instant he took his hand off it, the telephone rang. Henry jumped, as if he had set off an alarm. He reached for the receiver before the second ring.

His voice was hoarse. "Yes."

"Henry! This is Danny! I promised I'd call you if I came around. Well, I did. And I'm having a whale of a time at the Casino Royale. That's exactly twenty minutes away from your hotel. You got to come join me! Like old times. We'll have a late supper. Pick me up at the casino or just go to my suite, 7G—I told the concierge to let you in if you showed up—and call me at the casino from the suite. They'll know who I am, you bet. By the time you get there they'll be after me to lend *them* some money, the way I'm doing! What you say?"

Henry found himself saying, "Sure. Sure, Danny, I'll be around as soon as I can get there." And then a quick thought. "About midnight. I need a couple of hours."

Thirty-five

WHEN HE FIRST spotted Danny from behind, leaning over the roulette table, Henry was startled. Danny was wearing a tuxedo, even though formal clothes were no longer required by the casino. He looked suddenly like the young man Henry had known fifteen years before, radiant with energy and poise and life lust. Henry's eyes peeled Danny's clothes off, and he stared now at the dorsal side of the ardent collegian smothering his million-dollar whore. Another photograph flashed in Henry's mind, of Paul Hébert, his head lying in his own blood. His gaze wheeled to the casino bar, with its shaded mirrors, gilt, velvet and sconces. There was the bartender with his red jacket. It must have been on that very spot that Paul Hébert had approached Danny and made the deal. And over there, at the table where Danny was now playing, it must have been there that the beautiful blonde had raked in her winnings while Danny was dissipating all the money he had.

He thought then of Barbara's description of the young graduate student from the University of Chicago. "A really nice guy, lovely guy, a scholar who digs like a good reporter and who has bright and funny ideas—serious, a little bit of romance there, he liked to sit at FDR's desk—"

Henry began to walk toward Danny, who had just ordered a drink brought in from the bar. As Henry got closer, Danny began to gain weight. As he turned to lay down a bet, his chin looked a little paunchy, his hair a little sparse, with streaks of gray.

Henry stepped back.

No, not here. Danny had not seen him yet. He was intent on winning with the turn of the wheel.

Henry backed away, crossed the street and at the Negresco Hotel identified himself as the friend Mr. O'Hara was expecting. He was shown into Danny's suite. There was plenty of time. It was not yet midnight. He placed a phone call to New York, and then another.

A half hour later a hotel porter approached the American in the evening clothes playing at the roulette wheel. He was given, on a silver tray, an envelope. Danny read it. It was Henry. Danny must join him for that late dinner, already ordered to the suite at the hotel.

Danny had been winning. He could not leave that very second, not until that lovely little silver ball that was circling about the big wheel came to a stop. And yes! It dropped on the Red, which Danny was betting. If it had been so fifteen years ago there'd have been no need for Pauline. On the other hand, that was a stupid thought! He wouldn't have traded the memory of the night—and morning!—and afternoon with Pauline for, for—a diamond necklace! Danny thought this very funny, as he emptied the glass of champagne. By the law of averages, Henry wouldn't have to wait very long before the ball dropped into a Black pocket. Like—now. So he lost the final bet.

He had won a mere twenty-seven hundred dollars. But after all, he had spent almost three hours. Divided into twenty-seven, nine hundred dollars an hour; Danny was worth at least that! I mean, ask old Giuseppe, Giuseppe, yousa' think Danny Badboy no worth nine hundred dollars per hour?

That's right, Giuseppe, you bet your . . . Danny collected the money from the cashier, dropped a hundred-dollar note into the slot for the croupier *("Merci, monsieur, merci du part des employés")* and accepted a quick glass of champagne for the road. After all, he smiled inwardly, he had to go all the way across the street to the hotel for dinner. He gulped it down.

He bowed deferentially to his game companions. *"Bonsoir, messieurs, dames,"* he said, smiling, content.

Thirty-six

DANNY POUNDED on the door of 7A even though it was unlocked. He jostled the handle boisterously, up and down, up and down, settling finally for a thump-thump that thrust the door open.

"Hey there, Henry! How are you, brother! *J'espère que tout va bien!* Hey. Let's have a little gloom-chaser, what you say? Champagne, maybe? I mean, before we start eating—?"

Danny looked about the room. He had expected to see a dinner table set, with the usual Hotel Negresco apéritifs: olives, breadsticks, butter, a little paté. And where were the candles and flowers and the glimmering cutlery?

There was nothing. The suite was as he had left it. Just Henry, seated behind the coffee table with the telephone on it. Like a fucking judge, Danny half-muttered: Henry with his steno pad. Had Henry emerged from the womb with a steno pad? Danny thought it amusing to imagine this. He guessed that the waiters must be on their way.

"Sit down, Danny." Henry motioned to the couch opposite.

Danny plopped down. "Dinner not here yet, I can see. You got some champagne coming?"

Henry looked down at his pad. For twenty-four hours he had trained his mind on what he had to do and he knew now the meaning of the metaphor about sweating blood.

There was no levity in his voice. He began to speak—yes, Danny reckoned quickly, even as a judge might speak. The tone of voice was unsparing.

"At four this afternoon, Danny, Cutter Malone cracked; he told the D.A. he hadn't traveled with you at all on Tuesday, except from the Greenwich Library to the Pickwick Arms Hotel bar and then to the railroad station. He told the D.A. you had gone to Poughkeepsie to handle the problem of the Chicago graduate student. Malone told the D.A. that when you met him, you told him there wasn't anything more to worry about."

Danny didn't move. He simply changed color.

"An hour ago, the court issued a warrant for your arrest. The charge: murder and grand larceny.

"At three this afternoon, local time, I signed an affidavit. Here, in Nice. It says that we drove together to Boulevard Carnot in Cannes on September 6, 1949, that we overpowered the late Paul Hébert in his apartment; that we left him handcuffed and gagged; that as we were about to drive off, you left the car. That you told me you needed to go back to the apartment to retrieve your sunglasses; that you returned about five minutes later. That you were carrying your .22 Colt in your pocket.

"The police have located one Pauline Déboulard. She is prepared to identify the man she gave Paul Hébert's address to on September 5, 1949. The police files already have a picture of a person she was sleeping with, retrieved from the kitchen/studio of Paul Hébert the day of the crime. A negative you and I overlooked.

"The affidavit I have signed is not in the possession of Inspector Gilbert, the police investigator I've been dealing with. He has merely read it. I told him I would turn it over to the police only if he agreed to give me as much time as I wanted to talk with you here, tonight.

"That's the time I'm using up now. The police are stationed at both entrances to the hotel."

Henry paused. His exercise had deeply wearied him. He looked up from his notes, a heavy sadness etched into his face. He looked into Danny's eyes.

Danny's fingers clutched at the cushion he sat on. His mouth moved, but at first nothing was heard. Finally his jaw tightened. He spit out the words.

"You're a fucking coward, asshole."

"I figured you'd bring that up."

"Bring that up! It will hit the *hot wires,* what you did at Arno. You bet, asshole. *'Time* Correspondent Henry Chafee/Revealed Coward Under Fire 1944.' Cover story there? Asshole?"

"Danny. If you want to think about what to do . . . you can. As long as you want. They won't come up to take you."

"Think about *what?* Think about *what,* Henry?"

Henry paused. And then, "Do you really want to go back to New York?"

Suddenly, Danny understood. He looked slowly about the suite. His eyes rested on the little balcony.

"We're what, eight floors up?"

"Yes. Counting the lobby floor."

"That would do it, wouldn't it?"

"Yes."

Danny looked down at his cummerbund, hooked his thumb into it, and snapped it. A smile broke out.

"I could use a drink."

Henry walked over to the chest, opened the top drawer, removed a bottle of white wine and a second bottle, champagne. Both had been decorked. He brought out a glass, put it down on the night table by the couch where Danny sat, the two bottles alongside.

"Which do you want?"

Danny pointed with one finger to the champagne.

Henry filled the glass and went back to his chair. Danny reached over for it, raised it to his lips, held it, then, slowly, brought it down again, untouched. He put it back on the table. And spoke now with a strange calm.

"I do see your point, Henry. And I'm, well, sorry about the stuff just now, what I said. . . . Wasn't your fault, the Poughkeepsie thing. Though *this*"—he raised his voice slightly, circling his pointed finger vaguely, to suggest policemen surrounding the hotel— "*this* has to be your fucking fault; can't imagine how, after fifteen years, *the frog police* ran into Pauline, et cetera, et cetera, without you. God knows what put *you* on the trail.

"I think I got to tell you something, Henry. When I plugged that little pimp-gigolo-pornographer—*whatever* you want to call him—I didn't have one, not *un seule moment* of remorse. Hell, quite the opposite. I remember saying to myself when I held the pistol over his snotty nose: I've shot a lot nicer guys than"—the tone changed suddenly, back in the direction it had been—"*I* shot, Henry. You weren't so good at shooting, were you, Henry? You were too busy in the hospital, being taken care of like a war hero. The only person *you* ever shot was—"

Danny began a ribald laugh. "Yourself! *Henry Chafee!* Decorated for it! Nice touch that, wasn't it, Henry? You didn't like it much when I did that. But after all, it was your old buddy who set you up! Just being a little bit *mischievous*—so he gets you a medal for shooting yourself after you refuse to shoot the Nazis. Refuse to act like a man. Like a—"

Danny was distracted. He opened and closed his eyes. He was trying to focus them. He slowed the tempo of his talk.

"No," he said deliberatively, "I didn't give a shit about plugging that little bastard. But maybe I am just . . . just what, Henry? Ah, I am a *sinner!* Your sister—*dear* Caroline. I do love her, in a way. But I have a feeling every time she pours me a gin and tonic she is praying the tonic will *exorcise* me.

"Yeah." Danny looked over at the champagne. "So living with

Caroline hasn't been a bunch of roses, Henry. I know how you feel about her, and I don't give a shit; the hell with how you feel about her. . . . The hell with how *I* feel about her. *You* haven't been married to her for thirteen years. You haven't been told, no fuckee, Danny, Good Fridee, Danny." He laughed, and reached in the direction of the champagne, but stopped.

"No. No no no no, Henry. Caroline is a Wonderful Woman. Et cetera, et cetera. And I'm not suggesting I've been a chaste— wonderful word, chaste—Dixie-cup-dick husband. I bet you're a *chaste* husband to that Jew-girl Barbara, right, Henry? Did she check to see you were circumcised? Assuming she found any- thing down there? You *got* anything down there, Henry? Or did you leave it in Italy? In the foxhole?"

Henry Chafee's expression didn't change—the muscles in his face tightened. He waited.

"You're right, Henry. Some people pluck ripe apples if they're handy, some people don't. Not if there's a No Trespassing sign there. You don't. You wouldn't. You will die a respectable death and the pious will pray over you, you fucking bore. Me? Well, Henry, *I* was born to *take opportunities!*"

Now Danny reached for the glass, and brought it to his lips.

"I mean—so it didn't work out. The Martino raid. But it was a honey, wasn't it? I mean, sometimes things don't work out— that's true in every situation. It didn't work out for Alexander Hamilton, after all. Didn't work for Romeo—that's 'Romeo' as in 'Juliet'—come to think of it.

"You know, Henry, Romeo and I have *a lot* in common. I could give you any number of witnesses who would confirm that. Maybe my *foreplay* isn't so—poetic. On the other hand, maybe *Juliet* would have preferred it! Never occurred to me, that. But on the other point, do you think if I came up with, oh, three, four witnesses, to how, well, *super* chivalrous I am with the ladies, the frogs downstairs would let me slip out?"

He refilled his glass, drank it all. "Ah." He poured until his glass was full again, and spilled over. "I don't care. But I do see your point. . . . You know something, Henry? I've never *really* liked heights. You notice, I never took up skiing? Never climbed mountains, all that shit? You probably never noticed—after all, on Wednesday you didn't fly first class. But if you had, and you'd been looking at me, you might have noticed.

"Ah yes, you're saying weightily, since weightily is how you usually say things, dear Henry. I mean, what you're *thinking* weightily is: So Danny slips out of the Negresco Hotel—where does he go? Good point, Henry, very good point. There *is* that problem, the police in the good old U.S.A. They're all excited. About?

"That little creep from the University of Chicago. I bet that's what *really* did it to you, Henry. Not Paul Hébert, it was"— Danny's voice was mock funeral-parlor solemn—"the graduate student.

"But so—what was I *supposed* to do? Get in line in an academic procession? 'And summa cum laude, ladies and gentlemen, for Dr. Whatever his name—Max. Dr. Max Huxley—author of the prizewinning dissertation on The Great O'Hara Raid on Hyde Park. How Grandson Tried to Screw President Grandpa.'

"After the ceremony we all march off to the penitentiary, where they leave me off.

"I usually close my eyes on takeoff, in airplanes. No reason for you to know that. I've said that. But the idea of . . . jumping out the window . . . I mean, that's *creepy*. Creepy stuff, Henry. I'm just plain scared of things like that. I can understand now about the Arno business—you were just plain *scared* of getting up and running into—bullets. That's the last time you were scared, you bet. You certainly weren't scared of running tackles or heavyweight boxers. No—not heavyweight: You were middleweight, I remember. But you weren't scared anymore. Just that one time." Danny's voice trailed off.

"Well, I'm scared of jumping out of a window. Though I do see your point, Henry, never mind how much vino I've got in me, I see your point loud and clear. I wish I had my trusty old pistol—"

Henry reached in his pocket. "You have your old pistol and

you know you do. I looked in your bag. It's where you always kept it." Henry stood and opened the drawer under which he had kept the champagne. He lifted the familiar .22 Colt from it.

"God, Henry, you do think of everything." Danny stretched out his hands as if to catch a football. Henry obliged, lobbing the pistol across the room.

Danny caught it and brought it down on his waist. Almost absentmindedly he opened the magazine, sliding three bullets out, then reinserting them.

"Yes, I wouldn't confuse this little beauty with any other. Got it for Christmas when I was fourteen, last civilized thing my father ever did, that I can remember. I wonder if I inherited a lot of, you know—of this and that from *him?* But you never knew him, Henry, no. Before your time.

"Well, you can't put these things off forever, can you, and right now I'm wondering whether to have a little more of that— no. It's all gone. I'll have to dip into the wine. But please don't apologize, Henry. White wine is okay, especially," Danny examined the bottle, "a nice Pouilly-Fumé. So the question becomes, Shall I have a glass of wine? And you know something, Henry, when these great cosmic questions hit me—that one in particular, Shall I have another glass?—my tendency is to answer, 'Yes, Danny!—Yes, Danny *Badboy*, one of my dear . . . friends called me once. I'll have another drink.' "

He leaned over, recovered his glass, and drew it to his lips.

"There are right ways and wrong ways to do this thing, you know, Henry. Nothing worse than to do it wrong, I mean, *nothing* worse than fucking up on this kind of thing. I'd rather go to Sing Sing or wherever it is your friends in New York would stick me. Would stick me if I showed up. But you know something, I don't want you, sort of, *right here,* you understand, Henry? I mean—"

Henry stood up. "Danny, you tell me when, I'll go."

"Yeah, Henry, there's just one thing now, but it's important, and I know what your reaction is likely to be. But though I'm not in a position to lay down any *conditions*"—Danny tilted the glass, drank it down, and filled it again—"let me just put it this way: I got a half-million bucks in a Swiss account." He reached into his pocket, brought out his leather appointment book. "The details are there . . . last page. The number, which is all you need, just that number, and my I.D." He brought it out from his wallet, laid it on the coffee table.

"Now, dear Henry, you're going to say it's not *my* money, it's Giuseppe's. And therefore Hyde Park's. But I'm telling you, most of it came—no, *all* of it came, as a matter of fact—from my salary, stuff discreetly slipped away. Rainy-day stuff."

Henry was tempted to ask if it included returns from the sale of his mother's necklace. But no, no interruptions; nothing contentious.

"It belongs to Caroline and the children. Will you get it to them?"

Henry reasoned to himself: *Say yes. Whatever you end up doing, say yes now—give Danny that peace of mind.*

He nodded his head. "Yes."

"No fingers crossed?"

"No fingers crossed."

"Well"—Danny drank down the last of his glass—"I hate to leave an unfinished bottle, but these are special circumstances, wouldn't you say, Henry? Yes, time to go. And time for you to go—"

Henry walked toward the door to the corridor. He thought it best to say nothing. Because whatever he said might prove to be the wrong thing to say. He turned his head as he reached the door. He could see only the back of Danny's head, leaning over the end of the couch, the hair graying. His right hand was clenched around the empty glass. Henry needed to close his eyes, to reaffirm his purpose, to invoke the broad canvas and dwarf the scene in the room he was leaving.

He closed the door behind him, turned left for the elevator, thought better of it and engaged the staircase, down eight flights.

He arrived at the lobby. The concierge was jabbering in rapid, excited French to M. Gilbert. Someone from the seventh floor had reported hearing a shot. Gilbert motioned with his finger and four plainclothesmen materialized from the corners of the lobby. Another signal, and two elevators were summoned, while a third agent began the precautionary walk up the staircase.

Gilbert paused to address Henry. *"C'est fini, il paraît."*

Henry nodded, and reminded M. Gilbert, one more time: No word to America for forty-eight hours.

Henry would be with Caroline by then.

ACKNOWLEDGMENTS

I am most grateful to David Butler and Charles Benoit for helping me to research the chapters that deal with Vietnam. I leaned heavily on Dorothy McCartney of *National Review* for research. Tony Savage typed the manuscript, Frances Bronson coordinated the entire operation. Chaucy Bennetts did her invaluable job as copy editor, and Joe Isola as proofreader.

For general editing I am grateful to Sam Vaughan and to Bruce Tracy of Doubleday. I am indebted to Steve Rubin of Doubleday for his encouragement, and to Lynn Nesbit, my most helpful agent.

My thanks also to those who read my manuscript and gave me helpful suggestions, including my son Christopher, my wife Pat, my sisters Priscilla Buckley and Patricia Bozell, Charles Wallen, Jr., Thomas Wendel, and Richard Clurman.

ABOUT THE AUTHOR

William F. Buckley, Jr., is the author of ten novels that dealt with the cold war. He is the founder of *National Review* magazine, which he serves now as Editor-at-large. He writes a syndicated column and serves as host on the weekly discussion program *Firing Line.* He has written many nonfiction books, has won the American Book Award (for *Stained Glass),* and was awarded the Presidential Medal of Freedom in 1991.